Moonlight Scandals

JENNIFER L. ARMENTROUT

Moonlight Scandals

A de Vincent Novel

AVONBOOKS

An Imprint of HarperCollinsPublishers

First Avon Books mass market printing: February 2019
First Avon Books hardcover printing: January 2019

Print Edition ISBN: 978-0-06-289069-6
Digital Edition ISBN: 978-0-06-267458-6

FIRST EDITION

19 20 21 22 23   LSC   10 9 8 7 6 5 4 3 2 1

For you, the reader

Author's Note

I love beaded curtains, just so you know.

Chapter 1

Resting on her knees, Rosie Herpin drew in a deep, calming breath as she ignored the sharp pebbles digging into her skin. She leaned forward, flattening her palm against the warm, sun-bleached stone. Kneeling wasn't exactly comfortable in a wrap dress, but she wasn't going to wear jeans or leggings today.

She closed her eyes, sliding her hand down and to the right, tracing the shallow indentations painstakingly carved into the worn stone. She didn't need to see to know she'd reached the name—his name.

Ian Samuel Herpin.

Dragging her fingers over each letter, she mouthed them silently, and when she finished, reaching the N on the last name, she stopped. Rosie didn't need to keep going to know what the dates read underneath. Ian had been twenty-three. And she didn't need to open her eyes to read the single line etched into the stone, because that line had been carved into her brain.

MAY HE FIND THE PEACE THAT HAD EVADED HIM IN LIFE.

Rosie jerked her fingers off the stone, but she didn't open her eyes as she brought her hand to her chest, to right above her heart. She hated those words. His parents, bless them, had chosen that, and she hadn't the heart or the mind at the time to disagree. Now she wished she had.

Peace hadn't evaded Ian. Peace had been right there, waiting for him, surrounding him. Peace just . . . it just couldn't reach him.

That was different.

At least to Rosie it was.

Ten years had passed since their plans for the future—plans that had included college degrees, the house with a beautiful courtyard, babies, and maybe, God willing, grandbabies they could spend their days in retirement spoiling—ended with a gun Rosie hadn't even known her husband owned.

Ten years of replaying the time they did have together, over and over, looking for the signs that everything they had been and every-thing they were supposed to have become was a facade, because they were living two different lives. Rosie had believed that things were perfect. Yeah, they had problems like everyone had problems, but there was nothing major going on. But for Ian? His life hadn't been perfect at all. Things had been a struggle. Not a constant one. Not something he'd faced every day. What had preyed on his thoughts and emotions had been well hidden. His depression had been a silent killer. There hadn't been a single person, not his family or his friends or even Rosie, who had seen it coming.

Not until many, many years later, after a hell of a lot of soul-searching, did Rosie come to the shaky realization that their life hadn't been a total lie. She'd struggled through all the stages of grief before getting to that point. Some of it had been truth. Ian had loved her. She knew that was true. He'd loved her with everything inside him.

High school sweethearts.

That's what they'd been.

They'd married the summer after they'd graduated and both of them worked hard to make a life, maybe a little too hard, and that had added to what had troubled him. He'd spent long days at the sugar refinery while Rosie attended Tulane, working toward a degree in education. They talked about those plans—a future, one that she now knew Ian had desperately wanted more than anything.

She was twenty-three, almost done with her degree, and they'd been looking for their first home when Rosie got the call from the police while at her parents' bakery in the city and was told not to go home.

She'd been a month shy of graduation when Ian called the police and told them what he was about to do. They were just beginning the stressful process of applying for a mortgage when she learned that her husband of almost five years hadn't wanted her to be the one to come home and discover him. It had been a week before his birthday when their walking, living, and breathing all-American dream turned into an all-American tragedy.

For so many years, she never understood why he did what he did. So many years of being so damn angry and so damn guilty, feeling like she should've seen something, could've done something. It wasn't until she went to the University of Alabama and enrolled in the psychology program that she began to accept there'd been warning signs—red flags that most people would never have picked up on.

She learned through classes and her own experience that depression looked nothing like what people thought—like what she had thought.

Ian smiled and lived, but he'd done that for Rosie. He'd done that for his family and friends. He smiled, laughed, and got up each day and went to work, made plans and had lazy Sundays with her so she wouldn't worry about him or feel bad. He didn't want her to feel the same way he felt.

And he'd kept doing that until he couldn't any longer.

Guilt finally turned to regret, and regret lessened until it was a kernel of emotion that would always, no matter what, be there when she really let herself think about where they'd be, who'd they'd be, if things had been different. And that was, well, it was life.

He'd been gone now longer than she knew him, and while each month, each year, got easier, it still killed her a little to even say his name.

Rosie didn't believe you could simply move on from losing someone you truly loved, someone who was not only your best friend but also your other half. You didn't get back that part of you that you irrevocably gave to another person. When they left, that part disappeared forever with them. But Rosie believed you could come to accept that they were no longer there and keep living and enjoying life.

There wasn't anything she was prouder of than the fact that she did just that. No one, not a single damn person could say she was weak, that she didn't dust off her ass and pick herself back up, because you could never begin to understand the turbulent, ever-changing whirlwind of utterly violent emotions that came with losing someone you cherished more than anything in this world to their own hand.

No one.

She got not one or two degrees, but three of them. She went out and had fun, the crazy fun that sometimes felt like it was moments away from becoming the kind of fun that ended with the police showing up. She took what used to be a curiosity for all things paranormal, an interest she shared with Ian, and turned it into a legitimate side career where she'd met some of the best people in the world. Rosie also dated. Often. Hell, she'd just gone out with a guy at the beginning of the week she'd met while working at her parents' bakery. And she never held back. Never. Life was too damn short to do that.

That she had learned the hard way.

But today, on the tenth anniversary of Ian's death, it was hard not to feel like it happened yesterday. It was almost impossible to not be cloaked in suffocating sadness.

Reaching around her neck, she tugged on the gold chain she always wore. She pulled it out from under the collar of her dress, curling her fingers around the gold band. Her husband's ring. She lifted it to her lips and kissed the warm metal.

One day she would put this ring away somewhere safe. She knew that, but that one day just hadn't come yet.

Opening her eyes, she blinked back tears as she lowered her gaze to the bouquet of fresh flowers resting on the ground. Peonies. Her favorite, because Ian didn't have a favorite flower. They were half-bloomed mignon peonies, crisp white with pink centers that would eventually turn all white. Picking up the damp stems, she inhaled the rich, rose fragrance.

Rosie needed to get going. She'd promised to help her friend Nikki move today, so it was time to head back to her apartment, get changed, and be a good friend for the day. She leaned—

A soft, swift curse jerked her head up. Normally, she didn't hear a ton of cursing in a cemetery. Usually things were quite quiet. A faint grin tugged at her lips. Cursing and cemeteries typically did not go hand in hand. She scanned the narrow path to her right and didn't see anything. Leaning back, she looked to her left and found the source.

A man knelt on one knee with his back to her as he picked up flowers that had fallen into a puddle left by the recent rainstorm. Even from where she sat, she could see that whatever delicate bouquet he'd carried was ruined.

Placing a hand over her eyes, she squinted in the sunlight as she watched the man rise. He was dressed as if he'd come straight from work. Dark trousers paired with a fitted white dress shirt. The sleeves were rolled up to the elbows, revealing tan forearms. It was late September and New Orleans was still circling the seventh level of hot, currently as humid as Satan's balls in the afternoon, so she figured if she was close to dying in her black dress, he had to be minutes away from stripping off the shirt.

Still standing with his back to her, he stared down at the ruined flowers. His shoulders were tense as he turned in the other direction. His pace was brisk as he took the flowers over to an old oak tree festooned with Spanish moss. There was a small trash can there, one of the very few in the entire cemetery. He tossed the flowers and then pivoted, quickly disappearing down one of the numerous lanes.

Oh man, that sucked.

Feeling for the guy, she sprang into action. Carefully, she pulled half of the stems free and then leaned forward, placing the remaining in the vase in front of the Herpin tomb. She picked up her keys and as she rose, she slid her purple-framed sunglasses on. Hurrying down the worn path with patchy grass, she turned down the lane she'd seen the guy go down. Luck was on her side, because she saw him near the pyramid tomb. He hung a right there, and feeling a wee bit like a stalker, she trailed behind him.

Of course, she could yell out to him and just hand him the other half of the peonies, but shouting at a stranger in a cemetery just seemed wrong. Shouting in a cemetery at all felt like something her mother would side-eye her over.

And no one side-eyed quite like her mother.

The man made another turn and then stepped out of her line of sight. Holding on to the flowers, she walked passed a tomb with a large cross and then her steps slowed.

She found him.

He was standing before a massive mausoleum, one guarded by two beautifully erected weeping angels, and he was just standing there, as still as those angels, his arms stiff at his sides and his hands closed. She took a step forward as her gaze drifted to the name on the mausoleum.

de Vincent.

Her eyes widened and she blurted out, "Holy baby llama."

The man twisted at the waist, and Rosie was suddenly standing within mere feet of the Devil.

That was what the gossip magazines called him.

That was what most of her family called him.

Rosie liked to refer to him as *in her wildest dreams.*

Everyone in New Orleans, the state of Louisiana, and probably more than half the country knew who Devlin de Vincent was. Besides all the photos of him and his fiancée that were constantly posted in the Living and Leisure section of the newspaper, he was the eldest of three remaining de Vincent siblings, the heirs to the kind of fortune Rosie, along with most of the world, couldn't even begin to wrap their heads around.

What a small world.

That was all she could think as she stared at him. Her friend Nikki worked for the de Vincents. Well, she worked temporarily for them and currently had something going on with the middle brother. That whole situation was an absolute mess at the moment, and Gabriel de Vincent was currently on the Boyfriends Who Needed to Get Their Shit Together list.

But the de Vincents' notorious fame or her friend's on-again, off-again relationship with Gabe weren't the only reasons why she knew more about them than the average bear.

It was because of their home—their land.

The de Vincent estate was one of the most haunted locations in the entire state of Louisiana. Rosie knew this because she had been a bit obsessed with all the legends surrounding the land and the family, one that included a *curse*. Yes. The family and the land were supposedly cursed. How cool was that? Okay, probably not cool to those involved, but Rosie was fascinated by the whole thing.

From the research Rosie had done eons ago, it all stemmed from the land itself. New Orleans had been plagued with many virulent outbreaks in the late eighteen hundreds and the early nineteen hundreds. Smallpox. Spanish influenza. Yellow fever. Even the bubonic plague. Thousands of people died and many more were quarantined. Often, the dead and the dying were sent to the same place, left to rot away. The land that the de Vincent home sat on was one of the areas popularly used throughout many of the outbreaks. Even once the house was originally built, lands near the property were still used in the later outbreaks. All that sickness and death, mixed with heartbreak and hopelessness, were going to leave some bad vibes behind.

And boy did the de Vincent land have some bad vibes.

The house itself had caught fire multiple times. The fires could easily be explained, but all the strange deaths? There was the stuff her friend Nikki had told her. Then there was the de Vincent curse, and even more crazy?

Ley lines.

Ley lines were basically straight lines of energy that traveled all over the earth and were believed to have spiritual connections. The very line that extended from Stonehenge, moved across the Atlantic, and passed through cities like New York, Washington, D.C., New Orleans. And, according to her research, straight through the de Vincent property.

Rosie would do bad, terrible things to get inside that house and investigate.

But that was unlikely to ever happen. When Rosie had mentioned it to Nikki, she was shot down faster than her running after freshly baked beignets.

She'd never met a de Vincent before and definitely not *the* Devlin de Vincent, but she'd seen enough pictures of him to know that Devlin just . . . well, he just did it for her.

That indefinable thing that got her hormones revving like a 1967 Impala. Wide-shouldered and narrow at the waist, the man was tall, well over six feet. His dark hair was coiffed and styled short. He had the kind of face that was universally handsome. High, broad cheekbones and a straight, aquiline nose paired with a set of full lips that came with a perfect Cupid's bow. He had a square, hard jaw and a chin with a slight cleft in it.

The man was stunning, yet there was something cold about him, almost detached and a bit cruel about how he was pieced together. To anyone else, that might've dampened his attractiveness, but to Rosie? That only made him all the more beautiful.

Oh God, Rosie remembered something in that moment. How could she have forgotten? She wasn't sure, but his father had died recently. Lawrence de Vincent had died the same way the de Vincents' mother had—the same way Ian had.

By his own hand.

Lawrence de Vincent hadn't used a gun, though. He'd hung himself. Or that was what the gossip section of the paper claimed.

Her heart all but broke for him, for all the brothers in that moment. To have experienced what they did not once but twice? Good God. . . .

Devlin hadn't turned fully in her direction, but he was staring at her and she was staring at him, and this was so not how she expected her trip to the cemetery to go.

"Can I help you?" he asked, and goodness, his voice was as deep as an ocean.

"I saw you back there, when your flowers fell into the puddle," she said, inching closer to him. "I have extra. I thought you could use them."

The sunlight glanced off his cheekbones as he tilted his head to the side. He didn't respond.

So, she extended her arms, holding out the peonies. "Would you like them?"

Devlin still didn't respond.

She sucked her bottom lip in between her teeth and decided if she was in for a penny, she was in for a pound. Stepping around the stone

She did laugh again then. "No. Your back was to me and you were too far away. All I knew was that you were a guy."

The way he studied her made her wonder if he believed that or not, but there really wasn't anything she could say to change it if that was the case. A cloud passed overhead, and Rosie pushed her sunglasses up. She'd smoothed her curls back into a topknot this morning. If she hadn't, she was confident her hair would be a frizzy mess in the humidity.

Something . . . weird flickered across his face as he stared at her. She had no idea what it was as she spun the key ring on her pointer finger. "Well, I've taken up enough of your time—"

"These aren't for Lawrence," he said, and she thought it was strange that Devlin called him that instead of Father. He stepped forward, crossing over the stone. "You have me at a disadvantage."

"I do?" She watched him kneel, and that was when she saw the name. Marjorie de Vincent. Was that his mother?

Devlin placed the peonies in the vase. "You know me, but I don't know you."

"Oh." Rosie almost said who she was. It was on the tip of her tongue, but Rosie had kind of fixed Nikki up with a mutual friend who had been attempting to investigate the de Vincents for the local paper, unbeknownst to Rosie. She didn't know if Devlin knew anything about that, but there was no point in running that risk. "It doesn't matter."

He turned to her, brows knitted in a slight frown. "It doesn't?"

"No." She smiled as her gaze flickered from him to where she saw the father's name etched into stone. "You know, I'm sure you've heard this before, but it's true. You may never really understand why your father did what he did, but it gets easier to . . . deal with."

Devlin's lips parted as he stared at her.

She felt her cheeks warm, because of course he knew. He already had experience with this, with his mother, and here she was, dispensing unnecessary advice like an idiot.

He stepped toward her, coming over the stone. "What is your name?"

Before she could answer, a phone rang. For a moment she thought he wasn't going to answer it, but then he reached into his pocket, pulling it out.

"Sorry," he said. "I have to answer this."

"It's okay."

Devlin turned away, placing his hand on his waist as he spoke into the phone. This was her chance to make a clean exit. Taking just one more second to soak in the line of his jaw and the breadth of his shoulders, she slid her sunglasses back down as she backed up.

Turning with a soft smile on her lips, she walked away from Devlin de Vincent, knowing it was very unlikely that she'd see him again.

Chapter 2

*P*rincess Silvermoon was her trade name, but Rosie simply knew her as Sarah LePen. Princess Silvermoon was, no question about it, a really absurd name, but in Sarah's line of work, she had to stand out. Especially in a city where you couldn't throw a rock and not hit a tarot card reader or a psychic, and calling yourself a princess did get you a lot of attention.

But Sarah was the real deal Holyfield.

She was a psychic medium whose *feelings* were almost always premonitions, and not only that, she was able to communicate with honest to goodness spirits. Rosie knew it was more than Sarah relying on finely honed intuition or being able to expertly read people's body language. She'd seen Sarah in action many times over to know that she was connecting with someone, able to answer nearly impossible questions and impart shockingly accurate information to those who had her do readings.

Rosie had met Sarah through her friend Jillian several years ago. Jilly was the creator and co-owner of NOPE—the New Orleans Paranormal Exploration team, and in Rosie's opinion, one of the best paranormal investigation teams out there. Jilly brought Sarah in while NOPE was investigating a house out in Covington. They had a previous owner of the home who hadn't moved on and was making herself quite the nuisance in the home, banging around, stealing things and placing them in weird locations to scare the bejesus out of the kids. Sarah had managed to get the old lady to cross over, much to the family's delight. And as far as Rosie knew, they still lived in that house. But sometimes spirits could be stubborn. There'd been times that Sarah couldn't get them to cross over, and then it became up to the owners to either attempt to forcibly remove the spirits or learn to live with them.

Sarah had been engaged up until about four months ago, when a *feeling* had led her to come home earlier than normal, catching her fiancé with, as cliché as hell, his secretary.

So she'd recently moved into an apartment over on Ursulines, which wasn't too far from Rosie, and where she was currently begging for forgiveness.

"I'm sorry I'm late," she told Sarah as she dropped her bag on the couch. "Today has been—it has been all over the place. I had to help my friend Nikki move and I had to help Jilly with one of the ghost tours. You know how those things are."

"A mess and they always run over?" Sarah laughed as she walked out of her kitchen. Her blond hair was pulled up in a messy knot that looked Instagram ready. She was a gorgeous woman who reminded Rosie of an older version of the actress Jennifer Lawrence. When Sarah was *officially* working, she wore flowing gowns and brace-lets that sounded like wind chimes every time they clanked together. When she was off, like she was now, she wore black leggings and a black tunic. "You have no reason to apologize. It's okay. I have noth-ing else planned tonight. I never do on this night."

"But it's Friday—"

"And we have a standing date every year, on this date, so it's okay." She carried two small pillar candles and placed them on the coffee table.

Sarah was correct.

For the last six years, Sarah had attempted to communicate with Ian on the anniversary of his death. Like Houdini and his wife, Rosie and Ian had a code word. A word only they would know. It was something they'd come up with one night, after drinking about a gallon of wine and watching a marathon of *The Dead Files* on one of their lazy Sundays. Since he'd been just as into the paranormal as she was, it wasn't that out-there that they'd come up with a word that would prove a medium was really communicating with one or the other.

It had taken Rosie four years to get the point that she was even remotely ready for something like that. She didn't really have any questions for Ian. She just wanted to know if he was . . . okay. That's all.

And for the last six years, Sarah had never been able to reach him. Rosie didn't know what that meant. Sarah had always told her that didn't mean he wasn't around her. He just wasn't coming through. Maybe he wasn't ready to talk. Maybe he . . . maybe he wasn't *there*, wherever *there* was.

Either way, Rosie was in awe of Sarah, and maybe even had a little girl crush on her, too. The fact that she could talk to those who had passed absolutely fascinated Rosie. Sarah had been more than open about what it was like and how it was when she was a child, but Rosie really couldn't understand or even begin to know what it was like to hear voices that others could not, to feel what others couldn't.

Sarah and those like her, who were truly gifted, were heroes in Rosie's book.

"How was the tour?" Sarah asked.

"Not bad." Being familiar with the drill, Rosie walked into the kitchen and grabbed the other two candles. She brought them into the living room, placing them in the center of the coffee table. "It's just that a lot of people had questions, which I don't mind, but we got hung up near the Sultan's house."

Sarah rolled her eyes as she turned off the overhead lights. The room was cast in soft, flickering shadows. The blinds were already closed, shutting out the bright lights of the city. She'd already turned on music. Well, it really wasn't technically music. It was the low sound of ocean waves, background noise that helped Sarah concentrate and to drown out the sounds from outside.

Making her way back over to Rosie, Sarah knelt down on a thick, sparkly blue cushion. "You mean the house where there is absolutely no evidence of a Sultan or a Sultan's brother living there? Or any evidence of a bloody, horrific massacre?"

Chuckling, Rosie dropped down onto her pillow. It was also sparkly, but pink. "One of the tourists wanted to know why we weren't taking them to the Gardette-LaPrete House, and I tried to explain that there has never been any historical evidence that such a massacre took place there and while the place is beautiful, we don't include stories where there isn't some level of historical evidence. He argued, listed all these facts, which aren't facts, and anyone with a degree in Googling could've figured that out."

"Mansplained you, did he?"

"Yep." She crossed her legs. "I told that guy that no one was saying the house wasn't haunted. Just that there wasn't anything factual supporting the legend. Not even a single report in any newspapers about the murders, and with something as bad as this supposedly was, it would've been in a newspaper."

Sarah stretched her neck to the left and then the right as the flame of the candle danced over her face. "The place does give off weird vibes and I wouldn't live in one of those apartments, but ya know . . ."

"Yep. Either you believe the Gardette-LaPrete House murders are real or you don't. There is no in-between. Anyway, the debate caused us to run over. So, did you spend your evening arguing over a mass murder that may have never taken place?"

She laughed softly. "No. I kind of wish I had. I did a private reading with this couple who'd just lost their child."

"Oh no." Rosie's shoulders slumped. Those readings had to be the worst, and Rosie wasn't sure how Sarah managed to deal with them—the grieving family and friends who were so desperate to speak to their loved ones just one more time. But no matter how distraught those people were, Sarah wouldn't lie to them. She wouldn't tell them vague things like some mediums would to make them feel better. Sarah was always honest, even when it hurt. "Did you reach the child?"

Sarah brushed a loose strand of hair off her cheek. "No. Kids are . . . it's always hard with them, especially when the passing is recent. I tried to explain that, but they wanted to try anyway. They want to try again, but I was able to convince them to give it a couple of months." She smiled, but it was sad as she placed her hands on the coffee table.

"By the way, you're still planning on going to the Masquerade with me next week, right?"

Rosie nodded enthusiastically. "Hell yeah! I'm just glad you're still going, but thank you again for bringing me as your plus-one. I've always wanted to attend."

The annual charity Masquerade was where the wealthiest and most powerful of New Orleans rubbed elbows and God knew what else, so Rosie never had a chance to attend. She didn't hobnob with the highfalutin crowd.

Sarah normally attended with her ex, who got the exclusive tickets because he worked in the district attorney's office. As far as they knew, her ex wasn't going to be there. Rosie kind of hoped he would be, because their costumes were sexy as hell, and she wanted Sarah to be able to rub all that he threw away in his face.

"You're just excited because the house is haunted." Sarah grinned.

"Guilty as charged." The bedroom upstairs, the last one on the left that faced the courtyard in the back, was one of the most haunted locations in the city. Legend said a woman who'd been murdered by a jealous ex-lover the night before her wedding haunted the room, full-bodied-apparition type of haunting, and Rosie was *so* going to check it out.

Sarah shook her head. "Let's see if we can reach Ian. Okay?"

Rosie nodded. Sometimes Sarah needed personal effects, but she tried to make contact without them at first. Rosie wasn't holding her breath that tonight was going to be any different than all the previous attempts.

But she was going to try, because that was the promise they'd made each other. And maybe it was just a silly promise, one that Ian hadn't taken seriously, but Rosie did.

"Close your eyes and picture Ian," Sarah said, her voice soft in the darkness. "I'll let you know if he comes through."

In other words, that meant Rosie needed to shut up and let Sarah concentrate. So, she did just that, because Rosie knew that Sarah didn't want her talking until she asked her a question. After all, Rosie could accidentally feed information to Sarah, and because they were friends and Sarah knew a lot about Ian, it was already difficult for Sarah not to fall back on what she already knew.

Closing her eyes, she pictured Ian. Or tried to. It was . . . God, it sucked to acknowledge this, but it was getting harder to piece his features together. She had to try really hard for the details not to be blurry and it took effort. Rosie knew that was common, but it still burned a hole through her chest.

Ian was handsome.

He'd been tall and lanky. The kind of guy who could eat fried chicken wings smothered in every sauce known to man and hamburgers daily and never gain a pound. Rosie so much as looked at a basket of chicken wings and put on weight, but not Ian. He'd had dark brown hair that was cropped close to the skull. Rosie liked longer hair on guys, but the short cut always worked for Ian since it showcased his high cheekbones. His skin had been a little darker than hers, courtesy of his father, and his eyes had been a rich, deep brown. Rosie held the image of him in her mind—an image of him smiling, because goodness, he had a beautiful smile. A smile that was so infectious that you couldn't help but smile in return. And his laugh? Oh man, it had been just as—

"Someone is here," Sarah announced, causing Rosie's stomach to lurch. "The voice is faint. Very far away." There was another pause. "It's a female voice."

Jolting out of her thoughts, her eyes flew open. Sarah sat across from her, her eyes still closed.

Her pale brows knitted together as her fingers curled against the coffee table. "Rosalynn . . ."

No one called her Rosalynn except for her parents or her sister when they wanted to be annoying. Then again, her grandmother always called her that.

Sarah's head twitched slightly to the left. "You always . . . hated that name."

A wry grin tugged at her lips. Everyone who knew Rosie knew she didn't like her full name. Rosalynn June Pradine had been her full name before she married. After Ian's death, she hadn't changed it back. Didn't see the point in it, but anyway, her sister's name was worse, though. Their parents just had to be extra about everything and named the poor girl Belladonna, which meant she was named after an extremely poisonous plant also known as nightshade.

The weird name thing was unfortunately a family tradition on her mother's side. Her mother was Juniper *May* Pradine. Bella was Belladonna *February* Pradine. Yes, there was a trend there. Their middle names were the months their parents swore they were conceived in. Apparently that weird tradition started with their grandmother.

And her granny sure as hell knew she didn't like to be called that.

It obviously wasn't Ian coming through, but if it was her granny, Rosie couldn't complain. She'd come through before and actually told Rosie where her mother could find a necklace of Granny's that her mom had been searching for forever.

Exhaling slowly, Rosie watched Sarah lift her hand to the space behind her left ear. That's what she did whenever she was hearing someone. She would mess with that ear, tugging on it or rubbing her fingers behind it, or tilt her head in the opposite direction.

"*Whoa.* Wait." Sarah's head jerked. "There's another voice. It's louder. Very loud and it's coming through."

Rosie's brows lifted. That . . . that had never happened before. She leaned forward and then stopped as the flames on the candles flickered rapidly. As she frowned, her gaze bounced between the candles. The flames had moved like there was wind, but there wasn't even a ceiling fan running.

A chill skated down Rosie's spine as she lifted her gaze to Sarah as a sixth sense kicked in. Not the kind of sense Sarah had, nothing as finely tuned as that, but it was the same feeling she got on investigations, right before something freaky happened.

Sarah was rubbing at the back of her ear. "It's a male voice and . . . and he's saying . . . he thinks it's a pretty name." She shook her head. "He is talking about your name, too, but . . ."

Rosie ordered the hope swelling in her chest to chill out. Just because it was a male coming through and he knew she didn't like her full name didn't mean it was Ian. Her grandfather had come through once, just like her grandmother, three years ago, and so had a cousin.

Though, they'd never mentioned her name before. So that was . . . odd.

Sarah's lips pursed as her nose scrunched. "Who . . . I don't know. I keep hearing the word . . . 'peonies'? Yes. Something to do with peonies." She opened her eyes. "What is the deal with peonies?"

Her lips parted on a sharp inhale. "Peonies are my favorite flower."

Nodding slowly, Sarah closed her eyes again. "Okay. But it's something about . . . something about peonies today?"

"Today? I don't—wait. Yes." Her eyes widened. Holy crapola. . . . "I took peonies to the cemetery. I always do. Every year."

She tipped her head to the side. "You did something with those flowers, right? He's saying—*slow down*," Sarah ordered softly. "Yes. Okay. You gave those flowers to someone?"

Rosie's mouth dropped open. A shiver danced over her skin. Just because she was around the supernatural a lot, that didn't mean she still didn't get freaked out.

And she was a little freaked out.

There was no way, none whatsoever, that Sarah would've known that. She hadn't even told Nikki that she'd run into Devlin at the cemetery and spoken to him.

"Yes," Rosie said, her hands closing in her lap. "I did give the flowers to someone—"

"Half of them," Sarah corrected.

Rosie's heart skipped a beat.

"He's saying that was nice of you," Sarah continued, her eyes open now. She wasn't looking at Rosie, but staring into one of the flames. "He's . . . I'm sorry. He's kind of all over the place, and half of what he's saying isn't making sense."

Now her heart had sped up. Had Sarah finally connected with Ian? "He can hear me, right?" When Sarah nodded absently, she drew in a shallow breath. "What is our word?"

Sarah's gaze flew to hers. "This isn't Ian."

"What?"

"This isn't him," she repeated. "I don't . . . I don't even think this spirit knows you."

Okay. Now she was more than a little freaked out. *"What?"*

"This happens sometimes." She flinched as she refocused on the flame. Then her eyes widened. "He saw you at the cemetery. That is right."

Rosie leaned forward again. "What is he saying?"

"He keeps saying that he doesn't belong there. That he shouldn't be there." She curled her fingers around the lobe of her ear. "I think he means . . . he shouldn't be dead."

Well, that wasn't entirely surprising. A lot of dead people didn't think they should be dead.

"He's angry. Very angry." Her head twitched again. "What about the peonies—oh." She looked at Rosie again. "He's saying you shouldn't have given the flowers to him."

Her stomach twisted. Okay. Yet another detail Sarah didn't know. Rosie never mentioned a guy. Was this spirit talking about Devlin? "Why shouldn't I have?"

Sarah grew quiet. "Ungrateful," she muttered, her lips thinning. "Mistake. He made a mistake. That's what he keeps saying."

"Who?"

"I don't know. I can't get him to calm down. He's . . . God." She dragged her hand over her head, shoving the shorter strands back. "He's enraged. He keeps shouting that he doesn't belong there." Her chest rose with a deep breath. *"Death."*

Rosie cocked her head to the side.

"Death," Sarah repeated, making a sudden choking sound. "He's saying . . . something about his death. It wasn't supposed to happen."

"Really?" Rosie sighed.

"Wait." Sarah touched her neck. "He's saying—oh my God." Her eyes widened. "Nope. I'm done. I can't—I'm done. I'm closing off this connection."

"Okay." Rosie nodded jerkily. "Close it down. Close it—"

Sarah suddenly jerked back from the coffee table as her hands went out in front of her. Her eyes were wide. "He's here."

"Um, I'm not following."

"He. Is. *Here*, Rosie." Sarah's gaze latched on to hers. "Not in the metaphysical sense. Don't you—"

A loud thud came from above, like a giant hand smacked into the ceiling. Both of them jolted.

The candles blew out—every single one.

"Holy shit," Sarah whispered, and Rosie heard her jump to her feet.

Goose bumps rose all over Rosie's bare arms as she stared into the darkness and her heart thumped heavily. She strained to see or hear anything, but all she heard was Sarah rushing over toward the door. A second later, the living room flooded with light and Rosie was staring at the colorful pillows all along Sarah's couch. Slowly, she twisted at the waist, to where Sarah stood.

Sarah stared back at her. "Rosie. . . ."

"That happened." Her eyes felt like they were going to pop out of her head. "That really just happened."

Dragging in deep, rapid breaths, Sarah nodded. "He kept saying . . ."

"What?"

"He kept saying . . . God, I don't want to even say this out loud, but I need to." Visibly pale, she pulled away from the wall. "He kept saying, the . . . the devil is coming."

Chapter 3

The only two devils Rosie sort of knew were the perfectly sugared beignets that were to blame for her rounded hips and a de Vincent.

But could this spirit be talking about a de Vincent? Or was *it* a de Vincent? That just sounded out of this world, but . . .

Clutching the bottle of wine, Sarah sat down next to Rosie on the couch. All the lights were turned on in her apartment, and Sarah had put the kibosh on any attempt Rosie wanted to make to communicate with whoever the hell it was that had come through. Sarah claimed the spirit was gone now, but as Rosie sipped from her wineglass and Sarah drank straight from the bottle, she wasn't sure she believed her.

"Has that happened before?" Rosie asked as she pulled her leg up onto the couch.

Sarah stared straight ahead, her blue eyes focused on a pink-and-blue, bohemian-style wall tapestry hung behind the TV. "Yes. Not often, but sometimes a spirit will sort of . . . ride another spirit through the connection. I've done readings where complete strangers showed up and wanted to talk. I mean, sometimes the spirit knows the person, and the person just doesn't realize that, but there've been cases where it was a random spirit hitching a ride." She turned to Rosie as she lifted her hand to her neck. She began rubbing it again. "I think . . . I think he was trying to jump me."

Rosie sucked in a sharp breath. "Are you serious?"

She nodded.

"That's . . . that's not good." And it wasn't. Jumping wasn't the same thing as full possession, but it could still wreak havoc on a person's mind, body, and environment. It occurred when a spirit jumped into a person's body to communicate through them. People might find themselves saying things they normally wouldn't, having odd accents and even mannerisms that were unlike them. When a person was jumped, they might even experience how the spirit died, and that could really mess with someone's head.

And from her own experience with investigations, Rosie knew that only a very strong spirit or a very determined one could jump a living human.

"You know, I've let spirits in many times during readings, when they wait for permission, but this guy . . . he wasn't waiting for permission. He wanted in and he was furious."

Feeling guilty, Rosie touched Sarah's arm and winced when the woman jumped a little. "I'm sorry. I—"

"This is not your fault. You don't need to apologize, but I do need to tell you this, and not just because you're my friend." Still white-knuckling the wine bottle, she dropped her hand and twisted toward Rosie. "I'm pretty sure this spirit didn't know you personally, but I got the feeling that he . . . he hitched a ride with you and not another spirit and it wasn't a mistake."

Rosie's brows lifted as she nibbled on her lower lip. That wasn't something anyone wanted to hear. Not even her.

"Do you have any idea of who that could've been?" Sarah asked and then took another big, healthy gulp of the wine.

Rosie could easily be a spirit beacon, especially considering all the investigations she'd taken part in with NOPE over the years, but she didn't think it came from any of those cases. She looked away from Sarah, not sure if her suspicions were on point or not.

"What are you not telling me?" Sarah demanded.

Drawing in a deep breath, Rosie leaned forward and placed her wineglass on the coffee table. She hadn't really allowed herself time to think about her brief meeting with Devlin, because there truly was no point, but she couldn't help but feel like they'd had a . . . a moment, hadn't they? That indefinable connection that even strangers could make in a short period of time.

"Okay, this is going to sound crazier than what just happened, but when I was at the cemetery today, I saw this guy drop his flowers in a puddle," she told Sarah. "They were ruined and he'd tossed them, and I had more than enough flowers. I split the peonies and found the guy to give them to him, because that had to suck, you know?"

Sarah nodded slowly as she took another drink.

"I swear I had no idea who he was until I found him and he was standing in front of the de Vincent mausoleum. It was Devlin de Vincent."

"The *Devil*." Sarah let out a hard, short laugh. "That makes me feel better that he could've been referencing a nickname and not the actual devil."

Rosie snorted at that.

"You know, literally everyone seems to know his nickname, but no one knows why they call him that or how it got started."

She lifted a shoulder. "I don't know. I guess the nicknames for all the brothers started when they were in college up north, but yeah, I would love to know why they call him that."

"Ditto," murmured Sarah. "What happened when you gave him the flowers?"

"We chatted for a couple of minutes and then I left. I thought he was there because of his father. You know, he passed recently."

She blanched as she lowered her gaze. "Didn't he . . . ?"

"Yeah, he killed himself. I said that I was sorry to hear about his father's death, and he corrected me, said the flowers were for his mother," Rosie continued. "I figured he just wasn't ready to even acknowledge his father's death, and I totally understand that. Anyway, that's where the whole peony thing is from. I didn't even tell Nikki about that when I saw her tonight and you know she works in the de Vincent household. Do you think the spirit was him— Lawrence de Vincent?"

"God." Sarah leaned back against the cushion, lowering the bottle to her stomach. "You know, it's possible. He could've been hanging around Devlin or the cemetery, saw you, and attached himself."

"But why? I didn't know him and I don't know Devlin. That was the first time I saw him in person."

"Sometimes the reason why a spirit attaches to someone is never known."

Rosie's lips pursed. "Well, that's not cool."

She slid her a dry look. "Most people would be more freaked out about that possibility."

"Most people don't hunt ghosts." Rosie shrugged, but she was a little disturbed. Especially if this ghostie was an angry one. She wasn't about that kind of life. "I mean, hey, if I'm going to be haunted by a ghost, I figure a de Vincent is like the gold standard."

Sarah giggled and then smacked her hand over her mouth. "That's not funny."

"Yeah." Rosie grinned. "It kind of is."

Sarah let her head fall back against the couch. "But seriously, I don't know if that was Lawrence or someone else, but I do know he was angry and . . . I think . . . I think he said something else, right before I closed down communication." She exhaled roughly. "I don't know if I heard him right. He was trying to jump me and I don't need that, so I cut him off, but if he was Lawrence . . ."

"What? What do you think he said?"

She turned her head toward Rosie. "I think he said he was *murdered*."

Not unexpectedly, Rosie had one hell of a time falling asleep that night.

Back at her apartment and in her bed, she stared up at the glow of the dark stars stuck to her ceiling. They didn't glow green. They were a soft, luminous white, but yeah, they were still tacky.

Rosie loved them.

They reminded her of infinite space, and while that may be a weird thing to want to be reminded of, she sort of found it comforting that in the big scheme of things, she was just a tiny speck of flesh and bone on a giant rock hurtling around the sun.

The stars also helped her fall asleep. Usually. But not tonight. Tonight she could only think about the reading with Sarah and the question her friend had asked her before she'd left.

"Are you going to say something?"

Rosie snorted-laughed into the relatively dark bedroom. Was she going to say something? To who? Devlin? Yeah, that was not going to happen. Her reluctance had nothing to do with Rosie not believing Sarah. She totally believed her. Sarah had connected with someone who was very angry and quite possibly could've been murdered, but—and it was a big but—who in the world would believe Rosie if she came up to them and said something like that?

It was one thing for her to readily believe what Sarah told her, because Rosie had seen some bizarre shit, but someone who most likely didn't believe in the supernatural, even if their house appeared to be haunted, probably wouldn't be open to a virtual stranger walking up to them and dropping that kind of bomb.

Because it would, in fact, sound like she'd donned her crazy pants.

Groaning, Rosie rolled onto her side and her gaze traveled across the room, to the heavily curtained bedroom window. It was the only window in the room. She was grateful for investing in those blackout curtains, because none of the bright, flashing lights from the French Quarter seeped through that window.

Rosie sighed.

There was no way she could say anything about what happened tonight. She didn't know the de Vincents well enough to approach them, but she could tell Nikki. Even though her friend believed in the supernatural, she seriously didn't think Nikki would feel remotely comfortable telling any of the de Vincents what Rosie had heard, because again, it would sound a little insane.

Besides all of that, and all of *that* was enough for Rosie to keep her mouth shut, Sarah and she couldn't be sure that it was Lawrence who'd briefly come through. Wasn't like the spirit had entered with a name tag. Yes, it seemed like it was him. It made sense, after all. Rosie had been at the cemetery and given Devlin peonies. As creepy as it sounded, Lawrence could've been hanging around either his son or the cemetery and for some bizarre reason hitched a ride with Rosie.

Shifting onto her back again, she closed her eyes and blew out a ragged breath.

Anything was possible, which meant that spirit could've really been

Lawrence and it also meant that it could've been someone totally un-related to the de Vincents, and it was just a strange coincidence or it could've been another de Vincent other than Lawrence. For decades, that family had been plagued by deaths and all kinds of drama. They were cursed! Lots of their family members had died, many in weird and bizarre manners.

But what . . . what if it had been Lawrence? What if he had come through the reading and wanted it to be known that he hadn't killed himself? That he'd been *murdered*? That was a big deal. Wouldn't they want to know that?

If the shoes were on her feet, she would want to know. She figured she had a unique perspective on things, but this wasn't about her.

"Ugh," she moaned, rolling onto her stomach and planting her face in the pillow.

"The devil is coming."

Her thoughts kept turning, but finally, after forever, and after kicking half the blankets off her, she fell asleep. She had no idea how many hours passed before she was jarred out of dreams about lemon sorbet by the shrill sound of her phone ringing.

Groaning, she smacked around on her end table, blindly reaching for her phone. Her hand hit an empty plastic glass, knocking it to the floor.

"Damn it," she muttered, lifting her face from the pillow. Blowing a thick curl out of her face, she stretched over and snatched up her phone. Squinting, she saw Nikki's smiling face on the screen. It was a god-awful time in the morning; the kind of time that wasn't even really morning in Rosie's opinion.

She answered as she let her head fall back to the pillow. "Hello?" she croaked, and then winced. She sounded like she'd inhaled fifty packs of cigarettes.

"Rosie? It's Nikki. I know . . . it's early and I'm sorry," Nikki said, and even half-awake, Rosie thought her voice sounded weird, like her words were mushy. "But I need your help. I'm in the hospital."

NEVER IN HER life had Rosie woken up so quickly. The moment she hung up the phone, she all but flung herself off the bed. Fear had twisted up her stomach as she found a pair of black leggings that looked somewhat clean. She pulled them on, along with her oversized Got Ghosts! shirt. Her hair was way too much of a mess to even begin to do something with it, so she grabbed a scarf, shoving the curls out of her face.

Thank God and every deity she could think of that she kept a stash of those disposal toothbrushes in her Corolla. She brushed her teeth on the way to the hospital and when she got her first look at Nikki's bruised and battered face while she was waiting for her outside just as the sun crested the sky, Rosie's heart cracked wide open.

She couldn't believe what she saw as she ushered Nikki into the car or what she'd learned, and it wasn't until after she finally got Nikki settled in her bedroom that she sat down and really tried to process what had happened.

No one should have to go through what Nikki Besson had been through.

"God," she whispered, staring at her mug of untouched coffee. Scrubbing her hands down her face, she exhaled roughly.

Nikki could've died—she was almost murdered.

Hands shaking, she lowered them to her knees and looked over her shoulder, to the beaded curtain that separated the bedroom and living room. Last night, while Rosie was doing a ghost tour in the Quarter, one of her closest and nicest friends in the whole wide universe had been fighting for her life.

And in the process of fighting for survival, she had killed the man who attacked her.

Rosie shuddered.

Slowly, her gaze drifted back to the open laptop sitting on the coffee table that had once been a chess table. What had happened was already breaking news on the local news website. Luckily, Nikki's name hadn't been mentioned, thank God, but that couldn't last for long.

"Parker Harrington. . . ." Rosie shook her head in disbelief. She didn't know Parker personally, but she knew of him. The Harringtons were just like the de Vincents. Extremely wealthy with a long blood-line rooted in New Orleans and Louisiana. The Harringtons were so much like the de Vincents that Parker's older sister was engaged to Devlin de Vincent.

The man she'd met less than twenty-four hours ago in the cemetery.

The man whose father might've possibly come through Sarah and told them he was murdered.

And now his fiancée's brother had tried to kill Nikki—Nikki, who was possibly the sweetest and kindest person, who spent her weekends volunteering at the local no-kill animal shelter.

Nikki had defended herself with a . . . a wood chisel.

Another shudder rolled through Rosie as she leaned forward and picked up her mug. As far as Nikki knew, she couldn't return to her apartment for some time. It was a crime scene, and if Rosie knew anything, she knew the police would simply leave. They'd remove the body, but they wouldn't do any cleanup. Nikki would be left with that. Just like Rosie had been left to deal with that after Ian took his life.

There was no way she would let Nikki handle that. No way.

Guilt churned as she stared down at her light brown coffee. She liked it sweet with lots of sugar and cream. Actually, it was basically sugar with a dash of coffee. But right now, the coffee still tasted bitter. Rosie had been at Nikki's apartment for hours earlier in the day, and from what she could gather from Nikki, Parker had shown up an hour or so later. If Rosie hadn't left . . .

Being haunted by all the could've, would've, should've was worse than an honest to goodness ghost.

She took a sip of her coffee and was about to put the mug back down when there was a sharp knock on her door. She drew in a deep breath.

Call it a sixth sense or whatever, but Rosie had a good idea of who stood on the other side.

Gabriel de Vincent.

Nikki had told her he'd been at the hospital and she'd all but snuck out. From that very second, Rosie figured Gabe was going to ferret out where Nikki was and where Rosie lived. Standing, she stepped around the coffee table and crossed the short distance to her door. Throwing the dead bolt, she cracked the door open.

And she was right.

There stood Gabe, in all his hot, long-haired de Vincent glory. Her gaze drifted over his shoulder and her heart jumped into her throat at the same time her stomach dropped. Gabe wasn't alone.

Devlin was with him.

Chapter 4

*O*h my God, she'd been expecting Gabe, but not *him*, not his brother. For a moment, she was so shocked, all she could do was peek out at them. She opened her mouth, but he pulled off a pair of silver aviators, tucked the arm into the collar of his shirt, and then those stunning sea-green eyes met hers.

He was going to have so many questions and how could she answer them? He was definitely going to want to know why she didn't tell him who she was yesterday when it was now obvious she had some sort of tie to his family. Would he believe she honestly never thought she'd see him again? Because she'd honestly believed that.

Devlin stared at her from behind Gabe and he . . . he looked at her, looked right *through* her, his strikingly handsome face devoid of emotion and even a flicker of recognition. He had to remember her, though. They'd just met *yesterday*, for crying out loud, less than twenty-four hours ago, and she thought they had shared a moment.

"Figured you'd find your way here," she said to Gabe, and then looked at Devlin again, waiting for him to say something. Nothing. He looked at her impassively. "Surprised to see that one here."

Devlin stepped out to the side. "Excuse me?"

It struck her then, really hit her that he didn't recognize her. Wow. That was a pretty brutal wake-up call that she'd left absolutely no impression on the man.

Stung more than she should be, she focused on Gabe. "You here for Nikki?"

"Yes," he answered. "You going to let me in?"

She blocked the door. Part of her wanted to let him in, but the other knew that he and Nikki had a rough go of it recently. Almost everyone in her book deserved second chances, but she was pretty sure Gabe was on his third.

"Depends," she finally said. "Are you finally going to do right by my friend?"

"Who is this woman?" Devlin demanded.

Rosie sucked in a sharp breath as her gaze shot to him. He honest to God did not remember her! Maybe it was because she hadn't gotten much sleep. Maybe it was because her best friend had almost died and had been beaten within an inch of her life. Maybe all of that mixed with the fact that a man who'd seen her less than twenty-four hours ago didn't recognize anything about her. Rosie wasn't a mean person. Most of the time, she liked to consider herself pretty chill. Granted, she could turn into a possessed bitch-tigress when it came to protecting those she cared about, but she knew life was way too short to be an asshole and to take things too seriously.

But the bitch-tigress came out in full force right then. "First name Nonya, last name Your Business," she snapped, her gaze not leaving Gabe's face.

Gabe's lips twitched as if he were fighting a smile. "I'm going to try to."

"Trying isn't good enough, bud. Not anymore," Rosie shot back and she saw the surprise fill eyes identical to Devlin's. "You trying is pretty much like me trying not to eat the last cupcake in the fridge. It's not real successful."

"Okay," he said. "I'm going to do right by her. That's why I'm here. You going to let me in?"

Hoping she wasn't making a mistake, she stepped back and opened the door. "She's in the bedroom."

Gabe walked in then, nodding in her direction. "Thank you."

"Don't make me regret this," she said, keeping her voice low. "Because you will not like it if I regret this."

Gabe smiled, and Rosie had to admit, it was a nice smile. "I won't."

"Good."

He slid past her just as Devlin entered her apartment. She bet he had a nice smile, too. The man who'd spoken to her for a good ten minutes the day before didn't even look at her.

He was staring straight ahead, past his brother. "Is that really a beaded curtain?"

His tone knitted her brows. He sounded like . . . like he just spied a naked old man shaking his junk. Devlin hadn't spoken like that the day before. Sure, they hadn't had an epic-long conversation, but that . . . that cold revulsion hadn't been there.

Thrown off by his tone and irritated by her apparent utter forgetability, she fired back, "You got a problem with that? Are they not up to your taste or class?"

"I'm pretty sure that most people who are over the age of twelve find them to be tasteless."

"Behave," Gabe said to Devlin as he parted the beads, disappearing into the bedroom.

Swallowing hard, she turned to Devlin. If he thought beaded curtains were childish, good thing he'd never see the glow-in-the-dark stars on her ceiling. She opened her mouth but was at a complete loss as to what to say.

He stood not even a foot inside her apartment, stiff as iron bars. Standing like he couldn't bring himself to step any farther as he still stared at the beaded curtain.

For a moment, Rosie allowed herself to be dickmatized—you know, when you were either hypnotized by how attractive someone was or you were hypnotized by their dick, which therefore allowed you to look past unsavory traits about the person. That was what she was doing right then. She was allowing herself to ignore, just for a few seconds, the fact that man had absolutely forgotten her and was currently staring at her beaded curtains like they were a crime against man, and was just going to bask in his unequivocal attractiveness.

Devlin was dressed like he had been the day before, white button-down dress shirt neatly tucked into a pair of heather-gray trousers. His shoes were so polished Rosie could probably see her reflection in them. The de Vincents had good DNA, and it really showed when it came to Devlin. From the height of his cheekbones to the strong curve of his jaw, he had the kind of face she wished she had the talent to sketch, just to capture the angles and planes.

His hair was perfectly coiffed and Rosie had this wild urge to shove her fingers in his hair and mess it up. Unfortunately, even with all the attractiveness and even with what was an apparent one-sided connection, Devlin was turning out to be a douchebag of the highest order—the order reserved for rich, privileged pricks who treated the world like it was their oyster.

She crossed her arms over her chest. "You really have a problem with beaded curtains, don't you?"

He didn't look at her as he replied, "Who wouldn't? They're beaded curtains."

Never in Rosie's thirty-three years of life on this planet had she ever met someone who was so *offended* by beaded curtains. And she had seen a lot of bizarre things in her life. Once, she'd seen a book fly off a shelf by itself. She'd seen a dead person lift their arm—a postmortem spasm, but still, that had been freaky as hell, and a bit traumatizing. Twice she'd seen a full-bodied apparition, which to this very day was in the top five most amazing things she'd ever witnessed. Just last night, a complete stranger came through her psychic reading—a stranger who just might be this man's father. And she'd seen a lot of bizarre stuff on the crowded, narrow streets of the French Quarter on a daily, often hourly, basis.

But someone offended by beaded curtains?

That was a first.

Goodness, this morning—the last twenty-four hours—had not been normal at all.

"Are they even made out of real wood?" he asked.

Sighing, she arched a brow. "Yes. They're made of particleboard and yes, I bought them down at the local Walmart."

Devlin didn't turn his head toward her, but his gaze did slide in her direction. "Particleboard is not real wood."

"Isn't it made with wood chips, and the last time I checked, wood chips are wood."

"It's also made with sawdust and synthetic resin," he replied.

"So?"

"It's not real wood."

"Whatever."

"Whatever?"

"Yeah, *whatever*," she repeated.

Now he turned toward where she stood beside her coffee table. "You cannot 'whatever' away the fact that particleboard isn't real wood."

Rosie let out a soft laugh. "I cannot believe you're still talking about particleboard."

A look of surprise flickered across his face. "And I cannot believe you think particleboard is real wood."

Another giggle squeaked out of her as she spun around and walked over to her couch. "You're still talking about particleboard."

"I am not."

"Yeah, you are." She plopped down on her comfy couch, probably the only thing in her apartment that cost any real money. She picked up her mug, hoping the coffee hadn't cooled. "And those beaded curtains are freaking ah-mazing, particleboard or not. So, don't talk smack about my super-cool beaded curtains."

"They're beaded curtains," he said, sounding like he was pointing out a massive cockroach on her wall.

This man was testing her kindness and patience like no other. "Were you harmed by beaded curtains as a child?" She kicked her legs up on the coffee table and crossed her ankles. "Did they not want to be friends with you or something?"

His gaze sharpened. Hell, his entire face seemed to sharpen. "Besides the fact that beaded curtains are inanimate objects incapable of harming a person or being friends with one, a door would suffice, would it not?"

Smirking, she took a sip of her coffee. "Suffice? Fancy."

His nostrils flared.

"Look, I'm not the one who seems to be personally offended by beaded curtains, so excuse me for asking a genuine question. I mean, have you been smacked by a beaded curtain? Those things can sting."

"I am sure your question was genuine."

"Totes," she murmured.

He came toward her in a slow, measured step. "How often are you smacked by beaded curtains?"

She snorted. "More often than I care to admit."

There was an odd light to his sea-green eyes, as if that interested him. "Why wouldn't you just get a door? It would offer more privacy."

"Why don't you just walk out of the one behind you?" she retorted.

That odd look to his gaze intensified. "Did you just tell me to leave?"

"Sure sounds like I did."

He stared at her, and a long moment passed. "You know, most people would offer their guests a drink."

Her grip tightened on her mug. "Last I checked, you weren't a guest."

"And how do you see that?"

"Well, mainly because I sure as hell didn't invite you into my apartment to insult my beaded curtain."

"If I recall correctly, and I do, you opened the door and let me in."

She held his stare. "Your recollection is faulty. I let your brother inside. You helped yourself by walking in behind him and then proceeded to insult my interior design."

Devlin laughed—barked out a deep, husky laugh that seemed to surprise him, because he immediately snapped his mouth shut. The laugh didn't surprise her. Irritatingly, it caused a warm little curl low in her belly. She liked his laugh even though it seemed harsh.

"Interior design?" he scoffed, and Rosie stiffened. "It looks like a twelve-year-old obsessed with *The X-Files* and B-grade horror movies decorated your apartment."

"Okay, I draw the line with you insulting Scully and Mulder." She sat her mug on the end table. "Seriously."

And what was wrong with B-grade horror movies? Spending a lazy Sunday afternoon watching horribly plotted zombie movies was a favorite pastime of hers.

He turned from her, scanning the bookshelves lining the wall on either side of her television. "Is that an encyclopedia of ghosts?"

"Isn't that the clearly visible title?"

Looking over his shoulder, he pinned her with what only could be described as a droll stare. "How could there be an encyclopedia of ghosts?"

For a moment, she wasn't sure how to answer his question. Part of her wanted to describe exactly how that was possible. She resisted the pointless urge. "You're a de Vincent."

"Yes." He faced her once more. "Thank you for reminding me."

She ignored that comment. "You live in a house that is rumored—"

"To be haunted and the land and the family cursed," he cut her off. "Yes, I know. I do live there and I am a de Vincent."

"So, is your house haunted?" she asked, already knowing the answer to that question.

Devlin's lips thinned.

Unable to help herself, she clasped her hands together. "You know, I'm a part of a paranormal investigation team."

"Why am I not surprised?" he replied dryly, stepping around the coffee table. He was now at the other end of the couch. "What is it called? Lunatic Investigations?"

Now *her* mouth was thinning. "Good guess, but no. It's called New Orleans Paranormal Explorations."

"New Orleans Paranormal . . . wait." His dark brows lifted. "It's called NOPE?"

"Yes. Catchy, isn't it?"

The derision that clouded his striking face told her he thought it was the stupidest-sounding thing without him even having to open his mouth. "You're kidding, right?"

"No, I am not."

"Do you truly belong to one of those joke investigative teams?"

Rosie felt that inner badass tigress rearing its bitchy head once more. Okay, now he seriously had gone too far. "There is absolutely nothing funny about what we do. Be a nonbeliever. Fine. But don't stand in my house, right in front of me, and insult me."

"Nonbeliever?" he murmured.

Anger flushed her system as she glared up at him. If there was a single doubt left in her that said she should tell him about what happened last night with Sarah, it wasn't there anymore. If someone lived in a house like his and still didn't believe, he wasn't going to believe she possibly communed with his dead father. And that sucked, because if that spirit was Lawrence and if what he said was true, Devlin should know—his family should know.

But it wasn't going to come out of her mouth. "Why are you even here? Did Gabe need a chaperone?"

He finally moved again, taking another quiet step toward where she sat. "Why I'm here is none of your business."

Rosie threw up her hands. "You're in my house, so yes, it is my business."

"This is not your house."

"What?"

"It's your *apartment*."

"Are you for real?" She let out a short laugh, looking away. Why did so many good-looking guys have to be such douche canoes? "Man, you are something else."

"That I am."

"That wasn't a compliment."

"You sure about that?"

"Uh, yeah. I am."

"Hmm." He sounded utterly dismissive.

She had to force her hands to unclench. "I think you're the most uptight person I know."

"You know nothing about me."

"I know enough to know you need a hobby or a pastime. Maybe a different workout regimen to de-stress or you need to get laid. Something to loosen you up a bit."

His lips parted as he stared down at her. He looked *affronted*. Like if he had pearls, he'd be clutching them. "Did you seriously just tell me I needed to get laid?"

Rosie rolled her eyes. "Did you seriously just prove what I said?"

A moment passed. "Are you volunteering?"

Her mouth dropped open so fast she was sure she was catching flies. She was almost positive he was engaged to be married to Sabrina

Harrington. Then again, since Sabrina's brother was Parker, who'd just attempted to kill Nikki, perhaps that engagement was off.

A sudden sound came from her bedroom, drawing her attention. It sounded like a sob. Concern spiked as she pulled her feet off the table and started to stand.

"Don't."

Her head swiveled toward Devlin. "Excuse me?"

"Don't intrude on them."

Rosie stood and straightened, which put her right about chest level to Devlin. That little observation shot a trill through her system. Tall men were . . . they were just yummy. Unfortunately, this man's personality was anything but yummy. "Please tell me there's something wrong with my hearing and you did not just tell me what to do."

"My brother is back there with Nikki. She needs him and he needs to be there for her," he said, his voice low. "He loves her."

Rosie snapped her mouth shut and then asked, "Gabe loves her?"

Devlin's expression was bland as he nodded.

"Wow. You look so thrilled about that."

He crossed his arms, and her eyes narrowed into thin slits. "What?" she demanded, mimicking his movements and folding her arms across her chest. "You don't approve of his relationship with Nikki? You don't think she's good enough—"

"I do not approve of virtually any relationship," he said, cutting her off. "The age difference is a bit concerning, but if you're insinuating that I don't approve because she is the daughter of our staff, that is your mistake to make, not mine."

"Wait—you don't approve of any relationship? Aren't you engaged?"

"Not anymore."

Well, that cleared up her earlier suspicions. "But you were engaged."

"How does that have any bearing on this conversation?"

Rosie stared at him for what felt like a full minute before she could find the right words. "Were you not in a relationship while you were engaged? Did you not love—"

"You do not need to love someone to be in a relationship or be engaged to them," he cut in, and Rosie's eyes widened.

"Wow," she murmured, sitting back down. "Why would you do that to yourself?"

"Do what?" Confusion clouded his features.

"Marry someone you didn't love? Why would you put yourself through something like that?" she asked, honestly curious. "Put another person through that?"

A dark shadow crossed his features, and Rosie knew almost instantly that she'd crossed some unspoken line with this man. Then again, she figured he had an entire city's worth of lines to be crossed.

Devlin's face turned to granite as he stared down at her. "I find it ironic that you sit there in judgment of my *ended* engagement, as if you're a fountain of knowledge on such subjects, when you're so obviously not married or engaged, living alone in an apartment with beaded curtains and books about ghosts."

Rosie drew in a sharp breath that scalded the back of her throat. She may've tiptoed over a line with him, but he just dive-bombed over one with her. "I *was* married, you flaming asshole, and just so you know, we didn't have a lot, but I loved my husband and he loved me." Reaching around her neck, she tugged on the gold chain and pulled it out from underneath her shirt. "So, even though he no longer walks this earth, I *still* sit here on my fountain of knowledge, knowing exactly what it's like to marry for love and then lose it."

A flicker of regret widened his eyes and the line of his jaw softened just a bit. "I'm—"

"Don't apologize. I don't care," she snapped, snatching up her mug. Lukewarm coffee sloshed over the rim, onto her fingers.

Devlin stared at her a moment and then turned away. The conversation came to a grinding halt right then and there. Devlin retreated to the balcony doors that overlooked Chartres Street and stared at his phone. Rosie turned on the television, and yeah, she purposely opened up her DVR and played an episode of *The Dead Files*.

Devlin's heavy sigh once he realized what she'd turned on made her feel better about how messed up life could be.

As minutes ticked into an hour, Rosie checked in on her friend by quietly moving the curtain aside when she went to put her mug in the sink. The room was dark, but she could make out the shapes of Nikki and Gabe. He was holding her so close she could barely make out where one of them began and the other ended.

Seeing that got Gabe a step closer to being off the Boyfriends Who Needed to Get Their Shit Together list.

When she turned back around, Devlin was still standing quietly by the balcony doors. Her gaze drifted to her small kitchen and she felt like it was time for some rage cleaning. She was behind her sink, reaching for the door underneath to grab some cleaning supplies, when Devlin spoke for the first time in over an hour.

"You lied to me."

Her head jerked up. "What?"

He was still standing with his back to her. "Yesterday. When you said you didn't know who I was, you obviously did."

Rosie's mouth dropped open as she straightened. "So you do remember me."

He was quiet for a moment. "How could I forget?"

Her brows snapped together. "Sure seemed like you did when you saw me."

"I was surprised to see the woman who'd brought me flowers in a cemetery now standing in the same place one of my employees was," he replied, and Rosie's empty hands flattened on the counter. "The same woman who claimed she didn't know who I was, at first."

She tried to count to ten, but only made it to five. "I know it seems hard to believe, but I seriously didn't know who you were when I saw you drop the flowers."

"Then why didn't you tell me who you were once you realized?"

That was a good question. One she really didn't have an awesome answer for, so she went with the truth. "Because I figured I'd never see you again. Who I was didn't matter."

"But it does." Devlin then turned to face her, and she almost wished he hadn't. His intense stare unnerved her. "Because I know exactly who you are now, Rosie Herpin."

Chapter 5

*R*osie's stomach took a tumble as a fine shiver skated across her shoulder blades. "Yeah. I think we just established that. I'm the woman who was super nice to you yesterday and brought you peonies."

He stepped forward. "You're also the woman who introduced Nikki to Ross Haid."

Crap! That was true.

Damn it, if and when she saw Ross Haid again, she was going to straight up sucker punch the man in the throat.

She'd met Ross around two years ago, when he was doing a fluff piece on French Quarter ghost tours. He'd sought her out to do an interview, and they'd hit it off since she appreciated his quick-wittedness and he found her snark humorous. She never in a million years would've thought he'd use their friendship in the way he did.

"A man who happens to be a journalist hell-bent on destroying my family." Somehow, Devlin was even closer without her realizing it. "So, if you're wondering if I for one second believe that you didn't know who I was yesterday, you'd be mistaken."

Rosie felt warmth swamp her face as she struggled to keep her voice low so they weren't overheard. "Okay, let's get a few things straight. I didn't know Ross wanted to meet Nikki because of her working for your family or her involvement with Gabe. I would *never* do that to my friend."

He said nothing as he tilted his head.

"Ross also knows better than to come anywhere near me now, be-cause I was scarily angry when I learned that he used me to get to

Nikki and you don't want to see me scarily angry," she said, stepping toward him. "And, for the last time, I did not know who you were until I saw you standing in front of the de Vincent tomb."

Devlin was now so close that she caught the scent of his cologne. It was a crisp citrus scent mixed with the woodsy aroma of teak. In other words, he smelled really, really good and if he weren't such a douche canoe, her lady parts would've appreciated the cologne.

There was a slight curve to one side of his lips. A smirk. "There's something you need to know about me."

"I don't think there's anything I need to know about you." She unfolded her arms.

He let out a dry, sardonic sound that wasn't much of a laugh. "Well, you need to know that I know everything and if I come across something I don't, I find out. So, of course, I learned that Ross tried to go through Nikki to get to my family. It took *nothing* to discover that one Rosie Herpin was the connection between them. It was only your name I was given."

Okay. That was officially creepy. The need to point out that his ego was about the size of Lake Pontchartrain faded. "Given by whom?"

He ignored that question as he dipped his chin a fraction of an inch. "I should've made sure that I knew what you looked like. That was my mistake, but now I know."

"Who gave you my name?" she demanded.

Devlin smiled at her then, and it was a tight, cold one. "If you ever do anything again that jeopardizes my family, and that includes Nikki, you won't just regret it. Do you understand me?"

That smile and those words were encased in ice and they should've scared her, but all they did was seriously piss her off. "Are you seriously standing in my house and threatening me?"

His chin came down even farther, lining their mouths up like they were lovers. "I do believe we've already established that this is not a house but an apartment."

Rosie wasn't quite sure what tipped her over the edge, leaving bitch-tigress mode behind and going straight into slap-a-bitch mode. Could've been the insinuation that she would somehow put Nikki in harm's way or it could've been the fact that he had the gall to threaten her. Hell, it could've been his mere presence at this point that did it.

Either way, Rosie lifted her hand without thinking. She wasn't going to hit him, even though that would give her enough satisfaction that therapists across the nation would be concerned. She lifted her hand to push him back.

But that didn't happen.

Devlin had the reflexes of a damn cat, catching her wrist before she even had the joy of making contact. She gasped out of surprise and his eyes narrowed into thin slits. "Were you going to hit me?"

"No," she seethed, wishing her eyes could shoot out death rays.

"That's not how it appears to me," he said, his voice deadly soft.

"Well, I have a feeling a lot of things don't appear as they really are to you," she shot back, tugging on her arm, but he didn't let go. "I was going to push you since, you know, you're in my personal space."

"I'm not the one who got in your space." A muscle flexed along his jaw. "You got in mine."

Okay, that was kind of true.

"There's something else you need to know." He tugged on her arm, and before Rosie could react, her chest was suddenly flush against his. The contact was jarring, sending a riot of sensations through her. "I don't make threats. I make promises."

She drew in a deep breath and immediately regretted it, because it pushed her chest against his even more, and . . . God, her stomach was dropping and twisting in ways that were *not* unpleasant. She felt her nipples harden, and started praying that he couldn't feel them through the incredibly thin and worn shirt she wore and the lacy, nearly non-existent bralette she'd slept in.

She didn't back down, though. "I don't think you know how to use words correctly, because that, yet again, sounded an awful lot like a threat."

"Does it?" he asked, and his voice seemed deeper, rougher. His eyes took on a sudden, hooded quality. "If it was a threat, it doesn't seem to be working."

"Why is that?"

Devlin shifted just the slightest, and the next breath Rosie took lodged in her throat. She felt him against her stomach, thick and hard, and unless he had something weird in the front of his pants, he was totally turned on.

So was she.

And they were both apparently freaks, because she'd just tried to shove him and he had just threatened her, but here they were, utterly aroused, and there was a really good chance she needed to find a therapist stat.

Those thick lashes lifted and his eyes pierced hers. It was like he waited for her to say something or to pull away, but she did nothing but hold his stare as a lick of heat curled low in her stomach.

Devlin's gaze lowered and those full lips parted. "I think it's doing something entirely different."

It was. For a multitude of wrong reasons, it was, and Rosie bit down on her lower lip as her hips shifted of their own accord.

"Are we going to pretend like you don't feel me?" he asked, rather calmly.

"Yes," she snapped.

"How's that working out for you?"

"Just great." The moment those words came out of her mouth, she realized how ridiculous they sounded.

Devlin's lips twitched, and she just wanted him to—

Footsteps sounded from her bedroom, and both of them reacted at once. Devlin let go of her wrist as if her skin scalded him, and Rosie turned into a kangaroo, because she jumped back a good foot.

The curtains parted, rattling as the beads knocked off one another. She hoped she looked somewhat normal as Gabe and Nikki entered the room and not like she had just been seconds away from rubbing all over Devlin like a cat that was not only in heat but one that also had rabies.

Gabe had his arm tight around Nikki's shoulders and he didn't seem at all surprised that Devlin was still there, but the moment she saw Nikki, she wasn't thinking about whatever the hell had happened between her and Devlin. A little bit of shame rose in Rosie. While she'd been out here arguing and whatever with Devlin, Nikki had been in there, in pain and living a nightmare that had come to life.

Rosie cringed. Somehow the bruises looked even worse now. She hurried from where she stood. "Hey, honey. How are you feeling?"

Nikki tried to smile, but it was more of a grimace. "Better. I'm feeling better."

"That's good." She glanced at Gabe as she felt Devlin move closer to them.

"I'm going to Gabe's," Nikki said, and if her face wasn't so messed up at the moment, Rosie knew she'd see a blush.

"Okay. Is there anything I can do?"

"You've already done enough," Nikki replied.

"Thank you for getting Nikki this morning," Gabe chimed in.

"I haven't done nearly enough, so there's no need to thank me." Rosie leaned in, carefully kissing the one unmarred spot on Nikki's cheek. "Text me later, okay? When you feel up to it?"

"Will do."

Rosie then turned to Gabe and met his stare. "Take care of my girl."

"Always" came Gabe's response.

She held his gaze for a moment, long enough for him to understand she would, without a doubt, find a voodoo priestess to hex him if he did Nikki wrong again.

A slow, small smile tugged at Gabe's lips and then he turned, guiding Nikki to the door. Devlin was already there, opening it for them. Rosie trailed behind.

Devlin stepped out into the hall as Rosie gripped the side of the door. He turned and looked at her, opening his mouth.

"All the gossip magazines have it wrong," she said, meeting his blue-green eyes. "They call you the Devil, but they should call you the Dickhead."

And with that, she slammed the door shut in Devlin de Vincent's face.

"ALIVE OR DEAD?" There was a pause. "Or would you rather the subject simply disappears?"

Seated in the dimly lit private booth of the Red Stallion Sunday afternoon, Devlin de Vincent was currently deciding if someone lived, died . . . or, as Archie Carr had succinctly put it, simply disappeared.

Frankly, he wanted the *subject* dead and erased.

That would make him smile, but as he dragged his finger along the rim of the heavy glass, he knew he couldn't let his personal feelings involving this person get in the way. He had questions and he needed answers.

"Alive," he answered.

"That'll cost more."

Strange how taking a life would cost less, but then again, keeping someone alive posed risks. Dev understood that. "Figured."

"A lot more."

Slowly, Dev lifted his gaze to the man who sat across from him. Archie was his age, but life in private military armies had weathered and hardened the man, aging him well beyond thirty-eight. The man was finely tuned death, though, and Dev imagined that some of those deep grooves in the pale skin around Archie's dark eyes were a result of the deeds he carried out in exchange for monetary gain.

People lied when they said money couldn't buy you everything.

Money could secure anything. Life. Death. Love. Security. Protection. Absolution. Happiness, or at least, a facsimile of joy. It was Dev's experience that *anything* could be bought or bartered. Only the naive and the emotional believed otherwise, and Dev had never met a person who couldn't be bought one way or another.

"Figured," Dev repeated.

Archie studied him a moment and then nodded. "What do you have for me?"

Using his forefinger, he slid the closed file toward Archie. "Everything you need is in there."

The redheaded man took the file and opened it. A harsh, low chuckle sounded from him. "Interesting. Is this related to what's been all over the news this weekend?"

Dev said nothing, which was answer enough. Word of Parker Harrington's murderous intentions and subsequent death had dominated the news. It was only a matter of time before Parker's sister, his ex-fiancée, was reported missing by her family. Sabrina was out there. Somewhere. And he was going to find her before anyone else did.

Archie closed the file. "And once I've located the subject?"

"You know the place, over in Bywater."

"Same code?"

He nodded.

"Meanwhile, you've got yourself a gun, right? Just in case that crazy comes back to you," Archie said.

"Of course. There's something else I want you to do for me."

"I'm all ears." Archie tossed his arm along the back of the booth.

"I want you to look into something that involves my uncle."

Archie's brows lifted, wrinkling his forehead. "The senator."

"He's the only uncle left, isn't he?" Dev's fingers curled around his glass. "I want you to find anything you can on that intern of his."

Interest sparked in his eyes. "The one who went missing? Andrea Joan?"

"Yes."

He seemed to mull that over. "Do you think she's dead?"

Dev didn't answer for a long moment. "I hope she is. For her sake."

"Jesus," Archie muttered. He was one of the rare people who got what Dev meant, because he knew about one-tenth of what Dev knew, and Dev was guessing that was enough to keep the man awake at night. "On it."

"Perfect."

"Speaking of the senator. You did get my update about what you suspected?"

"The Ritz-Carlton while I was out of town?" Dev asked.

Archie nodded. "And many, many times before that from what my contacts have advised."

"Yes." Taking a drink, he welcomed the burn as the amber-colored liquid coursed down his throat. "I'll wait to hear from you."

Nodding, Archie scooted to the end of the booth and then stopped. He met Dev's stare. "I've seen some shit. Stared evil in the face to know that real evil *has* a face. And there've been times I've been terrified by what I've seen and who I've met. You? Never once seen you break a smile. You scare me a little."

Dev lifted a brow.

Archie grinned. "I'll be in touch."

Watching Archie slide out of the booth and disappear into the shadows, Dev finished off his glass of bourbon as he thought about what Archie had admitted.

"You scare me a little."

Even his brothers were afraid of him. They had no reason to be, but he understood why. After all, he was willing to go *there* to protect his brothers, do the unthinkable. But they didn't know what he knew, and it would stay that way.

He was their shield and that would never change.

"Another glass?"

Dev's gaze shifted to Justin, one of the servers who'd been at the Red Stallion for years. "Yes. Thank you."

Bowing, Justin plucked up the glass and disappeared. Dev glanced at his phone and started to reach for it, but stopped. His brother had his hands full at the moment. Both of them, actually. Letting his head rest against the tall booth, he exhaled a long, steady breath and for some damn reason, an image came to him.

Not just an image.

A person.

A person he'd met for the first time on Friday.

A person who searched him down in a cemetery to bring him flowers. A person who told him that his father's death would get easier to deal with, and she had said that like she had personal experience in the subject matter. A person who turned out to be connected to that annoying son of a bitch journalist. And she was definitely someone not scared of him. Not even remotely. She had not been feeling fear when she'd been pressed against him.

And he'd definitely been feeling . . . something.

Rosie Herpin.

A Creole last name to match the tawny complexion.

Another glass of bourbon appeared in front of him, but he didn't reach for it.

Beaded curtains?

The woman had the tackiest beaded curtains in her apartment. What grown adult with even a thumbnail-sized worth of taste would have cheap beaded curtains in their home? It wasn't the sixties or seventies, and Rosie wasn't a child amused by things that clanked together and made noise.

A day after his brother played the white-knight-in-shining-armor routine and retrieved their temporary housekeeper from what Dev was guessing was her best friend's apartment, this was what was lingering on the edge of his thoughts.

Beaded fucking curtains.

Dev had no idea why he was even thinking about the woman.

Actually, that wasn't entirely true. If he was going to be honest with himself for once in his life, it was because Rosie . . . *intrigued* him on several levels. One of the reasons being the fact she had looked at him like his mere presence in her apartment tainted everything in it, including the beaded curtains.

No one, besides his brothers, looked at him like that or dared to glare at him.

That . . . interested him. And he needed to spend only a handful of minutes with Rosie to know she was nothing like that conniving—

He cut those thoughts off. Shut them the hell down.

Dev thought about where Rosie lived. Not too far from Jackson Square. How in the hell she lived there, with all the noise, was beyond him. His gaze shifted to the glass of bourbon.

There were two types of New Orleanians. Those who thrived on the sounds, the smells, the sights, and the whole atmosphere of the French Quarter. And there were those who avoided the Quarter at all costs.

He was guessing Rosie was the former.

He was the latter.

Dev didn't know much about her. He could change that in seconds if he wanted to. One call and he could find out anything he wanted to know. Age. Birthplace. Family. Siblings. Education. Workplace. *Anything*. He could even find out exactly how this husband of hers had died.

Damn.

He'd been an asshole about that, hadn't he?

His gaze shifted to his phone again. The strangest thing had happened when he stood in Rosie's apartment that morning, waiting for his brother and arguing with her over what constituted real wood. He stopped . . . thinking.

Thinking about everything.

Dev couldn't even remember the last time when that had happened, and well, that had been a nice break.

Devlin didn't believe in coincidences, so there wasn't a single doubt in his mind that she knew exactly who he was when she found him in the cemetery. Had Ross been following him and sent her in? Quite possible since it was a favorite pastime of the reporter. Her apparent close relationship to Nikki and her association with Ross made Rosie dangerous.

So, of course, he'd become hard as a rock arguing with her.

He didn't even want to know what that said about him, but he knew the whole time he'd been with Sabrina, and that had been years, never once did he get so turned on, so easily.

That was why sex, and it hadn't been often, with Sabrina had been a chore, a means to an end that was never fulfilled. And there was no way Sabrina hadn't felt his impassivity when it came to her. He was also a means to an end for her.

Hell, he didn't want to think about Sabrina. He'd rather think about the woman who glared at him like she wanted to kill him with a single look.

What had she called him?

Ah, yes. A dickhead.

His shoulders lifted in a silent chuckle as he reached for his glass of bourbon. A woman who owned fucking beaded curtains actually interested him. A woman with hazel eyes—eyes that shifted from brown to green depending on how angry she was becoming.

Damn.

Hazel eyes.

It made him think of when he was a young boy. His mother had this friend who'd come visit every Saturday. This was before his brothers and sister were born, when it was just him and his mother and . . . *Saturdays*. Mrs. Windham would always bring her daughter with her. The girl was Dev's age, give or take a few months. All he could remember was that she had blond hair and hazel eyes. What was her name?

Pearl.

They used to play in the many rooms at the manor, because Lawrence was never home on Saturdays, and Dev could just be. One day, he was rushing from bedroom to bedroom, looking for Pearl. They'd been playing hide-and-seek or some silly game like that. He couldn't remember that exactly, but he did recall finding Pearl. He'd also found Lawrence with Mrs. Windham in one of those rooms.

His mother's friend didn't come back after that afternoon. Dev never saw Pearl again, and Saturdays changed. Everything began to change that one Saturday afternoon, and it wasn't until years later, when Dev was older, that he began to understand why.

When was the last time he'd thought of Pearl? Hell. It had been years.

His mind shifted back to Lawrence. The man was a virus that infected everything he touched, that much was true. Too many people who had business dealings with Lawrence, from his estate lawyer, Edmond Oakes, to several high-ranking city officials, had become tainted and twisted, either implicated or complicit in what Dev had suspected of Lawrence.

Hell, Lawrence was more than a virus. He had been a fucking cancer.

A shadow fell over the table, drawing his gaze. Justin stood there once more, holding a manila envelope. "Sorry to bother you, Mr. de Vincent, but this was left for you at the door."

"Was it?" He reached for the envelope, taking it from the man. "By whom?"

"It appears to have been placed in the mail slot just a few moments ago. No one saw who left it there."

Interesting. "Thank you, Justin."

The man nodded and then scurried off while Dev looked at the envelope. His name was typed across the center of the envelope. Turning it over, he tore the top, unsealing it. At first he thought there was nothing in it, but as he reached inside, he felt something smooth. Dev pulled out an eight by eleven photograph.

What the . . . ?

A photograph of him and Lawrence de Vincent, his *father*. It was taken at the last charity function Lawrence had attended with Dev before Lawrence's . . . untimely passing and only a few months after Dev's suspicions about Lawrence had been confirmed in ways he could've never imagined.

Neither of them was smiling as they stood side by side. Neither of them looked like he wanted to be there. And neither of them was doing a good job hiding their immense dislike and distrust of one another.

Dev remembered the night of the Ulysses Ball. It was that evening, in the car to the event, the man who'd raised Dev and made him who he was today had scornfully told him that he and Gabriel were not his children. Only Lucian and their sister, Madeline, were.

Hell, Dev had never felt relief like he had right then. Some might believe that Dev was a monster, but if they knew what he did about Lawrence, they'd know what Archie had said earlier was true.

Real evil always had a face.

His brothers hadn't known that Dev knew the truth before them. His brothers hardly knew anything.

Not even what Dev had learned before the night of the Ulysses Ball. A secret so fucking life-changing that he still, to this day, had no idea how to tell his brothers.

How to even deal with it himself.

If he could spare his brothers the knowledge of how evil, how spiteful the man who raised them was, he would. Damn, if he wasn't trying to go to the grave with what he knew. It would be . . . better that way.

But it wasn't the photograph that caused Dev's jaw to clench. It wasn't even what the photograph symbolized. It was the message scratched into the film by what looked to be a needle or some other thin, sharp instrument.

I know the truth.

Chapter 6

Rosie spent the better part of the weekend alternating between re-playing the verbal fisticuffs with Dickhead de Vincent, being furious with herself for the momentary lapse of sanity when she'd been pretty damn aroused by the Dickhead and worrying about Nikki.

Which meant she was antsy and unable to sit still for longer than a minute at a time. This left her with only one option.

Rage cleaning.

She attacked every inch of her apartment. The living room and kitchen were practically sparkling and by the time she finished the bathroom adjacent to her bedroom, she felt that an immune-compromised individual could safely eat off the floor in there.

The bathroom was Rosie's second favorite place in the apartment, coming in behind the balcony. The balcony only took first place because of its comfortable chairs and the view. After standing all day, either working the register or in the kitchen of her parents' bakery while her parents, with the best intentions, periodically demanded to know ex-actly when Rosie was going to put one of her three college degrees to use, it was nice to sit up there and people watch.

That special scene—the one reserved only for people ready to get married and have babies.

Rosie already had that, at least the get-married part, and she wasn't sure she'd have that ever again or if she wanted to.

By the end of those days when her parents and sister, Bella, were on her, Rosie wanted nothing more than to kick her feet up and drink wine out on the balcony, under the churning fans, doing nothing but people watching and listening.

The claw-foot tub and the balcony were what sold the apartment. She'd stumbled across it two years ago. Getting into the apartment had taken some patience since the tenant had left a lot of his personal belongings behind.

But it had been worth the wait.

Her apartment was rather small, but the bathroom was humongous in comparison. It was like the apartment was built around the bathroom. At least that was what she liked to think. In reality, the bathroom was probably originally a bedroom or something, but it was just amazing.

A double-sink vanity and long mirror offered more than enough room for all her makeup and hair stuff, which was quite impressive considering she did have a mean makeup addiction. She was constantly on the lookout for the perfect foundation. Her skin tone did not make that easy. Foundation often looked amazing in the soft lights of the bathroom, but once she stepped out under the sun, she either appeared ghastly ill or like she'd baked herself. So the drawers were filled with samples and half-used jars she hadn't parted with, because maybe one day, magically, the foundation would work. Not only did the bathroom have that amazing vanity with a space underneath for a chair, but it also had a beautiful porcelain tub that had probably been in this apartment since the dawn of time.

There was also a decent-sized detached shower with classic subway tile. She could lie down in the bathroom, stretch her arms and legs out, and make bathroom angels without touching anything. Perfect. And if she did that right now, she knew she'd be fresh and clean since she'd scrubbed the tile floor for about an hour.

Rage cleaning was a lot like depressed cleaning, which was what she did whenever she really allowed herself to sit and think about Ian. It was no big surprise that he was lingering in the back of her mind since it was the anniversary of his death, but there really wasn't a day that went by in the last ten years that Rosie wasn't reminded of him.

Hell, nearly every time she walked into Pradine's Pralines, the bakery run by her family since its creation, she thought about how Ian used to come here after school and study at one of the small booths at the front of the store.

Sometimes, when she was at the bakery, behind the register, and if she tried hard enough, she could see him sitting there, nibbling on the cap of his pen as he pored over his homework.

Those were the memories she held on to.

And Devlin thought she didn't know anything about marriage and love? What an asshole.

Irritated all over again, she stomped out to the kitchen and made a beeline for the bottle of moscato in the fridge. She poured herself a glass and walked over to where her laptop sat open on the coffee table.

She needed a distraction and she had the perfect one. The video that had been sent to her this morning was paused on her laptop. She'd already watched it about two dozen times and was prepared to watch it two dozen more.

And it wasn't even a video of puppies stumbling around and being freaking adorable either. It was better than that.

Plopping down on her couch, she balanced the laptop on her knees and hit play.

NOPE had caught something on film.

It wasn't a full-bodied apparition, but the shadow darting across the hallway was definitely not a floating dust bunny.

Setting her wineglass aside, she picked up her red-framed glasses and then brought the screen as close as she could to her face. She hit the play button again on the grainy image. The moment the shadow blob appeared at the end of the hall, across from the baby's room, she hit pause. Squinting, she tried to make out any sort of definition to the blob.

It looked like smudge on the camera or a flying grocery bag, but she knew that wasn't what it was. She hit play and then slowed the film down. It still looked like a grocery-bag-blob when it disappeared into the opposite wall. What followed could only be described as the sound of a sledgehammer hitting the floor.

Rosie knew the sound was coming, after all, but it still caused her to jerk and her heart to jump. Whatever was behind that noise was physical. It caused the camera to shake, and seconds later, she could hear the baby crying from inside his room.

"Damn," she whispered. A slow smile crept across her face.

Not a full-bodied apparition, but there was definitely something in that house.

Whatever was caught on the camera might not seem like much to the untrained eye, but it was some sort of evidence, and it gave her hope they'd find more, because they'd just installed the cameras in the Mendezes' home over in the Garden District on Friday. To catch anything this quickly was a good sign—to Rosie and her team.

Not to the poor Mendez family.

They'd contacted NOPE a little over a month ago. Maureen and Preston Mendez had bought the rather recently built home on Third Street a few years back. They didn't have any trouble until their son came into the picture. According to what the Mendez family reported, it started off as disembodied footsteps and other sounds, like unexplained bangs and thuds. Then they started catching movement out of the corners of their eyes, and items would go missing and randomly reappear in odd places. Things that could easily be ignored or chalked up to the house settling or one of them being forgetful, but the behavior had been steadily increasing over the weeks and months. Both the husband and wife claimed to see a shadow figure in the upstairs hallway, near their son Steve's room. The unexplained thuds grew louder, eventually shaking the entire house, like the one caught on the camera. Feelings of being watched and followed throughout the house had escalated into doors slamming and, according to the couple, the holy grail of hauntings.

Full. Body. Apparition.

Preston claimed he saw what appeared to be an older man in baby Steve's room, standing by the crib. He described the apparition as being solid around the head, shoulders, and chest, while the lower body was more see-through. Preston had been so caught off guard by the sight, he hadn't noticed the period of clothing or any other detail other than the room feeling colder than normal. The apparition had disappeared right before his eyes.

Afraid for their child's safety, especially since the FBA was seen in Steve's room, and more than just a little freaked out, the family called NOPE. Most ghosts never meant any harm. If they were active hauntings versus residual, they were often just curious. However, sometimes what people had in their homes weren't ghosts.

Sometimes it was something else entirely.

Rosie lowered the laptop and flagged the segment of film. Saving the video, she sent the file over to Lance Page, who had the technology to isolate the images and magnify without losing quality. Reaching for the cushion beside her, she snatched up her phone and quickly sent a text to Lance letting him know he had film heading his way. Before she put her phone aside, she scrolled through her texts until she came upon her friend Nikki's last text.

Face hurts like hell, but I'm okay.

Rosie stared at it for what felt like an hour but was only a few moments. She knew that Nikki was physically okay but emotionally? Mentally? That was a different story, and Rosie didn't need her third unused bachelor's degree, this one in psychology, to know that.

Dropping her phone on the cushion, she leaned forward and placed her laptop back on the coffee table. She tugged off her glasses and placed them on the laptop.

She glanced at the closed balcony doors. Night had fallen, but the hum of traffic and voices was still as strong as ever. When she closed her eyes, the most annoying image ever surfaced. She immediately saw Devlin standing before those doors.

Goodness, that man was good-looking, but he was also a certifiable douche nozzle—an attractive douche nozzle.

An arrogant, straitlaced, demanding, obnoxious douche nozzle about as warm and friendly as a haunted house.

A jerk who appeared to be very, very well-endowed. God. She did not need to think about that. She didn't even need to think about him in general, but he was in her thoughts whether she liked it or not.

Opening her eyes, she pursed her lips. Saturday morning and that man had been dressed as if he were attending a business meeting, wearing gray trousers and a white button-down. He looked amazing, though, just like he had at the cemetery, but she doubted he owned a pair of jeans.

Recalling the look on his face when she called him a dickhead, she giggled. She wished she'd had the foresight to have had her phone in her hand, because that splash of shock would've been amazing to capture on film. She would've changed her Facebook profile pic to it just to be an ass.

Another giggle escaped her as she glanced up at the llama-shaped clock her friend Bree had gotten her. God only knew where she found a llama-shaped clock, but Rosie wasn't complaining. The thing was amazing, and she had a soft spot for those adorably weird creatures.

It was close to ten, and she should be tired, having woken up so early yesterday and the same today to pull a shift at Pradine's to get ready for the church crowd, but she was wide-awake and antsy.

And there was only one thing that cured restlessness.

Du Monde beignets.

Sadly, that meant she was going to have to get changed. Even though it was nighttime in the Quarter and there'd be all manner of people walking the streets, Rosie was not going out there wearing nothing but a tank top, boxer shorts, and thick, knee-high socks.

Beignets were worth the effort, though.

Popping to her feet, she'd started to turn when her phone rang. A smile appeared when she saw Lance's name and the goofy pic of him wearing a headband with tiny plastic ghosts attached to springs.

"Hey, buddy," she answered as she picked up her wine. "Thought you were on shift tonight?"

"Nah. Got off early," he answered. Lance was an EMT, and boy, did his job never have a dull moment. "I saw the video. Haven't been able to take a closer look, but whoa, I can't believe we caught something already."

"I know." She took a sip of her wine. "It's freaking out there."

"We need to get back in that house and spend another night."

"Yes, but the family hasn't agreed to that yet." They wanted their help, but NOPE had only been able to log a handful of hours investigating. "And if they don't . . ."

Lance sighed. "If they don't, then I am suspicious as fuck that we're getting played."

"Me, too." Finishing off the wine, she carried her glass into the kitchen. NOPE debunked and discovered scams more than they found actual evidence, but that was the nature of the business. "Jilly said she'd be calling the family tomorrow with an update. You'll have the film enhanced by then?"

"Of course." There was a pause as Rosie placed her glass in the sink. "Doing anything tonight?"

"Nothing except I was thinking about walking down to Du Monde."

"Want company?"

Rosie grinned. Lance lived off of Canal, and that was a bit of a hike to Du Monde, but, like her, Lance was a night owl and was up for anything. "If you're sure you want to join me."

"Babe, I always want to," he replied.

Her grin faltered as she pushed away from the kitchen counter. There was something teasing about how he said that, but there was also something . . . *more*. Anxiety bubbled to life. Lance was cute and an all-around great guy, but he was one of her closest friends. She knew better than to cross those lines, no matter how easy it would be. And lately? Lance had been throwing off signals that could be read as him being interested in more. Dinner invites. Showing up unexpectedly at Pradine's with her favorite drink—salted caramel mocha—or surprising her with her favorite snack, those Graze box thingies that were all garlicky and yummy and *not* easy to come by. Or he could just be an awesome friend and she was reading way too much into it.

Probably the latter.

"You there, Rosie?" he asked.

"Yeah." She cleared her throat. "Sorry. Zoned out. Weird weekend."

"Then even more reason to shut the weekend down with beignets."

Relaxing, she rolled her eyes. "No truer words have ever been spoken. I just need about fifteen minutes to get changed. Okay?"

"Perfect. See you there."

Hanging up, she left her phone in the kitchen as she hurried into her bedroom, grinning when the curtains rattled obnoxiously behind her. Yanking a pair of patterned leggings out of the dresser, she toed off her socks, nearly falling over in the process.

She tried to picture Devlin spontaneously going to get beignets at ten at night, and burst out laughing. With her leggings halfway stuck around her knees, she fell backward, her butt hitting the bed.

Rosie was betting Devlin de Vincent was about as spontaneous as a dentist appointment.

DEV DIDN'T LIKE SURPRISES.

Especially when that surprise came in the form of his uncle, Stefan de Vincent, waiting for him in his home office Monday morning.

"I'm sorry. The senator insisted it could not wait." Richard Besson explained as Dev stalked down the hall of the second floor.

The older house manager was as much a part of this building as a de Vincent was, having run the home, along with his wife, since Dev was a child. Livie was out for health reasons for the time being, and their daughter, Nikki, had stepped in. However, Nikki was no longer a suitable replacement, even temporarily, for a multitude of reasons.

Dev briefly wondered what Besson thought of his daughter's relationship with Gabe. Even though Gabe was, by far, the most . . . likable of the brothers, he was still a de Vincent, and Besson had seen a lot in his time working here.

Besson also knew a lot.

The faint curiosity disappeared as his gaze focused on the paneled doors that led to his office. A muscle worked along his jaw.

"It's okay." Dev adjusted the cuffs on his shirt. "Can you please bring up a pot of coffee when you have a chance?"

"Of course." Besson started to turn.

Dev stopped as Besson started to turn. Lowering his arms, he shook out the sleeves. "Richard?"

A flicker of surprise crossed the older man's face. "Yes?"

He opened his mouth and then closed it. A moment passed as he considered what he wanted to say. He stepped toward the older man, keeping his voice low as he said, "I am sorry for what happened to your daughter. I will make sure nothing like that happens again."

Besson stared back at him for a moment and then cleared his throat. "I do not have a doubt that you will . . . ensure that my daughter is safe. Thank you."

Dev nodded. "We need to have a discussion later about a temporary replacement for Livie. Nikki is no longer suited for the job."

Her father opened his mouth.

"She's in a relationship with my brother," Dev said, catching the man's dark eyes. "I do not think you want her responsible for serving his food and cleaning up after him, too."

A faint smile crossed Besson's face. "No. I do not."

"Good."

The smile remained. "I'll have a fresh pot of coffee brought to your office momentarily."

Giving the man a curt nod, Dev pivoted and approached his office doors. He placed his hands on the panels and pushed.

His office was light and airy from the sun streaming through the east windows, but there was a dark cloud sitting with his back to the doors.

Lawrence de Vincent had been pure evil. His twin, Stefan, was just a fucking idiot in comparison. Dangerous in his own ways, but nowhere near as bad as Lawrence.

"Nice of you to finally join me," Stefan said.

Dev's lip curled as he closed the doors behind him. He hated the sound of Stefan's voice, because it sounded like Lawrence's. "Nice of you to show up unannounced after you haven't returned my calls all weekend."

"I was in D.C., Dev, and quite busy."

"So busy you couldn't use a phone?" Dev strolled across the office, and as he passed his uncle, he caught the faint scent of Cuban cigars.

Rich, sweet ones like Lawrence used to smoke. He stepped behind the desk, and only then did he allow himself to look at his uncle.

With the trademark blue-green eyes and dark hair with only a tint of silver to the man's temples, he looked every inch a de Vincent. Faint lines appeared at the corners of his eyes and lips. Whether it was because of a skilled doctor's hand or good genetics, the man was aging well.

Stefan looked just like Lawrence. After all, they were identical twins, so every time Dev had to cast his eyes upon Stefan, it was like looking at the one thing he truly hated.

His uncle probably came in at a close second if Dev had to list those he hated, and his uncle deserved every ounce of it, but if he had to compare the two men, Lawrence was worse.

Lawrence would always be worse.

"I was busy representing this fine state. Running the country is quite time-consuming." Stefan smiled as Dev sat, toying with the gold band of the Rolex wrapped around his left wrist. "But I figured you were calling me over what happened Friday night, and I am here now."

"So, you've seen the news?"

Stefan snorted. "How could I not? It's all over the damn place. The brother of a de Vincent fiancée killed while attempting to murder someone? The fuckers are eating this up."

"Fuckers?"

"The press." Stefan flicked his wrist. "They love nothing better than a de Vincent scandal. Especially that damn reporter for the *Advocate*. Ross Haid? While I was on the way here, I got a call from my office saying he was already there, asking questions."

Dev smirked. The mere mention of Ross Haid's name on any other day would've annoyed him greatly. Hearing that the reporter was bothering Stefan amused him. "Well, you do have a lot of experience with reporters digging around in your business, don't you?"

Stefan's lips thinned. "I have a lot of experience with the press making a mountain out of a molehill."

"A missing and presumed-dead intern is a molehill?"

"It is to me." Stefan lifted a shoulder in a casual shrug. "What did Parker do exactly?"

"You don't know?"

"I know that the press believes it was some sort of domestic situation. The victim's name has been withheld, but they believe he attacked someone and was killed in the process," Stefan answered. "I find that odd since I wasn't aware of Parker being in any . . . domestic-type relationship."

Not for one second did Dev believe that was all that he knew. "Parker attacked Nikki."

"Nicolette Besson?" Stefan let out a laugh. "The housekeeper's daughter?"

Dev kept his expression blank. "You mean Gabe's girlfriend?"

"What?" Another laugh as Stefan sat back in the chair. "Jesus. He's screwing that little piece—"

"Careful," Dev warned softly. "I doubt you would like what would happen if Gabe were to hear you speaking like that."

"As if you care how I speak about her." Stefan snorted with a roll of his eyes. A moment passed. "That girl always had a thing for him, didn't she? I guess he's a lucky man."

Tension crept into Dev's shoulders. That was an interesting statement for his uncle to make. Nikki practically grew up in their house when she was younger, spending many of the summers here while her parents worked. Of course, Stefan had been at the home on and off over the years, but Dev hadn't believed his uncle was that observant when it came to what used to be Nikki's schoolgirl, unrequited crush on his brother.

Obviously, Dev had underestimated his uncle's observation skills. He thought of the photograph he received on Sunday.

"Parker went after her?" Stefan asked.

"And you really didn't know that?"

"Of course not," Stefan exclaimed. "How would I?"

There was a knock on the door, and Dev lifted his hand, silencing Stefan. "Come in."

Besson entered and the scent of freshly brewed coffee erased that of cigars. The man was quick as a bullet, serving the coffee and then leaving. Dev figured that Besson wasn't exactly a fan of the senator even though he was too damn professional to show it.

That was why he liked Besson.

Stefan waited until the door closed. "You do not think Sabrina had anything to do with her brother—"

"I know for a fact Sabrina had everything to do with what Parker tried to do to Nikki. I also know that she has been stalking Gabe since college," he said, and when his uncle's gaze flew to his, he raised a brow. "And I also know that she and Parker were responsible for Emma's accident."

"Emma Rothchild?" Stefan froze with the coffee halfway to his mouth. "The woman Gabe used to be involved with *years* ago?"

Dev's expression smoothed out as he studied his uncle. When the news that Sabrina had been involved in Emma's death had come out, it had shocked Dev, who thought he'd known all that Sabrina was capable of. He'd misjudged just how . . . psychotic that woman was at the end of the day. It was a mistake Dev would have to live with.

"Jesus. You're not joking."

"Why would I joke about something like that?" Dev asked.

Stefan took a sip of his coffee. "Why would you lie about how my brother died?"

"Now, Stefan, you know Lawrence hung himself," Dev responded, picking up his coffee. It was dark. No sugar. No cream. A taste as bitter as a winter's night. "Let's not go down that road again."

"I'm never going to get off that road, Devlin." Stefan lifted his cup. "I know my brother did not kill himself."

"Hmm. Tell me something, Stefan." Dev sat back, crossing one knee over the other. He waited until Stefan took a drink. "Do you think I don't know you've been fucking Sabrina?"

The man sputtered, choking on the coffee. Liquid splashed across the front of his suit. His lips pulled back, baring his teeth. "What in the hell?"

Dev wanted to laugh, but he didn't. "Do you know where Sabrina is? Her family hasn't seen her since Friday morning."

"I have no clue where that woman is."

"So you're saying you have no idea where she is?"

"Yes!" Stefan slammed the coffee cup down on the desk with enough force to crack the china. Dev sighed. "And you're out of your mind if you think I've been sleeping with Sabrina."

"Oh I am quite certain you've been with Sabrina, and I know last week wasn't the first time."

"You have to be joking," Stefan said with a forced-sounding laugh. "If you truly thought your fiancée was sleeping with me, why in the hell were you still engaged to her? What does that say about you?"

Dev took a drink even though his stomach churned with a mixture of disgust and loathing. "I have my reasons—reasons, I might add, that are no longer necessary."

"You always have your *reasons*, don't you, Devlin?" The senator's jaw hardened. "You think I don't know what you're trying to accomplish with such an outrageous accusation? Diversion tactics. I bring up my brother and you always find a way to not discuss him."

"So, you weren't with her at the Ritz while I was out of town last weekend?" Dev asked.

Stefan's eyes narrowed. "Do you have someone following me?"

"Answer the question, Stefan."

His uncle's nostrils flared. "She came to see me while I was entertaining guests there. She was concerned about your engagement, quite upset I might add. I'm assuming the engagement is off."

"It is." Dev knew that excuse was bullshit. "Must have been one hell of an entertainment you provided for your guests. You can also safely assume that any donations the Harringtons might've been planning to make for your upcoming campaign for reelection are not going to happen."

Stefan sneered. "You know what your fatal flaw is?"

"I don't have many, but do enlighten me."

The sneer turned into a smirk as he leaned forward, clasping the arms of the chair as he began to rise. "You think you know everything."

Dev raised an eyebrow as he held his uncle's stare.

"And the truth is, you know nothing." Stefan stood, and Dev was rather unimpressed by that parting statement. He thought Stefan could do better than that. "Good day, Devlin."

He waited until his uncle reached the doors and then he spoke. "Stefan?"

His uncle stopped and then turned to him. "What?"

He thought about the gun he kept in the top drawer. His brothers knew where it was. Stefan didn't. Part of him wanted to pull it out and end Stefan right there, but he wasn't a murderer. Not like that. "If I find out you're hiding Sabrina or if you know where she is and have failed to tell me, I will not only take everything from you." Dev smiled then, a slight curl of his lips. "I will destroy you."

Chapter 7

Laughter spilled out from the kitchen, stopping Dev in his tracks Monday evening as he was shrugging on the Cucinelli sport jacket. He was near the back entrance to the kitchen, the one that was accessed by the long, narrow mudroom that led to the back staircases and the veranda.

The sound was so strange to him, he didn't move for several heartbeats. Wild, unfettered *happy* laughter was not something often heard in this home.

His brothers were in there, with their women. Dev figured they were making dinner since he'd advised Besson today that evening responsibilities would be suspended until further notice. The man needed to be home with his ill wife, and Dev was confident the household wouldn't collapse onto itself with no one here in the evening.

"I'm not sure that's how it's supposed to work," he heard Julia say, and he arched a brow.

Lucian and Julia had bought an old Victorian in the Garden District that was currently being renovated. Soon, he imagined that the home would be ready for them, and Lucian would be . . . gone.

Dev couldn't be happier for him.

He imagined Gabe wouldn't be too far behind Lucian, having already looked for a part-time residence in Baton Rouge to be closer to his son. And then it would be just Dev.

Ironic how things always came full circle.

He fixed the collar on the jacket and started walking. He made it a few steps when he felt a kiss of cold air along the nape of his neck. His step halted and he looked over his shoulder.

Something *dark* moved at the end of the long, narrow mudroom.

He wasn't sure what the hell it was, because he'd caught the quick movement out of the corner of his eyes only a second before it disappeared. Frowning, he turned around and scanned the end of the mudroom. The door to the stairwell was closed, and if someone was down there, there was nowhere for them to go or hide.

"So, is your house haunted?"

Rosie's question entered his thoughts, and a slight half grin tugged at his mouth. NOPE. That was the acronym for her paranormal investigative team. How . . . satirical.

"Dev?"

He turned toward the sound of Lucian's voice. The youngest de Vincent stood in front of the pocket doors that led to the pantry and kitchen. He held a bottle of unopened red wine in his hand. With the exception of the blue-green eyes, Lucian looked nothing like Gabe or him. Fair of skin and hair, Lucian took after their mother, and it was no wonder that all of them had suspected that Lawrence wasn't the father of Lucian and his twin sister. They'd all thought it was some unknown male, someone who was probably kinder to their mother than Lawrence.

Obviously it came as a shock when it was revealed that Lawrence was indeed the twins' biological father and Gabe and Dev weren't his children. That hadn't been the only earth-shattering shock in the last several months. There was also the whole mess with their sister, Madeline, and the truth about what had happened to their mother.

"What are you doing?" Lucian asked.

"Thinking," he replied.

Fair brows lifted. "Really? You're just standing in the mudroom thinking?"

"Appears to be the case."

Lucian sent him a wry look. "That's not weird or anything." He grinned as he stepped to the side. "Heard the senator was here this morning."

"He was, but I doubt he'll be back for a while."

"Is that so?" Lucian started walking toward the kitchen, obviously expecting Dev to follow. Dev sighed. "Does he know anything about Sabrina's whereabouts?"

"He claims he doesn't."

"Do you believe him?" Lucian asked as they passed the pantry.

"Not for one second," Dev answered. "It doesn't matter, though. I have someone looking for her."

Lucian nodded, and a moment ticked by as he met Dev's stare. "Hate everything that Sabrina has had a part of, and you know my intense dislike of that woman has and always will be unmatched, but I'm glad you're finally free of her."

He tilted his head to the side. "I'd chosen to be with her." That was partly true. The idea of their engagement had been introduced by Lawrence and there had been no greater supporter of merging the de Vincent and Harrington empires than Lawrence, but Dev'd gone along with it. Not for those reasons, though. "Wasn't like it was against my will."

"Yeah, you did, and yeah, I've heard you had your reasons—ones that I'll never fucking understand—but at the end of the day, she's not going to be your wife, so hallelujah, my brother, that is reason to celebrate." He lifted the bottle of wine. "Now you can find someone who isn't a grade A bitch."

Dev stared at his brother blandly. "I'm not currently in the market to find someone."

"And isn't that when you usually do?" Lucian turned before he could see Dev's frown and pushed open the kitchen door. "Look who I found loitering in the mudroom, thinking about deep de Vincent stuff."

Letting out an audible sigh, Dev caught the door before it swung back and smacked him in his face. He really should've just kept walking earlier.

The kitchen was the combination of what used to be two rooms, and it had been renovated over the years. His mother would've enjoyed this current reincarnation, with the white cabinets and spacious gray marble countertops. In the center was an island large enough to seat half a football team. She would've loved that.

Sitting on the stools were Julia and Nikki. Both women turned toward him. Julia smiled in his direction. Nikki didn't turn fully since her movements were still stiff and she looked like smiling would've hurt, so she wiggled her fingers. Neither woman truly liked him nor were they probably thrilled that he was in the kitchen with them. Dev knew that and really couldn't blame them. Truthfully, he wasn't sure if he cared about that or not. He knew he should—after all, his brothers cared for them deeply—but he was rather . . . ambivalent.

For the most part.

On the other side of the island stood Gabe in front of some sort of stainless-steel pot thing and an array of chopped vegetables.

"Lucian is cooking dinner," Gabe announced as the younger de Vincent joined him, placing the bottle of wine on the island. "Or attempting to."

"Hey. I know what I'm doing." Lucian reached across the island and tugged on the end of Julia's ponytail. "Don't I?"

"I'm hoping you do, because we're starving," she replied.

"You don't have faith in my culinary skills?" Lucian's eyes widened as he straightened. "What about you, Nikki?"

"Strangely I'm relieved I can only eat liquids right now," she replied.

Dev smirked as Gabe laughed under his breath.

"That's rude." Lucian picked up a package of beef. "Y'all are going to be eating your words figuratively and literally."

A frown tugged at Julia's brows. "I don't think you can eat your words literally."

"Oh you can."

Julia opened her mouth, but closed it and then shook her head. There was a fond look to her eyes, though, as she watched Lucian. The woman was in love with Lucian, that much was clear. One would have to be to put up with the youngest de Vincent.

"Why don't you join us?" Gabe offered as he walked to where Nikki sat. He didn't touch her as he leaned against the island, but it was apparent to Dev that he wanted to. "I can't promise that this Instant Pot thing is going to work—"

"It's going to work." Lucian turned to Gabe. "It's really not that complicated. You put the beef in the pot and you push a few buttons."

"What's an Instant Pot?" Dev asked, his gaze moving to the contraption on the counter.

"It cooks food." Lucian paused dramatically. "Instantly."

Something didn't sound right about that.

"It's kind of like a Crock-Pot, but it's more of a pressure cooker," Nikki explained, speaking slowly. Her words were also a little mushed, due to the busted lip and bruised jaw. "Supposedly you can roast beef in about thirty minutes."

That *really* did not sound right.

"I bought it today," Lucian said proudly. "At a store."

"Really?" Dev replied dryly. "All by yourself?"

"I was with him," Julia chimed in.

Lucian nodded. "That is true."

"Have dinner with us," Gabe chimed in again. "It would only be fair if all of us were poisoned at once."

"Well, while that offer is enticing, I'll have to pass. I have dinner plans." Plans that included a medium-rare fillet and none of this . . . family stuff. It was time to go. "Have a nice evening and enjoy your . . . Instant Pot."

Lucian's eyes narrowed, but Dev turned and left before either of his brothers said a word. He made it to the mudroom and to the outside door when he heard his name called out again. So close, he thought. He even had his car keys in his hand. He turned back around.

Nikki was in the mudroom, her small frame nearly swallowed by what he assumed was one of Gabe's old Harvard hoodies. "I won't keep you, because I know you're busy."

Dev waited, having no idea why Nikki wanted to talk to him since she usually went out of her way to avoid him.

She shuffled forward and then stopped. "I just wanted to say thank you for making sure my father isn't overworking right now, covering both the day and evening shifts."

He had no idea what to say, so he just stared at her.

"I know it's an inconvenience. I mean, you have Lucian in there trying to cook dinner with an Instant Pot." The side of her mouth that didn't look bruised to all hell tipped up in a small smile. "So, yeah, I just wanted to say thank you."

Why in the hell was Nikki thanking him? If he had Sabrina under control, like he'd thought he did, she wouldn't be standing there looking like she went toe to toe in a cage fight and lost. He really had no words.

Nikki's gaze lifted to his, and then she lurched toward him. Dev froze as she wrapped her arms around him. It wasn't a tight hug. Would've hurt her too much to do that, but it was a hug, and Dev couldn't remember the last time he'd been hugged. Possibly by her mother, Livie, after the death of his mother? That was over a decade ago.

Nikki pulled back and mumbled, "Thank you."

Still as a damn statue, he stood there and watched Nikki shuffle back toward the kitchen. A second later, he saw Gabe standing in the doorway. The son of a bitch smiled.

Dev needed to get the hell out of this house, and he did without a second more hesitation.

Smelling like she bathed in brown sugar and vanilla extract, Rosie stared at the space in the hallway, the area where carpet had once been, now covered with tacked-down blue tarp.

She shuddered as if someone had walked over her grave. Biting down on her lip, she looked over at the man standing beside her. He was also staring at the spot, and she imagined he was just as affected, if not more, by it.

That was where Parker Harrington had died.

It could've been where Nikki had died.

"Thank you," Gabe said, his voice rough as his head turned in her direction. "For coming over and doing this. Nic needs some clothes, but I don't want to pick out the wrong stuff."

"It's okay. Glad I can help out." Rosie turned back to the hallway. Gabe had come by Pradine's Pralines this morning and asked if she could help him get some clothes for Nikki, so of course, she had agreed. She only had to stop at the seamstress who'd been working on her costume for the Masquerade and pick up her dress first, which she had done and it was now stretched out on the back seat of her car protected in a garment bag. "Am I allowed to walk on the tarp?"

"Yeah. The carpet is pulled up under there, but it's safe to walk on."

Taking a deep breath, she walked forward with the old Vera Bradley weekender and tried not to think about the fact she was most likely walking on blood that had dried through to the subfloors. One would think that since she investigated creepy hauntings that this wouldn't freak her out.

But it did.

"Try not to think about it," Gabe advised, and Rosie realized the creep factor must've been written all over her face.

"Trying," she said as she all but tiptoed over the tarp. "Not really working."

She hurried across the tarp and down the short hallway. The bedroom door was left open, and as Rosie stepped inside, she realized the bedroom remained the way Nikki had left it.

Towels were scattered along the floor and bed, and she knew from what Nikki had told her, she'd been folding them when Parker showed up. A broken lamp was placed on the dresser, the shade ruined.

"I was here, you know?" Rosie placed the bag on the bed and unzipped it. Turning to the dresser, where she figured Nikki kept most of her comfy clothes, she knocked a curl out of her face. "Last Friday? I was helping her unpack, and I would've stayed later, but I had this thing I had to do."

Gabe was quiet from where he waited in the doorway.

Walking over to the dresser, she knelt and started opening the drawers. Luck was on her side, because she immediately found a stash of sweatpants and leggings. "If I had stayed, I would've been here. I could've—I don't know." She snatched up some pants. "Maybe if I was here, he wouldn't have tried to hurt her."

"You shouldn't go down that road." Gabe leaned against the doorframe.

Finding some lightweight shirts, she gathered them up. "Kind of hard not to."

"If you stayed, he could've attacked you or worse."

That was true, but it didn't really lessen the guilt. She carried her finds over to the bed, placing them in the roomy bag.

"I should've been here," Gabe said after a few moments. "If I hadn't made a mess of things with Nic, I would've been here. None of this would've happened."

Rosie looked over at him. He was staring forward, but she could tell he wasn't seeing her. He was seeing what had happened in here. "You told me not to go down that road, but you're obviously doing it, too."

His gaze shifted to her. "Kind of hard not to."

A faint smile tugged at her lips. "I just hope she can come back here and enjoy this. She was so excited about this place. I don't want that ruined for her."

"Me neither."

"Then I guess we make sure it doesn't."

Gabe smiled as he nodded. "Sounds like a plan."

Thinking of what Devlin had said about how Gabe felt about Nikki, she wondered if this was something Nikki was aware of yet. Probably not. Knowing Nikki, she'd be the last one to figure it out.

Rosie quickly gathered up enough clothing to last Nikki for almost two weeks, including undergarments. By the time she zipped up the bag, the thing was bursting at the seams and had to weigh a ton.

"I got this." Gabe appeared beside her when she went to lift the bag. He took the strap, hooking it over his shoulder like it weighed nothing.

Knocking a stray curl out of her face, she stepped back from the bed and faced Gabe. "I would like to see Nikki. I know she's at your place, and whatever, but I really would like to be able to visit her."

"I think she'd like to see you." Gabe turned to the doorway. "You're more than welcome to come over now."

Surprise flickered through her. She expected to have a massive argument on her hands, where she'd have to beg and plead. The de Vincents were notoriously private. "Really?"

"Yeah. I think that would be a nice surprise for her." He looked over his shoulder at her. "You look shocked. Did you think I'd say no?"

Rosie blinked slowly. "I'm sorry. I guess I kind of did."

He lifted his brows. "And why is that?"

"Well, your brother . . ." She trailed off.

Understanding flickered across his face. "Dev? Don't worry about him. It's unlikely that he'll even be there."

A weird feeling whirled inside her, a mixture of relief and, oddly, disappointment. Never seeing Devlin again would be for the best, so she didn't understand the disappointment at all.

But who cared? Because holy moon pies, she was going to get to see Nikki and she was going to set foot in the de Vincent manor, one of the most haunted places ever.

Chapter 8

*E*ven if Rosie wasn't following Gabe, she would've known how to get to the de Vincent manor because of all the research she'd done. She kept that piece of knowledge to herself since it made her sound like a creepy stalker and she doubted Gabe would appreciate knowing that.

She already kind of felt like a stalker, a cheap one, trailing behind Gabe's fancy-ass Porsche in her *Corolla*. She had no idea what kind of Porsche the man drove, but she imagined it cost more than she'd ever be willing to pay for a car.

Lance rang her just as she slowed and pulled onto the private access road. She let the call go to voice mail as she drove along the winding road crowded by tall oaks. Heavy Spanish moss clung to the trees, creating a canopy that nearly blocked out the autumn sun. It was really beautiful and eerie, and knowing that these trees and the moss had been here long before man had claimed this land had a humbling effect.

The trees cleared and rolling green hills came into view. The road kept going for at least another mile. Eventually she came upon more trees edging along the road. Rosie felt like she was driving into another state at this point, but eventually, a large gate attached to a small building that reminded her of a checkpoint came into view.

As she drove past the gate, she finally saw the house.

"Holy Mary, mother of God and baby Jesuses everywhere," she whispered, clutching the steering wheel as she tipped forward in her seat.

There were no pictures of the de Vincent home anywhere on the internet, not even aerial views, which seemed impossible in this day and age, but it was the truth. So, this was the first time she was seeing the place.

It looked as big as the White House!

The center part of the structure was three stories tall and each side was flanked by smaller additions that appeared to be two stories. Every part of the compound was connected by balconies and breezeways on each level. And as she drew closer, she could see the fans churning from the multiple balcony ceilings.

Thick columns surrounded the front of the home and continued along the entire structure. Shutters were black and large, bushy ferns hung from the wrought-iron railings on the upper levels, and the entire home was covered in vines.

That wasn't normal, to say the least.

Some of the older homes in the area had issues with the aggressive vines and ivy, but a house like this and covered entirely? Where the owners had the means to keep the structure clear?

Rosie needed to stop staring at the house and pay attention, because Gabe was heading toward the left wing and she was going to end up driving straight through the front door.

She followed him around to a separate structure she quickly realized was a garage—a garage large enough to store at least ten cars. How many vehicles did these people have?

Gabe didn't pull into one of the bays, instead parking in front, so Rosie did the same, pulling up beside him. She snatched her phone, shoving it into the pocket of her jeans, and her purse off the front seat, and then climbed out.

Gabe was already waiting for her at the trunk of her Corolla, the weekender bag in hand and silver sunglasses shielding his eyes. He'd pulled his hair back, the dark strands secured at the nape of his neck. "Follow me."

Rosie hurried to catch up with him. "What is up with all the ivy?"

"You know, that's a good question." He cut across the driveway and then stepped onto the veranda along the side of the house. "They come from the rose garden out back and have just spread out of control. Lawrence—our father? He used to have the vines pulled down yearly, but they always came back and quick, too. Weird, huh?"

"Yeah." She drew the word out as she stared at the green vine crawling over the exterior walls. "That is notably weird."

Gabe grinned as he started climbing the covered outdoor stairs. "Sometimes I wonder if the vines are trying to smother the house."

Her brows lifted. There had been examples of weird vegetative abnormalities at sites with high paranormal activity. The Hoia Baciu Forest came to mind, which featured an unexplained circle where no living thing grew and a ton of firsthand accounts of the paranormal, but she'd never seen anything like *this*.

"This is my private entry," Gabe explained as he rounded the second-floor landing. "Lucian's is over in the right wing for now, but he's moving out, and Dev is up there." He jerked his chin up.

Her stomach dipped for some dumbass reason at the mention of Devlin's name. They stepped out onto the wide, second-floor porch. She followed him around the corner and then saw comfy chairs lined up. There was a closed book, one that appeared to be an old historical romance based on the beautiful dress the model was wearing on the cover. The book rested on a wicker end table. The ivy had made its way to this level, spreading along the walls and even curling around the legs of the chairs. When she looked out over the railing, she wasn't surprised to see the ivy covering that, too. Down below, there was a huge lima-bean-shaped pool and a . . .

"Is that a *plane*?" she asked.

Gabe chuckled as he opened the door. "It's Dev's."

"He has a plane?" She turned to him. "Why would he need a plane?"

"He travels a lot for the company. I guess for him it's easier to have his own jet," he answered. "It does come in handy when you want to head somewhere on short notice."

"I imagine so." Actually, that was a lie. Rosie couldn't imagine waking up one day and randomly deciding to go to Paris or the Caribbean, walking outside, and hopping on a private jet. Like her brain formally rejected the notion and she was a fairly spontaneous person.

But she was not a super-wealthy spontaneous person.

"Rosie?" Nikki's voice floated from somewhere in the recesses of the house. "Is that you?"

Gabe stepped aside, allowing Rosie to enter what was definitely not an ordinary bedroom in a house. It was an *apartment*.

An apartment triple the size of hers.

Feeling way out of her element, her gaze shifted to Nikki. "Surprise?"

"What are you doing here?" Nikki shuffled toward her.

"I helped Gabe get some clothes for you." Rosie dropped her purse on a chair near the door. She met Nikki halfway, clasping her cool hands in hers. "I wanted to see you and he said I could come over."

"Really?" Nikki's wide, one good eye swerved toward Gabe.

"I didn't see a problem with it," he responded. "I'm going to take this back in the bedroom."

She stared at him for a moment and then focused on Rosie. "I'm glad to see you. I'm just surprised. They aren't really fond of having people over here."

"You were surprised?" Rosie giggled. "I was prepared to beg and plead to come see you, even hold your clothing hostage, but I didn't have to argue at all."

"That's . . . wow. Okay." She glanced in the direction Gabe disappeared. "Sit?" She didn't wait for Rosie to answer, leading her over to a couch. "I just woke up from a nap, so this was perfect timing."

"You look a lot better."

"You're such a liar, but thank you."

That wasn't entirely false. Some of the swelling had gone down and her left eye was open a little, but yeah, she still looked pretty terrible. "How are you feeling?"

"A lot better. I'm sore, but I'm alive."

Rosie glanced at the hallway and when she spoke, she kept her voice low. "How is everything with Gabe?"

"Good, I guess." Nikki leaned back into the thick cushions. "I mean, we haven't talked about anything, but he . . ."

"He has you set up here, in the de Vincent compound, searched me down to make sure he got the right stuff for you, and even allowed me to visit?" Rosie whispered back, remembering what Devlin had told her. "And his br—"

"Want anything to drink?" Gabe yelled from the hallway.

Rosie's shoulders slumped. "I'll tell you later."

Nikki studied her. "Okay."

Just about then, Gabe appeared and decided both of them needed a glass of sweet tea. It was strange, sitting in the de Vincent house, being served iced sweet tea by a de Vincent. It was so surreal, she hadn't even thought about whipping out the Electronic Voice Phenomena recorder she *always* carried with her.

Nikki must've been reading her mind, because she said, "I'm surprised you don't have one of those electronic meter thingies out and taking readings."

"A what?" Gabe asked, sitting down on a barstool that butted up to the kitchen island.

"An EMF meter. It detects electrically charged objects, like power lines and ghosts."

"Ghosts?" he repeated.

"Yep. See, it's believed that when spirits are around, they emit electronic charges into the air, and an EMF meter will pick up on that."

Nikki nodded. "I've actually seen her use one and it went off in the middle of nowhere, where there weren't any power lines or electricity nearby."

She was talking about that old cemetery near Tuscaloosa, where she'd met Nikki at the University of Alabama. "I don't have an EMF meter with me, but I do have the EVP recorder."

Interest filled Gabe's expression as he hooked his feet on the bottom rung of the stool. She realized then he'd taken off his shoes. "And what does that do?"

Grinning, she glanced over at Nikki and saw that her expression had softened as she stared across the room at Gabe. "So, EVP stands for electronic voice phenomena. The recorder can catch intentional voices—voices you hear with your own two ears—and it catches voices that you can't hear. Often it picks up just words or short phrases, but if you've got a place with a lot of EVPs, then you want to bring in a spirit box."

Gabe lowered his glass of tea. "Like a Ouija board?"

"Hell no, I do not mess with that shit." Rosie scooted forward. "Spirits sometimes need energy to communicate and there's evidence that white noise in radio frequencies can provide the necessary energy. A spirit box provides that energy."

"Why won't you use a Ouija board?" Gabe asked, and there wasn't an ounce of judgment in his tone. Just honest curiosity. "Figured ghost hunters would be all up in that."

"Only ghost hunters who don't care what door they may be opening or who they may be contacting," Rosie said, thinking of what happened with Sarah. Sometimes being a medium was like being a living, breathing Ouija board. "And not to mention, my mother would straight up knock me into next week if she knew I was messing with those things." She paused, looking over at Nikki. "I could take out the EVP recorder and see if we catch—"

"No. No way." Gabe held up a hand. "I do not want to know what ghosts may or may not be saying. I'd rather just pretend that everything about this house is completely normal."

"Gabe and his brothers have this remarkable ability to explain away everything they see or hear," Nikki chimed in.

"Like you don't?" Gabe laughed while Nikki huffed.

Excitement filled Rosie. Gabe seemed more open to supernatural stuff. Maybe she could tell him about the possibility of his father coming through. At least she would get it off her conscience. "So, what—"

"Uh-oh," murmured Nikki, her face turned to the glass balcony doors.

Rosie followed her gaze, and her stomach leaped to her throat. Every cell in her body seemed to freeze as she watched Devlin de Vincent open the balcony door and step into Gabe's living room.

Against her will, her gaze roamed over him. Fitted dark trousers. Tailored white shirt that showed off his shoulders and broad chest.

His dark hair was perfectly coiffed like before, not a single strand out of place, and there wasn't even a five o'clock shadow on his smooth jaw.

That didn't seem possible.

"Someone doesn't know how to knock," Gabe muttered.

Devlin didn't seem to hear his brother or even realize anyone else was in the room, because those stunning, clear sea-green eyes were latched on to her. He stopped just inside the living room, leaving the door open behind him. "What is *she* doing here?"

Rosie's spine stiffened like hot steel was poured down it and she stopped checking him out right then and there. He said "she" like she was some sort of venereal disease, and that was, well, freaking insulting. "I'm here to break shit and raise some holy hell."

Nikki choked on what sounded like a laugh.

Devlin stared at her, his handsome face cold and bland.

"I'm visiting my friend." Rosie rolled her eyes. "That's all."

"Is that so?" he remarked.

"Uh. Yeah?" she replied.

"Hi, Dev." Gabe raised his glass in his direction. "You don't know this, Rosie, but Dev has a preternatural ability of knowing whenever someone that is not family is in the house." He paused. "It's kind of freaky."

"While having a preternatural ability sounds interesting, that's not how I knew someone was here." Devlin didn't take his eyes off her. "Her car was parked in my space."

"You have assigned parking?" Rosie felt a laugh bubbling up her throat. "At your own house?"

His eyes narrowed slightly.

"He likes things to be organized," Gabe replied. "For everything, even his car, to have a place—*his* place."

"I can answer for myself," Devlin said dryly, and finally he focused on his brother, and she felt like she could take a full breath. "But thanks for speaking for me."

"You're welcome." Gabe took a drink.

Dev stared at his brother and then that unholy intense gaze came back to Rosie. "But you're not parked in my spot. You're actually blocking access to my spot in my garage."

She stared back at him, stuck for a moment, wondering if he was actually being serious. "Would you like me to move my car?"

"That would've been nice of you to suggest when I first mentioned your car was in my spot," he said, tone even.

Nikki stiffened beside her while Gabe sighed. "You don't have to move your car," he said. "Dev is fine."

Devlin's gaze still held hers and there was a challenge in that stare.

Swallowing down a mouthful of words that would probably get her kicked out of the house forever and a day, she stood. "You know what? I'll move my car."

"Rosie," Nikki started.

"No, it's okay." Rosie smiled at her friend and then whirled toward Devlin, keeping said super-big smile plastered across her face while she glared up at him. "I'm more than happy to move my car out of the way for him. After all, I wouldn't want him to get stressed-out over it."

"I'm not stressed-out over it." A slight frown pulled at his lips as he turned, watching her walk to her purse.

"Oh I don't know about that." Digging around in her purse, she pulled out her keys. "You seem like you're one more occupied parking space away from having a cardiac issue and I would not want to be the cause of that."

There was another choked sound, but this time it sounded like it was coming from Gabe. Keys in hand, she spun back to them. "I'll be right back."

"Okay," Nikki murmured.

Moving toward the doors—the doors Devlin blocked—she stopped and stared up at him. "Excuse me?"

He was still for a moment and then slowly, purposefully, he stepped to the side.

"Thanks, buddy." Walking past him, she patted his arm and then stalked right out the doors. Clouds had moved in, and the scent of rain was in the air. A storm was coming, both literally and figuratively.

Because, of course, Devlin was right behind her. She looked over her shoulder at him. "Are you following me to make sure I move my car?"

He arched a brow. "I'm not following you."

"Sure looks like you're doing that." Looking away, she kept walking. "Or are you worried that I'm going to damage your property?"

"Should I be worried?" He fell into step beside her, easily keeping up with her brisk pace that was close to leaving her winded.

Rosie rolled her eyes again as she reached the staircase and started down the steps. "Yes. Very worried. I'm one bad ma—" She reached the end of the balcony and could see the massive garage down below, and the vehicle that hadn't been there when she arrived. Her mouth dropped open. "A truck?"

Devlin stopped beside her. "That is what it appears to be."

Sort of dumbfounded, all she could do was stare. Parked on the other side of her Corolla was a . . . truck. Just an ordinary truck. Looked like a Ford. Not particularly a newer one either. It was black and had mud dried and splattered along the wheels. It wasn't a Porsche. Or a Jaguar. Or a Benz. Or any other number of luxury cars that cost the price of a town house.

This man owned a private jet, but drove a truck?

"Is there something wrong with a truck?" he asked.

She blinked and shook her head no. There was nothing wrong with it, but it was unexpected. Whatever. His choice, no matter how surprising it was, didn't matter. Turning, she stepped toward the staircase.

"I'm not following you, by the way," he said. "After you move your car, I will need to move mine."

Oh well, that made sense—

She gasped as Dev suddenly moved. One second he was beside her, and the next, he was blocking the steps below. She clutched the vine-covered railing. "How am I supposed to move my car if you're blocking the stairway? Or do you expect me to go traipsing through your house to get downstairs?"

Even though he was two whole steps below her, he was eye to eye with her. "Do you often traipse through homes?"

"Daily. It's how I get my workout in."

"That must be interesting to see."

"It most definitely is."

He leaned in suddenly, and Rosie sucked in a sharp breath, unprepared for him to be so damn close to her. She immediately thought of Saturday morning. Him. Her. Their bodies pressed against one another. Was he thinking about that, too?

His dark lashes lifted. "You smell like—"

"If you say something ignorant, I'm seriously going to push you down these steps."

The blue of his eyes seemed to deepen. "That wouldn't be very nice, Rosie."

There was another catch to her breath, because she was pretty confident that was the first time he'd said her name, and in that deep, slightly accented voice of his, it sent an unwanted thrill right through her.

"But what I was going to say before I was so rudely interrupted," Devlin continued. "You smell like vanilla and . . ." He trailed off as if he couldn't place how she smelled.

Rosie sighed. "Sugar. Brown sugar to be exact. I work at Pradine's Pralines and went straight from there to Nikki's place to get her some fresh clothing. You've probably never heard of the place—"

"I have. They have amazing pralines." He tilted his head to the side. "I didn't know you worked there."

"It's been family owned since the beginning and my parents now run it," she said, noting the flicker of surprise in his eyes. "I can't picture you eating pralines."

"You can't?" One eyebrow rose.

"Yeah, I picture you eating raw vegetables, lots of fat-trimmed steak, and beets."

"Beets?"

She nodded. "Isn't that what people eat when they're in a permanent state of constipation?"

His eyes widened and his mouth went lax. "Did you just suggest I was constipated?"

"That would explain the attitude, wouldn't it?"

"Then what would explain yours?"

"Mine has nothing to do with what I eat, but it's affected by who I'm around, Dev."

He came up a step, crowding her as he now stared down at her. "No one but my brothers call me Dev."

"Oh I'm sorry? Do I need permission to call you an abbreviated version of your name?"

"You should. After all, that's what's appropriate."

Rosie couldn't help it. She rolled her eyes so far back in her head, they'd probably get stuck.

"How would you like if I called you Rose?"

"That's actually a pretty nickname and I wouldn't mind," she shot back. "Rosa would make more sense since my first name is Rosalynn."

"Rosalynn? So Southern," he murmured in a way that irritated her.

"Okay, I won't call you Dev, *Dev.*"

"You just did," he said dryly.

"How about I just call you Dickhead, then? That sounds about fitting."

"You already did that."

"Then that's perfect. I'll just—" Her phone suddenly rang from her pocket. She pulled it out and saw that it was Lance calling again. "Excuse me." She held up her hand, silencing Dev as she answered her phone. "Hello?"

Dev stared at her—no, he *gaped* at her.

She smirked as Lance said into her ear, "I've been calling you all afternoon. What in the world have you been doing? I got news on the Mendez case."

"I'm sorry. I know. I've just been really busy today and right now isn't a good time."

"Is something wrong?" Lance asked, concern filing his tone.

"If it wasn't a good time, why did you answer the phone?" Devlin asked.

"Was that a guy's voice?" Lance asked as Rosie shushed Devlin.

"Did you just shush me?" they both demanded at the same time.

Rosie clutched her phone. "I didn't shush you, Lance. I'd never shush you. Look, can I call you back in a little bit? I'm in the middle of a very important argument with Devlin de Vincent over whether or not I can call him a dickhead instead of Dev."

Devlin's mouth dropped open, and for a moment she thought he was going to fall over backward. The shock pouring into his expression was the first real hard-core reaction she'd seen from him.

"Devlin de Vincent—*the* Devlin de Vincent?" Lance sounded like he might fall over, too.

"Yes." She met Devlin's stunned stare. "*The* Devlin de Vincent. So, can I please call you back? Like I imagine most things with him, I don't think this is going to take long."

Devlin snapped his mouth shut.

"Uh, yeah. Call me back as soon as you can," Lance muttered, sounding way confused.

"Thanks, babe." Rosie ended the call and slipped the phone into her pocket. "You're still here? I was hoping you'd go ahead and walk down."

"Who was that?" he demanded.

"The Pope. Can you please move out of the way so I can move my car before your precious truck gets a raindrop on it, even though it looks like it could use a bath?"

"No," he said.

"No?"

"No," he repeated, and then he moved in.

They weren't as close as they'd been on Saturday, but she could see the flecks of green in his blue eyes. Close enough that if she took a deep breath, her chest would brush his, and she knew that would be bad, because as terrible as it was, her body *wanted* that closeness. Her brain, however, was not on board with her body. Her brain was seriously considering the consequences of pushing him *lightly* down the stairs.

"I want you to listen to everything I say, because I will not ever repeat myself," he said, his voice so low, so soft that she could barely hear him. "I should not have to explain how incredibly rude it is to answer the phone in the middle of a conversation, one in which you're insulting the other person, but then to shush me? Even as a child, I was not shushed."

Her heart rate tripled. "I guess there's a first for everything?"

"You're not listening. If you were, you wouldn't be speaking."

Rosie narrowed her eyes. "I'm listening."

"Good. Silence must be a new thing for you," he continued, and when she opened her mouth, he placed his finger over her lips. So shocked by the contact, she was effectively silenced. "I am not done, Rosalynn."

Oh dear.

His thumb curled under her chin and his touch was oddly gentle in comparison to the hard line of his jaw. Then he dipped his head, bringing his mouth within an inch of hers.

Oh my good God, was he going to kiss her?

That would be a sharp turn in events, so sharp she just stood there as a hot flush swept over and an acute heaviness settled into her breasts and flowed down to her stomach and lower, much lower.

Wait. Bad Rosie. Bad. Bad. Bad.

She did not want him to kiss her. He was a dickhead douchebag of the highest order!

But yep, her nipples were hard, and yep, something was wrong with her, and nope, he did not kiss her.

"Being shushed was a first for me and it will be the last," he said, definitely not kissing her. "But most importantly? The insinuation you made on the phone about most things not lasting long with me? I can assure you, that is not the case." His finger slid over her lips, eliciting a gasp from her. "*That* takes longer than I'm betting you can last and you'd be begging me to stop while pleading with me to keep going the whole time. I can assure you, no one would ever fuck you longer or harder."

Oh.

My.

God.

Rosie was actually speechless. Utterly shocked into real, honest to goodness silence while her body and mind engaged in a full-fledged war with one another. Her mind was telling her to be offended, like kick him in the balls offended, and her body had liquefied as molten lava swept through her veins, sparking to life a fire—a *need* she'd never experienced before, not even with Ian.

Devlin dragged his finger back over her bottom lip, tugging on it before lowering his hand. "But that, my dear, is something you'll never have the honor of experiencing with me, because the mere idea of me even thinking about fucking you is laughable."

His words were like having a bucket of cold water dumped over her head. The fire was doused in a heartbeat. What he said . . . that was, wow. . . . Never in her life had anyone ever spoken to her like that. Ever. A horrible messy knot of emotion plugged her throat. His words stung more than they should, probably because she was getting close to that time of the month and was overly emotional.

Holding her wide-eyed gaze, he turned sideways and stepped aside. "Now you may go move your car."

A thousand retorts rose to the tip of her tongue. She could out-shade him to the point he was eclipsed by the shade she could throw in his direction, but he . . . he wasn't worth it. He wasn't worth a single second of her snarkiness or her time.

He wasn't worth *anything* to her.

But that didn't mean she wasn't going to serve it right back at him, because she was not the kind of woman to let a man stand there and talk to her like that.

Pushing the knot in her throat down, she held his gaze even though her eyes burned. "I think you misspoke. I think you meant to say that fucking me is an *honor* that you know you'd never be worthy of and that is why it would never happen, *Dev.*"

Something flickered across his face that looked an awful lot like respect—reluctant respect, but she didn't give a flying chupacabra's ass what Devlin de Vincent thought or felt.

Slipping past him, she walked down the steps without looking back and without saying another word.

She was a lot of things. A little out there. Definitely weird. Sometimes irresponsible and she probably drank too much wine and ate way too many sweets, but she'd never been a doormat for any man to wipe his feet on, and she sure as hell wasn't going to become one now.

Chapter 9

"What in the world were you doing with a de Vincent?" That was the first question Lance asked when Rosie met up with him at Jilly's place. He'd been sitting out on the porch, waiting for her.

Lance was a couple years younger, and with his head full of auburn hair and big brown eyes, he had a perpetual baby face. The man would probably still look like he was in his early twenties even when he was in his forties and he really was a good guy.

A good man who'd had a rough run of things after returning home from a tour in Afghanistan. It wasn't a topic he talked about often, but Rosie knew he'd done something along the lines of emergency medicine when with the army. Knowing that, she figured the man had seen things that no human should ever have to witness.

His girlfriend of several years had apparently gotten involved with someone else without telling him. It hadn't been exactly easy for him to adapt to civilian life and finding a job had been even harder. Combined with everything he'd experienced overseas and the life that seemed to have moved on without him once he returned home, he'd had a tough go at things at first.

But Lance was proof of human resilience. He got knocked down several times, but he picked himself up and here he was.

Rosie shifted the strap of her purse as she slowly climbed the steps. "You remember Nikki, right? My friend from the University of Alabama? She's dating one of the brothers—Gabriel. She was over at their house and I was visiting her," she said, leaving out most of the details since it wasn't widely known that Nikki had been involved in what happened with Parker. Not that she didn't trust Lance. What happened wasn't her story to tell. "And Devlin was there. He's a bit of a . . . dickhead, so I was arguing with him."

Lance's reddish-brown brows lifted. "Okay. First, I cannot believe you were at the de Vincent house, and second, you were arguing with Devlin de Vincent."

Rosie shrugged like she didn't care, but it felt forced. As stupid as it sounded because Devlin was a virtual stranger to her, but she did care, because she couldn't fathom how or why someone would be such an ass for no good reason. Sure, she wasn't particularly nice to him when he came to her apartment, but he'd acted like he hadn't known who she was and he'd been rude to her the moment he stepped through her door. The man she'd met in the cemetery, while distant, had been polite. That wasn't the Devlin she had now seen twice.

It was like the man wanted people to hate him.

"Believe it," she said, pushing thoughts of Devlin aside as the strap of her purse started to inch down her arm again.

"What was the house like?" he asked, and Rosie knew why he was asking. Like her, Lance knew all about the legends and rumors that surrounded the de Vincent place.

"I didn't get to see much of it, but there was something super weird." She told him about the ivy growing everywhere. "I've never seen anything like that in my life."

"All over?" Interest filled his brown eyes.

"All over the entire exterior," she confirmed.

"Hell, that is insane." Lance scratched his fingers through his messy, curly hair. "So, do you think you can get us access to the house? Or Nikki could?"

Rosie barked out a short laugh. "Yeah, that's not going to happen."

"Why not?" He frowned.

She caught the purse before it slipped right off her arm. Jesus, she hated this purse with its short straps, but damn it, the patchwork fabric was so cute. "Besides the fact that the de Vincents are notoriously private, I'm pretty confident Devlin loathes me."

"Loathes you? How in the world can anyone hate you?" He rose as she reached the top step and draped his arm over her shoulders. "You're fucking awesome."

Rosie laughed softly. "I know." She didn't want to spend another moment thinking about Devlin. "So, what's the update with the Mendez family?"

Sliding his arm off her shoulders, he opened the door for her. "I'll let Jilly give you the details."

Jilly was in the narrow living room, on the phone with her girl-friend by the sound of the one-sided hushed argument and her brisk pace in front of the leaning tower of books. Those two argued over everything, from what they were having for dinner to if a residual haunting counted as a real haunting or not, and the only thing they both agreed on was the fact there was no one else for them. They were complete opposites, from the way they looked and dressed, all the way down to Jilly being a vegetarian and Liz considering herself a meat connoisseur.

But Rosie doubted she knew two people who loved each other more than them.

She dropped into the old armchair as Jilly turned, throwing up her free hand. "You know I love you, babe, but I have to get off the phone. Rosie and Lance are here—yes." Jilly rolled her eyes. "Liz says hi."

"Hi," Rosie replied, grinning at Lance. "Is she working?"

"Yes. She'll be here soon. What?" Jilly whipped around and picked up her glass of wine. "Liz will be here in forty minutes. I'm hanging up." There was a pause, and her face softened. "You know I miss you. I always miss you, now shut up and get back to work so you can actu-ally get off work on time for once.

"Do you guys want anything to drink? No? Perfect." Jilly tossed her phone onto the couch, where it bounced off a fluffy chenille throw. "Glad to see you're still alive, Rosie."

Rosie arched a brow. "I miss a few phone calls and you guys assume I'm dead?"

"It's New Orleans." She tucked short dark strands behind her ear. "Anything is possible."

"That's a wee bit of an exaggeration," Rosie commented.

"Gonna have to agree with Rosie on that." Lance sat on the arm of her chair.

"Of course you do. You love her." Jilly smiled sweetly.

Rosie stiffened while Lance flipped her off.

Jilly ignored him. "Anyway, I did speak to Preston Mendez, and like he'd asked of us, I haven't showed his wife what we caught on camera yet."

Preston had wanted to vet anything we caught on film before it was showed to his wife, and their team had respected that even though Rosie felt Maureen should know. She got that he didn't want to upset his wife, but she was eventually going to have to see the film.

"Needless to say, he was quite disturbed by what was caught on film Saturday night," she continued, taking a drink of her wine. "He didn't hear the bang, but he did wake up when the baby started crying."

"Is he going to let us stay the night in there?" Lance asked.

Jilly shook her head. "He's still talking it over with his wife, but I think they're going to let us. I've only explained a hundred million times to him why we'd be able to gain more evidence if we were able to do an overnight."

"In the meantime, he should at least let us set up a couple of EVP recorders in the house," Rosie suggested.

"Agreed. But people are weird when it comes to knowing there's something in their house recording their conversations. You know this." Jilly sat on the couch. "But kiddos, it's time for me to tell you something really weird. Something I discovered while talking to Preston earlier, and it's either a really bizarre coincidence or it's fate."

Rosie glanced at Lance. "Do you have any idea of what she is talking about?"

"Not really."

"He doesn't know, but when he came over earlier, he said when he talked to you on the phone, you were with a de Vincent. Is that true?" Jilly was practically trembling with excitement or she'd drunk one of those five-hour energy drinks again.

Her brows knit together as she exhaled heavily. The last person she wanted to think or talk about was a de Vincent. "Yeah, I was, but what does that have to do with anything?"

Jilly laughed. "Here is where things get either super coincidental or get really weird. As you know, the Mendezes didn't have any activity in their home until they brought the baby home. We of course assumed that was the cause of the activity."

Rosie nodded slowly. "Yeah. . . ."

"But come to find out, at the same time they introduced the baby to their home, the house next door to them, which had been empty, was sold to a lovely young couple."

Rosie really had no idea where Jilly was going with this, and she wondered if she'd smoked some pot before they had come over.

"The house next door to them eventually went under an extensive renovation that has lasted months and is still currently undergoing renovation," Jilly explained, tipping her wineglass at them before placing it on the coffee table. "And what is the number one thing that stirs up ghosts?"

"Renovations?" Lance answered.

Jilly clapped. "Correct!"

Sitting forward, Rosie crossed one leg over the other. "Okay. There have been cases of renovations in one house stirring up activity in another house. And if that's the case, then that's good news for the family. Usually activity simmers down once the renovations are done."

"Or the spirit will make its way back to the house it originated from," Lance added.

"Either way, what does this have to do with the de Vincents?" Rosie asked.

"Because who do you think bought the house next door to the Mendez family?" Jilly bit down on her lip as she looked between the two of them. "Lucian de Vincent."

Rosie's jaw dropped.

"What?" Lance stiffened.

Jilly nodded. "Yep. Preston met him over the weekend. He happened to be out in the yard while Lucian and his girlfriend were there checking on the renovations. Now, you tell me, is this just a bizarre coincidence that someone who just happens to live in one of the rumored most haunted locations in all of the United States is moving in next door to the family who reported strange activity in their house around the same time?"

Rosie had no words.

"Ghosts can sometimes follow people—you know, the whole person is haunted versus the house or property, but . . ." Lance dragged his hand through his hair. "But man, what a small world."

Jilly grinned as she lifted her brows at Rosie. "So, since you're apparently now best friends forever with a de Vincent," Jilly said, and Rosie opened her mouth to correct that horrifically wrong assumption, but she kept talking. "You need to get us into the house next door to the Mendezes."

Rosie snapped out of her stupor. "Yeah, that's not going to happen."

Across from her Jilly met her gaze and her grin turned downright demonic. "I'm willing to bet my entire signed first-edition set of the Twilight series that it *will* happen."

"You're an asshole, you know that?"

Dev lifted his gaze from the glow of his computer to where Gabe stood. It was late, damn near midnight, and the columns of numbers— deposits from banks in China, Russia, and Uzbekistan—were giving him a fucking headache. Deposits from banks in countries where Dev knew damn well they did not do enough business to warrant seven-figure deposits.

It had taken the forensic accountant months to peel back layers of fake accounts and transfer numbers and all the false information provided by some of Lawrence's lawyers and financial advisers, then to ferret out where the deposits had originated from, and these banks were confirming the worst of Dev's suspicions.

So, at the moment, he really didn't have the patience for whatever Gabe wanted to talk about.

"I'm not quite sure what you're referring to, but I'm not exactly in the mood for this conversation." Dev minimized the spreadsheets before he sat back in his chair.

"You're never in the mood for anything, at least anything good." Gabe strolled on into the office and planted his hands on the backs of the two chairs seated in front of Dev's desk. "But I'll give you a refresher."

"Of course."

Gabe's jaw hardened. "The way you spoke to Nikki's friend today? That was unacceptable."

Tension crept into Dev's neck. "Unacceptable to whom?"

"To any decent fucking human being," Gabe shot back. "You made her go move her car and for what? You normally don't give two shits about your truck being parked outside the garage."

That wasn't exactly untrue, and to be honest, Dev wasn't sure why he'd demanded that Rosie move her car. The request was . . . immature and asinine. Even he could admit that to himself. He'd done it because he knew . . . he knew it would get a rise out of her and for some reason he wanted to do that. "You waited until midnight to have this conversation?"

"I waited until Nikki was asleep and wasn't going to have a goddamn nightmare to come to talk to you." Gabe pushed off the chairs. "Right now Nikki needs to be surrounded by her friends and family and people who give a damn about her. And if that means Rosie is going to be here to visit her, you need to get the hell over that."

"I don't care if Rosie comes to visit her," Dev replied.

"Really? You don't? Sure didn't seem that way. The moment you knew someone was here, you made her feel about as welcome as a cat in a room full of dogs."

Contrary to what his brothers believed, he didn't have a preternatural sense that told him when people were in the house, nor did he waste time worrying over what they were doing when they were there. As long as his brothers' guests didn't roam around and stayed the hell out of his line of sight, he couldn't care less.

His gaze lowered to the glass of bourbon on his desk. Gabe had no idea just how much of an asshole he had been to Rosie. Shit. Even Dev felt a stirring of . . . guilt. The woman, though, she pushed every single one of his buttons—buttons he didn't even know he had—but he had been unreasonable and uncouth toward Rosie. What he'd said to her . . . ?

Not only had that been completely uncalled-for, it also had been a lie.

Not the part when he said she'd be begging him to stop and pleading to keep going. Or the part where he promised no one would fuck her harder or longer. That was the truth. Saying that the mere idea of him ever fucking her was laughable was the lie.

There was nothing funny about that, and he'd thought about it a lot since Saturday morning. Enough that he was already convinced that she'd be . . . Exhaling roughly, Dev picked up the glass of bourbon and took a drink. Rosie would be like no other. He already knew that.

"Is that all you wanted to talk to me about?" he asked, lifting his gaze to Gabe.

His brother was silent and then he asked, "What in the hell did that man do to you?"

Every muscle locked up. Dev didn't even twitch a finger. "What man?"

"Don't play that game with me. You know I'm talking about Lawrence. What in the hell did he do to you to make you this miserable?"

For a moment he couldn't believe his brother had asked him that question, but then he remembered Gabe didn't know. Neither did Lucian. He stared back at his brother, wishing he would go back to Nikki. Not because he wanted Gabe to get the hell out of his face. But because he didn't want his brother digging up fresh skeletons.

"What did he do, Dev?" Gabe wasn't leaving. Not yet. "I need to know, because with every day that goes by, you're becoming more like him, and that fucking terrifies me."

Dev's jaw locked down as his right hand tightened on the glass. He couldn't even speak.

Gabe stared at him for a long moment and then barked out a harsh, short laugh as he shook his head. "Whatever. Good night, Dev."

He sat there and watched his brother walk out of his office, closing the door behind him. The glass was heavy in his hand as Gabe's words cycled over and over. *"You're becoming more like him."* Dev would never become Lawrence. Never.

Dev's body reacted without thought.

Standing, he cocked his arm back and threw the glass across the room. It smashed into the closed door, shattering upon impact. Liquor and glass sprayed the hardwood floors. He stood there, still, for several moments and then he drew in a deep, slow breath. He fixed the cuffs of his shirt and sat back down, turning his attention to the evidence of what Lawrence de Vincent had been involved in.

Chapter 10

The following afternoon, Dev stood in front of the floor-to-ceiling windows and stared out over the city, his mind running in what felt like a thousand different directions even though he was still and solid as the building he stood in.

He'd just finished a meeting with the city planning officials over plans to break ground on the project de Vincent Industrials was funding. What had begun as a new office had now morphed into an entire damn medical complex, but the state-of-the-art facility meant Dr. Flores remained discreet whenever his family needed medical assistance, and for that, there was no price tag.

After all, if it hadn't been for Dr. Flores's silence, the world would've easily discovered that his sister, Madeline, had been alive for the last ten years, and if that knowledge ever got out, there'd be a lot of questions. Ones Dev and his family would rather not answer, because of where those questions would lead.

The world didn't need to know that not only had his sister purposely disappeared, but she'd also been shacked up with their *cousin* and she had been a murderer.

Suppose that ran in the family.

His phone buzzed and he turned, walking swiftly back to his desk. He hit the intercom button. "Yes?"

The voice of Derek Frain, his assistant, came through the speaker. "Ross Haid is here to see you." There was a pause and the annoyance in Derek's tone was clear in the one word. "Again."

Dev's jaw clenched as he stared at the phone. The man had been dogged when it came to the de Vincent family, confident that they were involved in some grand conspiracy and misdeeds.

Ironically, Ross would be right, but he was barking up the wrong tree. As always.

But Dev knew what fueled Ross was way more personal than the need to write a must-read tell-all on the de Vincent family, and unlike his uncle and the rest of his family, he didn't avoid these meetings, which were becoming like clockwork, with Ross.

"Send him in," Dev ordered.

"Yes, sir."

No sooner had Dev sat behind his desk than his assistant opened the door and in walked the reporter from the *Advocate*. Derek didn't even need to ask if they needed anything. He simply closed the door behind him, leaving Dev alone with the reporter.

Ross smiled, flashing straight, ultrawhite teeth. "You don't look too happy right now."

"Do I ever look happy when you visit?" he asked.

Completely undaunted, the younger man stepped forward. "Thought you'd want to give a statement on the untimely and rather scandalous demise of Parker Harrington."

Dev leaned back in his chair. "We've already given a statement, as I'm positive you're aware of."

"Ah, yes, but I figured there'd be more than the standard thoughts and prayers BS, especially considering the brother of the woman you're engaged to tried to kill someone and Sabrina was reported missing." Ross sat in the chair in front of the desk.

"Then you'd figured wrong," Dev replied blandly. "And Sabrina is no longer my fiancée."

Interest sparked in Ross's dark eyes. "That's interesting."

"Not really. The engagement ended over a month ago." The lie rolled off his tongue as smoothly as the truth, but he always had a devil's tongue, didn't he? That's one thing Lawrence taught him. "You didn't know that? I'd expected a journalist with your talents would've known that."

His jaw hardened. "You know what I find even more interesting? Is that complete lack of information regarding Parker's victim. It's like this woman doesn't exist or is connected to someone or some *family* powerful enough to keep her information completely out of the public eye, and you know who that makes me think of? The de Vincents."

"Or it should make you think that whoever your inside person is in the police department is actually doing their job for once and keeping the victim's identity private."

Ross smirked. "I'm sure that's the case and has nothing to do with the new chief of police afraid of dying the same way as the old one."

He raised an eyebrow. "Dying of a heart condition? I'd sure hope not."

"Yeah." Ross smiled tightly. "I'm sure he died of natural causes, just like I'm sure your father hung himself."

Dev smirked. "You have such a fanciful imagination, Ross."

"Imagination? I'm lacking in the department."

Eyeing him, he crossed one leg over the other and idly clasped his fingers together. "You know, I'm actually glad you visited me today."

"Really?" Ross's response was dry.

"What's going on with Rosie Herpin?"

Ross's brows knitted together. "Rosie? What about her?"

"You of all people are going to play coy?" Dev met his gaze. "What is your relationship with her?"

"My relationship?" Ross coughed out a low laugh. "That's nosy of you to ask."

"Considering you have no problem being up in my business, then you should have no problem with me asking questions," Dev replied. "What is she to you?"

Ross didn't answer for a long moment. "Why would you be asking that kind of question?"

"Do you think I don't know that Rosie is who introduced you to Nikki?" Dev cocked an eyebrow. "Your friendship with Rosie is rather convenient."

"I've known Rosie for about two years." A muscle flexed along Ross's jaw. "Before I even knew who Nicolette Besson was."

"Really?" Dev's gaze flickered over his face. "If you're using her to get information, like you tried to do with Nikki, you're putting her in a very bad situation. Hopefully you wouldn't do that to an innocent person. That is, if she is innocent when it comes to whatever you're up to."

The reporter's nostrils flared and a long moment passed. "I will do anything to get to the truth."

"Will Rosie?" Dev asked. "Is she willing?"

Ross smirked as he gripped the arms of his chair. "I can see that I'm getting nowhere with this conversation. I'll show myself out."

"Wait." Dev smiled faintly when the reporter stilled. "I have another question for you. Something I've been curious about."

Ross lifted his brows. "I'm all ears."

"Do you think I don't know who your girlfriend was?" Dev asked. "Or is. Since she's still considered to be missing."

A change came over the man. His gaze sharpened as did his features. A tenseness filled him, settling into every line and shadow on his face.

"I know why you keep coming around. I know what you think and what you believe about my family and their involvement," Dev continued. "I even understand why you won't let it go."

The man's knuckles were turning white. "Do you understand, Devlin?"

"I do." And he did. He understood in ways he hoped Ross never had the misfortune of knowing.

"Then you have to know I will never give up until I know the truth of what happened to her," Ross bit out. "And don't you dare sit in front of me and tell me that none of you had anything to do with her disappearance."

Dev said nothing as he stared back at the man.

Ross's lips peeled back in a snarl. "All this time, you've never told me you knew. Why bring it up now, Devlin? Am I getting too close to the truth?"

"You've never been further from the truth," Dev said. "And if you continue down this road, you're never going to find it."

"Is that a threat?" A flush of anger crept into Ross's cheeks.

Dev shook his head. "It's advice. Free of charge. And another piece of advice? Don't send me another photograph with the words 'I know the truth' carved into it. This isn't a mystery novel."

"And how do you know that was me?"

"Because I'm not stupid, Ross."

"Fuck you." Ross rose to his feet. "You have no idea what I know. You have no idea how close I am to exposing every last one of you sons of bitches."

"Exposing us as what?" he asked, a little curious.

"For what you all are," Ross said. "Murderers."

Chapter 11

*T*he costume dress was . . . it was just wow.

Rosie twisted at the waist as she stood in front of the full-length mirror tacked to her bathroom door. Time had gotten away from her and she hadn't tried the dress on to make sure it worked before the ball. So, here she was, Friday, the night of the Masquerade, and she had just put it on.

Thank baby chupacabras everywhere, it worked—the dress definitely worked.

Rosie had found the old wedding gown in a thrift store, and when she purchased it in all its cream-and-ivory glory, she wasn't sure what could be done with it to make it into an appropriate costume, but it now looked nothing like the wedding dress she'd found.

A slow grin tugged at her lips. The gown was made of silk with nylon lining, enabling the seamstress to work her magic. It was dyed a crimson red and the beaded detail from the bodice had been removed, dyed black, and used as lacy trim around the collar of the dress, the edges of the loose, flowing sleeves, and along the hem of the skirt. Without the black corset, the bodice would be loose, but with it, her breasts never looked better and her waist never looked smaller, and she didn't even have it cinched as far as it could go.

She knew that some women would most likely wear petticoats or a taffeta underskirt to create the volume typical of the time period the Masquerade represented, but she was opting out of the heavy and cumbersome undergarment. She liked the way the dress moved against her thighs and hips. Why ruin that with a huge underskirt?

If Devlin saw her in this dress, he'd eat his words and then vomit them back up. Rosie smirked at her reflection. But alas, it was very unlikely he'd see her. Not that she wanted him to, but she didn't think for one second that Devlin would be at the Masquerade. Costumes were a requirement, no exceptions, and there was no way she could picture him even donning a mask. He probably threw a ton of money at the event and called it a day.

Rosie turned, checked out the back, and then twisted around. Her smile grew as she straightened the corset.

The beads rattled suddenly. "You look beautiful, baby."

Rosie's gaze lifted, and she saw her mother smiling at her in the reflection. Her mother had come over after work to help her get into the gown and the corset. Rosie looked nothing like her mother or her sister. Bella shared the same beautiful dark eyes and skin, along with the willowy, graceful frame that reminded Rosie of a graceful ballet dancer.

"Willowy" and "graceful" were two words no one in their right mind would've ever used to describe her. More like "sturdy" and "awkward."

An older cousin of hers used to tease her mercilessly when they were children, claiming that she was found in the bayou, and because she'd been young and dumb, she'd run straight to her mom, sobbing hysterically, because she'd been convinced she'd been an unwanted and/or stolen bayou baby.

That was probably the first time and definitely not the last time her parents wondered just how gullible she was, but kids—even family— could be so freaking mean.

It wasn't until Rosie grew older that she began to take after their father. But all three of the Pradine women had their great-grandmother's hair. Big, fat curls that were a mixture of brown and auburn, with Rosie ending up with a dash more auburn and her father's freckles. They were faint, and not even all that noticeable when she wore makeup, but they were there, proving that genetics were weird.

"Thank you, Momma."

Her mom eyed the dress as she sat in the old, oversized Victorian-style chair with emerald green velvet cushions Rosie had placed in the corner, by the balcony doors. "I cannot believe that was a wedding dress."

"I know, right?" Rosie turned from the mirror and walked over to the dresser. She picked up the mask. "You don't think this is too plain, do you?"

"Honey, with that dress, you could just paint a mask on."

Rosie laughed. The mask was a cheap one she'd picked up in a tourist shop. It was red with black lacing around the edges, simple compared to the ones adorned with feathers and jewels. "Have you seen me try to draw a stick figure? There is no way I am painting on a mask."

Her mother crossed her long legs. She'd stopped by after leaving the bakery, but there wasn't a speckle of flour on her. When Rosie left the bakery, she looked like she'd rolled around in it. "You leaving your hair down?"

Rosie nodded. She'd let the hair part in the middle, and right now, as long as the humidity stayed in check, the curls wouldn't look like a giant frizz ball. "I know everyone will probably have their hair up, but no matter what I do, it will look great when I walk out of here and then look like a porcupine died on top of my head within fifteen minutes tops."

"That sounds like a bit of an exaggeration," her mom replied. "I like it down, though. Makes you look sexy."

She wrinkled her nose at her mom. "I could die a happy woman if you never refer to me as sexy again, Mom."

Mom rolled her eyes. "Is Sarah coming here or . . . ?"

"I'm meeting her over at the house."

There was a pause and then, "So, do you have any other plans for this weekend besides the ball?"

Placing the mask on the dresser, she shook her head. "Not really."

That could change if Jilly had any success in getting the Mendez family to allow them to do a longer investigation. There hadn't been any more activity caught on film, and right now, Jilly was also trying to convince them to allow NOPE to bring in Sarah to see if she could communicate, but they were hesitant to do that, which both she and Lance found odd, but people were weird, even normal ones who believed their house to be haunted.

Of course, Jilly was now convinced that the activity was coming from the house Lucian had bought and, in Jilly's opinion, that explained why there were long gaps in activity. She was still hounding Rosie about getting access to the house. Just today, she'd left a message so long that the voice mail cut her off when she got to the tenth reason why Rosie needed to ask one of the de Vincents or Nikki about the house.

"That's perfect, then," Mom said.

Her eyes narrowed on her mother as she straightened the corset. "Why is that perfect?"

Her mother smiled and it was that smile Rosie knew all too well. It was too eager, too helpful, and she had the glint to her brown eyes. Rosie braced herself. "Well, there is this lovely male friend I think you'd be thrilled to meet."

Rosie's mouth opened as her fingers stilled around the bottom half of the corset.

"He's friends with Adrian," her mom continued. Adrian was her sister's husband. "He's a respiratory therapist, divorced but not recently. According to Bella, he's very—"

"Mom," Rosie cut her off.

"What?" She fixed a perfect look of innocence on her face. "I'm just letting you know that there is a guy who I am pretty sure is available this weekend and would love to meet you."

Rosie lowered her arms. "Please tell me you did not pimp me out again."

"I would never do such a thing." Her gasp of outrage wasn't effective considering her mother had not once but three times set her up on dates without Rosie's knowledge. "Finding you a date is not pimping you out."

"Well, it kind of is the same thing," she replied, returning to the corset. "It's not like I don't date."

"Using Tinder is not dating."

"Mom." Rosie wrinkled her nose. "Like you know what Tinder is."

"Oh I totally know what it is, and quite honestly, I'm jealous there was nothing like that back when I was single. Love your father with all my heart, but it would've been nice to have this neat little dating app on my phone."

Shaking her head, she inhaled her breath and her ribs expanded against the boning in the corset. These things were the worst, but they were sexy as hell. "You'd be swiping right nonstop."

Her mother snickered. "But seriously, Erick—his name is Erick—would love to meet with you. I'll text you his number."

Rosie closed her eyes and said a little prayer. It wasn't a good prayer. Started with *Baby Jesus, please help me*, so she doubted her prayer would be answered, but it was worth the shot. "You got this guy's number?"

"For you. Not me."

"Well, yeah, obviously." Rosie paused. "Or at least I hope so."

"I didn't agree that you'd go out with him, but I hope you do text him." She rose from the chair and walked over to where Rosie stood. Her mother's eyes searched hers. "I just want you to be happy, baby."

"I am happy. Do I not look happy? Because I am. I'm finally getting to go to the Masquerade, so I'm actually freaking thrilled."

"I know, but that's not what I meant." She smoothed her thumb over Rosie's cheek. "I want you to find that happiness you had with Ian."

Rosie's breath caught. "Mom. . . ."

"I know, baby. I know it's been ten years and you've moved on. I know this, but I . . . I worry about you. You're my daughter, and I worry that you're not going to let yourself find that kind of love again, and really, what is the point of all of this, of life, when you don't have someone to share it with?"

The back of her throat burned. "I do have people to share it with. You. Dad. Bella. My friends."

"That's not the kind of sharing I'm talking about."

Drawing in a shallow breath, Rosie withdrew from her mother's grasp and stepped back. "Maybe . . . maybe I'm not going to find that kind of love again," she said, lifting her gaze to her mother's. "Maybe he was it for me. Maybe he was the one, and I'm not someone who gets to have multiple 'the ones.' And I'm okay with that."

Her eyes turned sad. "Are you really, Rosie?"

Did it really matter if she was? Because if Ian was the one and only for her, it didn't matter if she was okay or not with it. Real life wasn't always full of happily-ever-afters, and a lot of people never got to experience that. Often it was the exact opposite of happily-ever-after.

And maybe that was it for Rosie. Her happily-ever-after wasn't going to be found in a man or a woman. It was going to have to be found within herself.

She'd thought that was already true for her, but after moments like this, she wasn't so sure.

Chapter 12

$\mathcal{I}$ have a strange feeling about tonight."

Clutching the long skirt of her gown so she didn't face-plant a side-walk outside the private home on St. Charles, Rosie stopped midstep and turned to look at Sarah. Rosie had just been dropped off and had found Sarah waiting for her near the corner of the street.

Sarah looked amazing in a similar costume. Being that she was a good head taller than Rosie, had the quintessential peaches-and-cream complexion, and had a mass of blond hair piled atop her head in an elegant updo.

She was dressed like Rosie, wearing the red mask with black lacing and the same long, black-and-red gown with the flowing sleeves and a corseted, lacy bodice so extremely low cut there was a chance the world was going to see Sarah's girls at some point tonight.

Not that Rosie had any room to talk. If she bent over, there was a high probability she would spill out, and maybe even pass out, be-cause the first thing Sarah did when she saw Rosie was to tighten the corset on her in such a manner she was amazed that her ribs hadn't broken.

But when Sarah said she had a strange feeling, Rosie listened. "Like a bad, 'let's go home right now' strange feeling? Or just a strange feel-ing in general?"

Ignoring the annoyed looks from others in period costumes having to walk around them, Sarah closed her blue eyes and stepped closer to Rosie. "It's a fairly strong feeling."

Rosie waited for more of an explanation, feeling a fine shiver curl around the nape of her neck. The evening air was cool, but she knew it was more than just the temperatures causing her to shiver. "I'm starting to feel like I shouldn't have accepted your invitation."

Laughing at that, Sarah tilted her chin to the side, and Rosie was amazed she didn't topple over with all that hair piled up on the top of her head. "If I told you that you were going to lose a finger tonight, you'd still be here. You've wanted to attend the Masquerade for years."

"True." A man walking past them dressed like, Rosie assumed, the vampire Lestat momentarily distracted her. It was quite the authentic costume. She refocused on Sarah. "But you have a strange feeling."

"It's not a bad feeling. It's just that I heard this voice." A streetlamp flickered on, casting a dim yellow glow on the cornstalk fence that lined the front of the mansion. Sarah turned, lifting the two ivory envelopes to fan herself. Of course the Masquerade didn't do online tickets or invites. They were old-school, paper all the way. "It was more like a whisper."

"A whisper?" Rosie was used to this when it came to Sarah, the random whispers and feelings. "Do you know what the whisper said?"

Sarah nodded and a strand of hair slipped forward, brushing the mask. "'If there is no risk, there is no reward.'"

"Really?" Rosie replied dryly. "Did a ghost whisper a motivational speech in your ear?"

"Funny, right?" She lifted a shoulder. "Did you ever tell any of the de Vincents what happened during our reading?"

Rosie was also used to Sarah's rapid change of subject. "No. I don't think they'd believe me, and well, they have their hands full with a lot of things," she explained, thinking of Nikki. "It's not the easiest thing to bring up in a conversation with a stranger."

Surprise widened Sarah's eyes. "I'm sort of shocked that you didn't immediately find one of them and tell them."

Rosie pressed her lips together. It was hard to explain why she hadn't said anything. Granted, most people would understand why, because it sounded legit crazy pants and it did bother Rosie that she hadn't shared that info, but it would require her talking to a de Vincent and possibly drawing the attention of Devlin.

Which was probably inevitable since she planned on visiting Nikki again soon.

Sarah studied her a moment and then nodded. "We should get going."

And then with that, Sarah was walking off into the steady throng of people entering the narrow opening in the fence. It was a good thing Rosie liked weird, because damn, Sarah could be really weird sometimes.

Holding on to her dress, she caught up with Sarah and got a look at the stunning Greek Revival mansion that sat near Loyola University. Rosie had seen it a hundred thousand times it seemed, but never like this. Never on the night of the legendary Masquerade, where the most powerful and the wealthiest in New Orleans rubbed elbows and the sweet Lord knew what else. But Rosie really wasn't interested in any of them.

She dragged her hand across the small beaded clutch, feeling the small, square voice recorder. Rosie grinned. Her one and only goal tonight was to catch the voice of the ghost of the murdered bride.

She most likely wasn't going to get the chance again, so maybe whatever voice Sarah had heard had imparted a very important message, if not an incredibly cheesy one. There was no reward without risk.

A team of security guards stood at the gate, which was why it was taking so long to enter, but Sarah flashed their invites and they were soon through, their steps slowing as they entered the property. There was white-and-black lace everywhere, a sea of taffeta and feathered masks and elaborate hairpieces. Ladies painted with fake moles, faces powdered white as rice cakes, and necks glistening with what appeared to be real emeralds and sapphires.

The cloying scent of perfume and cologne mixed with how close everyone was left Rosie a little dizzy. Well, the corset probably had something to do with that, but she pushed through it. There was wine inside, hopefully the really expensive kind she'd never buy, because she was parched.

"It's really beautiful, isn't it?" Sarah curled her arm around Rosie's.

It truly was. The mansion sat back from the street, and it seemed like every inside light was turned on. The large front yard was lit with soft white fairy lights and paper lanterns hanging from poles. The wide walkway led up to a set of steps that were as long as the width of the house.

"Thank you for inviting me," Rosie said, squeezing her arm. "I know I've thanked you already, but it bears repeating. This is an amazing experience."

Sarah leaned into her, lowering her voice as they reached the steps. "An amazing experience to sneak upstairs into that bedroom?"

Sliding her a coy glance, she feigned an affronted gasp. "How dare you suggest such things."

"Uh-huh." Sarah laughed as they climbed the steps. "If you get caught, I don't know you."

Rosie grinned. "I'll make sure I shout your ex-fiancé's name from the rafters for all to hear."

"That's my girl."

Cooler air teased her heated skin as they crossed into the wide, oval foyer. Voodoo magic had to be the reason they were able to cool the inside with all the bodies crammed together and the doors left open, but she was damn grateful for it. She'd been expecting the place to feel like a sauna, but it was rather airy.

It was hard to get a sense of the space, with the laughter, the hum of conversation, and people everywhere. There was so much to hear and see, she was a little overwhelmed, and it reminded her of trying to navigate the streets during Mardi Gras. She scanned the hidden faces and costumed bodies. If there was anyone here she knew, which was unlikely because she didn't hobnob with the highfalutin crowd, she wouldn't recognize them—her eyes widened. Holy baby llamas, the men were wearing . . .

"Breeches," Rosie whispered, a slow grin tugging at her lips as her gaze swiveled over *a lot* that was on display in gray, tan, and black super-tight, super-fitted breeches. Many of those legs were paired with pretty authentic-looking riding boots. She hadn't noticed that outside for some reason. "They're wearing breeches."

"That they are."

Rosie couldn't look away. "Do you think they're wearing codpieces under their breeches?"

Sarah snorted.

"You know, so they'd be historically accurate?" Rosie whispered. "Because some of those . . . packages do not look real."

"I really hope what I am seeing is not the result of codpieces," she replied and then added, "Some pretty nice butts in the bunch, though."

A woman in front of them looked over her shoulder, her bright red lips tilting into a faint smile as she blatantly checked them out, her gaze lingering below their chins. "Lots of pretty . . . things here tonight," the woman replied and then winked before turning back around.

Sarah and Rosie exchanged a long look.

"We need to find something to drink stat." Sarah kept her arm around Rosie's. "It should be to the left, in the grand room."

Rosie let Sarah lead the way and as they broke away from the crowd, she could see more of the grand house. She took in the oak walls and the stunning cypress grand staircase. Rooms were adorned with plaster medallions and elaborate moldings she figured were original.

Sarah was right. Not only was there an open bar in the grand room, the crowd was also much lighter, which was surprising since that was where the liquor was. There was a small group of women by the large window, eyeing the men who stood at the bar.

"Let's get some sweet, sweet moscato in you." Sarah grinned. "And get some expensive as hell whiskey in me."

"Sounds like a marvelous plan," Rosie said as they neared the bar.

"Excuse me, gentlemen," Sarah said in a voice that just dripped with Southern sugar. "May we scoot in?"

Two of the men closest turned and damn if their stares weren't as blatant as the woman in the foyer. "Of course," one of the men murmured. He stepped aside, as did the other. Both had fair hair and brown eyes, strong jaws and nice smiles. With half of their faces obscured, that was all she could make out of their features. They were handsome, she decided as she smiled at them, because most men were handsome when they wore a mask.

"Thank you," she said.

"What are you boys drinking?" Sarah asked, and as they answered, Rosie caught the attention of the bartender. Or her breasts did. Whatever worked. She ordered their drinks and then turned to the two men, resting her hip against the bar.

"I want you to find that happiness you had with Ian."

Her mother's words crept into her thoughts, unwanted but there and annoyingly loud, too. Did she want that again? Yeah, she did, but she didn't—realizing one of the men was speaking to her, she pulled herself out of her thoughts. "I'm sorry?"

"It's okay." His smile was warm. "I was saying my name is Theo. Yours?"

"Rosie," she answered, accepting her glass of pink, sparkling wine.

"I like it. Are you from here, Rosie?"

Sipping her wine, she peeked over at Sarah. Her friend was well on the way to forgetting about her ex. "Born and raised. How about you?"

"From Baton Rouge, but I like to think I was adopted by New Orleans," he answered. "Been here for four years."

"Well, you know what they say about New Orleans? She either accepts you with open arms or spits you right out."

"No truer words have ever been spoken." Theo toasted to that.

Rosie was about to ask what brought him to New Orleans when *it* happened—the sensation of warm fingers traveling down her spine. It came out of nowhere, and before she knew what she was doing, she looked over her shoulder. Her gaze had landed on him with unnerving accuracy.

The man leaned against the bar, his legs crossed at the ankles and his arm resting on the top of the bar. He was drinking some sort of amber-colored liquor from a short glass and he was staring straight at her. Their gazes met, and the strangest awareness whipped through Rosie, causing goose bumps to spread across her flesh despite the long sleeves.

Wait a second. . . .

Even with a black mask and being too far away to see his eye color, she recognized the perfectly smoothed-back black hair and granite jaw.

Crap on a crusty cracker, it was Devlin de Vincent.

She couldn't believe it. At no point did she really believe that he'd be here. Nothing about him gave the indication that he'd be at a Masquerade *and* wearing a mask, but that was him and he looked . . .

Her gaze dropped. He was wearing black breeches and he looked . . . A shiver whipped its way through her, but this one was feverish, as if she was standing too close to a flame.

Oh dear Lord, why was God so cruel? With great effort, she lifted her gaze. In that mask and those pants, he looked like something straight out of a fantasy.

One side of his lips twisted into a smirk as he raised his glass in her direction.

Honest to God, she had the absolute worst luck. She really didn't want to see him, especially after what he'd said to her at his house.

Before she turned away from him, she lifted her glass of wine and extended her middle finger along the glass, flipping him off.

Rosie refocused on . . . hell, what was his name? She couldn't remember, and he was now staring at her in a way that said he'd been talking again and she hadn't been listening. How could she? Even with her back to Devlin, she could feel him, staring at her.

She couldn't be in this room, and besides, she didn't come here to flirt with handsome men whose names she couldn't recall or to have holes drilled into her back.

Murmuring her apologies to the man before her, she caught Sarah's eyes. With one look, she knew where Rosie was off to. Ignoring Devlin's presence at the end of the bar, she walked as slowly as possible from the room, hoping her ass swayed in an enticing way and not like she had a limp.

The only good thing about seeing him tonight was what *he* got to see. Her and the amazing dress that made her breasts look absolutely divine, so at least there was that.

Determined to not spend one moment stressing over Devlin's unexpected appearance, she entered the still-packed foyer. There was something going on toward the back of the house, where a band played. She slipped past a group standing near the grand staircase. With her glass of wine in hand, she walked up the steps just like her mother would've taught her to do.

Walk like she had every reason to be where she was, and like always, it worked. No one stopped her. No one called out as she trailed a hand along the beautiful wood. She made it to the second floor with a smug smile.

She could totally be a spy.

Or a ninja.

Better yet, a ninja-spy.

Turning to the right, her foot caught on the edge of a runner. She tripped, throwing her free hand out to catch herself. A miracle occurred and she didn't spill her drink.

Okay, she definitely could not be a spy or a ninja.

Shaking her head, she made her way down the hall that led to the back of the house. *Please be unlocked. Please be unlocked.* She reached for the handle on the last bedroom to the left. The door swung open, and she breathed a sigh of relief.

She flipped on the light and got a look at the room as she stepped inside, leaving the door ajar. It was pretty small and sparsely decorated. There was just a bed and a nightstand against one wall, a dresser against the one near the door. A standing mirror stood next to a curtained window. Everything was new so, for some reason, she didn't feel that bad when she placed her wineglass on the nightstand.

What she was doing up in the room without permission was pretty unethical, but no one in her position would've passed up the chance. Both Lance and Jilly had done it—multiple times and they'd been caught a lot.

Opening her clutch, she reached inside for the voice recorder.

"Rosie" came a deep, all-too-familiar voice. "What a surprise."

Chapter 13

$\mathcal{D}$ev had recognized her the moment she walked into the grand room with the tall blonde, before she even became aware of his presence. How could he not? Every woman at the ball was dressed either to entice or impress, but no one—not a single woman here— carried it off as well as Rosie. She was walking temptation and eyes followed her.

That dress . . .

God. Unlike most of the women here, she didn't wear the ridiculous underdress that increased the volume of the skirt. Her dress was more of a sheath of red and black, clinging to her round hips and thighs with every step, and it was cut low and cinched at the waist by a corset. That dress . . .

Fuck.

He wanted to find a burlap sack and cover her with it.

He also wanted to rip that dress off her with his teeth.

The bourbon he drank had scorched his throat as his gaze lingered on the voluptuous swell above the delicate black lace. He'd only seen Rosie in loose shirts, but the brief moments that their bodies had been pressed together, he'd felt enough to know her breasts were plump and ample. Seeing her in that dress made it nearly impossible to ignore how beautiful her body must be, with all those hidden, soft curves.

It hadn't helped when he was finally able to drag his gaze up to her face. Her full lips were painted a soft red and those eyes were striking behind the simple red-and-black mask. She was going against the trend in many ways. Her hair was down instead of swept up in some complicated style. Those thick curls brushed her heart-shaped face and fell past her shoulders, longer than he'd expected. Rosie wore no jewelry except the gold chain—the chain that held her deceased husband's ring—and that made her more elegant than those with thousands of dollars' worth of diamonds adorning their necks and ears.

Rosie was simply breathtaking.

Not that he hadn't noticed that about her before, even when she wore loose clothing and had her hair pulled back. From the moment he'd seen her in her apartment, he'd thought she was beautiful, but he recognized now how utterly stunning she was. And he'd known a lot of beautiful women, those born that way and those who achieved it through a gifted surgeon's hands. None of them could hold a candle to Rosie, because she was a fire.

His senses sparked alive and his body burned just by seeing her, and he knew that had nothing to do with their often volatile conversations or what he suspected about her.

Dev simply reacted to everything that was her, and damn, that was rare and he didn't like it. At all.

That he was surprised that she was at the Masquerade would be an understatement to say the least, but he was learning that Rosie had a habit of popping up unexpectedly.

He thought about what Gabe had said to him and a twinge of guilt surfaced, but Dev doubted her appearances were so random. Possibly more like extremely calculated, because how could she not think he would be here?

When she left the room, he followed even though he knew he shouldn't. He had no idea what Rosie was up to, but he was sure it involved that damn journalist and that meant he needed to stay the hell away from her, but curiosity had quickly taken hold when she climbed the cypress staircase and made her way to a smaller bedroom in the back of the house. What in the world was she up to? Nothing good if he was to judge the wide-eyed stare now meeting his. She looked like she'd just been caught trying to steal the queen's jewels.

"What are you doing up here?" she demanded, pulling her hand out of the clutch.

"I have a better question." Holding on to the glass of bourbon, he leaned against the door he closed behind him. "What are you doing at the Masquerade?"

"Attempting to have a nice, lovely evening without any drama," she retorted, and that lovely and rather distracting chest of hers swelled when she took a deep breath. "But apparently that's not going to happen."

He smirked. "That's not what I meant by the question, and you know that." He paused. "You've never been at this event before. I would've noticed."

"Oh really?" She snapped her clutch shut.

Dev nodded.

"There are hundreds of people down there. How would you know if I've been to this event before and you just haven't noticed?"

"There is no way I would not have noticed you. Not if you were dressed like that."

She was quiet as she appeared to decipher what he meant. "I'm not sure if that was a compliment, but knowing you, it was probably an insult."

"It wasn't an insult," he replied. "You look beautiful. Stunning, really. If you'd been to this event before and looked like this, I would've noticed you right away."

Rosie's lips parted, drawing his attention. He'd never been much of a kisser. Hell, he never once kissed Sabrina, mainly because he hadn't wanted that woman's mouth anywhere near his, but he'd never wanted to know more what a woman's mouth tasted and felt like than he did in that moment.

"Are you drunk?" she asked.

He arched a brow. "I wish."

She looked around the room before her gaze drifted back to his. A moment passed and then she said, "My friend had an extra ticket and she knew that I've always wanted to attend the Masquerade, so she invited me."

Interesting. "The blonde you walked in with?"

Rosie eyed him as she nodded.

"But that doesn't answer why you're in this room instead of with your friend and enjoying the party."

"I am enjoying the party."

"Alone? In a bedroom upstairs where I'm sure guests were not expected to roam?" he queried.

Those tantalizing lips thinned. "Did you think that maybe I saw you and was attempting to hide?"

"Not for one second do I believe you would ever run from me."

Rosie rolled her eyes.

"What are you doing in here?"

"I'm measuring the door space for beaded curtains. What are you doing?"

A surprised laugh burst from him, the sound unfamiliar even to his own ears. "I'm sure the homeowners will be appreciative of the additional decor, but I seriously doubt that's what you're doing, or at least I hope not."

Her eyes narrowed. "You didn't answer my question. Why are you up here?"

"I followed you," he admitted.

She blinked. "Well, not only is that creepy, that's also annoying."

"Why is that?" He took a sip of the bourbon, watching her through half-open eyes.

"Because I'm sure you followed me just so you can insult me, and I'm not going to give you that luxury." She picked up her wineglass and stepped forward, lifting her chin. "So, could you move away from the door?"

"I didn't follow you so I could insult you. Pretty sure we've established that when I said you looked beautiful."

"Really?" came her dry response. "Considering every conversation I've had with you, with the exception of the day in the cemetery, has ended with you insulting me. Why would tonight be any different?"

Tonight was different. He didn't know why he knew this. Maybe it was instinct, but he knew tonight was like no other that came before. "Are you always this argumentative?"

"Are you always such a douche canoe?" she snapped back. "Oh wait. Don't answer that. I already know. You are."

"Douche canoe? I haven't heard that word since I was . . . thirteen."

"So?"

"So who still says that?"

"Me." She smiled then, and it went straight to his dick, hardening him. "I'm bringing it back in style."

He smiled faintly at that. "Thought I was a dickhead."

"You're both. A dickhead and a douche canoe."

"That's rather impressive."

"Not really." She took a drink of her wine.

He watched her run her finger along the stem of the wineglass and found himself oddly jealous of the wineglass. He wanted her to touch him like that, but considering the fact she most likely hated him, that wasn't going to happen . . . then again, she'd felt him the morning in her apartment, and he would swear that he saw arousal in her eyes and in her shallow, short breaths.

"I think . . . I think I should apologize to you," he said, lifting his gaze to hers.

"For what?" she asked, taking another sip of her wine.

He felt his dick harden when her tongue darted out, catching a droplet of wine on her lower lip. "You're going to make me say it, aren't you?"

"Is the sky blue? Yeah." She smiled tightly. "Because when you said 'apologize,' it sounded like you were choking."

"It did not."

"Choking on your arrogance," she added.

"Okay. I acted like a dick."

"Which time? In my apartment when you insulted my interior design or when you suggested that I had ulterior motives for giving you flowers at the cemetery?"

He opened his mouth, but he didn't get a chance to say anything, because apparently Rosie was not done.

"Or when you insinuated that I was out to do something nefarious to your family just because I introduced my friend to a guy?" She stepped toward him, lowering her glass, and for a second he thought she might throw the contents at him. "Or are you apologizing for making me move my car and feel completely unwelcome while visiting my friend? Wait. There's more. Are you apologizing for saying that the mere idea of having sex with me was laughable?"

He was learning Rosie had a remarkable memory. "Yes. I am apologizing for all of that. I'm . . . sorry."

She tilted her head. "You could not sound less genuine if you tried."

"It was genuine." And that was—well, it was true. Maybe he'd misread Rosie? Maybe he was making her guilty by association? He wasn't sure, but he did . . . feel guilt, and he didn't feel guilt about a lot of things. "I was a dick to you."

"Yeah, you were, but you can't undick yourself."

He blinked. "Undick myself?"

A giggle snuck out of her, and he didn't even fight it. Didn't hesitate. He grinned in response to the sound, surprising himself.

"Yeah, undick yourself." She finished off her wine and then lifted a shoulder in a shrug. "I don't think it's possible."

"Anything is possible when I put effort into it."

She snorted.

He tipped his head back against the door. "So you don't accept my apology?"

"Not really. Words are meaningless. Actions are everything."

"That I will agree with." He raised his glass to her and then finished it off, welcoming the bite of bourbon. "You're a mystery to me, and that's . . . different," he admitted, setting his glass on the dresser. "I could find out everything I ever wanted to know about you by making a single phone call, and yet, I haven't. That alone is a mystery."

She opened her mouth, closed it, and then said, "Okay. I don't even know where to start with all that, so I will just go with wow, that would be a huge violation of privacy."

"It would be."

Rosie stared at him for a moment. "And that's all you have to say about that?"

"It is," he replied, straightening and pulling away from the door. "But I haven't done it."

"Do you think you deserve a gold star by your name for not being a stalker?"

It happened again. The smile he couldn't stop and didn't even try to. "I think so."

"Wow." Rosie laughed, and it wasn't bitter or cold sounding. "You are . . . something else."

"I'll take that as a compliment."

"Of course you would." She lifted a shoulder. "Well, if you did make that creepy phone call, you're not going to find out anything interesting. I've lived a pretty boring life."

"Now, that's a lie," he murmured, taking a step toward her. "I doubt there's a single thing about you that's boring."

Her gaze met his and a long moment passed before she said, "Do you really want to know what I was doing up here?"

His interest was more than piqued. "I do."

She watched him for a second longer and then turned, walking back to the nightstand to place her glass there. His gaze drifted over her, lingering on the sway of her lips.

Christ.

Was his mouth watering? Because it felt like that.

Rosie faced him. She was opening her clutch. "This room is haunted."

Dev opened his mouth and then snapped it shut.

"Legend says that a bride was murdered by a jealous lover in this room, the night before her wedding," she continued, pulling out a slim black rectangular object. "Supposedly, you can pick up EVPs of her voice. That's why I came up here."

He shouldn't have been surprised, but he was. "EVP?"

"Yes. Electronic—"

"I know what it means." He walked over to where she stood beside the bed. "Did you find anything?"

She didn't answer immediately. "No. You interrupted me. But you know what an EVP is?"

He nodded as he reached his hand out. "May I?"

She hesitated for a moment and then handed it over. Their fingers brushed as he picked up the simple black recorder. Turning it over, he checked to see if it was turned off. It was, but that didn't mean it hadn't been on this entire time.

God, even he knew he sounded paranoid.

Dev shook the thought out of his head as he handed the recorder back to Rosie. When she slipped it back into her clutch, he asked, "You're not going to try to . . . investigate the room now?"

She pinned him with a droll look. "With you in the room? Yeah, I'd rather get a lobotomy."

"That's excessive."

Closing the clutch, she placed it on the bed, and he liked that, because it meant she wasn't planning to leave right then. He shouldn't like that, because he needed to be downstairs at some point, when they started the auction.

"You don't believe in ghosts," she said, glancing to the right of them. Their reflection was in the standing mirror. "So, having you here would make the whole endeavor not only pointless but also painful."

Dev didn't know why he said what he said next, giving voice to words he never said to even his brothers, but tonight . . . yeah, tonight was different. "I never said I didn't believe in ghosts."

Her eyes widened behind the mask. "I'm pretty sure you did."

He shook his head as he stared down at her. "I don't believe in a lot of what ghost hunters do or psychics and that kind of stuff. I think most of them are scammers or delusional, but I never said I didn't believe. There is just a lot of crap and very little truth when it comes to that kind of stuff."

She looked like she didn't know what to say at first and then she asked a question she'd asked before. "Is your house haunted, Devlin?"

He dragged his teeth along his lip, considering how he could answer the question. "Things . . . things have a way of happening there. Stuff that cannot be easily explained."

Excitement sparked in those lovely eyes. "Like what kind of stuff?"

"Unexplained noises. Things move without anyone interacting with them." He sat on the high bed and stretched his legs out. "I've seen . . ."

She sat next to him, her posture stiff due to the corset. "Seen what?"

His gaze slid to hers. "I've seen shadows. Movement out of the corner of my eyes when no one else is in the room or hallways."

She leaned toward him, placing a hand on the bed next to his thigh. He inhaled deeply, catching the scent of . . . coconut. "So, you think your house is haunted? Then why the attitude when I first asked you?"

He looked at her mouth again and had to spread his thighs. "Because I'm a dickhead?"

A tiny grin appeared. "Sounds about right."

"I can only believe what I've seen and what I've experienced," he said.

"But if you've seen things and heard stuff at your house, how can you be so dismissive of ghost hunters and other people's experiences?"

"Because like I said, I think most of them are scammers or delusional."

The grin faded. "Do you think that about me?"

He didn't know what he thought about her. "I think you believe in what you're doing."

Her eyes narrowed. "Nice choice of words."

He lifted a shoulder.

"I don't get it," she said after a moment. "You've experienced supernatural activity and yet universally doubt anyone else's claims? I don't get that."

Dev leaned back, resting on his arm as he angled his body toward hers. "I saw something just this week." He felt one side of his lips curl. "A black shadow at the other end of the mudroom. I thought of you when I saw it."

"I'm sure that filled you with happy thoughts."

"I wouldn't exactly say happy," he murmured, shifting his gaze to the mirror. "Have you ever seen anything, with your own eyes?"

"Yes," she said quickly. "I've seen ghosts and I've heard them."

For some reason he thought about that Saturday afternoon when he was a kid, the last time his mother's friend brought Pearl to the house. "So, you believe in life after death?"

Rosie dipped her chin and several curls fell over her shoulders, brushing the tops of her breasts. "There is something after death. If there wasn't, there wouldn't be spirits. And if there wasn't, then what would be the point of all of this? All the joy and sadness, all the failures and successes? We go through all this life and then for us to just die and that be it? I don't want to believe that." There was a pause where she pressed her plump lips together. "I can't."

Dev felt his chest tighten as she lifted her gaze to his. Just like before, words formed on the tip of his tongue. Words he'd never spoke out loud to another human being.

Maybe it was because she was a stranger to him but at the same time she wasn't. Maybe it was because she knew so little about him and he knew so very little about her. And maybe it was because she wasn't impressed by him. She wasn't enthralled or wasn't trying to entice him. He knew there was a good chance that she could be working with Ross, but what he did know for sure was that she was not remotely afraid of him.

So maybe he knew why he said what came out of his mouth next. "I died once."

"What?" She reached up, her fingers going to the thin cord securing the mask in place.

"Don't." He caught her wrist. "It's . . . easier this way."

She stared at him and then her gaze dropped to where he brought her hand to the bed. A long moment passed. "You died?"

"I probably should've elaborated." A wry grin tugged at his mouth. "When I was young—a young boy, actually—I was . . . I was injured quite gravely. I died, but I was revived."

"Oh my God." Her body rocked forward as she placed both hands on the bed by his thigh. "I've never experienced anything like that. I mean, I've spoken to people who have, but . . . What happened to you?"

His brothers hadn't been born yet and they didn't even know about this. The only people alive besides him who knew what happened that night after he found Pearl's mother in the room with his father were Besson and his wife, Livie, and it was going to stay that way. "I was a kid, messing around. Got myself hurt."

She stared at him for a moment as she reached up with her free hand, fiddling with the chain around her neck. "Do you remember what happened when you . . . ?"

"Died?" Dev's fingers seemed to move on their own accord, finding their way under the sleeve of her dress. "It was many years ago and some of the memories have lost their clarity, but I remember bits and pieces. As cliché as it sounds, there was a white light. No tunnel. But there was a bright light. It was all I could see and . . ."

Her fingers stilled around the necklace. "And what?"

Part of him still couldn't believe he was saying any of this and he couldn't even blame the bourbon. "I heard my grandmother's voice."

Even with the mask still in place, he could see her face soften as he dragged his finger along the inside of her wrist. "That had to be very special, wasn't it? I mean, I'm sure as a young boy you were scared and confused, but to hear a loved one who's passed? That . . ." She drew in a heavy breath and when she spoke, there was a wistfulness to her tone. "That had to be amazing."

Suddenly, there was something he wanted to know—no, needed to know. "How did your husband die?"

Rosie pulled and he let go. She straightened as she dropped her hands into her lap. "We don't know each other like that for that kind of conversation."

"I just told you that I died and heard my grandmother's voice. How much more do we need to know each other before you tell me that?"

She was quiet and then she laughed. "That's a good point and I hate even admitting that to you."

"I always make good points."

Rosie wrinkled her nose. "That's yet to be seen." She stared down at her fingers and then looked up and over at him. "I have . . ." She bit down on her lip and looked away.

"What?"

She shook out her shoulders. "I have a favor to ask. You're probably going to say no, but you just told me that your house is haunted and—"

"You're not investigating my house," he replied dryly. "And you haven't answered my question."

"I'm not asking to investigate your house. Not really." She narrowed her eyes. "Your brother is renovating a house over in the Garden District. I want to get into that house, along with my team."

Devlin tilted his head back. "To do what?"

"We have a client who lives next door and has been experiencing a pretty dramatic haunting. We think it's stemming from the house Lucian is having renovated," she explained. "Can you talk to Lucian and get him to let us check out his house?"

"Let me get this straight. You want my brother to let you into his home to see if it's haunted?"

She nodded.

Dev honest to God had no idea how to respond to that, but then he watched her suck her bottom lip between her teeth. As shitty as it was, he realized he had bargaining power, and there was something he wanted. Lots of things he wanted, actually.

"I'll get you into the house."

"What?" Surprise pitched her tone. "You're for real?"

A half grin tugged at his lips. "On one condition."

"What condition?"

He sat up and leaned in close enough that he heard her inhale. The scent of coconuts teased him again. "It's a pretty big condition."

"Okay? What is it?"

What he was about to say was not planned. It was not calculated in the ways he wanted it to be and how he was accustomed to. His condition was . . . simply something he desired.

"Kiss me," he said, voice low. "That's my condition. Kiss me."

Chapter 14

Rosie was almost positive she hadn't heard him correctly. "I'm going to need you to say that again."

Those thick lashes lowered. "The condition is a kiss."

Okay.

She had heard him correctly.

"You want to kiss me?" she repeated, feeling foolish for even asking that question and for the flutter that picked up in her stomach.

That small grin appeared again. "I do." He paused. "Very badly."

The flutter now moved to her chest and felt like a nest of butterflies was going to beat its way out. "It's the dress, isn't it?" she said, half joking.

"It is." He lifted one hand and placed just the tip of his finger on the black lace that rested against her shoulder. The light touch caused the muscles in her stomach and much, much lower to tighten. "And it's so much more than that."

"Really? How so?"

He slowly, so damn slowly, dragged his finger down the collar. "Do I really need to explain why I want to kiss you?"

"Considering just a few days ago you said that the idea—"

"I know what I said," he cut in, and his finger reached the swell of her breast. Her entire body jerked as a sweet, heady flush invaded her system. "That was a lie."

She was finding it difficult to get enough air into her lungs, and she was totally blaming the corset for that.

"So, what do you think?" He dragged his finger to the center of her bodice, to where her breasts met. An ache filled her, potent and swift as he curled his finger over the center of her dress, tugging lightly on it. His lashes lifted and those remarkable eyes pierced hers. "About my condition?"

Never in a million years did Rosie think she'd be in this situation. Not even in her most out-there, impossible fantasies could she have dreamt up this moment with Devlin de Vincent.

And she had some pretty far-out-there fantasies. One involved a Santa suit, but she wasn't going to focus on that at this moment.

From the moment he walked in this room, everything had turned surreal. The fact that they weren't at each other's throats and he'd shared something so personal with her was testimony of how bizarre tonight was turning out to be, so why was she so shocked that he wanted to kiss her?

Tonight was . . . it was just different.

Her gaze roamed over his face. Maybe it was the masks. As stupid as that sounded, it made her feel like it wasn't really them. She wasn't sure why, but the only thing she did know was that, despite all the things they'd said to each other, she wanted to kiss him.

And Rosie had learned a long time ago to do what you wanted before you didn't have a chance to do it again.

"Okay," she whispered. "I agree to your condition."

Devlin held very still, his breath dancing over her lips. "Then do it."

Her stomach pitched as if she were on a roller coaster about to plummet down a steep hill. Placing her hand on the bed, she leaned in and tilted her head. A stuttered heartbeat later, her lips touched his. It was just the lightest brush of her lips against his, but he made this sound that sent a wild, hot shiver through her. It came from the back of his throat, a deep groan that curled her toes inside her heels. His lips were soft and firm, and when she touched the tip of her tongue to the seam of his mouth, he opened for her.

Rosie shuddered as her tongue touched his. He tasted of bourbon, and while she wasn't a whiskey girl, she found that he tasted delicious. Sinful. *Wicked.* Slowly, she lifted her hand and placed it against his hard chest. She swore she could feel his heart beating under her palm. The moment she touched him, everything changed about the kiss.

Rosie might've started the kiss, but Devlin now had complete and utter control.

He deepened the kiss, tasting her just like she'd done to him. One hand slipped under the weight of her hair, curling around the nape of her neck, and those deep, slow, nerve-frying kisses changed. There was a barely restrained hunger to how he moved his mouth over hers, as if he was barely holding back.

Another shudder rolled its way through her as heat simmered low in her stomach. Dizzy and breathless, she moaned into his mouth as her fingers curled around the front of his shirt. He kissed her as if he wouldn't allow a single part of her to be left unexplored.

The way he kissed wrecked her.

Then the hand that was against the center of her breasts moved, dragging over the swell of her breast. Her body reacted, she pressed into his palm, suddenly, desperately wanting more.

He made that sound again and he broke the kiss. "Rosie," he sighed against her mouth. "What are you?"

She didn't understand that question, but it didn't matter, because he was kissing her and kissing her until the thrumming in her core spread and her entire body pounded.

His fingers brushed over the tip of her breast and her back arched. She did what she'd wanted to do since she saw him in her apartment. She lifted her hand and sifted her fingers through his hair. The strands were soft, not at all stiff, and longer than expected. How he got them to stay back without some sort of stiff product was beyond her, but she was grateful for it, dragging her fingers through the hair, tugging on the ends as she reached the back of his head.

She was drowning in his kisses, falling so far, and she could feel him tumbling in behind her. The kisses were becoming frantic, deeper, and rougher. She pulled on his hair again.

Devlin groaned, baring his teeth as he pulled back. The mask he was wearing was still in place, and those pale eyes burned. "I do not think my condition is going to cut it."

Swaying slightly, she held on to him as his finger moved back and forth over her breast. "It's not?"

"No." The one word was harsh, guttural. It sent a thrill down her spine. "I want to make an amendment to the condition."

Through half-hooded eyes, she stared back at him and spoke in a voice that sounded husky. "What kind of amendment?"

"I need more than a kiss."

Her heart rate tripled as she slid her hand out of his hair, vaguely pleased to see it mussed. "Do you have any idea of what you would need?"

He pulled his hand around from her breast. "I have so many ideas."

This was quickly spiraling out of control. Rosie knew that and she also knew there were several reasons why she should pull the brakes, or at least pump them, but if this was a car, she was about to hit the gas pedal and drive them both off a cliff.

Her gaze met his. "Then why don't you show me?"

A ravenous, predatory glint filled his eyes. Without saying a word, he took her hand and rose, pulling her up with him. She expected him to pull her into his arms, but that's not what he did. He turned her around, so her back was to his front. He let go of her hand and placed his on her shoulders.

"Do you see us?" he asked.

At first she didn't understand what he meant, but as her gaze darted over the room, she saw them, in the standing mirror.

She drew in a shallow breath. "I do."

"I want to know." One hand skimmed down her arm, over her waist, to her hip. The other roamed down and those long, elegant fingers of his curled around her breast. Liking that—liking it too much—she bit down on her lip. "What are you thinking when you see us in the mirror?"

What was she thinking? She gave a little shake of her head. Their reflection was nothing less than decadent sin. Him towering behind her, one hand on her hip, the other opening and closing around her breast. Their masks in place and their lips parted.

"I'm thinking that I . . . I want to find out what your amendment is," she said.

"You're impatient, aren't you?"

"Always."

Devlin made a sound that reminded her of a rough, unused chuckle and then he stepped into her and using the hand at her hip and her breast, he pulled her back against his front.

She felt him, all of his iron-clad strength. He was so much taller, but somehow he lined their bodies up, pressing his hips against her ass, and she felt him there, hard and thick.

"Tell me, Rosie, are you going to pretend again?" His breath drifted over her temple. "Pretend you don't feel how badly I want you?"

Instead of using words, she pushed her hips back and rolled them. His deep groan turned into a grunt and his hand tightened on her hip as he swiveled his hips against her ass.

"Okay," he breathed. "You're not pretending."

"Nope." She let her head fall back against his chest. "Are you pretending?"

He seemed to shudder against her. "No. Yes. Both?"

"That sounds confusing."

"And complicated, Rosie. So very complicated." His teeth caught her earlobe, nipping at the tender skin. She gasped and shivered. "I want you to watch us."

She could barely catch her breath. "I'm watching."

"Good," he murmured, kissing her neck as he fisted the skirt of her dress. "I don't want you to miss a moment of this."

Neither did she, so she watched him pull up the skirt of her dress, inch by inch. Revealing first her calf and then her knee, until her one thigh appeared in the reflection and her legs went weak. He stopped.

Devlin kissed the space behind her ear and then pressed his cheek against hers. She could see him watching in the reflection as he lifted the skirt to her waist, pulling the material to the side, baring her.

He growled out, "Fuck."

She liked the way he said that, so her hips wiggled a little in response.

"No panties?"

"I didn't want a panty line," she explained, feeling her face start to heat. "And I hate thongs."

"Mmm." His hips pushed against her rear and she felt him straining against her. "Naughty."

She let go of her bottom lip and grinned. "You don't approve, Devlin?"

He squeezed her breast, eliciting a moan from her as the wicked bite of pain was immediately followed by a flood of pleasure. "I've never fucking approved of anything more." He turned his head then, dragging his lips across her cheek as he still stared at her. "Beautiful. Just beautiful. Lift your leg."

A harsh exhale left her. Resting her hand on his arm, just above where he held her dress, she balanced herself as she lifted her leg, placing her foot on the edge of the bed.

She was bare and open to his eyes, and oh God, his stare was greedy and devouring and she wanted to be devoured. Consumed. *Taken.*

"You are . . ." He kissed her jaw and then straightened his chin so he was looking at the reflection again. "You are exquisite. Absolutely delectable. Look at you."

She was looking.

"You are . . . complicated."

That word again. "Complicated." She felt that to her core. Yes. Felt it as her thighs quivered—as her entire body quivered. She held herself very still, letting a man who filled her with equal parts irrational rage and lust look his fill, letting a man who was a stranger with the ability to cut deep with words *and* make her lose her mind with kisses. *Complicated.* And she wasn't a shy woman. She liked to think she was quite adventurous when it came to sexy, fun times, but this was different and new to her. It left her feeling vulnerable and raw and strung too tight. She'd never felt like that, not with *anyone.* So, yes, this was complicated.

"Hold your dress," he ordered softly.

Rosie did what he asked without question. She held her dress so she remained exposed to him—to them.

With his hand free now, he moved to her bare thigh. Her heart was trying to beat itself out of her chest. She noticed it right off the bat. Not how her skin was darker than his or how large his hand was against her thigh, but how his palm felt. How rough his hands were.

They reminded her of Ian's. Hands of someone who used them, and that shocked her, because she didn't think he'd have palms and pads callused over. She'd thought his hands would be smooth and pampered. Protected.

She jerked back against his erection and he grunted out, "Wider."

She opened up as far as she could go without losing her balance. That hand on her thigh didn't move for the longest time. Felt like an eternity as cool air washed over her heated flesh.

"There's something else I remembered." He slid his palm along her inner thigh. Drawing closer and closer to where she ached and pulsed. "From the night when I died? There wasn't a tunnel," he said, and she trembled as his finger trailed the crease of her thigh and then out, his palm smoothing over her outer thigh. "But it was so damn cold. Never felt that kind of cold before. It was deep, unending, and beyond physical. Do you understand? It wasn't my skin or bones that were cold. It was me. Felt that coldness ever since."

She swallowed hard, and maybe under different circumstances she could recall if other people who'd had near-death experiences felt the same, but she couldn't at the moment. There was just one thing she wanted to know. "Are you cold now?"

"No." His hand slipped under her thigh and he carefully moved her foot, closing her legs until just a hint of her most vulnerable place was visible to his eyes. "I'm on fire now."

"Good," she whispered. "I don't want you to be cold."

He stilled behind her, his hand under her leg. A long, tense moment passed and then he said, "You'd let me in you, right now, wouldn't you?"

She trembled, not ashamed to admit the truth, but a little afraid of doing so as he skated his fingers over her hipbone. "I'd let you do just about anything right now."

"I know." He kissed her temple, and for some reason, that caused her heart to squeeze, her chest to spasm. "That makes this dangerous."

"Why?"

His fingers danced over the delicate sensitive skin of her mound. "Because I want to bend you over and sink so deep inside you, that you'd feel me for days."

A bolt of pure lust jolted through her. "How's that dangerous?"

Devlin didn't respond to that, but he lifted his head so he could see their reflection again. Their eyes met in the mirror, and then he touched her lightly, right in the center, drawing his fingers along her folds. Her breath caught as her hips twitched. That lazy finger of his trailed up over her clit, spreading her wetness. Then it slipped in her, just the tip of his finger, and she felt it coil deep inside her, a tightening of muscles that was so sharp, so swift that she thought she might come right then.

Devlin made this ragged sound and she felt him tense behind her. She waited for him to thrust his fingers in, to fuck her that way hard and fast. She waited, her breath coming out in short, shallow pants. She waited—

Suddenly, Devlin pulled his hand away from her. "Someone's coming."

The man must've had amazing hearing, because all she could hear was blood pounding and the unspoken pleas that were about to spill out of her mouth. "What?" she gasped.

"Terrible timing." He pulled her leg off the bed, and because she was still frozen, he pried her hand free, letting her dress fall, wrinkled, into place. "I don't want anyone else seeing that."

A wild giggle crawled up her throat as he pulled her away from the bed, still keeping his front pressed against her back.

"Dev?" a male voice called out from the hallway. "Are you up here? You're needed downstairs, on the stage, and everyone who is anyone is getting antsy."

He cursed swiftly under his breath as he curled a strong arm around her waist. "Yes," he called out over her head. "I'll be out in a moment."

"All right" came the response dripping with curiosity. "I'll be waiting. Out here." There was a pause. "In the hallway. By myself."

Rosie's lips pursed.

"Of course," Devlin muttered as his erection pressed into her.

Rosie smacked her hand over her mouth, smothering the giggle that finally broke free.

"You think this is funny?" he asked, turning her around so she faced him. There was a lightness in his eyes that she'd never seen in them before. "I can barely walk and I'm needed onstage where I'll be standing in front of hundreds of people."

"I'm sorry," she said, fighting back another laugh as she placed her hands on his chest. "Do you want me to take care of it? I'm rather fast and good at it. Or so I've been told."

The lightness vanished, replaced by stark hunger. "God." He cupped her jaw. "That suggestion is not helping."

"But it could," she teased, starting to slide her hand down his stomach.

He caught her wrist. "You are . . . trouble."

"That's my middle name. Well, my middle name is June. Trouble is my nickname. That sounds better."

"Rosalynn June?" He tilted his head.

"Yeah," she drew the word out.

He stared at her a moment. "Well, Rosalynn June, while I'd love to have your mouth wrapped around my dick, I have a feeling that is going to make things worse."

"Oh no, it will make this much, much better. I pro—"

"I'm getting bored waiting" came the voice again, from outside. "I'm coming in."

Devlin spun from her. "If you come in here, I swear to God—"

The door swung open, and there was this tall blond standing in the doorway, wearing a feathered mask that looked like someone had taken a Bedazzler to the thing.

Devlin stepped so he stood in front of her, halfway blocking her.

"Well, what in the world are you doing in here, Dev?" the man asked, a slow grin appearing on his lips and spreading into a wide smile. "With . . ." He leaned to the side, trying to see around Devlin. "Who is this?"

"If you do not leave this room, I will physically and quite painfully remove you," Devlin responded, and Rosie's eyes widened.

The man didn't at all appear worried. "But I'm curious, Dev. And you know what happens when I'm curious."

Something clicked into place. What did Devlin say about people who called him Dev? It was only his brothers?

"Leave," Devlin responded.

The man sighed quite loudly. "Fine." He looked at Rosie, and she thought that maybe his eyes were like Devlin's. "Bye, mystery lady, I sure hope we meet again."

Devlin exhaled roughly through his nose as the man backed out of the room, closing the door behind him. After a moment, he turned back to her.

Rosie's gaze dropped. "You're still hard, just FYI."

His lips twitched. "Yeah, I'm aware of that, thank you."

Unable to help herself, she grinned up at him. "The offer still stands."

He groaned as he glanced at the closed door. "Trouble," he repeated under his breath. "Fucking trouble."

"Sorry?"

His gaze slid back to her. "No, you're not."

"I'm not." She glanced up at his messy hair. "Here. Let me fix this, at least."

Devlin locked up as she stretched on the tips of her toes and smoothed the strands of his hair back. As she fixed his hair as best she could, he watched her as if he didn't understand what she was doing.

"There." She settled back onto her feet. "It's not perfect, but you don't look like . . ."

"I was seconds away from having my fingers in a wet pussy?"

Holy crapola, he really just said that.

Not one to embarrass easily, she sure as hell felt her body start to burn with a mixture of that and yearning. "Well, you're still hard, so yes, you do look like that, but hopefully you can resolve that before you get onstage."

Devlin huffed out a low, short laugh. "I need to go."

"I know." She stepped back.

He didn't move for a long moment. "I don't want to."

Her breath did that silly thing, catching in her throat again. Some people didn't think that was real. The breath-catch. Rosie knew it was real, and something between them shifted in that moment. Strange that it wasn't when he was flirting with her or when he was kissing her or even when he was touching her. It was now, when he was standing before her, open and . . . and *human*. Not coldly remote and detached, and she realized she . . . liked this Devlin.

She liked this Devlin, the one who admitted that his house was haunted and told her that he'd died once. She liked this Devlin, the one who wore a mask and kissed . . . God, kissed like a man who could very well carry through on everything he'd said that day on his steps. She liked this Devlin, the one who barely touched her and nearly brought her to the brink of release, who looked at her like a man starved.

Guilt surfaced, stirring to life. Because she liked this Devlin, she wanted to tell him about his father—about what happened during the reading with Sarah. It seemed so wrong that she hadn't told him, because if she was in his shoes, she would want to know.

But now was not the time.

"I know," she repeated finally.

Devlin stared at her a moment longer and then nodded before walking away. He stopped at the door and faced her. "My condition about Lucian's house? You just met Lucian, by the way." There was a wicked little half grin on his face. "All you needed to do was ask him. He would've let you in. His girlfriend is terrified of ghosts and would definitely want to know if their new place is haunted. You didn't have to go through me."

Her mouth dropped open as the loudest laugh she ever let loose erupted out of her. "You jackass."

Catching her gaze, he winked and then bowed. "I'll be in touch."

Chapter 15

Lucian was waiting for him in the hallway, looking bored as he leaned against the wall, beside one of his paintings. It was a painting of the bayou, captured at dusk, and rendered so realistically, it looked like a photograph instead of a painting.

Dev's youngest brother was annoying but he was also an extremely talented painter.

"You really didn't need to wait out here for me," he said, walking past his brother.

"Who was she?" he asked.

Dev made it halfway down the hall before he realized Lucian hadn't moved. He stopped and turned around. "What are you doing?"

"Waiting." A mischievous glint filled his eyes. "Who is she, Dev?"

Anger pricked over his skin, making him itchy. He wasn't sure what pissed him off more. Being so close to feeling what he knew was surely fucking heaven or the fact that he knew his brother could be like a rabid dog with a chew toy when he wanted to be. He was also self-aware enough to admit that he'd allowed desire to override common sense, something he'd never allowed before. He didn't regret what happened. He just didn't know how to . . . process it, especially since he knew what he'd shared with Rosie was something he spoke about with no one and what if she was somehow working with Ross?

Really too late to question that now.

"Where is Julia?" he asked.

"Downstairs, making friends." Lucian grinned. "Not that kind of making friends I think you were just doing in that room. I'm actually sort of sorry that I interrupted."

Dev's jaw hardened. "That would be a first."

"I know, right?" His brother's gaze slid back to the room Dev had just come out of. He knew it was only a matter of time before Rosie walked out, and if Lucian was still out here, he would bombard the woman with questions. Lucian often had no filter and saw no need to develop one.

"Come on," he called to Lucian. "I need to be downstairs and I assume you want to return to Julia?"

His brother hesitated and then pushed away from the wall. He quickly fell in step beside him. "Are you going to tell me about her?"

Dev really didn't want to, but he figured Lucian would recognize her if she did investigate his house. To say that he was shocked that he'd agreed to that still unnerved him. He hadn't been lying when he'd told her that all she had to do was go to Lucian, but her relationship with Ross, whatever it was, made telling her anything a risk, but again, it was a little too late for that and there was always the chance that Rosie hadn't been lying when she said she hadn't known about Ross's intentions.

"She's a friend of Nikki's. We were actually talking about you," he said as they reached the top of the stairs.

Lucian looked over at him. "Okay. I was not suspecting that."

What he was telling his brother wasn't necessarily a lie. He was just omitting a whole slew of other events that had taken place in that room. "I'll fill you in after the auction."

His brother was quiet as they went down the steps and a sea of costumed people greeted them. The silence, however, didn't last. "So, she's a friend of Nikki's and you guys were talking about me— the latter is interesting, but there is something I want to know. Who is she to you?"

Dev stopped at the bottom and then, as if he was compelled, he looked over his shoulder and then up the stairs. Something stirred deep inside him as he caught a glimpse of her waiting just out of view. He didn't know what that something was, and fuck him, he wanted to

find out, and that . . . that wasn't like him. Wanting to find out anything about Rosie wasn't smart, not right now. Not ever.

"Dev?" Lucian said his name quietly, and without looking at him,
he knew his brother was watching him closely.

"I don't know," Dev said finally, and that was the damn truth. "I
really don't."

"ARE YOU SURE you're okay if I leave with Theo?" Sarah asked, having
taken off the mask.

"Of course." Rosie had a lot of questions, namely how she ended up
talking to Theo, the guy who'd been talking to Rosie before she bolted
out of the grand room, but that was going to have to wait since Theo
was waiting at the bottom of the stairs.

She and Sarah now stood out on the wide porch, under one of the
slowly whirling ceiling fans. The Masquerade was coming to an end,
and half of the attendees were already gone or tipsy from the endless
supply of champagne and whiskey.

Sarah's gaze searched hers. "And why are you leaving? You met
someone."

"Not really," she replied, and that wasn't exactly a lie considering
she'd met Devlin before.

Her friend tilted her head. "You know, I *know* you met someone.
Like my psychic spidey—"

"Stop," Rosie laughed. "Get going and don't behave yourself tonight."

"Wasn't planning to," Sarah replied slyly, grinning as she glanced
over her shoulder to where Theo waited. "You have a ride?"

Rosie nodded as an older couple all but stumbled down the steps.
She planned on Ubering home. "Have fun."

Sarah smiled as she moved toward the top of the steps. She stopped
and turned back to Rosie. "Remember what they say about dancing
with the devil, Rosie."

Her mouth dropped open as she stared at her friend. The *devil*.
Rosie could only think of Devlin.

"But what they don't say is sometimes you need to get burned."
Sarah winked. "Have a good night, Rosie."

She honest to God had no response as she watched Sarah literally skip down the steps. There really hadn't been time or the opportunity to tell Sarah about what had gone down in the room upstairs with Devlin. Or that she was out here waiting for him, because she was.

Keeping secrets from psychic friends was hard sometimes.

She drew in a deep breath and stepped back into the shadows. Leaning against the railing, she didn't let herself think too much about what she was doing, because even as bold and often ballsy as she was, she might chicken out. Unlike what Sarah was about to engage in, she wasn't waiting to continue what she and Devlin had started upstairs.

Although, she wouldn't be against that.

But the reason why she was out here waiting was to finally tell Devlin what had happened when she did her reading with Sarah. Her stomach tumbled a bit at the thought, twisted up in nervous energy. Since Devlin had admitted that his house was haunted, she figured he wouldn't think she was entirely insane for bringing up a psychic reading, but she wasn't sure how he'd respond. All she knew was she couldn't wait any longer.

And she didn't have to.

Three of them stepped out of the house at the same time. In the front was a tall, curvy brunette who was wearing a gown similar to hers. Her hair was curled and pinned up. She still wore her mask as she stared up at the man whose arm was curled around her waist. A man she now recognized. It was Lucian. He'd pushed his mask up, causing strands of blond hair to stick up in every which direction. He was saying something to the woman, causing her to laugh. Behind them was Devlin, mask still impeccably in place.

Drawing in a deep breath, she started to step out of the shadows, but before she could make a move, Devlin turned and looked directly at her.

Her heart skipped just like Sarah had when she went down the steps. How in the world did he know she was standing there? A hot, tight shiver curled low in her stomach, tangling with the nervous coils.

"Excuse me," he said to his brother, stepping away from them, toward her.

Lucian turned, and she had the distinct feeling he could see her clearly. "Questions, Dev. I have many, many questions."

"Come on." The woman beside Lucian threaded her arm through his. "You promised me late-night beignets and mocha."

"I did." Lucian still eyed where Rosie stood. "And what did you promise me in return?"

"Lucian!" The woman laughed as she smacked his arm hard. "Let's go."

Chuckling, Lucian finally looked away as he let the woman drag him down the steps. Thankful that it was dark where she stood, she felt her face warm as Devlin slowly stalked toward her.

"I'm sorry," she began as he got close enough to hear her. "I know it's late and I swear I have a pretty valid reason for waiting for you. Well, it's a weird reason, and I'm not sure if you'd find it valid or not, but I can assure you, I'm not out here waiting for you like a stage-five clinger. I'm—"

"Come with me." Devlin took her hand and then didn't give her much of a choice.

He led her away from the railing, around the side of the porch that wrapped the house. She had no idea where he was taking her when he walked her down a short set of stairs and into the dark, empty courtyard in the back, an area that had been emptied out over an hour ago.

She glanced around at their surroundings. There were warm, yellow solar lights spaced throughout, casting light onto trees, but that was all she could see. "I don't think we're supposed to be back here."

"I'm *the* de Vincent," he replied, stopping as he turned to her. "I can be back here."

Rosie opened her mouth to point out just how arrogant that sounded. Also to point out that it was so dark back here there was no way anyone could tell if he was *the* de Vincent or not.

But she never got the chance.

Curling an arm around her waist, Devlin lifted her up. A startled gasp escaped her as he pulled her into him and pushed her against what felt like a tree all at the same time.

The sudden, unexpected feeling of being trapped between the hard length of his chest and the rough, unyielding bark of a tree overwhelmed her senses. She clutched his shoulders, dragging in short, shallow breaths.

Before she even had a chance to process that, his mouth came down on hers in a brutal, raw kiss that took those scattered senses and blew them up. Her lips parted, and Devlin deepened that kiss, slipping his tongue over hers, stealing her breath and nearly all her common sense.

Goodness, the man could kiss.

Because he kissed like he was ravenous for her, only her, and like before, she reveled in the knowledge she'd never been kissed like that before. He kissed roughly, like he innately knew that she could take it and in taking it, she would want more.

And damn, if she didn't want more.

She wanted to wrap her legs around his hips so she could feel that thickness pushing against her belly in a much more interesting place, but the dress had trapped her legs against his.

Devlin broke the kiss and pressed his forehead against hers as his arm tightened around her waist. "I don't care why you were outside waiting for me."

A full-body shudder hit her, and she bit back a moan as he placed a kiss along her jaw and then lower. Her head was a mess and her pulse was pounding like a jackhammer in her veins. Red-hot desire was pumping through in a way that nearly clouded everything.

"I'm just fucking grateful that you are here," he said against her neck, where her pulse beat wildly. "You know how crazy that is?"

In a weird way, she did. Her grip tightened on his shirt as he lifted his head. Moonlight cut over the black mask and the high curve of his cheekbone. "I have something even crazier to tell you."

"Can you tell me later?" His lips brushed hers, eliciting a fine tremor from her. "Agree that you can tell me later, at my place."

Rosie wanted to laugh, because again, this was the Devlin she liked. When she'd waited for him outside, she had no idea how he'd respond.

If he'd regret whatever they did in that bedroom or if he'd pretend as if he didn't know her. She'd thought she'd prepared herself for anything, but she was wrong.

She hadn't prepared herself for this.

Sarah was right, though. She was dancing with the devil and she wanted to get burned. Badly.

"Rosalynn." He murmured her name in a way that actually made her like the sound of it.

Rosie closed her eyes. "Okay," she whispered. "But I need to tell you something first, all right?"

Devlin made this sound that was sexy as hell and then he nipped at her bottom lip. "Do you have to tell me I'm a dickhead? Because we've already established that."

She couldn't stop the grin. "No."

"Do you want to tell me that the beaded curtains in your house are made of wood?" he asked, flicking his tongue along the seam of her mouth. "Because, Rosie dear, particleboard is not real wood."

That brought a laugh from her, one that came from deep within and seemed to have a strange effect on Devlin, because he made that sound again and then dropped his forehead to the space between her neck and shoulder. He was still for a moment and then lifted his head. "What are you?"

That was the second time he'd asked that question and the second time she had no idea what he'd meant by that. "I don't understand."

"I don't either." There was a quick pause and then he lifted her even higher and this time, when he rolled his hips into her, his erection found the place she ached most. "What do you have to tell me?"

Her hands spasmed on his shoulders as the ache between her thighs pulsed. "It's really going to sound out-there, so you have to promise to hear me out."

"Everything about you is out-there." He shifted his hips again. "And I mean that as a compliment."

She really thought he did. "My friend is a psychic—"

Devlin chuckled deeply. "Why am I not surprised?"

She bit back a giggle that was lost in a gasp as he caught her ear between his teeth. "It's really hard to focus and keep talking when you're doing . . . all that stuff."

He rolled his hips again. "I'm positive you can multitask." His lips brushed her temple. "What about your psychic friend?"

She had to take a moment to collect her thoughts. "Remember the Friday we met in the cemetery? Before you insulted my beaded curtains?"

"I remember." He slid his hand up over the curve of her waist, to her breast.

Her head fell back against the tree. "I had a reading done with her that night. She told me something that is really going to sound—"

"Unbelievable?" His mouth was making its way down her jaw again as his thumb moved back and forth over her breast. "It's going to sound out-there?"

"It is." She opened her eyes and stared above, to the faint twinkling stars blanketing the sky. A huge part of her didn't want to keep talking. The fingers at her breast were driving her to distraction and if she lowered her chin, his mouth would be at hers again. "During the reading, something . . . bizarre happened. Someone I didn't know came through. I think . . ." Anxiety sliced through her stomach, dampening the lust fueling her every heartbeat. "I think it was your father."

Devlin didn't just still. She could feel the muscles under her palms tense. Felt his entire body go rock hard. He slowly lifted his head. "Come again?"

Rosie lowered her chin and wished the mask was gone and she could see his expression. "I think your father came through and spoke to me."

A long moment passed and then Devlin asked, "And what did he say?"

The flatness in his tone reminded her of the day in her apartment. She wet her lips. "He kept saying that it . . . it wasn't supposed to be him, and he was angry, very angry."

"Is that so?"

She swallowed. "He said he was murdered, Devlin."

His reaction was swift.

Devlin let go, and without the warning, her feet hit the ground and she went toppling to the side. He caught her before she fell over, holding on to her shoulders long enough to straighten her and then he let go.

He let go of her, but he didn't step back. "What did you say?"

"I think it was your father who came through," she repeated, and then briefly told him about the peonies. "He said he was murdered, Devlin. And if I were you, I'd want to know."

"So, you're telling me that a psychic told you this? Who is the psychic?"

"That doesn't matter." No way was she throwing Sarah's name out there. Not until she knew how Devlin was going to proceed with this information. "I just thought you should know."

"Or did you think I should know that you think my father was murdered?" he challenged.

"What?" Rosie frowned. "I don't even understand what that means."

"You don't?" he bit out, his grip firm on her shoulders. "You seriously expect me to believe that a psychic told you this and not, oh I don't know, your friend Ross Haid?"

"What?" Yanking free from his grasp, she took a step back. "This has nothing to do with Ross. I haven't spoken to him in weeks and why would he think that?"

"That's a good question, Rosie." Arctic air seemed to blast through the garden. "Maybe you can fill me in."

"Oh my God, Devlin, I have no idea why he would think that, but maybe he knows something. Maybe you should listen to him!"

Devlin stepped toward her, and she saw the hard glint of his pale eyes in the moonlight. "Unbelievable," he growled, and not in that holy guacamole kind of way, but in the he was pissed kind of way. "Un-fucking-believable."

Rosie couldn't be all that surprised by his response. Although, him bringing up Ross was unexpected. "I know that sounds—"

"Like something a lunatic would say?"

Air hissed between her teeth as she drew in a sharp breath. "Excuse me?"

Devlin let out a dry, hoarse laugh that lacked all humor. "You must think I'm an idiot if I'm going to fall for this psychic bullshit."

Her mouth dropped open. "Where else do you think I would've heard this?"

"Really?" His tone dripped derision. "Was that what tonight was about? You knew I'd follow you. You pretend to be whatever the fuck you're pretending to be, to get me to talk about my father?"

"Pretending? How in the world was I pretending?" Rosie held up her hands. "You need to check yourself, bud. You followed me upstairs earlier. I did not want you to do that."

"Sure."

Her eyes narrowed. "Did I seem remotely happy about you being up there?"

"You seemed really happy when I had my fingers between your thighs," he shot back. "And surprise, surprise, it sure as hell didn't take a lot of convincing to get to that point either."

That was it.

That *right* there.

"You're such an asshole." Her hands balled into fists. "God. You're such an asshole and you know it. There's no way you don't know it."

"Might be an asshole, but at least I'm not a scheming liar."

"Are you calling me a scheming liar because I thought you'd want to know that there was a chance your father didn't kill himself?" The back of her throat stung with the words blistering inside her mouth. "Seriously. You're a dickhead."

"Positive that's already established."

She threw a glare at him he couldn't even see but made her feel better. "Forget I said a thing to you about this."

"Already did."

Her skin about caught fire as anger poured into her like a raging storm. This was not the Devlin she liked. "This is the real you, isn't it? Not the Devlin who was upstairs or the one who was just teasing me. This is who you are."

Devlin said nothing to that, and the wealth of disappointment that settled on her was like a coarse, thick blanket. She stepped back and started to turn away.

"Guess coming back to my place is out of the question now," he said, and the way he said it, she could feel the smirk she couldn't see.

Whipping around, Rosie stormed up to him and made sure that when she lifted her hand and extended her middle finger, he saw it. "Screw. You."

He sighed heavily. "Sounds about right."

She added another middle finger just for the satisfaction of it.

"Classy, Rosie."

"You may have more money than sin, but you wouldn't know class if it smacked you in the face," she retorted.

"Yeah," he drew the word out. "Let me make one thing clear. You do not want to go around telling people Lawrence was murdered. You don't want to make that mistake."

She threw her hands up. "Who would I tell besides you? And obviously that was a mistake."

"I'm being serious, Rosie."

"Me, too." She started backing away, not only furious, but also so damn *disappointed*. "You have no idea. Tonight was . . ."

"Was what? An act? A ploy to get me to start spilling family secrets so you can run them right back to Ross?"

Huffing, she shook her head. Tonight hadn't been an act or a ploy. Tonight *had* been beautiful. "You're so wrong about everything you have no clue. Goodbye, *Dev*. Do not be in touch. Like *ever*."

Chapter 16

"Gabe told me that he loved me," Nikki announced on the phone Saturday morning, and Rosie let out a squeal, dropping the jeans that she was folding. Nikki laughed, sounding a million times better than the last time Rosie chatted with her. "I can tell you're happy."

"I am!" Rosie was on her knees in front of her narrow closet, having woken up early with the random need to organize raging through her. "Okay, so remember what I was trying to tell you when I visited, but Gabe walked in?"

"Yeah?"

Shifting the phone to her shoulder, she picked up the jeans she dropped and began folding them. "I was trying to tell you that Gabe was officially off the Boyfriends Who Needed to Get Their Shit Together list."

"I think he's definitely off that list," Nikki agreed. "But why did you think that? Pretty sure you wanted to smack him."

"Oh I still want to smack him for all his past misdeeds." There was also another de Vincent she wanted to smack into next week, but she refused to even think of his name at the moment. She reached inside, grabbing another pile of jeans she hadn't worn in, like, a year but wasn't ready to part with. She cleared off the floor. "But it will be a friendly smack."

She laughed in Rosie's ear. "I should be back in my apartment in the next week. Gabe wants me to wait, but I need to do it now."

"I totally understand. The longer you wait . . ." She trailed off as she saw something she'd never noticed before. There was a thin gap in the back of the closet, where it connected with the wall. Was the section coming apart? That meant a call to the landlord.

"I know. The longer I wait, the harder it's going to be," Nikki finished, reclaiming her attention. "But Gabe is going to be there and that's going to make it easier."

Smiling, Rosie plopped onto her butt and reached for the next pile of jeans she hadn't worn in a while. "Nikki, I am so happy for you I could cry."

"What? Don't cry!"

"I can't make any promises, because I'm feeling all kinds of hormonal right now, but honey, you got a second chance with a man you've been in love with for freaking years," Rosie said, sighing happily as she started folding the jeans. "Do you know how impossible that is? You're like a unicorn."

Nikki laughed again, and each laugh sounded lighter than the one before. "I feel like a unicorn. Seriously. Anyway, did you end up going to the Masquerade last night?"

Holding on to a pair of jeans, she lowered it to her lap as she straightened her head and took ahold of the phone. "Yeah. I went."

"Did you have fun?" Nikki asked. "Doesn't sound like you had fun."

Rosie wasn't sure how to answer the question, because she did have fun, lots of fun, and then she didn't. She was really trying not to even think of him, because when she did, she wanted to start throwing things.

Or organizing.

Which was why she was up tearing apart her closet at dawn.

Worst part, when she had first woken up, the anger from last night hadn't returned yet. Oh no, she woke up feeling something entirely different, as much as she hated the word for it. Her mind immediately replayed the night before, the part in the bedroom and at the tree, the part before everything took a sharp turn into Crapsville, which left her hot and needy and digging around in her nightstand for the delightful little toy known as the Womanizer.

But now that she was up and moving around, what she felt when she thought about him wasn't lust and desire. More like a hefty dose of rage at him and herself, because she should've known better. A douche-bag was a douchebag, even if there were moments of nondouchery.

"Rosie? Are you there?" Nikki asked.

She blinked. "Sorry. Zoned out. Yeah, I had a lot of fun. So did Sarah. I think she met a guy last night."

"Really? That's good."

Rosie thought it was good for her, too. Not that Sarah was looking for anything long-term right then, but she was happy to see her friend enjoying herself after experiencing such a nasty breakup.

"What about you?" she asked, and Rosie's eyes widened.

There was no way Nikki knew about Devlin, because she was more likely to give up beignets before Devlin told anyone about what happened between them. Not that she believed Devlin would hide what happened for nefarious reasons, and she wasn't giving him credit where it wasn't due, but she had a feeling Devlin rarely shared anything with anyone.

Which was why she was so surprised that he'd talked openly with her—*her* of all people. And that was why she'd felt like she could tell him about what happened with Sarah during her reading.

Boy, had she been wrong.

"I just had a really good time," Rosie said finally. She wanted to tell someone—hell, anyone—about what had gone down with Devlin, but it felt way too six degrees of de Vincent to talk about it with Nikki. "The house was absolutely beautiful. I'm sure you'll get to go next year."

"Maybe," she said, and then there was a sharp, audible inhale that brought a frown to Rosie's face. A second later, there was a laugh and she heard Nikki saying, "*Gabe*, I'm on the phone."

"Oh dear," murmured Rosie, grinning. "I'll let you go."

"It's okay. I can chat—" There was another gasp that sounded an awful lot like a moan, and Rosie's eyes widened.

"Just call me later," Rosie cut in, laughing since she really didn't want to hear whatever it was that was about to go down. "Focus on making some sweet, sweet loving with your man."

Nikki's answering laugh was cut off when Rosie hung up. She

tossed her phone onto the pile of folded jeans and then flopped back onto the furry, gray area rug. Closing her eyes, she let her arms flop to her sides.

Last night seemed like a weird dream/nightmare. She still couldn't quite figure out how they'd gone from verbal fisticuffs . . . to his hand between her thighs and her telling him she'd let him do anything . . . to her ending the night by giving him not one but two middle fingers.

Everything sure escalated quickly.

"God," she whispered.

Actually, she knew exactly how that happened. It all started with a kiss but boy, oh boy, that man could kiss. Rosie was a sucker for a good kisser. It was true.

If she hadn't told him about Sarah's reading and had just left the Masquerade, who knew what could've come from what happened in the bedroom. She wasn't foolish enough to believe that a relationship could've arose. Before she'd met him outside, she'd seen him in the main room of the house, where they held the auction. He'd all but been swallowed by women in fancy gowns and men in masks.

Standing in the background, watching him with people like him—in other words, watching him with people who were so rich, they owned, like, six homes and had nannies and housekeepers and personal assistants. That was a pretty eye-opening experience. He blended right into them, and she did not. Her family wasn't poor. They were hardworking middle-class people who spent every day earning what they had. She didn't assume that none of the wealthy people at the gala had earned their money. She knew that many had, but Devlin lived and breathed in a world that was so incredibly foreign to her it didn't seem real.

And if she had just left the gala at that moment, then last night could've just been a really good time. Last night would've been something that simply *happened*, because she wasn't foolish or naive. It wasn't the start of anything. It was just two people who really didn't get along, getting along *really well* for a few brief minutes, reacting to the fact that they were obviously attracted to one another. And that's how last night should've ended, but she had to do what she thought was the right thing. Ugh. She didn't regret telling him what had happened with Sarah. If anything, she regretted being foolish enough to think the Devlin wearing the mask was really any different from the arrogant, snide, and judgmental Devlin she was all too familiar with.

The disappointment, though? It was real. There was no shaking that, because . . . because Rosie hadn't felt like she had last night with Devlin since . . . since Ian, and that had been something so beautiful that had become something so ugly. She'd almost admitted that to Devlin last night and she was so damn grateful that she'd kept that little piece of herself hidden.

Rosie opened her eyes. They felt weirdly wet.

What did her mee maw always say? Crying did nothing but ruin your makeup. A small, tired grin pulled at her lips. Her mee maw sure loved her mascara.

It was time to pick her ass up and get over it, because there was nothing really to get over. She'd told her mom she'd help out this afternoon at the bakery and Jilly and Lance wanted to get together this evening to discuss the Mendez case.

And thanks to Devlin's parting words, she now knew she didn't even have to rely on him to gain access to Lucian's new home. She would just need to talk to Lucian and she probably should've asked Nikki to give him her phone number.

Sitting up, she reached for her phone and typed up a not-so-quick text to Nikki, asking her to give her number to Lucian and explaining that it was about his new house. Her text sounded a wee bit bizarre, but she'd sent weirder texts to Nikki. She didn't expect a quick response considering how Nikki had ended the call, so she got back to organizing her closet, proud that she was being smart, realistic Rosie and had completely bypassed Devlin.

And doing that meant she most likely wouldn't see him again, especially since Nikki would be moving back into her apartment soon and it wasn't like she and Devlin hung out at the same places.

Perfect.

After all, hadn't her mother said she had someone she wanted her to meet? A friend of her sister's husband? Seemed like now was the most opportune time to explore that connection.

SWEAT RAN DOWN Dev's bare chest while the hard riff from "Freak on a Leash" poured out of the earbuds as his feet pounded off the treadmill. He'd been at it for about an hour and the muscles in his calves and thighs screamed, but he pushed himself. He pushed to the point his body was about to break and then, only then, did he pull back.

He hadn't gotten to that point yet. He was close but not there.

If he stopped now, it was only a matter of time before he found himself with his hand wrapped around his dick, pissed off at the world while jacking himself off, and wasn't that a messed-up combination?

Truth was, though, he'd had a damn hard-on since last night, even had it when he stood there and heard Rosie say that shit about Lawrence, and even knowing that he got played like a damn fiddle, it took almost nothing for him to get as hard as a rock.

He'd already taken matters into his own hand, literally, three times since then. Once when he got back here, then in the middle of the night, and once again when he woke up this morning, and still, if he allowed himself to even think about how she felt under his hands or how her mouth tasted, he immediately—

"Fuck," he grunted, feeling it happen right then, even as he ran, even when he was so damn pissed off. Arousal powered down his spine and into his groin.

Slamming his thumb down on the controls, he upped the speed until the entire damn treadmill rattled.

Dev's jaw clenched as he tried to shove thoughts of Rosie and all that untapped sweetness out of his mind and failed—failed fucking spectacularly.

What the hell had he been thinking? Keeping an eye on her did not involve his tongue and his fingers.

Goddamn himself.

He'd slipped up last night, making mistakes he really couldn't afford, and he didn't make mistakes. Not ever. But damn if he hadn't . . . hadn't what?

Kissed her? Touched her? Opened up to her? All of them and more?

He'd told her shit he never should have, things he didn't even talk to his brothers about, and even more bizarre was the fact that he'd wanted to take her back to his place. Not this place, the de Vincent manor, but the place he had that his brothers didn't even know about, and she'd been fucking playing him.

Obviously, Ross put her up to it.

Or did he? a really annoying voice whispered in the back of his head. Rosie seemed genuinely angry and upset when he brought up Ross, but then again, for all he knew, she could just be a damn good actress. That could've all been an act.

All except her moans and the way her body responded to him. That hadn't been an act.

But that didn't mean anything at the end of the day, now did it?

A person could hate you and want you all in the same breath. Look at Sabrina. Dev was confident that woman despised him. Hell, she'd been obsessed with his brother Gabe since college, and yet, she'd wanted Dev. Well, she wanted to fuck him and fuck *with* him, and often, too. And it hadn't just been her doing what she could do to get the last name de Vincent.

Blinking the sweat out of his eyes, he cursed under his breath. Maybe that was why he was rocking what felt like a permanent erection. He hadn't been with Sabrina since everything went down. Actually, a good month or so before that.

Hell, he hadn't been with anyone.

He wanted that to be the reason, but he'd never lied to himself before, and he sure as hell wasn't going to start now.

It was because of her—of Rosie, and she was under Ross's thumb. That was the only logical explanation, because the idea of Lawrence coming through a psychic reading to tell her, a complete stranger, that he was murdered was the definition of preposterous.

He might acknowledge that there was some weird shit going down at his home, that he himself had experienced that weird shit, but the spirit of Lawrence out there telling random people who just happened to have a connection to Ross Haid that he was murdered?

Fucking absurd.

Pressure clamped down on Dev's chest, warring with the steadily increasing burn.

Ross was playing a dangerous game and he was involving Rosie in it.

That pressure on his chest doubled. God, he didn't want to think about it. Either way, this wasn't going to end well for Ross.

It wasn't going to end well for Rosie.

But what if she wasn't—

He cut that thought off. Didn't matter. He'd find out soon enough, when and not if Ross came skulking around again, suddenly knowing about Dev's near-death experience. There was no way the journalist wasn't going to bring that up.

And if, however unlikely, she was telling the truth, then . . .

Wouldn't that be even worse?

A better question, then—was Rosie a threat?

Dev didn't like the idea of that and he sure as hell didn't like that he had a problem with that idea. The woman should mean nothing to him—she *didn't* mean anything. His hands curled into fists as he ran. No one but his family mattered. That was the way it had been. That was the way—

His phone suddenly rang, cutting through the heavy thump of drums. A quick glance and he knew it was Archie. Stopping the treadmill, he answered the call.

"What do you have for me?" he asked, riding the treadmill belt to the edge and then off, onto the floor.

"She messed up" came the gravelly reply. "She used a credit card in Texas on Tuesday. Booked a hotel in Houston. Sabrina checked out yesterday. It's not much, but I know what car she's in. Apparently she didn't tip the valet, so he was more than willing to talk shit. She's in a black Mercedes. Got the tag number from the hotel."

"Black Mercedes?" Dev frowned as he picked up a towel and dragged it over his chest. "Sabrina didn't drive a Mercedes."

"And neither did Parker or anyone in her immediate family, according to what vehicles they have registered." The kind of data Archie could get access to made him worth any amount of money he charged. "The tags are bogus, though."

Tossing the towel into the laundry shoot, he turned to the door. "How are you sure?"

"They were thirty-day temps that didn't come back to any dealer," Archie answered.

"Shit." He ran his hand through his damp hair. "Then it's a dead end?"

"Not necessarily." There was a smile in Archie's rough voice. "Luck was on our side for once. The valet is a bit of klepto and had been rooting around in her glove box. Saw her insurance card. I have the company name and I'm confident I can get the necessary info like registration and real tag number. Should take a few days, if that. Meanwhile, I got some buddies who work for the Texas State Police, and they're on the lookout for her."

"Perfect." Leaning against the wall, he stretched out his aching calves. "Anything on the intern?"

"Nothing that half the world hasn't already heard and what you don't already know, but I'm still poking around."

"Good." He pushed off the wall. "Call me as soon as you have an update."

"Of course."

The call disconnected and Dev slipped his phone into his pocket. Some of the tension eased out of his shoulders. He may have screwed up last night, but at least they were getting somewhere when it came to Sabrina. And there was good news buried in all that. Sabrina appeared to be far enough away from here, which was good news for his brother and his nephew. He knew Gabe stressed about Sabrina's whereabouts. Couldn't blame him for that.

But Sabrina wouldn't be a problem for much longer. And last night with Rosie?

He wasn't going to make that kind of mistake again.

Needing a shower, he strode across the room and opened the door. He drew up short.

Gabe stood in front of him, his hair pulled back from his face in a bun, but he wasn't dressed as if he were about to work out. Unless he was prepared to run in his jeans.

And barefoot.

"I was just looking for you," Gabe said, blocking the doorway.

"Can it wait?"

"Sure, but I'm thinking you're going to want to hear what I have to say now." There was a grin on his brother's face that caused Dev to narrow his eyes. "I was just sitting out in the garden, enjoying this rather cool morning with Lucian and Julia and Nic. You know, doing the family thing you never take part in."

"Okay. Thanks for sharing."

"You're welcome," Gabe replied. "The strangest damn conversation came up. You see, Nic was talking to Rosie this morning."

Having no idea where his brother was going with this and knowing it could lead anywhere, Dev kept his expression blank. There was a chance Rosie could've told Nikki about what had gone down between them. They were girlfriends. They talked about shit like that. "Good to know."

"And, well, after they got off the phone, Rosie texted her. Took Nic a bit to see the text, but Rosie had the strangest request . . . and the strangest story." Gabe planted his hands on the doorframe and leaned in. "Rosie wanted Lucian's number."

Son of a bitch.

A weird sense of emotion slammed into him. Instead of being what he figured was a normal gossiping with her friend about what they'd done, ending with him being harassed by his brothers over it, that wasn't the case. Rosie wasn't normal. Instead of feeling relief, he was irritated . . . and amused.

"Because, apparently, she believes that Lucian and Julia's new place is haunted and wants to investigate? Of course, I'm sure you know how Julia reacted to that. That was her one condition when they were looking for a new house. No ghosts." An unholy light filled Gabe's eyes. "Lucian was more than happy to give Nic his number, especially after Nic mentioned Rosie was at that gala thing last night. Interestingly, Lucian's never met Rosie."

Dev drew in a deep, calming breath that did fuck shit to calm him. Rosie had gotten Lucian's number. Unbelievable.

"But then Lucian got to talking and you know how that goes. He brought up this . . . woman he saw you with last night."

Of course he did.

Why would Dev ever have to worry about Rosie saying anything when Lucian probably already wrote a short story about what he saw and published it.

"Come to find out, Lucian did meet Rosie." Gabe did a dramatic pause that their younger brother would be proud of. "Last night. You were all—hey. Excuse me."

Pushing past his brother, he stalked toward the back staircase. He heard Gabe call out his name, but he didn't stop.

Did Rosie really think she could just go around him straight to Lucian? That Dev would allow that to happen? He had said that she could've just asked Lucian herself, but he hadn't been serious.

Well, this was just . . . wholly unacceptable.

Chapter 17

*D*ev watched as Lucian stepped out into the hallway, closing the door to his private apartment behind him. The plain white shirt he wore was covered with grayish charcoal smudges.

His brother must've been working.

"What's up?" Lucian asked.

Dev's gaze flickered to the closed door. He figured Julia was in there, and he found that interesting—that his brother could work on his paintings and sketches with Julia there. He thought painting was a solitary endeavor.

"I know Rosie wants your number," Dev said, cutting to the point. "I do not want you to get in contact with her."

Lucian leaned against the door and arched a brow. "Didn't know you were in the position to dictate what I can and cannot do, Dev."

"I've spent your entire life trying to tell you what to do, mostly for your benefit, but this time, I am asking you not to call her."

"Asking?" Lucian laughed. "That sure as hell didn't sound like a request at first."

Dev stared at him.

"She's the woman you were with last night," Lucian said after a moment. "Wasn't she? Nikki's friend. Rosie."

"You already know the answer to that."

"Yeah, but for some reason, I want to hear you admit it."

Dev frowned. "Why?"

"Because it would amuse me."

"Well, since I live to amuse you, yes, she was the woman you saw me with last night, and yes, I was planning on filling you in on what we were talking about."

His brother wiped his hands along his jeans. "So, the shit about the new house being haunted is true?"

"As true as any paranormal team would claim," Dev muttered.

"Shit, Dev. Julia knows now. She's all for having a team go in and clear whatever is in that house out. There's no way I'm going to get out of that," Lucian said. "That's like the only thing Julia had on her wish list. Not an updated kitchen or a large tub in a master bathroom. She's specifically asked for no ghosts."

"Your house is most likely not haunted," Dev told him, thinking that only in New Orleans would that be on someone's list. "Rosie is . . . I don't know if we can trust her motives."

"What?" His brows lowered.

"Look, she's friends with that reporter—"

"Fucking Ross Haid?"

"Yes."

"Shit." Lifting a hand, he dragged it through his hair, leaving behind streaks of charcoal. "For real? But she's friends with Nikki and—"

"She hooked Nikki up on a date with Ross before she and Gabe got together. Ross wanted to use Nikki to get information on us."

"Did Rosie know that was why Ross was interested in Nikki?"

Valid question. "I don't believe in coincidences."

"They're a real thing, dude."

"Look, all I'm asking is that you don't have contact with her. We don't know what her agenda is."

"After seeing you two together last night, pretty confident I can tell you what her agenda was." Lucian added a grin. "And yours."

"You don't know what you saw last night," he replied. "You can have someone take a look at your house. Ghost hunters. Psychics. I don't care. Just not Rosie. That's what I'm asking."

Lucian tipped his chin back. A long moment passed. "Okay. Because you're actually asking, I won't contact her."

For a moment, Dev thought he might be having a fever-induced hallucination, because was his youngest brother finally agreeing with something he asked? He stared at him and saw that he wasn't messing with him.

Pigs just sprouted wings and flew.

"Thank you," Dev said, and he said this knowing he rarely said that to anyone, especially his youngest brother.

Lucian nodded.

"I'll let you get back to work." He started to turn.

"Dev?"

He faced Lucian. "Yes?"

"Did you ask Rosie if she was working with Ross?"

"Yes, I did."

"And what did she say?"

"She said she wasn't, but I don't expect her to admit to it," he replied.

"Hmm." Lucian pushed away from the door.

The frown returned to Dev's face. "What?"

"Nothing." Lucian lifted a shoulder. "Just wondering if it ever occurred to you that she just might be telling the truth?"

Yeah, it had occurred to him.

Just about every damn time he thought about her and Ross and that shit she told him last night. It occurred to him that she could be telling the truth.

But that didn't make her any less dangerous.

It didn't make him any less smart.

What he did know was that there was no way he could allow Lucian to spend time with Rosie. His brother was too damn chatty and Dev couldn't risk Lucian blurting only God knew what to Rosie.

He was doing this for his brothers—like always.

At least that was what he kept telling himself.

THE SATURDAY EVENING rush hadn't even hit yet, and Rosie was ready to press the rewind button on the entire weekend.

Nothing was going right. It started about five minutes after she finished organizing her closet and her mother called, asking if she could come in early. One of their regulars was sick.

No big deal, except Jilly called a moment afterward, wanting an update on Lucian's house. Rosie had tried to explain she was working on it, but Jilly seemed to think Rosie could snap her fingers and a house key would appear in her hand. Rosie was pretty confident that Nikki would get Lucian's number for her or just give hers to Lucian. Everyone just needed to be patient, because she wasn't going to make Devlin hold up the end of his *bargain*. She would rather pluck every single strand of hair from her body with a rusty pair of tweezers than even speak Devlin's name again.

Devlin de Vincent was now on the Do Not Speak in Her Presence list.

It was a new list.

Coffee was also on the list since she wanted some afternoon caffeine boost and her freaking coffeemaker decided to shit the bed on her. The day kept getting steadily worse.

Rosie had decided to walk to Pradine's, and she nearly died on the way when a cab hopped the curb and almost took her out, causing her to drop the coffee she'd picked up on the way—the coffee that had cost a ridiculous amount of money considering it was just freaking coffee.

A block from Pradine's, the entire sole of her ankle boots peeled back. Literally peeled back like an invisible can opener got ahold of her foot. And they were her favorite walking boots, worn suede with a small heel. Super cute.

Ugh.

So, she was wearing flip-flops even though a chilly autumn was in full effect and her toes were freezing while the boots were sitting in her parents' office at the bakery, because her mother swore she could fix them, but Rosie knew she was just going to slather Gorilla Glue on the damn shoe and call it a day.

Worse yet, her mother had jacked up the cling-wrap roll under the counter, the one her father had installed eons ago, to the point they needed a degree in rocket science to untangle the damn thing.

Rosie's knees were starting to ache—she'd been on them so long trying to fix the stupid thing while her mother stood beside her, hands planted on her hips. Rosie dragged her nail along what she hoped was the end of the roll while her younger sister, Bella, worked the register.

"That roll of plastic wrap is testing me." Her mother leaned over her, closing the glass door to the freshly baked chocolate muffins.

Stopping, Rosie turned her glare on her mother. "How is it testing you? You messed it up."

"And I'm supervising while you're fixing it, like a good owner and mother would do," she replied, winking when Rosie pursed her lips.

From somewhere beyond her mother, she heard Bella snort.

"What did you do to this thing?" Rosie muttered, turning the roll again, because what she thought was the end of the cling wrap wasn't. "I do not get paid enough to mess with this."

"You're lucky you get paid at all," her mother retorted.

"It's just plastic wrap," Bella chimed in. "It can't be this difficult to manage."

"Just plastic wrap? Have you ever tried to find the tangled, jacked-up edge on a three-foot ball of plastic wrap?" Rosie took a deep breath. "Giving birth has to be easier than this."

"Are you out of your mind? Giving birth is not easier," Bella shot back. "I would know, because—"

"You have two beautiful babies and I'm childless and joyless and going to die cold, alone with fifteen cats who are going to feast on my dead carcass," Rosie finished for her, exasperated. "So, why don't you come over here and fix this with baby-birthing magic?"

"But you're doing such a good job of it," her sister responded. "By the way, Mom mentioned you'd be interested in meeting Adrian's friend."

Rosie closed her eyes. "I did not tell Mom that. I so did—"

"That's not how I recall the conversation," her mom cut in.

"Satan is a liar," Rosie muttered under her breath as she opened her eyes. This morning, when she thought about taking her mother and sister up on the offer to meet Adrian's friend, felt like a lifetime ago after the afternoon she'd had.

"What did you say?" her mom asked.

"Nothing," Rosie sighed. "I don't want to be introduced to anyone right now."

And that was the truth even though she'd briefly considered it this morning. She'd smartened up, though, realizing that wanting to meet someone new because she was ticked off about someone else wasn't exactly the brightest idea.

Somewhere between her coffeemaker breaking and almost dying by cabdriver, she'd decided to swear off all men.

At least for the next month or so.

"Oh my . . ." Her mother kneed her in the back, causing her to grunt. "That is one tall drink of water walking down the street."

"Mom," she muttered, shooting her a look from where she was hidden. It was pointless, though, since her mom was staring straight ahead, a notably creepy smile on her face.

"And may I add to the fact that is one *fine* tall drink of water?" she continued, and Rosie rolled her eyes. "He's walking like a man who knows how to keep you up all night."

"He looks like he knows how to and he's proud of it," Bella said, and Rosie wrinkled her nose. "If I wasn't married . . ."

"Ditto, my sweet child, ditto."

Rosie had this theory that once you had children, you were suddenly able to openly discuss what it would be like to sleep with the same guy as your mother. It was like some kind of weird baby bond a mother and daughter shared. Her theory could be grossly incorrect, but empirical evidence was suggesting she just might be onto something.

"If Dad hears you talking like that," Rosie muttered, finally getting the roll of plastic wrap unstuck. That was a useless threat. Her father would either just laugh at her or attempt to one-up whatever man she was talking about.

"Wait," Bella whisper-yelled in a way Rosie was sure some of the customers heard her. "He's coming in here and he looks . . . Oh my God, I know who that is."

It was probably the guy down the street who dressed like Ronald McDonald.

The doorbell dinged and then Rosie heard her mother speak, suddenly sounding like she was an extra in *Gone with the Wind*. "Well, hi there, sweetheart. How can I help you?"

Rosie's head fell to the side as she squeezed her eyes closed tight. Her mother was a mess.

"Hi" came a deep, familiar voice. "I'm hoping you can help me."

Rosie's eyes snapped open. That voice . . .

"I'm looking for someone I believe works here?" There was a pause. "Her name is Rosie."

No.

No way.

Slowly, Rosie lifted her head and looked up at her mother as her mother looked down at her.

"There is a Rosie who works here." Her mother narrowed her eyes at her. "And I happen to know exactly where my very lovely and very single daughter is."

Oh my God!

Rosie went to stand up, but lost her balance, and landed on her ass just as a shadow crossed the counter. An all-too-familiar face appeared, and Rosie was positive she was hallucinating.

"Found her," he said, and unless she was also having auditory hallucinations, it really was him, standing in her family's shop, staring down at her, smirking.

Devlin.

Chapter 13

"What are you doing here?" Rosie blurted out.

Devlin looked down at her with a hint of curiosity settling into the coldly handsome lines of his face. His hands were on the counter, his long fingers splayed, and it wasn't until that moment she realized how large those hands were. It was an odd thing to notice, especially considering she'd been up close and personal with those hands and fingers, but it was an odd day—odd couple of days.

"What are you doing sitting on the floor?" he asked, sounding like he couldn't fathom why there'd ever be a reason for her to be sitting on the floor.

Irritation spiked. "I'm meditating."

He tilted his head to the side. "Seems like an odd place to do that."

"Now, she's telling you a fib. She actually fell over," her mom clarified, all helpful like. "She's a little clumsy, but my girl is well educated. Did you know she has three degrees?"

"No." A flicker of surprise made its way across Devlin's face. "I did not."

"But I am sure you know she's stunningly beautiful."

Rosie slowly turned her head toward her mother—her soon to be *dead* mother.

Her mother smiled, flashing those pearly whites. "Well educated and pretty as a peach pie, but she's about as clumsy as a three-legged alligator."

Rosie's mouth dropped open. A three-legged alligator? First off, she wasn't clumsy and second, a *three-legged alligator*?

"She is beautiful," Devlin replied, and he did this in the same monotone voice he used the first couple of times they met. She felt this weird, totally uncalled-for lurch in her chest. There was no need for that lurch, because she did not like this man. Not at all, and it was really time for Devlin to leave.

Because she saw her mother's face soften, saw her mother shift her gaze to where Rosie was still sitting on the floor and then back to where Devlin stood.

Her mother was hearing a brass band's second line and no doubt already picturing fluttering handkerchiefs and twirling parasols.

It was official.

Devlin had obviously crawled out from the bowels of hell to torture her, because apparently she'd racked up some bad karma or something.

"Do you have a moment to talk?" Devlin asked, and her gaze flew back to his. "That is, if you're done meditating?"

"She has time," her mother answered for her.

"So much time," Bella piped up.

Oh my God, she was going to hurt both of them! "Actually, I don't have any time. I'm very busy—"

"Sitting on the floor?" A single dark eyebrow rose.

"Yes," she snapped. "I have stuff to do down here."

"Like what?" he asked.

"Stuff." She crossed her arms. "Important stuff."

Bella was suddenly beside her. "She's just being funny. She has nothing to do."

"Bella," Rosie snapped, unfolding her arms and putting her hands on the floor. "As you can see, I'm very—"

"Talented at fixing plastic cling wrap," Bella cut in as her sneakers got awfully close to smashing Rosie's fingers. "Which is what she has been working on all afternoon, but guess what?"

"Hmm?" Devlin murmured.

"It's her dinner break!" Bella announced this like Rosie was just nominated for a Nobel Prize, and it was ridiculous. All of this was ridiculous.

Rosie and Bella didn't even have assigned lunch or dinner breaks.

"Perfect," Devlin said.

Her mother moved in on her and she had that look she often got when the teen version of Rosie didn't want to get out of bed. The look that said she would haul her ass out of said bed and kick it all the way to school.

She didn't for one second doubt that her mother wouldn't yank her off the floor and all but throw her into Devlin's arms.

Rosie popped to her feet, and immediately realized there was an audience of sorts on the other side of the counter. Beyond Devlin stood three regulars, customers who came into Pradine's so regularly they could practically work there. Cindy and her husband, Benny, with their matching gray hair and lined faces, were watching Devlin and them like they were at a tennis match. Standing next to them was Laurie, a quiet younger girl who spent a good part of her afternoons studying at one of the small tables near the windows. She went to college at Loyola.

Rosie smiled at them.

Laurie grinned as she ducked her chin, letting her thick black hair fall forward and hide her face.

"Good afternoon, honey." Cindy wiggled her brows in Devlin's direction as she curled her arm around her husband's. "What a lovely change of scenery today."

Her husband snorted. "Scenery is always lovely to me." Benny winked in their direction.

"That's my boy," Mom replied with a big old smile. "Whatever you like, it's on the house."

"I don't know." Cindy looked Devlin up and down like he was for sale. "You guys got yourself a de Vincent in here. I feel like I need to pay you just for that."

Bella giggled.

Devlin glanced over his shoulder at the older couple and then back to Rosie. He looked so thoroughly confused and out of his element that it took everything for Rosie not to laugh.

Did he never socialize with the common folk?

That thought made it even harder for her not to lose it, because in a way, the de Vincents were American royalty.

Except Devlin was definitely a frog and not a prince.

But then the worst possible thing happened. Rosie heard her father's deep voice booming from the recesses of the kitchen.

"What in the world is going on out there?" he demanded, and as he spoke, his voice grew closer. "Is there a party I'm not invited to?"

Rosie's eyes widened. There was no way she could let her father come out here and see Devlin. He'd have questions. Lots of them. Awkward ones. She sprang into action, bolting out from behind the counter. "You want to chat, we're going to do it outside."

"Why?" Bella called out. "There's plenty of space here."

Rosie shot her sister a scowl and then turned to Devlin. He stared at her like she'd spoken in code, but he nodded at those gathered around the counter and followed her outside, to a cloudy, overcast sky. It was going to be another rainy day.

Stopping under the black-and-gold-striped awning, she crossed her arms, tipped her head back, and glared death rays up at him. She opened her mouth.

Devlin beat her to it. "Do you always speak to people like you're barking at them?"

"Barking? Are you calling me a dog?"

His head tilted to the side. "That's not what I'm saying, but you do remind me of one of those little dogs. The fluffy ones that nip at people's ankles when they want attention."

Rosie could not believe him. She *seriously* could not believe him. "Did you seriously just say that I remind you of a Pomeranian?"

"I wasn't thinking of a Pomeranian, but now that you mention it . . ."

"Did you come here just to insult me more?" she demanded, keeping her voice low as people passed them on the street. "Like you searched me down using some sort of nefarious means just to tell me I'm like a small, yappy dog?"

His chin dipped and his lips twitched as if he wanted to smile. "I didn't have to use nefarious methods to find you."

"Oh really? Then how did you know I was here?"

"You actually told me you worked here."

She opened her mouth then snapped it shut. He was right. She had mentioned it.

Devlin smirked.

"Whatever. Did you not get all your insults out last night? Pretty sure I made it painfully clear that I never want to speak to you or see you again."

"You did make that clear, but it looks like our paths are just destined to keep crossing," he replied blandly.

"No. Absolutely not. Our paths are going in two very different directions. You're east. I'm west. So, peace out—"

"I wish that was the case."

Her lips thinned. "Do you realize you're standing in front of me, at my parents' bakery, after accusing me of being a scheming liar and basically a lunatic, and you just insulted me again?"

"How did I just insult you again?"

"You just said you wished our paths wouldn't cross."

One side of his lips kicked up. "I did say that, but do you realize you've been insulting me since you opened your mouth?"

"I do, but I'm allowed, because you're a giant—"

"Dickhead," he finished for her.

"Yes. And if you remember correctly, you're officially beyond un-dicking yourself. Goodbye—"

"I'm here because of our deal."

Rosie's eyes narrowed. "You have got to be kidding me."

Those thick, dark lashes swept up and that intense, pale gaze met hers. "Do I look like I'm kidding?"

"You look like you need a foot up your ass."

He laughed, sounding surprised. His expression smoothed out so quickly, though, that she wondered if she'd heard the laugh or not. "You asked for Lucian's number."

"I did."

"So you could get into his house."

"Sounds about right." She glanced at a woman leading a small girl into the bakery. "So, I'm still confused by why you're here."

"I'm here, because you're not going to involve my brother—"

"I'm not involving your brother in anything," she cut him off. "And I swear if you suggest that I'm somehow up to anything other than what I told you about Lucian's house, I am going to lose my mind right here and I will not be responsible for my actions."

His tone was dry. "I wouldn't want that to happen."

"No." She held his gaze. "You would not."

Something shifted over his features. "On second thought, I think I know what happens when you . . . lose your mind a little. Perhaps I would be interested in that happening, Rosie."

There it was again, an unwanted shiver accompanying the way he said that and her name. How in the world could a man, a man she did not like, cause such a reaction?

"Me losing my mind out here would be nothing like the way I lost my mind last night," she retorted. "I asked for your brother's phone number to see if he'd let my team into his house. You know that."

"What I was going to say before I was so rudely interrupted—" he stepped into her, so close that the sides of what had to be ridiculously expensive loafers brushed her cheap Old Navy flip-flops "—I don't want you involving Lucian in some kind of paranormal investigation."

"And why not?"

"If you knew my brother, you wouldn't have to ask that question," he said, his voice dry. "I made a deal with you. I plan to see it through. I will get you into Lucian's house."

She inhaled sharply through her nose. "I'd rather swim in Lake Pontchartrain and then bathe in the Mississippi River than even stand here and talk to you. You do realize that, right?"

He stared at her and then bit out, "Fuck."

Rosie felt her face flush with warmth. He said *fuck* the same way he said her name. Deep. Husky. *Hot.* And she hated that—the purely physical reaction to a word, to *that* word. To him.

"You're making this so difficult," he said.

She forced her words to come out steady and unaffected. "I would say I'm sorry, but I'm not. Nothing about this needs to be difficult, because there's no reason for you to be here and there's no real reason why Lucian can't just let the team into his house."

"I think you misunderstood what I said about you making this diffi-cult. It's not the fact that I'm here, talking to you about Lucian's house." Heat flared in those blue-green eyes, and as he held her gaze, she began to feel like she was standing too close to the sun, moments away from being burned. "You're making this difficult because I actually . . . like you."

"Okay. You must have issues coming out of the wazoo . . ." Move-ment out of the corner of her eye caught her attention and she turned to the bakery. Her mother and sister stood at the window, their faces planted to the glass.

Holy balls, they were ridiculous.

Rosie grabbed Devlin's arm and led him away from the window, out of the path of prying eyes, as she tried to ignore how solid and warm his arm was under the thin white shirt. Her hand slid down his arm when he resisted, but she kept pulling until he followed. Stopping at the corner of the street, she turned to say something to Devlin, but whatever she was about to say died on her tongue.

He stared down at where she'd grabbed him. Rosie's heart lurched. Somehow, she'd taken his hand. She was holding his hand! What kind of voodoo magic had possessed her to do that? Because seriously, she had no idea she'd taken his hand. None. So, she wasn't responsible for that. At all.

Rosie started to pull her hand away, but he stopped her, folding his fingers through hers.

Slowly, he lifted his gaze from her hand to her eyes. "I am sorry for . . . how things ended last night between us and I'd like to make it up to you."

"Come again?"

There was a slight curve of his lips. Not really a smile. Not even a half grin, and nothing like the smiles he allowed while he was wear-ing his mask. "I would like to make it up to you."

Rosie looked around them, half expecting someone to jump out of one of the cars parked along the street with a camera. He couldn't be real, but when she looked back at him, she saw the truth in his gaze. He was being for real.

He wanted to make it up to her?

"We've moved past that point." She tried to pull her hand free. He held on. "Like way past that point of you making it up to me."

"You haven't even heard how I plan to make it up to you."

"I really don't care."

"Oh I think you will." There was a slight warming to those pale eyes. "I'm making another amendment to our condition."

Her mouth dropped open again, and she was sure she looked like a fish out of water. "There will be no more amendments. Why? Because last night didn't happen. It was a figment of our imaginations."

His brows knitted together. "Do you think I'm going to forget what happened last night?"

"I already have." So not true.

And Devlin called her bluff. "Now, I know that's a lie." His voice lowered. "There is no way you forgot what it felt like to have my hand between your legs."

Rosie gasped. She was the furthest thing from a prude, but they were standing on the side of the street! Then again, people in New Orleans had probably heard weirder conversations than this one.

"And I sure as hell haven't forgotten that you said you'd let me do anything," he continued, and much to her horror, that hot, tight shiver returned *and* he saw it. "There it is. You haven't forgotten a thing, Rosie."

God, she loathed this man.

"Do I need to remind you of how much of a dick you were? I don't think I do, but if you'd like me to list the ways, I can."

"No." He sighed. "That will not be necessary."

"Good. So, can we just move past all of this? Lucian can let the team into his house, and you and I never have to cross paths again. That sounds—"

"The amendment," he cut in, the corner of his lips twitching when she narrowed her eyes. "I think you'll enjoy this amendment."

"Devlin—"

"I'll get you into the house—only you. No team of people. No strangers. That is my brother's home. I do not want random people prowling around."

She opened her mouth.

"I doubt that you'll find anything—"

"Just like I wouldn't find anything in your home?" she snapped. "Or did you forget that you'd admitted that your house was haunted?"

"I didn't forget, but that doesn't mean I believe for one second there is a ghost using my brother's home as a time-share."

Well, when he put it that way it did sound dumb. "Can you let go of my hand?"

"No."

"No?"

"I'm afraid you'll run away from me if I do."

"I want to," she retorted.

"And that's why I'm not letting go." His thumb moved on the center of her palm in a slow, idle sweep. "When you're done investigating the house, then that is it. You won't have to worry about our paths crossing again and I won't have to worry about you contacting my brother," he said. "And you won't have to worry about seeing me again."

"That's your new amendment?"

He nodded. "I'll take you into the house tonight."

"Tonight?" she squeaked.

"Tonight or never. Those are your options."

She gaped at him. "I have plans for tonight."

"Like what?"

"What do you mean like what? You say that like it's not possible for me to have plans." Other than meeting up with Jilly and Lance, she really didn't have plans, but he didn't need to know that.

"If you want in to Lucian's house bad enough, you'd change your plans."

She tugged on her hand again, and he didn't let go. "What if my plans are unchangeable?"

He stared at her a moment. "Then I guess you don't want to investigate Lucian's house bad enough."

Rosie clamped her jaw down so hard it was a miracle that she didn't crack a molar. There was a part of her that wanted to tell him to forget it, but Jilly would legit strangle her if she passed up this opportunity.

"Fine," she said. "I'll take one for the team."

"Take one for the team?" Devlin smirked. "You wanted in this house, Rosie. We made a deal, and I'm going to stick to it."

"I wanted in this house without you," she corrected. "And I would've had no problem with you honoring the deal if you didn't have—"

"To be a dick. Got it. Meet me at the house tonight at nine." He let go of her hand. "And don't be late."

Rosie resisted the urge to tell him she had a problem with the time. "You don't be late."

He started backing up. "I'm never late, Rosie. See you tonight."

As he pivoted around and prowled off, she muttered under her breath, "*I'm never late.* Blah. Blah, asshole."

Stringing together an impressive combination of curse words, she stalked back into the bakery.

Her mother and her sister were waiting for her in front of the counter. That was a problem, because Cindy and Benny were still waiting to be served, and so was Laurie.

And they were also standing there, staring at her just like her mom and sister were.

"Hello?" Rosie gestured toward the customers.

Her sister ignored that and marched straight to where Rosie stood and clasped her cheeks with her warm, sugary-scented hands. "Okay, you need to spill everything right now."

"I don't know what you're talking about."

Bella's eyes widened. "Oh no. No. No. You are going to tell me exactly why Devlin de Vincent just came in here looking for you and why it looked like you two were either seconds away from making out or punching one another."

Pulling away from her sister, Rosie headed for the counter. "It did not look like that."

"It so looked like that," her mother chimed in.

Bella followed. "I want all the details. *All* the details, Rosie."

"There's nothing to tell you. We were just talking. That's all."

"Honey, you do not just talk with a man who looks like that." Cindy raised her graying brows. "Trust me, I know. Bennie and I rarely talked when we first met."

"True," Bennie murmured as he leaned into the counter.

Rosie stared at them and then shook her head. "We were just talking, so can we please get back to work and let this go?"

"Mmm-hmm." Her mother came behind the counter. She focused on the couple, but Rosie knew what mmm-hmm meant in Juniper Pradine speak. So did Laurie, based on the sympathetic look she was shooting in her direction. Everyone who came into Pradine's on a regular basis knew what it meant.

Mom might be dropping the conversation, but she sure as hell wasn't letting it go.

Chapter 19

"This is freaking amazing." Jilly's eyes were wide.

Liz bobbed her blond head. "Totes McGoats."

"Are you sure none of us can go with you?" Lance stood in the corner of Jilly and Liz's place, his arms folded across his chest. He'd come straight from work, still dressed in the navy blue EMT uniform. "I don't like the idea of you doing this alone, at night with some dude."

"It's not some dude," Jilly answered before Rosie could. "It's Devlin de Vincent."

"That doesn't mean she'd be safe with him." Lance frowned. "Probably less safe considering who he is." His gaze narrowed on her. "I didn't think you guys liked each other."

"We don't, but I'm safe with him." As crazy as it sounded, Rosie believed that. He might be a dickhead, but he didn't give her bad vibes in that kind of way. "He's . . . prickly, but he's not dangerous."

Lance didn't look convinced.

When she woke up this morning, she really had not foreseen how today was going to play out. What she really wanted to do was crawl into bed with a bottle of moscato and a bag of chips—sour cream and onion to be exact. Not that she wasn't excited about investigating this house, but after dealing with her mother's and Bella's incessant questioning all evening, she wasn't sure she had the mental fortitude to deal with Devlin.

Zipping up the backpack chock-full of equipment, Jilly knocked her short black bangs out of her face. "If we can capture evidence that supports that the haunting is coming from the house next door, it would be a huge relief to Preston and his wife."

"I think it would only be a relief if the haunting stops or the ghosts stay in the house next door," Liz mused.

Jilly looked over at her girlfriend. "Yeah, but at least if it's not originating from their house, there are easier things we can suggest for them to do to put an end to the haunting."

Liz plopped down on the couch. "I feel like whatever we suggest, they're not going to do it anyway."

"Can we not have this convo again?" Jilly placed the backpack on the coffee table.

"We're so going to have this convo again." Liz grinned as she twisted her long hair into a rope. "Look, I still stand by what I said when we saw the apparition on film. We needed to hold off on telling the family until we know more. Now they've almost shut us completely out. It's too much for them."

Jilly straightened. "How is it too much when they called us in the first place?"

Rosie slid an inconspicuous glance in Lance's direction. A reluctant grin tugged at his lips.

"This isn't your first rodeo." Liz let go of her hair and it slowly began to unravel. "You know people react differently to hauntings once there's actual hard-core proof."

That was true.

Some people were relieved, even excited to learn that they weren't seeing or hearing things. Others were hoping the team would find a logical, not supernatural reason for their haunting. Sometimes the latter, when confronted with supernatural proof, decided that ignoring it and pretending it wasn't happening was the best route to go.

That didn't mean the haunting went away.

Rosie picked up the heavy bag, slinging it over her shoulder. "Here's the deal, though. If I do capture evidence tonight, I have the feeling that the owner—Lucian—will want to do something about it, but I'm not sure it'll be our team that will handle it."

Frowning, Jilly looked over at her. "And why not? We're the best damn team in this city."

"Devlin and I really don't get along." When Liz opened her mouth to ask a million questions, Rosie rushed on. "It's a long, convoluted story that really doesn't even entirely make sense, but if something is in that house, be prepared for us to be shut out."

Jilly popped her hands on her hips. "That's BS. If you find a spirit, it's our spirit."

"I'm not sure that's how that works," Rosie said, glancing down at her phone. Her Uber driver was a few minutes out.

"It is in Jilly Land, population Jilly." Liz bit down on her lip, failing to hide her smile when her girlfriend looked down at her. "What? It's true."

"Why don't we cross that bridge when we get there," Lance suggested, ever the mediator. His gaze found Rosie's again. "I really just don't like the idea of you going there by yourself with him. It's not smart."

Nothing that involved Devlin felt smart, and she had a feeling that tonight was going to be one giant hot mess. But sometimes spirits reacted to what was around them, and the good Lord knew, she and Devlin could sure create a charged environment.

"Everything will be fine." She smiled at Lance, hoping to reassure him. "The only thing that is at risk is my patience."

Liz snickered. "Do you have everything?"

"I believe so." She paused. "Did you pack a bottle of wine in this bag?"

That got a laugh out of the girls, but Lance grunted something about no one listening to him. Curling her hand around the strap of her bag, she headed outside with the team in tow.

"How long do you think you're going to be at it?" Jilly asked.

Rosie's mind jumped straight into the gutter, because when she thought about being *at it* with Devlin, an image of them in that mirror formed. Her body flushed with heat.

This was such a bad idea.

"Rosie?" Lance asked.

She blinked. "Sorry. I don't know. A couple of hours, if I'm lucky? I have no idea how this is going to go. He's not exactly a believer." Which she still found bizarre but whatever. Headlights appeared in the street, slowing down. "I think my car is here."

Liz sprang forward, hugging Rosie. "Make us proud."

She drew back, wrinkling her nose. "I'll try."

They followed her down the steps and narrow sidewalk to where the car pulled up to the curb. "Call us when you're done," Jilly said. "No matter how late it is."

"Do not forget," Lance warned. "Because I will come to your house and make sure you're still alive."

"Wow." Rosie laughed, opening the back door. "Wish me luck. I'm going to need it."

"You'll be fine," Jilly said.

Liz nodded. "You'll make us so proud we'll throw you a party."

"You look like you need an adult," Lance mumbled.

ROSIE WAS LATE.

Dev glanced down at his watch. Ten minutes and counting to be exact. Not that he was entirely surprised. Not for one second did he think she'd be on time. Knowing her, she was late on purpose.

He stood on the porch of Lucian's home, crossing his arms over his chest as he glanced to the house next door. Trees blocked most of the home, so he could see only the top of a Victorian-style turret. He was a little curious about the people who lived in that house. Were they sane was probably the most pressing question.

His gaze flicked back to the street as a car drove past. There were a lot of things he could be doing with his time, but here he was, standing on a porch at night, waiting for a paranormal investigator who just might be working with a reporter who was determined to bring his family down.

Oddly, he was kind of looking forward to it.

Not because he was looking forward to seeing her, but because this was a good opportunity to determine just how much of a threat she was. Did she really believe Lawrence's spirit had visited her or was she lying?

That's what he told himself as a car slowed down and then stopped. He jogged down the steps and went to the gate. Under the soft glow of the streetlights, he saw her as she pulled a large backpack out of the back seat. Her hair was pinned up into a mess of curls, but there was something elegant about the look and the length of her neck. Dev unlocked the gate as she turned to him.

Even in the dark he could read the writing on her black shirt.

GIRLS DO SHIT BETTER. The SH was grayed out, making it appear as if it said GIRLS DO *IT* BETTER.

Waving goodbye to the driver, she slowly made her way to the gate. So slowly, Dev was positive that a turtle would walk faster. "You're late," he said, opening the gate for her.

"Am I?"

He eyed her as she walked past. Not for one second did he believe she didn't realize that. The bag she carried looked like it was weighing half her body down. "Hold on."

Stopping, she turned to him. It was dark by the driveway, so he couldn't make out her features as he walked to her and reached for the backpack. The moment his fingers curved around the strap, she gave a little jolt. He lifted the bag. "God. What do you have in this bag?"

"A small child," she replied. "Thanks."

Felt like she had a toddler in there. Extending an arm, he said, "Let's get this over with."

"You sound so thrilled about this. You know, you didn't—" She tripped over something on the ground. He reached for one flailing arm, catching her as she let out a loud laugh. "Whoops."

"So, you are as clumsy as a three-legged alligator?"

Rosie snorted. "Only when it's pitch-black out and I have no idea where I'm walking." She paused. "You can let go of my arm now."

Was he still holding her arm? Yep. There was definitely her smooth skin under his palm. "Are you sure? The last thing we need is you breaking a leg—"

"And then suing a de Vincent for damages?"

His lips twitched. "You wouldn't do something like that, now, would you?"

"Depends on how badly you annoy me tonight." She started walking toward the steps.

There was a lightness in her voice that he . . . he enjoyed, and he realized that even when she was irritated with him or when she was turned on by him, there wasn't a coyness in her tone or a hidden, biting undertone. Sure, she had one hell of a mouth on her, but there was something real about it. Unlike with Sabrina, where everything that had come out of that woman's mouth had been well practiced and also carried a hidden agenda.

Rosie waited for him at the top of the stairs.

"The door is unlocked. You can go in."

She opened the front door and stepped into the lit foyer. He'd already been inside, turning some of the lights on downstairs. Immediately, his gaze dropped to where the worn, faded jeans hugged her rather lovely ass. Heart shaped. Perfect. He could already imagine what it'd feel like cupped—

He stopped that train wreck of a thought. If he let his mind wander down that road there'd be no way for him to stay remotely objective or alert. The situation last night had quickly spun into something he hadn't been expecting.

Dev was not repeating that tonight.

"Wow," she exclaimed softly.

Joining her, he closed the door behind them. "What? Do you already feel the presence of a spirit?"

Rosie looked over her shoulder at him. "I'm not a medium."

He knew that. "Well, that's disappointing."

"Uh-huh," she murmured, turning back around as she walked to the right, into the large living area and kitchen. "I was saying wow, because this house is really beautiful, even in this state of renovations."

Dev looked around. All he saw was scattered tools, workbenches, and tarp covering the cabinets and kitchen counters that had been installed. "Lucian said they would be done soon. I am not sure if that's the case."

A little grin appeared as she walked around an island. "Is the upstairs done?"

"As far as I could see everything was except the master bathroom."

She lifted a shoulder. "Then I guess they can't be that far from being done." She came toward him, and he couldn't help but notice her face was nearly bare of makeup. There was a pink gloss on her lips that made her mouth look sweet. That seemed to be all. Everything that was shining through her was her. No artifice. Physically, at least, as far as he could tell. Everything else? That he couldn't answer. Or he didn't want to.

Rosie reached a hand out. "Can I have the bag?"

"Where would you like me to put it?" he asked instead, thinking the thing was too damn heavy for her to be lugging around.

"Um." She turned. "I guess that counter is fine."

He carried the bag over to the island and placed it down. "What do you have in here?"

"Equipment." She came to stand beside him and unzipped the bag. He caught the faint scent of her. Coconut. "Everything that I need to investigate."

"This should be interesting." Angling his body toward her, he leaned against the island.

"You will be shocked and awed." Reaching inside, she pulled out a small device. "You've seen this before. It's an EVP recorder."

"Ah, yes. The most high-tech of ghost-catching tools."

Rosie huffed out a laugh. "You'd be amazed by what you can catch on this." Turning to him, she lifted her gaze. Those eyes were more brown today than green. "This is all I need right now."

"And what do you need from me?" The moment that question came out of his mouth he realized how that sounded.

Dev wasn't the only one.

There was a soft inhale from Rosie as her gaze flew to his. Her lips parted and when she wet her lips, he felt a bolt of pure red-hot lust shoot down his spine.

Damn.

This was not good.

Clearing her throat, Rosie turned her attention from him to the almost finished kitchen. "I just need you to stay out of my way."

His gaze flickered over her profile. How did he not realize how thick her lashes were last night? "I'm not sure if that's possible," he admitted.

"You need to make it possible," she retorted, walking away from him.

Dev hesitated a moment and then pushed off the island. The house smelled of raw wood and paint as they ventured into the den area.

"My team did some research on this home. Nothing that isn't already public record," she added. "It was built in 1859 and the previous owners stayed in the home for a pretty long time. This is the first major renovation I'm betting. So, that's good news."

"It is?"

She looked up at the tray ceiling. "Yep. See, if a house has a serious haunting problem, then you'd often see a property change owners multiple times in rather short periods. Unless the owners are de Vincents."

He arched a brow at that.

Wandering out of the den, she walked into a sitting area that led to a sunroom. "Renovations can stir up spirits, because the surroundings are changing. Sometimes the activity settles down once the renovations are complete and sometimes the activity gets worse."

"Or sometimes the house just stops settling."

She laughed at that. "Houses stop settling soon after being built. If a house is making 'settling' noises decades later," she said, and yes, she used quotation marks, "then you have a foundation problem. Anyway, we're thinking this renovation stirred up some ghosties or . . ."

"Or?" He stopped at the entryway to the sunroom. This area of the house was dark as none of the light switches had been put in yet.

"Or a ghost followed Lucian from your house."

He was beginning to really regret admitting that the manor was haunted. "Is that possible?"

"Oh yes. Spirits can form an attachment and go wherever the person they're attached to goes. From house to house. . . ." She faced him. "From cemeteries to homes."

Dev's eyes narrowed. "From cemeteries to psychic readings?"

"Yes." She held his stare. "And if you happen to be with a medium, you won't need one of these to hear what they're saying." She waved the recorder around. "Getting rid of those hauntings can be tricky, so let's hope that's not the case."

A muscle flexed in his jaw as she brushed past him. The slight touch was a jolt to his system. He pivoted and suddenly he needed to know. "Why?"

"Why what?" she tossed over her shoulder.

"Why are you so into this stuff?" he asked.

Slowly, she turned back to him as she stood in the archway between the dimly lit den and sitting room. "I woke up one day and thought *I want to hunt ghosts.*"

"It was a serious question, Rosie."

Giving a little shake of her head that caused a thick curl to fall across her forehead, she sighed heavily as she lifted a shoulder. "So, you really want to know?"

"I'm asking, aren't I?"

"Yeah, well, I can't imagine why you'd want to know anything about me." She looked down at the recorder, so she missed the way his jaw clenched. "It wasn't anything cool like with Jilly or Liz, my friends who actually started NOPE. They saw ghosts as kids and it inspired a lifelong obsession. Me? I just . . . I've always been interested, since a teen, and I guess it's because spirits are . . . proof that there is something after death. That we just don't die and cease to exist. I hated the idea of that, so that's what got me to start looking into things like hauntings and reincarnations. Even the occult."

"The occult?"

"Yeah. Like Wicca. I went through a stage as a teenager where I wanted to study Wicca, but quickly gave up on that, because I'm lazy and that requires a lot of work."

Nothing about Rosie seemed lazy. "Your mother said you had three degrees. Is that true?"

"Yeah."

"There's nothing lazy about three degrees," he pointed out, a little awed that the woman standing before him with an EVP recorder had three college degrees.

"True, but you obviously have no idea all the work that goes into practicing the Wiccan way." There was a smile in her voice that he couldn't see. "Anyway, that's what started this for me. This need to prove to myself that all of this—life and love and hurt and death and hate—all of it had a purpose. I guess I could've found Jesus or something. That seems more . . . acceptable, but I'm more likely to catch a Civil War soldier's voice on this recorder than the voice of God, so . . ."

A reluctant grin tugged at his lips. "Do you believe in God?"

"Yes. I do. I may not go to church every Sunday, but I'm a believer." She paused. "Do you?"

"Yes," he said after a long moment. "If there's a heaven . . ."

"There's a hell," she finished.

He already knew where he was probably ending up upon death.

"Anyway, like I said, nothing interesting." Rosie rocked back a step and then turned. "We need to turn the lights off."

"I've seen . . . things in my house in broad daylight."

She stopped again. "Well, aren't you special?"

"Very."

"Uh-huh." She inclined her head. "You know, spirits show up at any time during the day. Evidence suggests that spirits really can't tell time."

"That must be annoying."

"Always late for appointments, huh?" she replied, and from where he stood in the dark, a wry grin pulled at his lips. "The reason why we do a lot of our investigations at night is because *we* are more open and susceptible to the activity."

"In other words, we see and hear things when it's dark and quiet."

Rosie's sigh echoed through the empty room. "I'm going to get started."

He found that he wasn't ready for her to do that. Part of the reason why he decided to let her in here was for him to get a read on her.

"What are your degrees?" he asked, and he knew damn well that question had nothing to do with her association with Ross.

Walking through the den, she said, "I have a bachelor's in English with a certificate in teaching. Never used it. Went back and got a degree in business, and that bored me out of my mind, but figured it was useful. Then I went to the University of Alabama and majored in psychology."

"That is . . ."

"Scatterbrained?" She laughed as she went into the kitchen and he followed her. Finding the light, she turned it off.

"No. I was going to say impressive."

"Wow." Rosie whirled on him suddenly. "Did you just compliment me?" Snapping forward, she patted his chest quickly and then hopped back. "I am *shook*."

"I wouldn't get that excited." His tone was dry, but he was fighting a grin.

"I am so excited." She twirled, straight up twirled in front of him. She was so good at that he wondered if she'd taken dance. "My life is complete. Devlin de Vincent thinks I'm impressive!"

"All that really isn't necessary."

"But it is!" She skip-walked out of the kitchen, through the living room. "Who needs to find a ghost tonight? My life is complete!"

Standing in the kitchen, he lifted his gaze to the ceiling and Devlin . . . smiled. It felt like it stretched the skin of his mouth, and wasn't that screwed up? He was confident she was making fun of him, but he was . . . amused.

Because Rosie was . . . God, she could be just as bad for him, for his family, as Sabrina, but she was so . . . *her*. Not even remotely impressed by him in the slightest.

He shook his head and then found her in the foyer just as she was turning the light off.

"I'm hitting record," she warned.

He inclined his head.

Rosie studied him a moment and then turned as her thumb moved over the side of the small device. Walking to the center of what would become the living room, she looked up at the ceiling. "Hi," she said, clearing her throat. "Is anyone here with us?"

Dev arched a brow.

"Anyone who wishes to speak to us?" She was quiet for a few moments as she slowly walked around the room. "My name is Rosie. Can you tell me your name?" There was another break of silence as she roamed into the foyer. "Why are you here?"

That was the question of the night, wasn't it?

Rosie stopped by the stairs. "Are you alone?"

"Obviously not," Dev muttered. "We're here."

She turned to him. "Really?"

"What? Seems like a foolish question. Obviously it's not alone. We're here."

"That's not what I meant when I asked the question," she explained. "I'm asking if there is more than one spirit here."

"How do you even know there is a spirit here?"

Rosie stared at him.

"And your question wasn't very clear," he continued, following her into the open foyer. "What if it answers yes, but it's talking about us being here and not another ghost?"

"Fine," she said, sounding exasperated as she whipped around. "Is there another *spirit* with you?"

Dev grinned at her back as he slipped his hands into his pockets.

"Why are you here?" she asked.

Knowing she wasn't talking to him, but unable to help himself, he said, "I have no idea."

Shoulders slumping as she drew in a deep, very audible breath, she turned to him. "I'm not talking to you, Devlin."

"Oh," he murmured. "My bad."

Her eyes narrowed, and after a moment, she refocused. "How old are you?"

"I have a question."

Rosie's head fell back. "Of course you do."

"When you ask how old the spirit is, do you mean their age when they died or how long they've been stuck in this cold, barren existence?"

She lifted her head. "You do realize we're being recorded right now, right?"

He smirked.

"And that means that someone else may be listening to this recording other than me?"

The smirk faded. His eyes narrowed. He hadn't agreed to that.

Grinning, she moved away from him. "Can you tell me if you're upset about what they're doing to this house?"

Dev snorted.

Shooting him a narrowed glare over her shoulder, she then looked away. "How many of us are here?"

Hadn't she already asked that question?

Rosie roamed into what was to become a dining room. The chair rails were in place and the crown molding was propped in the corner. He leaned against the doorframe.

"Do you have anything you want to say to—"

A loud bang interrupted her. The sound was a shock to the silence and for a moment it sounded like it came from every which direction and then he heard it.

The sound of footsteps, right above them.

Chapter 20

$\mathcal{D}$ev's gaze flew to where Rosie stood. In the darkness with only the silvery moonlight streaming in through the windows, he couldn't make out her expression.

But he heard her.

"I think that came from upstairs," she whispered. "Is it possible someone is upstairs?"

"No." Pushing away from the door, he walked back into the foyer and looked up the stairs. He'd been upstairs before Rosie arrived. "Unless someone climbed the balcony."

Rosie moved silently, joining him in the foyer. "We need to investigate it."

He was already climbing the stairs. "Stay down here."

"What?" she demanded in a low voice.

Stopping halfway, he looked over his shoulder. "Just in case it is a person hell-bent on murdering one of us, can you stay down here?"

"It's not a serial killer," she whispered as she crept up the steps behind him. "You just said no one could be up here."

"I also said that someone could've gotten in through the balcony."

"By jumping from the patio down below like a kangaroo or a superhero?" The excitement was clear in her voice. "You know there's not a person up here."

Dev couldn't be sure. It was far more likely that it was an ax murderer than a spirit, so he really didn't want Rosie charging up the stairs, into God knew what.

"I'm not staying downstairs," she said. "That's not why I came here, to cower whenever there is a random noise."

Irritated, Dev realized he had only two options. Tie her up to something to keep her downstairs, and that sounded a hell of a lot more fun than it should've, or let her come up.

Sighing, he turned around and started up the stairs again. "At least stay behind me."

"Yes, sir."

His jaw clenched as he reached the top of the steps and flipped the hallway lights on. The hall split in two directions. Both were empty, but the noise seemed to come from above the dining room, which would be either the master bedroom or the guest room next to it. Both could be accessed from the balcony. He started in that direction with Rosie practically on top of his back. He opened the guest bedroom, but there were no lights to be turned on in that room. Crossing the room to the balcony doors, he found them locked. When he turned, he saw Rosie heading for the master.

"Damn it," he growled, stalking out of the room. He caught up to her in the hallway. "Didn't I say stay behind me?"

"I am," she insisted.

"No. No, you're not." Stepping around her, he approached the double doors that led to the master. He pushed the door open and scanned the large room as his eyes adjusted to the moonlit room. "Hmm." Spying something on the floor, he went into the room and bent over, picking it up. "I think I found the source of the noise."

Rosie walked over to him, the green light on the recording still shining. "A worker's helmet?"

"Yes." He turned to the workbench that sat in the corner. "It must've fallen off and rolled across the floor."

She stood in the center of the room, staring at him as pale moonlight glanced off the curve of her cheek. "Does a rolling helmet sound like footsteps to you?"

Well, not exactly. "What we heard in a dark, quiet house that you think might be haunted sounded like footsteps. That doesn't mean they were footsteps."

"And there is no way what we heard was a helmet rolling across the floor," she argued. "And by the way, how did it fall off the bench and roll across the floor? Invisible wind?"

He started to smile, but stopped himself. "It probably was just placed on the edge of the bench and us walking around disturbed it. And, by the way, all wind is invisible."

"That's not what I meant. Whatever. I'm going to get the EMF meter."

"EMF what—"

Rosie was already gone from the room.

Shaking his head, he placed the helmet back on the workbench and decided to check the other rooms, which he did. Nothing was out of place and there was no ghost hiding in a closet. He had no idea what they'd heard, whether it was the helmet or a spirit, and he doubted anything Rosie was doing was going to prove it either way.

Rosie was currently walking from room to room with some kind of electronic magnetic reader while asking the same damn questions she'd asked downstairs.

As he quietly trailed behind her, he could practically picture Gabe's and Lucian's faces if they saw him right now. Lucian had been amused when he'd gotten the keys from him earlier, but he imagined they would either be shocked or they would've passed out from laughter.

The EMF detector didn't pick up on any weird readings according to Rosie, but that hadn't deterred her. It felt like an eternity she spent upstairs, moving from asking vague and open-ended questions to more detailed ones. Was the spirit around during the Civil War? Was their death recent? As they walked back into what was to become Lucian and Julia's master bedroom and the rough-in bathroom, she waited several seconds, sometimes even minutes before asking another question.

Dev was learning that this ghost-hunting stuff took a hell of a lot of patience.

There was a good chance that if he was with anyone else, he'd be bored out of his fucking mind. Then again, he wouldn't be doing this with anyone else, but he found the whole thing with Rosie quite . . .

entertaining. Rosie was very serious about this. She remained alert as minutes turned into hours. If there was so much as a floorboard creaking somewhere in the house, she would become very still and quiet and listen for about five minutes, and if he made a noise during that time, like breathed too loudly, she'd hush him.

He didn't find the hushing as annoying as he did the first time she'd done it.

But even as entertaining as it was to just stand back and watch Rosie, by the time they made it back downstairs, he almost shouted with relief when she turned off the recorder. "Are we done?"

She laughed as she picked up the backpack and placed it on the covered counter in the kitchen. "Not quite."

For some reason, he wasn't sure if he was relieved to hear that or disappointed. "You've literally asked every question known to man. What more can you do?"

"Lots. I need to take pictures."

"Pictures?"

She nodded as she pulled out a small camera. "Sometimes you can catch a spirit or an orb—"

"Or a particle of dust?" he suggested.

Rosie sent him a droll look. "Sometimes you can catch spirits on film. We use a camera that produces high-resolution images," she explained. "Often, once you load them up, you'll find things in the pictures you couldn't see with your own eyes."

"Is it necessary?"

"Yes." She looked over at him. "You can always leave and come back when I'm done. No one is forcing you to be here."

That was true.

But he didn't leave.

Instead, he trailed behind her once more, going from room to room while she took pictures.

"I hear Nikki is moving back into her apartment soon," she said as they walked through the living room.

"That's what I hear."

"Guess that makes you happy."

He lifted a shoulder. "She grew up in that house. I'm used to seeing her around."

She snapped a picture and the flash was nearly blinding. "I imagine it won't be long before Gabe and Nikki are living together. With Lucian moving out, you're going to be . . ." She paused and then sang, *"All by yooourseeelf. You're gonna be, all by yooourseeelf."*

He slowly turned to her. "Please don't do that again."

She giggle-snorted as she turned, snapping another picture at, literally, a corner. "That's a hell of a house to be living in with no one else there."

"It is." Dev wasn't sure how much he planned on being there once everyone was gone.

Rosie moved toward the stairs and then stopped, turning to him. "I want to ask you a question that's just a nosy question that would be normal asking anyone else."

"Then why wouldn't it be normal asking me?"

She lowered the camera. "Because you'll probably think I'm asking for some nefarious reasons."

"Possibly," he admitted. "Guess you won't know if you don't ask."

Rosie laughed at that and started up the steps once more. "I guess not."

He waited for her to continue as he followed her. "So, you're not going to ask?"

"Haven't decided yet."

Dev frowned. "Ask, Rosie."

She reached the top of the steps, stopping to take a picture. "What happened with you and your fiancée?"

That was not a question he was expecting, and suspicion blossomed. "What do you mean?"

Taking a picture of the other side of the hallway, she then started walking again. "I get why you two aren't together. I mean, what her brother tried to do . . ." She trailed off. "I guess if you really cared about someone, you'd work through that, even as crazy as that is."

"I guess you would," he murmured.

Facing him, she inclined her head to the side. A moment passed. "I forgot."

"Forgot what?"

"That you said you didn't love her—well, you didn't say that exactly, but that's what it sounded like." Rosie turned and walked into the closet bedroom. "Why would you be engaged to marry someone you didn't love?"

Dev wasn't sure how he could answer her question. He had to be careful. If she was working with Ross, he could use this information to either embarrass his family or hold it over his head to get the information Ross thought Dev could provide.

Rosie took another picture. "You don't have to answer my question."

"I know." He waited out in the hallway as she moved around the room, taking a picture of the wall. He opened his mouth, closed it, and then tried again. "The Harringtons were friends of Lawrence's and we went to the same schools and university. Lawrence always had an eye on their business and I think . . . he liked the idea of our two families being joined."

She angled her body toward him. "You basically had a financially arranged marriage?"

He coughed out a dry laugh. "I guess you could look at it that way. He wanted one of us to marry one of the Harringtons, but . . ."

"But what?"

He stepped out of the way as she came out of the room. "But it didn't work out."

"Well, I guess it's a blessing in the long run." She moved toward the other door. "You won't be stuck with someone you don't love. Rather be alone than that."

Dev didn't have a response for that. He never loved someone other than family. "You've heard she's missing, right?" he asked to see what her response would be. "Sabrina?"

"That's what I've heard." Rosie walked into the master. "That's kind of insane. Makes you wonder if she had anything to do with what Parker tried."

His brows knitted as he stared at her back. Sabrina was behind what Parker had tried to do. Either Nikki hadn't told Rosie that or she was playing him.

"Hopefully someone finds her," she continued, snapping a picture. "For Nikki's sake at least, because I know it freaks her out even if she hasn't really said anything. It would freak me out."

Dev watched her take several pictures in the master. "You loved your husband?"

"With every breath I take." She came out of the room. "I'm done up here."

He nodded as they started back downstairs. "You said with every breath you take. In present tense."

"Yeah," she said, sounding confused. "Just because he's no longer here, doesn't mean I'll stop loving him. A part of me always will."

Dev started to ask her what happened to him, but stopped himself. That piece of knowledge didn't tell him anything about her being a risk and it was . . . it was too personal. He didn't need to know.

Returning to the bag in the kitchen, she placed the camera on the counter and pulled out something that reminded him of an old AM/FM radio. "Before you ask, we're not done yet. I need to use the spirit box."

"A spirit box?"

A worrisome smile appeared as she nodded. "Oh you're going to hate this."

ROSIE WAS SO RIGHT.

From the moment she turned on the spirit box and it started rapidly flipping through radio channels, scanning radio frequencies at an alarming rate, Devlin looked like he wanted to pick it up and throw it through a window.

Or throw himself out the window.

She had to struggle not to laugh through the whole thing. There weren't any voices coming through the frequencies, so she did Devlin a favor and didn't mess with it for long.

The moment she turned the thing off, Dev rubbed at the center of his brow. "That was the most obnoxious thing I've ever heard. I'm convinced that could be used as an effective torture device."

Rosie giggled as she turned the kitchen lights back on. It was pretty bad. "All I need to do is set up some cameras and then we'll be done."

"Cameras?"

"Just two small ones. One upstairs in the master bedroom, where the helmet walked across the floor." She grinned when his eyes narrowed. "And then probably one down here . . ." She twisted around as she pulled a camera out of her bag. "I think in here is good. Gets you a decent view."

Devlin offered to help, but she waved him off. It would take longer explaining how to set it up than it would for her just to do it. By the time she came back downstairs, Devlin was leaning against the island, thumbing through his phone. It was late, close to two in the morning, and the man looked as pristine and crisp as he did when she showed up.

She, on the other hand, felt like she was starting to sweat sugar.

Walking back to her bag, she glanced over at him and couldn't help but wonder what he was doing afterward. Was he going straight home to bed or did he have someone, somewhere, waiting for him? After last night, she imagined he had a legion of women he could call up, no matter the time, and be ready for him.

As long as he kept his mouth shut.

She bit down on her lip as she placed the recorder and the EMF meter back in the bag, along with the spirit box. Devlin hadn't kept his mouth shut tonight and he'd been . . . nice to talk to. Even when he was being annoying with the questions while she was doing the EVP reading, she was having . . . fun.

With Devlin de Vincent.

Fun with him wasn't something she exactly thought was possible. Well, fun outside of making out with him. That had certainly been fun.

What came afterward had not been.

Yawning, she zipped up the bag. It was time to get her butt home. "Do you know if someone will be here tomorrow?"

He watched her from where he stood just inside the kitchen. "There can be."

"We just need someone to come in at some point and get the cameras out. I left the boxes by them," she explained. "Someone can leave them out on the porch."

"I can bring them to you."

There was an annoying little wiggle in her chest. "That won't be necessary."

He arched a brow. "Why not?"

"Just won't."

Devlin's gaze turned knowing. "I'll make sure they're on the porch tomorrow afternoon."

"Perfect. So what will happen next is, we're going to review the tapes. See if we find anything. If we do . . ."

"If you do, then contact me."

She leaned forward, crossing her arms. "I don't have your number and you probably don't want to give it to me."

"I think I can trust you with my number."

"You never know. I could post your number online."

"Or write it in a bathroom stall. Call for a good time?"

"More like call if you want to be annoyed but yeah," she replied.

Devlin laughed softly. "Got your cell phone on you? I'll give you my number."

"Yep." She pulled it out of the front pocket of the bag and after Dev gave her his number, she pulled up her Uber app. "Well, that's all I'm going to do tonight. Thank you for doing this and not . . ."

Both his brows lifted. "And not what?"

"And not making . . . me want to throw myself down a flight of steps." She grinned as she pulled her bag off the counter. "So, thank you for that."

Devlin stepped forward and without saying a word, he took her bag from her. They were quiet as they walked outside. As he locked up, she looked to see if there was an Uber nearby. Luckily, one was less than five minutes away.

"Well, I'm going to call an Uber," she said when he turned to her. "Thanks—"

"I can take you home."

Surprised, she wasn't sure what to say at first. "I'll just call—"

Devlin pinned her with a look. "Get in the truck, Rosie."

It was kind of stupid to turn down the offer. Right? She glanced down at her phone and then made up her mind. "Can you say please?"

Coming to stand at the passenger side, he opened the door. "Can you please get in the damn truck?"

Rosie flashed a smile. "Since you asked so nicely and said please, yes, I shall take you up on your offer."

"Honored," he murmured as she climbed in. Devlin leaned in and placed the bag next to her feet.

Relaxing, she leaned back and closed her eyes as he opened up the gate. Tonight hadn't been bad at all. She'd gotten several hours of recording, and hopefully, the recorder had caught the noise they heard. Not for one second did she think that was the helmet, so maybe the recordings would pick up a voice or something.

Dev returned to back the truck out, but he had to stop again to close the gate. Once he was back in, she opened her eyes.

He was looking at her in that intense way of his. "Are you cold?"

"A little."

Turning on the heat, he then tossed his arm over the seat and started down the street. Her gaze roamed over the interior. This truck was not new, but it had been kept well. Nice and tidy.

Curiosity filled her. "Okay. I have to ask. Why this truck?"

"Why not?"

She looked over at him. "It's a pretty old truck."

"So?" His gaze was focused on the road.

"So? Look, I'm not talking smack about it. My car is pretty old, but you're worth what? A gajillion dollars? And you drive an old, outdated truck?"

"I'm not worth a gajillion dollars," he replied, and she rolled her eyes as she wiggled into the comfy seat. "I like the truck." He glanced over at her. "Why? Is there something wrong with it?"

"No," she laughed. "Why would you think there was?"

"You're asking about it?" he pointed out. "That's why."

"I'm just surprised. Figured you'd be in a Porsche or, like, a Ferrari or something."

He refocused on the road. "I have a Porsche."

"Of course," she demurred.

"I don't have a Ferrari."

"Gasp. What does the club think of that?"

"Club?"

"I assume rich people belong to some kind of private, secretive rich-people's club," she explained. "I imagine this rich-people's club has rules. Such as what kind of car you must drive."

"You are . . ."

"What?"

"Odd."

Rosie let out a tired laugh. "So, no rich-people's club?"

There was a heartbeat of silence. "There are clubs."

"Knew it!"

He pressed his lips together. "I do not belong to them."

"Oh. Well. That's boring." She sighed dramatically. "I was hoping you could tell me about their rules and tell me my theory is correct."

"What theory?"

"That the Illuminati is real."

The laugh that came from him was deep, but short. Too short. "Odd," he repeated. "You are odd."

"You know," she said, letting her head rest against the seat as she watched him. "You're allowed to laugh and smile."

His gaze shot to hers. "I know."

"Do you?"

At the stoplight, he stared at her for a few moments and then turned back to the road.

Oh no.

Apparently, she'd gone too far, because he didn't speak for several minutes.

But then he did. "Sabrina hated this truck. I think she rode in it once."

Okay. She was not expecting that statement. "Sabrina sounds like a bitch."

He snorted as he turned onto the highway. "I'm curious about some-thing myself."

"Ask. I'm an open book."

"You are not an open book," he replied, dropping one hand to his lap. "How did you meet Ross?"

"At a secret club for conspirators and scheming liars."

"That's what I thought."

She grinned as she closed her eyes. "We met about two years ago. He was doing this piece on ghost tours in the Quarter."

"Two years ago?"

"Yep. I haven't even known him all that long." She covered a yawn. "We were friends. I mean, never really personal or anything, but we've shared drinks and always chatted when we saw each other. Not recently," she added before he latched on to that. "When he showed interest in Nikki, I honestly thought it was legit."

When he didn't respond, she opened her eyes. He was focused on the road. It took a moment to see that they were close to Canal Street. She glanced back at him. "You don't even seem tired."

"I'm not much of a sleeper," he responded. "So I'm usually not even in bed by this time."

"Wow." She blinked. "I could sleep for twelve hours if I didn't have stuff going on."

"That must be nice."

"Why aren't you much of a sleeper?"

"Haven't been." The truck slowed as traffic picked up. There were always people out, especially on the weekend. "Not since I was young."

Rosie mulled that over and she thought she'd figured out what that meant. "Not since you had the accident, the one where you had a near-death experience?"

"Not since then."

That was the last thing Devlin said. The rest of the short trip to her apartment was in silence, and she wasn't sure if it was because something was said or if he didn't have anything else to say.

He pulled up to the curb and started to reach for the keys. "I can walk you up."

"No need," she replied, unbuckling her seat belt and reaching for the bag. "Thanks for the ride, Devlin."

She started to reach for the door, but then looked back at him. Their gazes collided and held. A warm, unwanted feeling curled in her lower stomach. "We . . . we got along tonight."

"We did." Those thick lashes of his lowered. "Which probably means we should end this now before that changes."

She looked away then, but her eyes went to the stupidest place imaginable. His mouth. There was no forgetting the way his lips felt against hers. The warmth in her stomach spread and there was a little reckless, utterly dumb part of her that wanted to invite him in.

But common sense won out. "Good night, Devlin."

Devlin drew in a deep breath, and Rosie saw how tightly he was holding on to the steering wheel. His knuckles were nearly bleached white.

"Good night, Rosie."

Chapter 21

Jilly picked up the cameras while checking in with the Mendez family Sunday afternoon. They were boxed and waiting for her, and Rosie just knew that it had been Devlin who'd gone over there, taken the cameras down, and placed them on the porch.

Liz and Jilly were going to review the tapes, and Rosie was planning to have the audio cleared by tonight, Monday by the latest, and that meant her ears needed to be glued to her headphones, but that wasn't what she was doing.

Instead, she was still in bed, lying on her side, and internet stalking Devlin de Vincent.

Not exactly one of her proudest moments.

But here she was, for the last . . . Lord, how many hours had she been at this? Too many hours, but there was a lot of stuff out there on the internet about Devlin, from when he was a child up until the more recent weeks, where news of his broken engagement with the missing Harrington heiress was discussed.

There were articles about their mother and some of them seemed to revel in how her life had come to a jarring end, going into grotesque detail about how she'd jumped from the roof of their home. All these old, archived articles mentioned something that Rosie had forgotten.

The sister had gone missing the same night their mother had committed suicide.

Madeline de Vincent.

No one ever talked about her now, did they? In the news, at least. She wasn't sure if the brothers did. If they wondered what happened to their sister. She imagined it must've been the hardest for Lucian since he and Madeline were fraternal twins.

There were several pieces on their father's death, and it made Rosie think about how he never called the man Father or Dad. It was always Lawrence. And that was . . . odd.

And she'd found a plethora of pictures of Devlin and his ex-fiancée. Rosie had a vague memory of what the woman looked like, having briefly seen her pictures in the papers over the years, but she had forgotten how beautiful she was.

There was a picture of them that she found herself staring at for a creepy amount of time, but she couldn't seem to pull her gaze away from it. They stood side by side, both dressed as if they were at some kind of gala. Devlin looked . . . goodness, he looked like a god dressed in a black tux, and Sabrina looked like a goodness. Her blond hair was pulled up in a chic, elegant twist and her pale skin as flawless as her bright red smile. She wore a gorgeous black strapless dress that was tight down to her knees and then billowed out.

If Rosie wore a dress like that, she would look five inches shorter and about fifty pounds heavier, but someone as tall and thin as Sabrina was, she looked like a Parisian model.

They were utterly beautiful together.

And there wasn't an ounce of warmth between them in the photo.

In any of the photos of them.

But it was so evident in this one, it was painful to even look at. Their posture and stance were stiff as a board. Sabrina's smile was perfect, but the slight narrowing of her eyes showed annoyance. Devlin, on the other hand, looked cold and aloof standing beside her. What little she did know about their relationship was evident in the pictures of them.

These two people didn't love one another. Rosie wasn't sure if they even liked each other. Why would combining two fortunes be worth being stuck, even if it was only by name, to someone you couldn't stand? There had to be more than that.

At least Rosie hoped so, because what did that say about Devlin to have gone along with his father's wishes for so long?

Closing the laptop, she rolled onto her back. There were things mentioned in the most scandalous of articles, stories about how many deaths and mysterious illnesses plagued the de Vincent family over the many decades. The curse was brought up. They were stories that Rosie had already known, because they fed the whole mythology of the de Vincent curse.

But these deaths and disappearances were very real. These were once living and breathing people. Family. Not myths and entertaining stories to be gossiped about. If this was her family, she'd probably feel the same way Devlin did when it came to protecting his family. There really was no wonder he was so . . . paranoid.

A kernel of guilt blossomed in her stomach when she thought about how she'd researched the curse and the haunting. She had done so without really ever considering the fact that these were real people. She was so detached from it all until now.

She dragged her teeth over her lower lip as her thoughts wandered their way back to the one thing she had noticed; the one thing she couldn't unsee.

Not that what it said about Devlin should matter to her, but there wasn't a single picture of him smiling and these photos she found on the internet spanned *years*. He wasn't smiling in the ones taken with his brothers or his father. Not even older ones when he was a teenager and with his mother, who was as blonde and fair as Lucian. He was always so incredibly . . . still in the pictures. If his eyes were closed, he would appear to be standing asleep or . . . dead.

God, that's how he appeared, as if he were dead.

Rosie didn't know a lot about near-death experiences beyond a few cases she'd read on the internet or the psychological and biological explanations of what people experienced when death was seconds away. But she had read about those experiences changing someone.

She wondered if Sarah had any insight on that that went beyond the science of it all, because Googling it would be a rabbit hole she really didn't need to fall down.

What was Devlin like before his accident? He'd been young, so even if he was a happy and carefree child, that didn't necessarily mean he'd be the same as an adult. The personality was nowhere near set in stone at that age, but what if . . . what if the death had changed him?

"Too far," Rosie murmured as she tucked a curl behind her ear. "I'm going too far."

She didn't know Devlin well enough to even begin to hazard a guess if his near-death experience had any impact on him.

And it didn't matter if it did.

If there wasn't anything to find at Lucian's house, there wouldn't be any reason to be in contact with him again. And if they did find something? Rosie knew what she needed to do.

She would remove herself from the case.

That was the only smart option. She and Devlin might've actually gotten along for several hours and she might've seen a different side of him, one that included smiles and laughter, but the man was complicated.

Too complicated.

And despite all that, he'd sparked an interest in her that needed to be squashed. She may not know everything about Devlin, but she knew enough that her interest would only grow, especially if the Devlin from last night was the real one, and that interest mixed with the attraction she felt even when she was mad at him . . . She was certain that meant only one thing.

It would not end well for her.

ROSIE FINALLY DRAGGED her butt out of bed and reviewed the EVP recordings. Okay, that wasn't exactly true. She reviewed the EVP recordings while lying in bed. Once she was finished, when it was close to seven in the evening, she headed over to Liz and Jilly's house.

"Hey." Liz led her into the living room, where Jilly was watching the film from Lucian's house. "So how was last night?"

"It was actually good. We didn't kill each other."

Hitting pause on the laptop, Jilly pulled off her headphones. "I heard that. Good news."

Rosie grinned as she sat in the moon chair they had under one of those hanging spider plants. "Yeah, so that's kind of why I'm here."

"I thought you just missed us." Liz pouted as she sat by Jilly.

"I did. I swear."

Jilly smirked. "No, you didn't. So anything on the EVP?"

"Work. Work." Liz leaned in, kissing Jilly's cheek. "Good thing I love you."

"Good thing you're interested in the same things," Rosie pointed out. "So, I've finished the EVP recordings. The crash and footstep sound I texted about when I got home this morning? It was picked up on the recorder. It's pretty muted sounding but it can be enhanced."

"Awesome." Jilly placed the headsets on the coffee table.

"And there were a couple of things I've flagged for Lance," Rosie continued, sliding down in the thick, cushioned chair. "There were a couple of other things that the recorder picked up. I swore one of them sounded like a name, when we were upstairs in one of the bedrooms, but I can't make it out."

Interest sparked in Liz's eyes.

"I'm not sure what or if we've caught anything that will be conclusive, but I think we're going to need to bring Sarah in, just in case. Have her do a walk-through."

"Agreed." Jilly let her arms rest on her knees. "You can do the walk—"

"So, back to the other reason why I'm here." Rosie drew in a deep breath. After internet stalking Devlin and realizing that the more time she spent with him, the more she got wrapped up in him, she knew what she needed to do. "I'm going to remove myself from this—"

"Narrative?" Liz supplied helpfully.

Rosie laughed. "Kind of. I'm going to step away from this investigation."

Jilly stared at her. "Come again? You can't be for real. You've been obsessed with the whole de Vincent curse and haunting since I've known you. I know this isn't the de Vincent manor, but this is one of their homes. I know you don't seem to get along with Devlin, but I cannot believe you do not want to be involved in this."

"Did things not go well last night?" Concern filled Liz's gaze.

"No, things were actually pretty cool. I mean, he was a bit distracting during the EVP recording." She paused, smiling. "Actually, he was kind of funny, but with my friend being involved with Gabriel, it just feels weird."

Both of them stared at her.

"And even though I didn't kill him last night, we haven't really gotten along . . ." She trailed off, thinking of just how well they had gotten along Friday night before she told him about the reading. "Anyway, I just think it's best for you guys to take this one over."

"Wow," Jilly murmured, still staring at her.

Liz leaned forward. "Did something happen between you two?"

"What?" Her stomach dipped. "Why would you ask that?"

"Because I've never known you to not want to work on a case," Jilly replied, glancing at Liz before refocusing on Rosie. "And you pretty much squeaked out 'what?'"

"I did not." Her brows lowered.

Liz grinned. "You did."

"So, I'm going to say something happened between you guys."

Sliding even farther down in the moon chair, she sighed heavily. "I . . . okay, something did happen between us, and I'm not trying to hide it or anything like that, but it just feels weird to be a part of this investigation now. So, yeah."

Jilly closed her laptop. "We're going to need a little more detail than that."

Rosie lifted her hands. "We kind of made out Friday night at the Masquerade. It's not a big deal—"

"Um. That is kind of a big deal," Liz said. "Isn't he engaged?"

"They broke up," she explained. "We made out and it was great. The man can kiss and . . . stuff, and we got along last night, but we really don't like each other."

"I always make out with people I don't like," Liz said blandly. "That's why I'm with Jilly."

Jilly snorted. "I feel like there is so much more you're not telling us."

All Rosie did was lift her brows and her hands again.

There was. There was a lot she wasn't telling them and she wasn't going to, because she figured enough people, including her, had whispered and gossiped about the de Vincents. And even if it wasn't a de Vincent, Rosie wasn't the 'kiss and discuss with the girls' type. She had no problem listening to other people talk about their love life, but for her, it was something private. She kept her business in her business.

Both girls knew this.

Liz groaned. "Okay. Fine. I will try to forget that my friend was all up close and personal with the Devil, but kudos to you for that. You basically made out with a celebrity."

She grinned, but really didn't want to think about the fact that she did make out with him, because it made her want to do it again, and she also knew that inevitably he'd tick her off again. "I'm going to text him your numbers, since I am sure he'll freak if I gave his away. So, just a heads-up if you get a random call or text from an unknown number."

"Cool." Jilly leaned into Liz. "We'll take it from here. I'm sure Devlin will be thrilled to work with us."

A slow smile pulled at Rosie's lips as a little bit of disappointment flickered in her chest. "Yeah, I'm sure he will be."

Chapter 22

Dev sat in his office in the city Monday afternoon, staring at his phone. His jaw worked as he read the text message for the twentieth time.

No matter how many times he read it, Rosie's message didn't magically change. And it was a rather long message. An actual paragraph. Who sent texts that long and ended it with a . . . chicken-head emoticon?

He had no idea what the chicken head represented, but the rest of the message was pretty clear.

She was pawning him off on a friend she called Jilly, and she wasn't in the position to pawn him off since, in his opinion, there was nothing about this situation that warranted pawning.

Then she typed—thanks for confirming what I already knew. That rich people do have secret clubs. A small grin had appeared the first time he read that. And then—I really hope Lucian doesn't have a spirit problem, but if so, Jilly will take care of it.

And that was the end.

This text was a brush-off. What he imagined people received after a date that went well, but one person no longer wanted to see the other. He'd never in his life been on the receiving end of a brush-off.

Dev did not like it. At all.

What in the hell?

He reached for his phone and stopped just before he picked it up. Was he going to call her? Yes, that was exactly what he'd been seconds away from doing. But why? There was no reason to contact her.

Dev picked up the phone anyway. Fuck being blown off. He would—

The phone rang suddenly, catching him off guard. He recognized the number.

Archie.

He was going to have to deal with Rosie later.

"What do you have for me?" Dev asked as he rose from his desk and turned to the glass wall behind him. The design gave an amazing view of the city, especially at night.

"Something fairly messed up, man. Got the insurance company to give me the VIN," he explained, and Dev was a little curious to know how he'd managed to pull that off. "Which led me back to who the vehicle was registered to. You're never going to guess who they came back to."

"Who?"

"One Lawrence de Vincent," he answered.

"What?" His hand tightened on the phone as he turned from the window. "Lawrence didn't have a Mercedes. The man only drove Porsches. You'd think they were cutting him some deal based on his loyalty to them."

"That may be, but that's what the records show." There was a pause. "I'll be in contact when I know more."

A muscle flexed along Dev's jaw as the call disconnected. Why in the hell was Sabrina even in possession of a car registered to Lawrence—a car that Dev had no idea the man owned? And how in the world did his father's estate lawyer miss this car when it came to settling the estate?

Dev doubted that he had.

Which meant that bastard had hidden the car and who the hell knew what else.

That was unacceptable.

Walking back to his desk, he snatched up his keys and stalked out of the office. Derek rose as he walked past. "Cancel all my afternoon meetings."

His assistant knew better than to ever question the orders. He nodded as he sat down, one hand heading for the keyboard, the other going for the headset attached to the phone.

Too impatient to wait for the elevator, he took the stairs down the ten floors, making his way to the front entrance. Lawrence's lawyer had an office less than four blocks from his, and he was about to get an unexpected visit. Entering the main level, he nodded at the receptionist and crossed the lobby, walking under the art deco murals on the ceiling that had been designed to match the Empire State Building. He stepped through the double lobby doors and then out into the cloudy day and air that held a surprising chill to it.

He took one damn step to the right when he heard his name and immediately recognized the voice.

"Devlin, what a convenient surprise. I was coming to see you."

Jaw clenching down so hard it was a wonder he didn't crack any molars, he slowly pivoted. His uncle was stepping out from a black town car, adjusting the jacket of his gray suit.

"Stefan." Dev waited by the revolving doors. "Surprised to see you here."

A half grin appeared as he walked up to him. "Now, why is that?"

"Figured after our last conversation, you wouldn't come around for a while."

"You would figure that." The amused set to Stefan's expression reminded Dev so much of Lawrence, he wanted to lay Stefan out on the sidewalk. "I need to have a word with you. Can we go up to your office?"

"I don't have time right now," Dev replied. "If you want to talk, then you're going to do it out here and make it fast."

The amused expression slipped off his face as if it were a mask. He stepped closer to Dev, away from the doormen. "You won't even give me the barest amount of respect, will you?"

Dev was about two inches taller than Stefan, so they were nearly eye to eye when he met Stefan's gaze. "No."

His jaw worked. "One of these days, you will regret this . . . attitude you have toward me."

"Doubtful," Dev sighed. "What did you need to speak to me about?"

Stefan ran his fingers along the band of his watch. "I ran into an old friend a few days ago at this dinner and he had the strangest thing to tell me."

"Is that so?" Indifference dripped from his tone.

"Yes. Surprisingly the topic of conversation turned from Lawrence's death to you." The muscle along his jaw was working overtime. "Which was very interesting, don't you think?"

Impatience ticked through Dev like a bomb counting down. "Can you get to the point of whatever it is that you have to say?"

"This friend of mine lives in Nebraska." Stefan paused when a car honked. "Had the strangest thing to tell me. Now, he lives in Omaha, but ran into a couple from some little village out in the middle of no-where. They were very excited. Had heard a de Vincent had come to their town a few months ago. The heir, to be exact."

Dev tensed, but kept his expression bland. "And?"

"And I'm curious." Stefan smiled then. "What in the world would you be doing in Nebraska of all places?"

Staring at his uncle, he couldn't decipher if Stefan knew why Devlin would be there or if Stefan knew what was in Nebraska. There'd been no evidence that he had, but Devlin knew better than to completely underestimate him.

"I was looking at property." That wasn't exactly untrue. "Thinking about expanding our resort portfolio."

"In Nebraska?" he replied smoothly, too smoothly. "Who would travel there for vacation?"

"A lot of people, Stefan." He cocked his head. "People who would rather be surrounded by wilderness instead of beaches and people. People who want to get . . . lost for a little while."

"Interesting."

He smirked. "Not really. I need to go."

"I'm sure you do." Stefan stepped back to the waiting car. "Oh by the way, a little piece of advice from someone who knows." He winked. "You should be more careful with your . . . indiscretions."

Dev's eyes narrowed. "Excuse me?"

A faint, knowing smile curved the older man's lips. "Engaging in a tryst with a woman at the gala so soon after Sabrina's disappearance is, well, quite scandalous, Devlin."

The fine hair along the nape of his neck rose. "I didn't see you at the Masquerade."

"Late arrival." Stefan lifted a shoulder. "I'd expect you of all people to be more careful. Honestly, I was quite surprised to see you lead the woman into the courtyard—a dark courtyard. Hopefully I was the only one who saw and recognized you."

Dev didn't give a shit if anyone saw him leaving with Rosie. What he cared about was if Stefan overheard their conversation. Anger flashed through him. "Did you follow us?"

"Unlike some, I wouldn't stoop to that crass behavior." He glanced down at his watch as he delivered that rather pathetic insult. "I need to go." He started to turn, but stopped, facing Dev once more. "From what I could see, she's a very . . . beautiful woman. Not at all like Sabrina, I am sure." Those eyes, nearly identical to Dev's own, lifted to meet his gaze. "I'm sure she must be something . . . unique to have caught your eye."

Dev said nothing as he kept his expression utterly blank, but inside, a slow inferno was building into a blinding rage. He knew not to let it show, no matter how badly he wanted to warn Stefan to not even think about Rosie. If he did that, it would only draw more attention to her.

And that was not the kind of attention he wanted Rosie to have, no matter what she may know about him or be involved in.

"That makes her . . . interesting." Stefan flashed a smile that didn't reach his eyes. "Very interesting, indeed."

"I'M SORRY, BUT Mr. Oakes is very busy." The frazzled receptionist stepped around the desk, hurrying after Dev as he stalked down the hall. "I'll tell him that you stopped by."

Dev ignored her. After the run-in with Stefan and having to wait to make sure he hadn't been followed, he had little to no patience.

"Mr. de Vincent, please. You cannot go—"

Too late.

Placing his hands on the wooden paneled doors—doors that his brother had made—he pushed them open.

A strangled-sounding curse came from behind the desk, from Edmond Oakes, to be exact. Who currently had his hands full and probably his mouth, too. There was a woman on his lap, a much younger and blonder woman than his wife of twenty-some years.

"I'm so sorry, Mr. Oakes. I tried to stop him," the receptionist gasped. "He wouldn't listen."

"Jesus, Devlin," Edmond said from somewhere behind the woman. "You could've at least knocked."

"I could've." He strolled forward and dropped into a chair. He arched a brow as the woman scrambled off the man's lap, clasping the edges of her blouse together, revealing his father's estate lawyer.

Edmond Oakes was a man getting up there in years—a man who was about one more glass of bourbon away from liver failure if his yellowish complexion was any indication. The front of his dress shirt was unbuttoned, revealing a white undershirt that stretched across his chest and looked like it was mere moments away from bursting. His dyed brown hair was a mess, and Dev knew that when he reached under the desk, he was buttoning up his slacks.

Dev had no idea why Lawrence used this man for his estate. He wasn't particularly noteworthy or well referred. His gaze flickered to where the lithe woman was buttoning up her blouse, her back to them. The woman glanced over her shoulder at Dev. She was young. As young as Nikki, probably in her early to midtwenties.

He refocused on Edmond. Well, there was something the aging lawyer had in common with Lawrence. Obviously.

Right now, his ruddy eyes were doing their best to glare a hole straight through Dev. "Sorry, Ms. Davis, we'll have to pick this up later."

Ms. Davis grinned as she nodded. "Of course." As she swayed her way past Dev, she winked. "Hello, Mr. de Vincent."

He nodded and waited until he heard the door close behind them. "How old is she, Edmond?"

Lawrence's lawyer snorted as he rose from his chair. Both the dress shirt and undershirt were untucked. "Old enough. Ms. Davis is my new assistant." He ambled toward the liquor cabinet that took up more space on the wall than law books did. "She is my personal scheduler."

"Personal scheduler? Is that what they're calling it nowadays?"

He huffed. "Care for a drink?"

"No, but please, help yourself."

Edmond did just that, pouring himself a glass of whiskey. "What can I do for you today, Devlin? I assume it's something fairly important since you didn't even attempt to make an appointment."

"It is." Dev rested his cheek on his balled hand and watched the lawyer shuffle back to his desk and sit down. "I want to know why I was unaware of a black Mercedes owned by Lawrence."

The man froze with the glass halfway to his mouth. "Excuse me?"

"Lawrence owned a black Mercedes. I was unaware of this since it was not included in the estate papers you went over with me," he said, watching a red tint seep across the man's face, following the faint spider veins. "Now, I imagine a lawyer with your many, many years of experience would've discovered unclaimed property and not have left it off the estate. Or it was on the estate, a part that was kept from me."

Edmond tipped the glass back, downing the contents in one impressive gulp. Baring his teeth, he shook his head as he placed the empty glass on the desk. "Now, Devlin, you know that when a person requests the contents of their estate to be private—"

"Do I remotely look like I care about privacy laws regarding Lawrence's estate?"

"Devlin—"

"I'm sure that I look like I care about why there was a Mercedes on the estate that I'm unaware of and why Sabrina Harrington is in possession of this Mercedes."

Edmond's gaze shot to his as he pulled his hand away from the glass. "You're going to have to ask Ms. Harrington that question."

"And I'm sure you've heard that Sabrina is missing," Dev replied. "So, asking her is going to be difficult."

He coughed out a dry laugh. "I'm sure that with all the . . . power at your fingertips, you can find Ms. Harrington and ask that question."

Dev smiled faintly as Edmond's hand twitched.

The man swallowed as the silence stretched out between them. "Devlin, you have to understand that I cannot, by law, share any details that my client had entrusted me to keep private."

"That's fine." Dev kicked his feet up onto the man's desk, crossing his legs at the ankles. "Then you have to understand that I've given you this opportunity to prevent what's about to happen."

Edmond stilled, even his hand. "What is about to happen?"

"Well, you're a phone call away from losing it all."

"Excuse me?"

Dev raised his brows. "You didn't understand what I said? I can repeat myself. You have been given an opportunity to preserve your way of life. I can change that with a simple phone call and what will happen after that phone call will probably be justly deserved."

"Are you threatening me?" His voice was guttural as he gaped at Dev.

"I have a question for you. What do you think your wife would do if she found out you're fucking your *personal scheduler*? Divorce you? Take half of everything? That would be terrible, but that isn't even the worst I can do to you." Dev smiled again, a small icy smile. "I know you provided false information for Lawrence—information that has ties to banks in countries like Russia and China. I also know what those banks were used for. Tell me, Edmond, do you know what those banks were used for?"

Blood drained so quickly from Edmond's face that for a moment, Devlin thought the man might have a heart attack. Both hands thudded off the desk and he leaned forward. "Devlin, I swear to you, I have nothing to do with what that money involved. I just did what your father asked me to do. He's a de Vincent, just like you. No one denies a de Vincent."

"I guess you can tell the Feds that, but I'm sure they'll use words you're well familiar with," Dev said. "Complicit. *Accessory*."

Edmond looked away, his chest heaving with short, deep breaths. Maybe he *was* having a heart attack. Dev hoped he gave him the information before that happened.

"Well . . ." Dev pulled his legs off the desk, dropping them to the floor. "I see you've made your choice—"

"Wait," Edmond rasped as his head swiveled toward Dev. "I just need a moment."

"Take as long as you need." Dev paused. "But don't take too long. I'm a busy man."

Edmond reached for his phone and hit a button. The receptionist answered immediately. "Yes, Mr. Oakes?"

"Bring me the de Vincent file. The one with the red label," he said, his voice hoarse. "I need it now."

"Of course."

Disconnecting the call, Edmond's gaze shifted to Dev. "She'll have it for you within a few moments."

"Perfect."

Luckily for Edmond, the receptionist hurried into the office with the file. She placed it on the desk and then quickly excused herself.

Edmond picked it up and opened it. Appearing satisfied with the documents, he closed it and inched the folder across the desk. "There's something you need to understand."

Dev doubted that as he picked up the file.

"I'd heard about how . . . ruthless Lawrence could be. Positive everyone in the city knew that, so it was never my goal to ever work for the man." Edmond collapsed back against his chair, and Dev was guessing he'd had no idea today was going to go like this when he had the blonde on his lap. "But like you, Lawrence had a way of making people do what he wanted. He discovered I had a bit of a gambling problem and . . . and here we are."

"So, here we are." Dev picked up the file.

"I told Lawrence you'd find out." He dragged his hand down his face. "You got what you came for. Now get the hell out of my office."

Chapter 23

"Jesus Christ," Dev muttered, staring down at the estate papers.

Not only had Lawrence owned the Mercedes and left it to Sabrina upon his passing, Dev had discovered that Lawrence owned a property in the French Quarter, a building that apparently housed a business and an apartment. Something about the address was familiar to him.

Chartres Street.

In the estate, the property was listed as being held under de Vincent Properties, but it wasn't a property in their portfolio, so that left the question of who was managing it and why was it kept separate?

Better yet, did Lawrence really think he wouldn't eventually discover this place? The Mercedes was one thing—one really fucked-up thing—but an entire property? Eventually, something would've come up on it. Taxes. A claim. Something.

Dev sat back, slowly shaking his head. He knew that Sabrina had a closeted relationship with Stefan, but not Lawrence. So why in the world would Lawrence leave a car to her?

Then again, maybe Sabrina had a relationship with Lawrence.

God.

Disgust swirled through him like a windstorm. He never knew what had connected Sabrina to Stefan. Was it just sex? The woman did have a . . . unique appetite for men with power, even if it was only perceived that they wielded that power. But Lawrence? The man Sabrina believed to be his father? But if she had no problem sleeping with his uncle, he may be giving her too much credit thinking she would have a problem with his father.

Dev just didn't get it.

It was one of the questions he needed Sabrina to answer. Why did she want to marry him when she'd been all twisted up in her infatuation with Gabe, sleeping with Stefan, possibly Lawrence? There had to be more to it, and with her having a vehicle Lawrence had left her, he knew it probably meant she was wrapped up in what Lawrence was involved in.

Lawrence was a disease and Dev had a feeling he'd only scratched the surface of how infectious he'd truly been, how many people he'd involved.

But he really couldn't blame all of Sabrina's actions on Lawrence, now, could he? That woman hadn't been stable. Dev had known it—known it for a long time. It was why he'd involved himself with her, because if he hadn't? He thought of Gabe, and his stomach twisted. The problem with his plan when it came to Sabrina was the fact that he thought he could control her.

He'd been dead wrong on that.

Sitting forward, he brought up Google and quickly typed in the address of the property. The map appeared and to the left of the page was the picture of the property.

"Holy fuck," he whispered, recoiling from his computer. "No way."

He immediately recognized the two-story black-and-brick Creole town house. It was one of many in the Quarter, but he'd been at this one. Recently. There was no forgetting the voodoo shop on the first floor or the apartment on the second level.

Or the woman who lived in the apartment.

Lawrence owned the building that Rosie Herpin lived in.

Dev barked out a short, harsh laugh as he stared at the picture on the web page. Even if he believed in coincidences, this would be too much. Rosie was way too connected. Friends with Nikki. Tied to Ross Haid. Claimed that the spirit of Lawrence had told her he was murdered, and now she was living in a property owned by de Vincent Properties and hidden by Lawrence.

Hell . . .

He picked up the papers again, his free hand curling into a fist as anger flushed through him. There were several properties owned by them throughout the state of Louisiana, so why would this one be hidden?

Dev needed to find out, and that meant he needed to discover not only who was managing the building, but also what could possibly be in that building that Lawrence had been hiding. And someone with beautiful hazel eyes and a fiery attitude that went straight to his dick had a hell of a lot of explaining to do, starting—

Thump.

Dev stilled.

Thump.

What in the hell? Lowering the papers to his desk, he lifted his head.

Thump.

There it was again, a distinctive thump against . . . against the floor, from the room down below.

Lawrence's office was directly below his.

Now, that made no sense, because no one was allowed to be in the room. Not even Besson.

He closed the file and then reached into his desk, grabbing the key to the office below. He took the outside entrance since it was quicker, coming in through the back door on the main floor. He stalked down the empty hall, reaching the closed doors of Lawrence's office. He turned the handle.

The door was locked.

"The hell?" His eyes narrowed as he heard the sound again. *Thump.* It was definitely coming from within the office.

Shoving the key into the lock, he pushed open the door. Cool air wafted out as he stepped into the room. Faint sunlight seeped under the blinds and crept across the hardwood floors. The oriental carpet had been removed, but other than that, the office looked the way Lawrence had left it.

His gaze lifted to the ceiling fan. It whirled slowly and it was by no means the source of the sound, but he knew that fan would've been turned off. Besson wouldn't have left it on when the room was sealed up.

He thought about what Stefan said about Nebraska. That was something he was going to need to check on. Just not right at the moment.

The edges of the key dug into his palm as he stared up at the ceiling. Took no amount of effort for him to see Lawrence hanging from that fan. Dev's upper lip curled. What that man—

An icy breath of air blew along the nape of his neck. Dev twisted at the waist, but no one stood behind him.

No one he could see, at least.

He dragged his teeth over his bottom lip as he scanned the office. There was nothing that could've been making that sound or causing the blast of icy air.

Walking out of the office, he closed and locked the door. He took only one step before he heard the noise again. A distinct *thump* coming from the office.

EYES GLUED TO the laptop screen, Rosie reached blindly for her wineglass. She knew if she looked away for just a second, she could miss something in the film from the Mendez house.

Ghosts didn't exactly lollygag around.

So far there'd been nothing but a few dust bunnies floating by. She guessed ghosts also played it low-key on Sundays.

Blowing out a long, low breath, she kept her gaze focused on the screen. Jilly and Liz had reviewed the tapes from Lucian's place and given her an update this afternoon. Nothing remarkable had been on the film, but there was what they thought might be orbs. They sent it to Lance to go over and were waiting for Devlin to reach out to them.

As far as she knew, he hadn't since she'd texted him.

Her fingers brushed the side of her glass and she snatched it up before it toppled over. Taking a sip, she wiggled her sock-covered toes as she scooted farther down into the couch.

The Mendez family still hadn't given them permission to do any more longer, extensive investigations, especially after the activity seemed to have died down, but they'd allowed the cameras to be set up again and to keep running. For now. Rosie had a feeling that would change if the activity continued to decline.

And that wasn't uncommon. Sometimes there was a burst of activity and then nothing for months or even years.

She straightened her glasses as she stared at the hallway on the screen. The time of the film at the bottom right hand read 2:34 A.M., and Rosie let out a sigh. This was the only part that sucked when it came to investigations. There were a lot of nothingburgers to get to the Big Mac, and that was if you ever caught anything.

And there were people like Devlin who had no idea how much work went into something like this. It wasn't a hobby. It was like a job—one you didn't get paid for—but she guessed after Saturday night, he had a whole new understanding of what it took.

God, she was so distracted.

She hit pause on the film and downed the rest of her wine in a gulp that Sarah would've been proud of. Setting her glass aside, she let her head fall back.

She was done with him, but the part of her brain that wanted to know the exact moment Ian had decided to end his life was the same part that had led her to study psychology at the University of Alabama. She liked to figure people out.

And Devlin? The man gave her whiplash. Believed in ghosts but apparently only the ones who haunted his house. Had a near-death experience, but believed psychics were a crock. Obviously trusted no one, but had shared something so incredibly personal with her and he barely knew her. Accused her of being in on some major conspiracy to take his family down, but also wanted to bring her back to his place for some naughty shenanigans. Irritated the crap out of her, but could also bring her to the heights of pleasure with a kiss and a brush of his fingers.

She could've done a graduate thesis on this man.

Staring up at her ceiling, she pressed her lips together. Why was she thinking about him? There'd been men she'd actually had relationships with who she thought about less, which was freaking ridiculous, because she had—

A knock at her front door snapped her out of her thoughts. Sitting up, she clutched the laptop before it slid off her bare legs. She glanced at the time. It was close to nine at night and while it wasn't all that late, she wasn't expecting anyone.

Then again, since her place was in the Quarter, there were often random friends showing up unannounced to basically dry out before they attempted to head home.

Setting the laptop on the coffee table, she rose and walked to the front door as she tugged the ends of her long, thigh-length gray cardigan together. She was just wearing a tank underneath and sleep shorts, so she wasn't exactly dressed for company.

She unlocked the dead bolt and cracked the door open just enough to see who stood outside, and it was enough to send her heart exploding right out of her chest. She was shocked into a frozen state of silence as her gaze crawled over smoothly coiffed black hair, aqua-blue eyes framed by impossibly thick lashes, and a jaw hard enough to cut through granite.

Devlin de Vincent was at her apartment.

Again.

Chapter 24

*L*ike she was under some kind of bad-life-choices spell, she opened the door the rest of the way, getting a full view of Devlin. The first dumb thought that entered her head, she spoke out loud.

"It's after nine at night and you're wearing trousers and a dress shirt. Just like Saturday." She shook her head, a little dumbfounded. "Amazing."

His brows snapped together. "Excuse me?"

"Do you own jeans? Sweatpants? Pajama bottoms?" she asked. "Do you sleep in black trousers?"

"Of course not."

"I don't believe you," she whispered.

Devlin stared at her for a moment and then checked her out. His gaze swept over her. "Jesus."

She stiffened. "What?"

"What are *you* wearing?" His gaze was so intense as it glided over her legs, it felt like an actual touch. His head tilted as he reached her thighs. "Are there tacos on your shorts?"

"Yes, sir. Taco Tuesday is a national holiday."

He bit down on that plump lower lip, and she hated that she felt that bite in the pit of her stomach, in the warm little tremor that unnerved her.

God, what was he doing here?

"It's Monday, Rosie."

Another lick of heat curled in her stomach, and she was thoroughly annoyed by that—by all of this. "I'm preparing for Taco Tuesday, thank you very much."

"Hmm." His gaze lifted, and he bit down on that damn lip again.

It was then when she realized that the sides of her cardigan had parted, and she didn't have to look down to know he could probably see just how affected she was by him.

Which meant this conversation had exceeded its limits.

"Stop ogling me," she demanded. "And tell me why you're here. I sent you a text and told you to contact—"

"I know what you texted me." Dev slowly brought his gaze to hers and there was a warmth in his stare that she recognized from the night of the Masquerade. "I'm not here because of the text, and it's really hard not to *ogle* you."

"Then you need to try harder—actually, that doesn't matter." She started to close the door. "I'm just going to pretend you're not stand-ing here, close the door, and go back to doing what I was doing."

Devlin caught the door before she could close it. "I need inside your apartment."

"And I need a million dollars, but you don't see me knocking on your door."

He arched a brow. "Well, it would be the right door to knock on if you were in need of it."

"Nice." Rosie rolled her eyes. "I honestly don't know why you're here if it doesn't have to do with the text I sent about Lucian's—wait." Concern blossomed in the pit of her stomach and spread like wildfire. "Is Nikki okay? Did something happen?"

"Nikki's okay," he told her. "As far as I know, she's still being waited on hand and foot by my brother."

"As it should be." Relief seeped into her. For a horrible second there, she'd thought something had happened, so she was happy to hear that it hadn't. Only one question remained. "Are you drunk?"

"What?"

"Are you drunk?" she repeated.

He stared at her like she'd asked him to do complicated mathematics in his head. "I'm not drunk."

"Then why are you here, Devlin? I'm pretty sure or at least hopeful that you understood that my text was—"

"A brush-off?" His expression was about as bland as white paint. "Yes. I understood exactly that you were brushing me off, Rosie. But again, I am not here because of that."

Well, hearing it put like that made it all kinds of awkward. Worse yet, she was—oh God—disappointed that he wasn't there because she was trying to cut off contact with him and lessen the chances of them being around each other, and that, well, that made no sense. But that was what she felt in her chest, a sensation like a balloon deflating.

And that was completely messed up.

She shifted her weight from one foot to the next. "Then why are you here?"

"Lawrence owned this building."

Now, she was not expecting him to say that. "Come again?"

His gaze sharpened as he watched her. "I just discovered that this entire building belongs to de Vincent Properties. The shop below and this apartment."

Rosie opened her mouth, but it took her a moment to figure out what to say to that. She was shocked. Honest to God, she had no idea who the owner or owners of this building was. She only dealt with the property manager, but if the de Vincents really owned this building, that was . . .

Wow. That sounded a lot like what Devlin had said Saturday outside of the bakery. Their paths really were . . . destined to cross. As silly as that sounded, a fine shiver tiptoed its way down her spine.

This was . . . too surreal.

First it was her obsession with the de Vincent manor and the legend that surrounded it. Then it was her friendship with Nikki that connected her to the de Vincents. She'd been at the cemetery at the exact same time as him and there was no forgetting the spirit that had come through her reading, the spirit who could very well be his father. And now this? Where she lived was owned by the de Vincents?

That was just way too many coincidences, so much so that even people who weren't superstitious would begin to think there was some kind of higher power involved—a higher power with a sick sense of humor.

But something . . . something was going on here. Something really weird.

A little stunned, she moved aside. Devlin's gaze lifted to hers once again and there was a questioning glint to them.

"You can come in." Her voice sounded hoarse to her own ears. "I didn't know your family owned this building."

Devlin walked in, and she closed the door behind him, throwing the dead bolt. "Really?" he asked.

"Yes. Really." She crossed her arms, feeling chilled and too hot all at the same time. "I don't understand. I mean, I have no idea who owns this building. I just deal with the property manager."

Dev wasn't looking at her. He was scanning the living room and kitchen like he was looking for something. "Who is your property manager?"

"Wait a second," she said, sort of dumbfounded. "You really just learned that you own this building? Like today?"

He strode forward, toward the kitchen area. "Yes."

"How is that even possible?"

Dev moved behind her counter. "That's a good question. I knew every property that is held in our portfolio, all except this one. This property was listed under Lawrence's estate." He stopped and looked at her. "And you had no idea that this building was owned by us?"

"Uh. No. Like I said. I only deal with the property manager. I just assumed he owned the building." She walked over to the fridge and pulled a business card that had the property manager's information on it out from underneath a magnet. She already had his number saved in her phone. Placing the card on the counter, she inched it over to him. "You can ask him yourself. His name is Carl Tassi. I have his phone number."

"Thank you," he said, picking up the card. It went into his pocket and he then knelt down, disappearing out of her view.

"What are you doing?" she asked, and then she heard the cabinet door open. "What the hell?" Darting around the counter, she skidded to a stop. "Why in the world are you going through my cabinets?"

He leaned in. "There has to be a reason why this property was hidden."

"If there is a reason, you sure as hell aren't going to find it with the cleaning supplies."

Devlin shot her a look as he closed the doors and moved on to the next cabinet.

Oh my God!

"Dude, you cannot just bust up into my house and start going through my stuff!"

He peered inside the cabinet that housed her one million mixing bowls. "We've already had this discussion, Rosie. It's an apartment. Not a house."

"Oh my God!" She said it out loud this time as she threw up her hands. "This is seriously not happening."

Devlin rose and slipped past her, moving to the other row of shaker cabinets.

"I apparently drank too much wine, stood up, and fell over and hit my head," she continued as she turned to him. "That is the only explanation for this."

"Does that happen often?" he asked as he rummaged through her cabinets like a trash panda in a dumpster.

"Yeah, at least twice a week. I'm a wino. No," she snapped. "What are you looking for?"

"I don't know." He closed the door on the last cabinet and then pivoted, walking out to the living room.

"You're searching my apartment for something and you don't even know what that something is? Did you eat bath salts today? Should I call someone? An adult? Caregiver?"

Devlin shot her a droll look over his shoulder.

"Do your loved ones know where you are?"

He sighed—sighed like he was exasperated with her when he was in her home, uninvited, going through her stuff! This was pure insanity.

She followed him to her bookcase, where he started peering behind the shelf. "Okay. Seriously. This is just out-there, and coming from me, that's pretty bad."

Stepping back from the bookshelf, he turned to her. Their gazes collided as he took a step toward her. "I want to believe you. As unexplainable as that is, I want to believe that you have nothing to do with Ross—nothing to do with Lawrence. I want to, but I don't believe in coincidences."

Her mouth dropped open. "I told you how I met Ross. And you know I've never met your father. Ever."

"Thought you met Lawrence during your psychic reading?" he queried.

"Thought you believed that was a crock of shit?"

Devlin snorted. "Do you have a closet?"

"Uh. Yeah." Her brows bunched together. "Duh."

He turned toward the beaded curtains and his lip curled. Rosie's eyes rolled, but then he started forward, toward those curtains.

"Don't you dare!" She shot forward.

"Both Lawrence and my mother had this habit of stowing things away in closets. If something was hidden here, something that he didn't want me to know about, it could be in there." He parted the beads like Moses before the Red Sea. She swore to God and the Holy Ghost he didn't even touch the damn things. He took one step into her dark bedroom and stopped so fast that she crashed into his back. "What in the hell?"

"What?" She shoved past him, thinking there must be a full-bodied apparition in her bedroom.

No ghost.

Devlin was staring up at her ceiling. "Are they . . . glow-in-the-dark stars?"

"If you make one snide comment about them, I will roundhouse kick you through a window." Stomping over to the light switch, she flicked it on. "I swear."

Slowly, he lowered his chin and looked over at her. "You know how to roundhouse kick someone?"

"No, but I'm a damn fast learner."

He stared at her for a moment and then his gaze flipped to the bed. Luckily it was made, but he stared at the bed so long it started to make her feel a little uncomfortable. Not in a bad way, but in a way that made her realize her hormones were completely, utterly out of control. Like she was experiencing a midlife crisis or something.

He glanced over at her and she felt that stare again, an intense sweep of his gaze before he turned from her. "Is that the closet?"

"That's the bathroom."

As if he didn't believe her, he opened the door. "That's a surprise."

"What? That I didn't lie? Spoiler alert. I haven't been lying to you. At all."

"I wasn't expecting your bathroom to be so big is what I meant." He lifted a shoulder and then closed the door. A second later, he was at the closet door. "Surprised there isn't a beaded curtain here."

"Oh go choke on a di—"

"This the only closet?" He opened it before she could say a word.

"Yeah, some of us don't have walk-in closets the size of a small house." She hurried over to him and managed to dip under his out-stretched arm, getting in between him and the closet. "You are not going to mess up my closet. I spent all Saturday morning rage orga-nizing that thing."

He stared down at her, expression piqued with confusion. "Rage organizing?"

"Yes, it's something that humans do when they are pissed at people or situations," she explained. "But you obviously wouldn't know what that is since you don't seem to experience human emotion."

His brows lowered. "I experience human emotion."

"Keep telling yourself that, buddy. Maybe one day you'll be a real boy, too."

Devlin's lips thinned.

"Ah! Wait. I am wrong. There's an emotion. Irritation. Anger," she said, glaring up at him. Mad at him. At herself. At how destiny really did keep throwing them together. "So you should understand rage cleaning. Maybe you should try that. Give your staff a day off."

His eyes widened just the slightest. "No one ever speaks to me like you do."

"I'm going to go out on a limb here and suggest that more people need to tell you how they really feel." She planted her hands on her hips.

He dipped his chin. "And how do you really feel?"

"Pretty positive that's obvious," she retorted. "I don't like you."

A slow half grin appeared. "Thought you weren't a liar."

"I'm not," she seethed.

"But you're lying right now, Rosie."

"Am not."

"Oh but you are. You're saying that you don't like me, but we both know that's not true."

Rosie laughed—laughed right in his face as she rose onto the tips of her toes. "You're delusional if you think that's the case just because one out of five times we get along. And as you remember, I'd know, considering I do have a bachelor's in psychology."

He smirked. "Well, what does that bachelor's in psychology say about you telling me you'd let me do anything to you while grinding on my dick just a few nights ago?"

She sucked in a shrill breath and for what felt like an eternity she had no response. He had her there. "It would say that I had temporary insanity."

His head came down even farther as he whispered, "You're lying again, Rosie, and I already don't trust you, so you're not helping yourself here."

"I couldn't care less about you trusting me. I'm not here for your issues." Anger and something hotter and brighter burned through her. "What happened between us at the Masquerade was a one-time-only thing."

"Was it?"

"Yep. You could kiss me right now and it would be about as thrilling as making out with a piece of sushi."

His hands came down on the doorframe, right above Rosie's head. "Is that a challenge?"

She snickered. "No, it's just the truth. You may be a pretty face and a nice body, but I'm about as turned on as a—"

Devlin moved so quickly she didn't have a chance to react. His hand curled around the nape of her neck a second before his mouth came down on hers.

There was nothing soft or questioning about this kiss. It was harsh and rough, and it was like striking a match to a pool of gasoline. There was no room for thought or common sense. Rosie's entire body exploded in reaction, and she wasn't sure how what happened next even happened, but he was kissing her like he wanted to devour every breath and she was kissing him back, clutching at the front of his shirt, wrinkling the crisp, pristine bastard.

An arm folded around her waist as he pulled her out from the doorway of her closet and pushed her against the wall. He pressed into her as his hand slid from the nape of her neck to her jaw. She felt him against her stomach, thick and hard, and molten lava poured through her veins.

This was wrong, so wrong, and she couldn't stop herself even if she wanted to. Her leg moved of its own accord, rising up his. Devlin seemed to know what she wanted, because he lifted her and pressed in again, but this time—oh my—this time the hardest part of him was pushed against the softest part of her.

And he didn't let up.

His mouth moved over hers, and she could taste his desire in his kiss, feel it when his tongue moved across her teeth and then her tongue, and in the way his hips rolled into her as the hand that had been at her jaw slid down. Her cardigan slipped off her shoulder as she squirmed against him, clutching his shoulders when his hand grazed her breast and then went down, under her shirt.

She was drowning in him and she couldn't breathe, and didn't care. Her heart was thumping and her pulse was pounding throughout her body.

"Okay. Okay," she gasped, dragging in air when he broke the kiss. "You've proved your point."

"Have I?" The hand under her shirt closed over her breast. The contact of his palm against her breast stole the breath she'd just gotten into her lungs. "I'm not sure if I've made my point yet."

Rosie moaned, her back arching as those nimble fingers plucked at her taut nipple.

"But that sound you just made?" He kissed her as the arm around her waist tightened and then he dropped his mouth to her neck. "I think I'm well on my way to making that point."

"Asshole," she moaned, her skin red-hot and body aching.

He chuckled against her skin. "That's not nice."

She slid her hand into his hair and pulled, lifting his mouth from her neck. Her eyes opened. "It may not be nice, but it's true."

Those pale blue-green eyes were on fire. "You want me to stop?"

Rosie pressed her lips together as she glared at him. She needed to say yes before this spiraled even further out of control and it was already pretty damn out of control.

He slipped his hand out from underneath her shirt and clasped her hip. "Rosie? Do you want me to stop?"

Did she?

"No," she whispered.

A deep growl rumbled out of him. "Thank fuck."

Devlin pulled her away from the wall and set her down on her feet. Then he let go and stepped back.

She stared at him, watching his chest rise and fall heavily, and she could see how aroused he was. His erection was straining the front of his gray trousers. "Are you stopping?" she asked.

"Hell no," he said, voice gruff. "I'm just . . . savoring the moment."

Rosie felt herself flush even more. "Why?"

His gaze lifted to hers. "Because you're a beautiful danger."

Her heart squeezed. "I'm not a danger."

"Then what are you?" He took one long step and was right in front of her.

She closed her eyes as she felt his hands on her hips. "I'm just . . . Rosie."

"You're not just anything." His warm breath coasted over her forehead as he hooked his fingers around the hem of her tank top. "That's the biggest lie you've told so far."

Rosie opened her mouth, but he lifted her top, gathering the material in his hands and shoving it up under her arms, exposing her chest.

His lips parted. "God."

It seemed impossible, but the ache intensified in her breasts to the point it was almost painful. "You like?" she asked, keeping her arms at her sides.

"Yeah."

She felt dizzy as the cool air of the room teased the tips of her breasts. "A lot?"

"Yeah."

"That's . . . that's nice." She bit down on her lip. "But I still don't like you, Devlin. None of this means I like you."

His lips kicked up on one side. "I don't care."

"Good."

"Because I know the truth."

Then he dipped, lowering his hot, wet mouth to her breast. Rosie cried out as he licked and nipped at her, drawing her nipple deep into his mouth and then letting the puckered skin slip out. He moved to her other breast, and with each tug, each tiny bite of his teeth, it sent a pulse straight to her very center.

"What . . . what truth?" she asked, her head lolling back as his one hand slid down the center of her stomach.

"You may not like me." He blazed a path of kisses across her breasts. "But you like this."

She groaned as his hand slipped inside her bottoms, cupping her. Her hips twitched and churned as he kept his hand pressed against her heat.

"You like this a lot," he said, his finger dragging along the wet, pulsing center. "Don't you?"

Rosie clamped her mouth shut, but her hips tipped into his touch.

"I like it. I liked it Friday night." His mouth moved up her neck, to her ear. "I liked it so much that I fucked my own hand more times than I can count since then. All I had to do was think about how soft you were, how wet. Then I remembered how your mouth tasted and I imagined you taking my dick into your mouth. I never came quicker in my life."

Oh God, who knew Devlin had this kind of mouth on him?

Her entire body melted. "I . . ."

"What?" His finger kept moving, back and forth idly. Never slipping inside her. "What, Rosie?"

"I liked it, too." She moved her head forward, letting it fall against his chest. "I did it, too."

His finger stilled against her. "Did what?"

"Thought of you." Her fingers curled around the front of his shirt. "Thought of you when I touched myself."

Devlin froze and then he grunted out, "Fuck."

"I came . . . thinking about what you did," she whispered. "Even though I don't like you."

"Same." He pulled his hand out of her bottoms and then he pulled them down, yanking them past her thighs. They slid the rest of the way, pooling at her feet. Using his thigh, he pushed her legs apart, spreading them. "I'm going to give us both new material."

And he did.

Devlin de Vincent dropped to his knees before her. His large hands clasped her thighs and then his mouth was *on* her.

Rosie's entire body jolted as her eyes flew open. The breath she took was stuttered as his tongue ran the length of her and then slipped in. "Fuck," she gasped, her hand going to his head, into his hair. *"Devlin."*

He growled against her flesh as he dragged his tongue to the sensitive bundle of nerves. His mouth closed over her, and she about doubled over.

"Oh God." Her hips jerked as his hand came around her thigh and up, and then he was thrusting a finger deep inside her.

And then he . . . he *feasted* on her.

Shudders rocked her entire body. Harsh puffs of air and soft groans. Her legs began to shake as muscles deep inside her tightened and tightened, and her hips moved shamelessly, riding his mouth and his fingers.

Thick lashes lifted and he peered up at her as he worked another finger inside her.

That was it.

Her release happened all at once, crashing into her like a tidal wave that shattered every piece of her. She came and her legs nearly gave out on her. Having no idea how she managed to keep standing as he dragged every little tremor from her, she was panting for breath by the time he lifted his head.

Rosie trembled all over as she looked down at him and watched him run his tongue over his mouth. The mere sight of that sent another twist of pleasure through her.

"Yeah," he said. "That is definitely new material."

It really was, she thought as he rose in front of her, his body tight and thrumming with unreleased desire. He curled his hand around the nape of her neck and brought his mouth to hers.

The kiss . . .

The taste of him and the taste of her mingling on their tongues did something to her. It was like being drunk. It was like falling underwater and holding yourself there until your lungs burned and your vision dotted. It was being consumed by blinding lust and there was no sense, no will, no end.

"You still don't like me?" he asked against her mouth.

"No." Her hands slipped down his chest, to his belt.

His lips curved into a smile against hers as his grip tightened on the back of her neck. "Then prove it."

Chapter 25

*T*his was not why he'd come here tonight. What he'd come for—
what he suspected about her? None of that mattered. Everything in
Dev's head had clicked off the moment his mouth had touched hers
and he was lost from that moment on.

It was like Rosie had some kind of superpower, silencing the constant churning of his thoughts.

And all that mattered right now was that Rosie knew what he wanted
and that she wanted it, too.

His eyes drifted shut as she tugged his shirt free from his pants and
then attacked his belt. She pulled it loose and then made quick work
of the button and zipper. He could still taste her on his mouth as she
pulled his briefs and pants down, freeing him.

"This doesn't mean I like you." Her voice was husky and brought a
faint smile to his mouth. "I still think you're an asshole."

"I know."

Rosie took him in her hand, and the smile faded from his lips as he
groaned. His eyes opened and his chin tipped down. She was watching him, staring up at him as she dragged her hand along his length,
from base to tip. She kept watching him as she smoothed her thumb
over the head of his dick.

"Hell," he grunted.

She leaned in, kissing the center of his chest, through his shirt, and
hell if that didn't cause this weird pressure to clamp down on him.

It was unexpected.

Potent.

Confusing as fuck.

But then she was working her way down, onto her knees just like he'd been before her. He felt his muscles tighten as her warm breath danced over his dick.

Unable to look away, he watched her as he moved his hand up into the mass of curls. She was the picture of sin. The sweater had fallen to her elbows and the tank top underneath was still up under her arms. Those mouthwatering breasts and their plump nipples peeked out from underneath the shirt. The gold chain and ring she always wore was there, the ring resting between her breasts, and she was bare the rest of the way, all the way down and between those pretty thighs.

Dev knew he could come just looking at her like this, her breasts out and all that heaven between her thighs glistening.

She leaned in and that wicked, sharp tongue of hers replaced her fingers.

A cyclone of sensation slammed into him, rocking him to his core. Watching her taste and lick every inch of him, feeling that hot, wet tongue on his sensitive skin, was damn near a religious experience.

"You really don't like me, do you?"

A small smile appeared on her lush, swollen lips. "Not at all."

"I can tell." He tugged her head back, just the slightest. "Rosie?"

Her eyes were heavily hooded. "Yes?"

"Show me just how much you hate me."

That grin increased as she squeezed him with her hand. "If you'd shut the hell up for five seconds, I will."

A rough laugh crawled its way out of him, but it ended on a groan as she wrapped that mouth around the head of his dick and sucked him deep.

Rosie—damn, she knew what she was doing. Then again, the heat of her mouth had blown his senses right out of his head, so he wasn't quite sure if it was just her or her talent.

Fuck.

It was just her.

But she worked him with her mouth and tongue and her hand. Both of them. One cupped his sac and she blew his mind again.

Took no amount of time for him to start moving in and out of her mouth, and he tried to keep it shallow, told himself to keep it controlled and hold himself back.

Rosie moaned around his dick, telling him she was enjoying this as much as he was, and any semblance of fucking control snapped.

He thrust into her mouth as he held the back of her head, completely, utterly lost as release powered down his spine and up the backs of his legs.

The weirdest damn thing happened. The overhead light, the one set in a ceiling fan, flickered rapidly. It went off once and then came back on, the light burning intently before settling. Had to be a power surge, but then he felt the first pulse hit his dick and he did something he'd never done with a woman before.

"Rosie," he shouted her name, and the sound branded his skin and echoed in his head and hit him straight in the chest. He'd never called out a lover's name. Ever.

She didn't try to pull away and she took him, everything in him as he spent himself, his entire body shuddering as he rode the release, and she kept going until nothing was left of him. Nothing.

Only then did he pull her head back, and she stared up at him with glazed eyes. She was . . . God, he struggled to find the right words to describe her in that moment. She was so beautiful, like an angel cloaked in sin, and he wanted . . .

Rosie started to stand.

"No."

Her eyes cleared. "No?"

"No," he repeated. "I'm not done with you."

THEY LAY SIDE by side on the floor, both breathing in large, deep breaths. Rosie wasn't sure she could move. Hell, she wasn't sure exactly how they both got down here, lying on the fluffy area rug. What happened after Devlin told her he wasn't done with her was a blur of deep, shattering kisses and greedy, grasping hands that ended in a second orgasm that was just as powerful as the first, this time with their hands. They hadn't even had *sex* sex and she'd already experienced more pleasure than she had in the ten years since Ian passed.

And that was . . . God, she didn't even know what to think about that.

But the heat and the glow of all that desperate passion was fading and as Rosie lay there, staring up at the ceiling, she wondered how two people could go from arguing like that to lying half-dressed on the floor. This was the second time this had happened. Her eyes closed as she drew in a shallow breath.

Our paths are destined to keep crossing.

Rosie trembled.

What had they just done? She wasn't regretful. Good Lord, there wasn't a cell in her body that could regret it, but this . . . what did this mean?

"Nothing," she whispered.

"What?"

She opened her eyes. "I still don't like you."

He turned his head toward her. "You made that claim, and I just proved that not to be true."

"What we just did doesn't mean I like you." Rosie wasn't sure if she was lying or not, and that left her uncomfortable. The man could be a handful, in more ways than one, but there were moments, very brief moments, she saw glimpses of what she thought he *could* be if he allowed himself to. She sat up and looked around for her bottoms. They were by the beaded curtains. How in the world did they get all the way over there? Her gaze landed on him. His shirt was still rucked up, exposing the tight ridges of his abs. His pants were still open and his cock was half-exposed, glistening and semi-hard. She flushed and looked away.

The man was complicated.

The man was, she thought, a little broken.

The man was absolutely stunning.

And that was a trifecta of run for the hills, but she wasn't running, was she? Unless going down on him counted as running away as fast as she could? Doubtful. It was also doubtful that what they had just shared changed anything significant between them.

"What we just did doesn't mean anything." She said that and she wished it was true, wanted it to be so true for a plethora of reasons. "I mean, I don't think it meant anything for you either, right? It was fun and . . . yeah, it was fun."

Devlin didn't respond to that as she rose on shaky knees. She fixed her shirt and pulled her cardigan closed as she stepped over him. She didn't make it very far. His hand snaked out and wrapped around her calf, halting her. "You think I'm a monster, don't you?"

Her breath hitched as she looked down at him. "I . . . I don't know what I think, but a monster is a pretty . . . severe thing to think about another person."

"Yeah." He let go of her calf. A moment passed as she made her way to where her shorts lay. "Glow-in-the-dark stars and beaded curtains."

Picking up her shorts, she glanced over her shoulder at him. He was still lying there, staring up at her ceiling. There was a relaxed look about him she hadn't seen before, a softening of his jaw and expression. He looked . . . *human*. That would be a weird thing to think about anyone except for Devlin, so it was a big deal. Innately, she knew that very few people saw him like this, relaxed and . . . loose.

And that made him—what? What did that make him to her? Rosie shook her head as she pulled her bottoms on.

"Sounds like an old country song, doesn't it?" His hands rested on his stomach as he let out a deep breath.

"It kind of does." Dressed and decent once more, she turned to him. "It sounds like a country song you'd hate."

A small curve of his lips appeared. Not a full smile, but a smile nonetheless. "There's something wrong with your lights, by the way."

Her brows lifted. "What do you mean?"

"They were flickering earlier. Went off and came back on."

"That's strange. It's never happened before." She walked over to the bed and sat on the edge. Another stretch of silence passed between them. "This . . . this isn't healthy, you know that, right? Arguing and then making out?"

"Confident we just did more than what most would consider making out."

"You're right, but that doesn't change that it's not exactly the healthiest thing."

Lifting his hands, he dragged them up his face and through his hair. "Isn't just about everything that feels good not healthy?"

A short laugh escaped her as she curled her fingers around her knees. She focused on the closet as he lowered his hands to his waist. She knew what he was doing, tucking himself away and zipping up his pants. "Can I ask you something?"

He didn't respond as he sat up.

So, she took that as a yes. "You really still don't trust me, do you?"

"Do you really want me to answer that question?" He leaned back and his body was so long, he was able to rest against the bed, beside her legs.

"Yes."

He was quiet for a long moment. "I don't."

She sucked in a soft breath and she wasn't exactly surprised by it, but she was . . . Rosie wasn't sure how she felt about that.

"I know there are things about me that make you suspicious, but I've done nothing to earn your distrust," she said. "Being called a scheming liar isn't exactly on anyone's top list of things they want people to think about them, especially when they've been nothing but honest."

"I shouldn't have said those things to you," he said after a moment. "Not that this is an excuse, but in my defense, I was a little blindsided by the whole psychic-reading thing."

"I get that. I mean, it's why I didn't say anything about it at first and why I didn't bring it up Saturday night, but there's a football field's length between being blindsided and being a dick."

"I know." He drew in a deep breath. "There's bad history between Ross and . . . my family. You're connected to him and I was caught off guard, so I . . . jumped to a conclusion that I hope is wrong."

"You *hope* is wrong?" Rosie sighed. "It is wrong, Devlin. I wasn't lying when I said I haven't spoken to Ross in weeks. What I told you about the reading I did was also the truth, no matter how crazy it sounds."

He pulled his lower lip between his teeth. A moment passed. "People hound my family, Rosie. They have for years. People try to use us. People try to make money and their careers off our tragedies. I cannot be too careful. None of us can."

Rosie could understand all of that. She really did, because she knew how bizarre the thing with Lawrence sounded and she got that there were a ton of people out there who would want to somehow manipulate the de Vincents. After all, she was able to find what looked like his life in pictures on the internet. She understood all of that, but that didn't excuse his behavior. "Look, I get that you have your reasons for always assuming the worst about someone, but you have been an ass to me more than you've been nice, and while what we just did was fantastic and amazing, it doesn't make up for what came before that, you know? I'm not going to be anyone's verbal punching bag."

He fell quiet again.

She studied him. "I don't think it's just me. I think it's pretty much everyone you don't trust."

"I trust my brothers."

Well, at least there was that. "Why do you have such difficulty trusting people? It has to be more than strangers trying to use you. It has to run deeper than that."

Devlin snorted. "A lot of people simply aren't worthy of trust, Rosie."

Her brows lifted at that. "But how do you know who is when you don't even give them a shot?"

He didn't respond.

"I have another question."

"Of course you do."

"Why do you . . . call your father Lawrence and not, I don't know, Dad?"

His shoulders tensed so much she could see it and he didn't respond for so long she figured he wasn't going to, but then he did. "He was not a good man, Rosie."

She stilled. "I . . . I didn't know that."

"The truth about most evil people is they are extremely skilled at making people believe that they are good," he told her. "And Lawrence was very talented at that and he was also evil. He wasn't just bad or mean. I think Ross knows some of it. My brothers know some of it, but they don't know everything. They don't know what he was truly capable of."

Rosie bit down on her lip. She wanted to point out that he was sharing something with her that you'd have to trust someone to share, but she knew better. She stayed quiet. Maybe it was the psychology classes and training in college, but she knew if she opened her mouth and pointed that out, he would shut down, and she didn't want him to.

"He was like a . . . disease, infecting everyone he came into contact with," he continued, his tone distant. "Sometimes they didn't even know."

"I'm . . . I'm sorry," she said, wishing there was something more she could say.

"The man is dead." Devlin tipped his head back and she saw his eyes close. "And the world is a better place because of it."

She jolted. That was a pretty harsh thing to say about your father, no matter what, but then again, she didn't know his father. If her dad was a serial killer, for example, she'd probably feel the same way as Devlin, and that had to leave your head a bit of a mess, wouldn't it? To hate your own flesh and blood, even if that hate was warranted.

Devlin turned his neck to one side and then the other, as if he were working out a kink. "Lawrence was involved in things that weren't exactly on the up-and-up, so it doesn't take a leap of imagination for me to think there was a reason for him hiding this place."

"He knew you knew about what he was doing?"

"I didn't think he did." Devlin paused. "But I am beginning to think I was wrong about that assumption."

Rosie toyed with the hem of her cardigan. She wanted to ask him if it were possible that whatever Lawrence was involved in had led to his death, suicide or murder. "And you said Ross knows about some of this stuff?"

"Some. Yes."

It hit her then. "That's why you're telling me this, because it's not exactly anything he doesn't know and it's not too detailed."

Devlin didn't respond, but his eyes opened.

"Whether you believe I'm telling the truth or not, that's on you. Not me. And I don't think there is anything I can do to change that."

Devlin pulled one leg up. "And you don't think it's odd that you're living in the apartment of a building Lawrence owned but kept hidden from me?"

"I think it's odd as fuck, to be honest. It's also a little creepy, but I like creepy things."

He made a noise that sounded like a laugh. "Obviously."

"Maybe it's . . . fate. You said our paths were destined to cross and maybe that's true. I don't know, but I do know there are things that happen that no one can ever explain. So, maybe there's a reason? Some higher force at work here," she said, feeling a little vulnerable for admitting that out loud. She then waited for him to laugh or suggest that sounded idiotic. And then she felt a lot more vulnerable.

Because what if it was some kind of weird fate? What if it was destiny? That might sound corny and foolish to some, but so did spirits and curses. So did angels and demons. There were a lot of things out there that people had never seen with their own eyes but believed in. There were a lot of things out there that no one could explain.

So, Rosie let it go.

Let all of it go when it came to them—the text she sent, the decision to put a wall up. There was obviously something there between them, staggeringly red-hot chemistry and maybe . . . maybe even something more. There was no denying that, and they could find out if he'd just let down the walls *he* built.

She took a deep, cleansing breath and made up her mind. "I am lying when I say I don't like you. I do. I'm starting to . . . really like you. Not even sure why." She let out a shaky laugh. "But I do. That's why I stepped back from the whole Lucian investigation. It just . . . I don't know. I'm rambling." She let out a nervous breath. "You can trust me, Devlin."

Silence greeted her.

Rosie squared her shoulders and tried again. "We could just start over. Hi." Leaning forward, she extended her hand. "I'm Rosie Herpin. Ghost hunter extraordinaire."

He didn't say a word. Not for several moments, and in that time, there was a change in him. Almost like she could see him patching whatever holes or cracks that had formed in those walls. They were immediately paved over.

"People can't start over, Rosie." Devlin pushed to his feet. "I should leave."

It was like a blast of arctic air entered the room. *"I should leave."* Those words cycled over and over. Stung, she recoiled and for a moment she was frozen. Wow. That was all she could think. Wow. She just sat there, skin chilled and the back of her throat suddenly burning as she watched him walk toward the beaded curtains.

"I'll see myself out." Devlin parted the curtains, and the soft rattle echoed. "Goodbye, Rosie."

She didn't open her mouth. She didn't say anything. And Devlin didn't look back. Not once as he walked out of her apartment.

Chapter 26

He was an asshole.

He was also an ineffective asshole.

Smirking at that, Dev downed the rest of his bourbon as he walked through the living room of his home, toward the kitchen. Not the living room of the de Vincent manor. He didn't want to go back there tonight. He just couldn't. So, he went to his place at the Port.

The spacious apartment with floor-to-ceiling views overlooking the Mississippi from the living room and the city from the bedroom was furnished with all the necessities, but it currently looked like a home staged for sale. He didn't come here a lot. Sometimes weeks went by before he returned. Sometimes he told his brothers he was going out of town, but in reality he came here and just vegged out.

But this was his place that not even Gabe and Lucian knew about.

He guessed at this moment he was more like Lawrence than he cared to admit. Didn't he keep just as many secrets? Big ones. Life-shattering secrets.

Putting the glass on the island, he grabbed the bottle of bourbon. Tonight had not gone as planned. Shit. He hadn't even checked out her apartment fully, but was that why he really went there? Did he expect to find some secret stash of information?

Who was he kidding?

Dev had seen the opportunity to search Rosie out and he'd seized it, no matter how illogical his reasoning was after the fact.

Truth was, he'd wanted to see her. He'd wanted the *quiet* that came with her. He'd wanted to get lost for a little while.

And that was so incredibly reckless, wasn't it? To go after what he truly wanted. To be selfish, if only for a little while? He hadn't that luxury since he was a child.

"You can trust me, Devlin."

He took a drink straight from the bottle as he walked into the bedroom. Standing at the windows, he stared out over the twinkling lights of the city. His grip tightened on the bottle as he closed his eyes and pressed his forehead to the cool pane of glass.

He felt the presence before he heard the click of a door opening. It wasn't the main door. No. It came from one of the other bedrooms. He probably should've checked the rooms before he cracked open a bottle of bourbon. Turning from the window, Dev waited and he didn't have to wait long.

A shadow in the hallway grew closer to the dim lights of the bedroom. The form stopped at the door.

Dev took a drink from the bottle. "Thought I told you it wasn't safe here."

Silence greeted him and then, "I don't think you used the word 'safe.' More like not 'easy' for me to be here."

"Same thing." Lifting a shoulder, Dev turned back to the window. "When you come here, you need to be careful. You've already been seen once and no one can see you."

"I know." There was a pause. "Obviously."

Dev took another drink. "Why are you here?"

"This is going to sound strange."

A wry grin twisted Dev's lips as he thought of Rosie. "I'm getting used to strange."

"Good." There was a heavy sigh. "Because I had a weird feeling. You know, like there was something going to happen, but I couldn't remember what. Like I missed an appointment. Had those feelings on and off my whole life. At least now I know why."

The grin faded from his face as he took another drink. This one had a bite to it, scorching the back of his throat.

"Are you okay, Devlin?"

Dev closed his eyes as he lowered the bottle and told a lie that was getting harder and harder to live up to—a lie that would not be believed right now. "I'm fine."

FALLING ASLEEP WASN'T the problem. Rosie had locked up after Devlin and curled onto her side, squeezing her eyes shut against the burn. She didn't remember falling asleep. She just knew she woke up and the sun hadn't even crested the sky yet and the stars glowed a luminous white from her ceiling.

Her chest ached as she stared up at the ceiling. Her chest hurt and she was wide-awake and she knew why. Devlin. She'd let her guard down just a fraction, and he'd slammed the door shut right in her face.

She knew better than admitting to him that she did like him. Worst part, she'd admitted that to herself, which was way more damaging than being embarrassed. And yeah, she was embarrassed. Who wouldn't be after admitting that you liked someone and told them they could trust you, and then they literally walked right out the door after you said those words?

But it wasn't even the embarrassment that was the part that caused her to be wide-awake in the early morning hours.

What in the hell was wrong with her?

Groaning, she scrubbed her palms into her eyes until she swore she could see dazzling white lights.

There was nothing wrong with her. She was just interested in a guy who really didn't deserve her interest—a guy she couldn't, for the life of her, even begin to figure out.

But there was a part of her that wanted to. A huge part, and it was more than him just being a puzzle she wanted to piece together.

Dropping her arms to her sides, she flopped onto her side. All the relationships she'd had since her husband passed and not a single one of them had woken her up in the middle of the night for good or for bad. Now, there had been many nights with Ian where she woke up like this, and there had been good and bad reasons for that.

There'd only been two men in her life who had that kind of impact on her. One of them she thought she knew like the back of her hand and didn't. And the other? She couldn't even begin to know or understand.

For what felt like the hundredth time, she told herself this was for the best. The last thing she needed was someone like Devlin randomly bursting into her apartment, looking for God knew—

Wait.

Rosie sat up. What was he looking for? She didn't know, because he didn't know, but he believed something was here—something hidden, which sounded bizarre. However, once again, there was a lot of bizarre stuff that existed in the world.

She tossed the covers off and swung her legs off the bed. He'd gone to her closet like he thought something would be hidden in there.

Her breath caught as she remembered seeing the piece of the wall in the back of the closet. It had looked like it was just coming apart, probably the result of a bad remodel, but . . .

Maybe there was something here.

Sounded legit ridiculous, but she popped up from the bed and hurried over to the light switch. She flipped it on, wincing when she was pitched out of the darkness into the bright light. Opening the closet door, she hesitated and really thought about what she was about to do.

"Am I really looking in my closet at four in the morning?" she asked the silent room. "Yep. Yes, I am."

Pushing her hair out of her face, she knelt down and carefully picked up the stack of jeans she would never wear and placed them outside the closet. Squinting, she leaned in, pushing hanging clothing out of the way. It was too dark. Rising, she snatched her phone off the bed and turned the flashlight on. She returned to the closet. With the bright light, she saw the separation between the walls.

"Okay," she said. "Either there is nothing back there and I'll cause the whole closet to collapse on me or . . . worse yet, I expose a nest of spiders or . . . I find something. Like a . . . skeleton." Her nose wrinkled. "That's dark."

Propping her phone against the wall, she slipped her fingers through the crack and pulled. The wall gave an inch or so. Praying that she didn't unearth bones, spiders, or bring the whole building down on herself, she pressed her lips together and then pulled again. Half of the section of the wall gave as if it weren't even connected to anything, but it caught on another section.

The piece of drywall cracked and then gave way, too. Plaster spewed into the air. Planting her face into her arm, she leaned back, her fingers gripping a section of the wall.

Rosie opened one eye and groaned. "Ugh."

White dust covered several of the hanging shirts. Probably should've taken the clothes down. Too late for that. Sighing as she pictured the massive amount of laundry she was going to have to do, she turned over the piece of wall. There were hinges, rusted over, but this section wasn't just a piece of a wall. It was a kind of door.

That she'd ripped off.

"What the hell?" Rosie picked up her phone and leaned in, shining the light into the hole she'd created.

At first all she saw was wood beams—stable wood beams—and then she tilted the phone down. Something . . . something was definitely inside there. Square and thick. There were several things in there, actually.

Her heart began thrumming as a cold chill snaked down her spine. Part of her couldn't believe she'd actually found something.

Thinking this was way too surreal, she reached inside, picked the first item, and pulled it out.

A dust-covered photo album.

Rosie twisted away from her closet and dragged her fingers over the album, brushing the dirt off before setting it aside. Leaning back into her closet, she reached inside and picked up something cool and smooth.

"An . . . iPad?" Turning it over, she saw that it was most definitely a dusty iPad. "Okay, this is . . . this is wow."

Having no idea if anything else was left in there, she picked up the phone and leaned in, shining the light down into what appeared to be a cubbyhole. Something else was in there. A slim, rectangular box. She picked it up and recognized the velvet under her fingers.

A jewelry case.

Heart still thrumming heavily in her chest, she sat back on her knees and opened the box. "Wow," she whispered, eyes widening as she stared down at a diamond tennis bracelet. A beautiful, well-kept bracelet.

Unbelievable.

Her gaze lifted to the closet as she held the jewelry case. Devlin came here thinking he'd find something hidden and there was—holy crapola, there was a diamond bracelet, an iPad of all things, and a . . . photo album.

Rosie looked over at the album as she placed the case on the floor. Her stomach pitched as she picked up the album. Curling her fingers around the dusty edges, she hesitated before she opened it up. She didn't know why she took a moment, but that chill came back, skipping over her shoulders, and there seemed to be some small voice in the back of her head that told her not to.

To put the bracelet, the iPad, and the album back in the wall, because even though God didn't put these items there, someone did for some reason.

Rosie opened the album.

There were two photos on the first page—one was of palm trees and the second was of a glistening beach and sparkling ocean water. She turned the page and saw a photo of a man lying in a patio lounge chair, shirtless and in red-and-blue swim trunks. A pair of sunglasses and a baseball hat shielded his face. The picture below that was of a younger woman with blondish-brown hair, probably a few years older than Nikki. She was wearing sunglasses, too, smiling widely at the camera as she held two large tropical-looking drinks.

Rosie turned the page and gasped as she stared down at the next photo—the picture of a couple at night, standing in front of lit tiki torches. No sunglasses. No hats. Both wore pastel blue-and-pink leis. The girl was really pretty and vaguely familiar to Rosie, like she'd seen her before, but it wasn't the woman who caused her to gasp. It was the man standing next to her, with his arm thrown over her shoulders as he smiled at the woman.

She knew him. "Oh God."

It was Ross Haid.

Chapter 27

*H*ere you go."

Rosie was jarred out of her daze as the white-shirted waiter placed her root beer on the table in front of her. "Thank you."

The young man smiled. "Do you need anything else?"

"No. I'm waiting for someone." She picked up her glass as the waiter nodded and then backed off to take care of his other tables.

Looking up from where she sat in her booth, tucked next to the eye-catching, stunning spiral staircase that led upstairs, she saw Ross Haid yanking open the door to the Palace Café.

There had been several moments in Rosie's life where she wanted to throat punch herself.

This was one of them.

But after what she found in *her* apartment, she needed to talk to Ross and this wasn't a conversation one could have over the phone, because seriously, *what the hell*? Why were there photos of Ross, a reporter who was after the de Vincents, hidden in her apartment—an apartment owned by the de Vincents. If Devlin had found this . . .

God.

She wouldn't be able to blame Devlin for thinking she was somehow involved in whatever insanity that was going on, because this—this was certifiable.

Rosie toyed with the napkin as she watched Ross cut between the mostly empty tables. The restaurant wasn't ridiculously cramped yet since it was still early in the day, but give it an hour, and all the tables outside and inside would be filled even though it appeared as if it were seconds away from pouring.

A tentative smile appeared on his handsome face as he slid into the booth across from her. "Got to say, Rosie, I'm still surprised that you called me this morning and wanted to meet."

Not as surprised as she was, considering the last time she'd talked to him, she'd basically threatened physical harm if she saw him again.

"I don't plan on having a long conversation with you, Ross. I still *really* don't like you." And there was a world of difference in her tone when it came to how she said that to Devlin and how she said it to Ross.

Ross knew it was true. The smile faded from his face as he sat back and shoved a hand through his blond hair. "I deserve your anger. I should've been up-front with you."

"If you were up-front with me, I never would've set you up on a date with Nikki." She tugged the paper off her straw. "That's why you weren't up-front."

"I was interested in Nikki and not just—"

"Don't want to hear it." She lifted a hand, silencing him. "Because I am *this* close to kicking you in the balls under this table and it's not why I'm here."

A muscle flexed in his jaw as he looked away. "Then why are we here?"

"I have something I think you might find interesting." Rosie took a sip of the drink, loving the taste of the sassafras root. She reached into her purse and pulled out the photo. "Here."

His brows knit as he stared at her for a moment and then he glanced down. The blood drained from his face so fast, he looked queasy. His hand shot out as he snatched up the photo. "Where . . . where did you find this?"

"In the closet of my apartment," she explained. "There was a photo album full of vacation pictures. Looked like Hawaii."

Ross didn't respond as he stared at the photo of him and the mystery lady.

"So, I want to know why there's a photo of you and some woman hidden in my closet."

He gave a slow shake of his head as a tremble ran down his hand, shaking the photo. "You found this in your closet?"

"Yep." She crossed one leg over the other. "That's bizarre, right?"

"I . . ." His gaze flew to hers. "Did you find anything else?"

"No," she lied smoothly. "Just the photo album."

"Did you bring the album with you?"

Rosie shook her head. "Just this picture. I want to know why this was in my closet."

Swallowing hard, he laid the photo facedown on the table and then placed his palm over it. "You don't know who she is?"

"No. Should I?"

"God," he muttered, closing his eyes. "How quickly people forget."

Rosie had no idea what he meant by that.

"I saw you last Friday—at the Masquerade."

Surprised, Rosie jolted. "Excuse me?"

His eyes opened and that brown-eyed gaze slid back to Rosie's. "Recognized you immediately, even with the mask. Surprised as hell to see you there. You left and headed upstairs," he continued. "And Devlin de Vincent followed shortly after."

She bit down on the inside of her lip. Had it been that obvious? Did others notice? A better question formed. "Did you follow us?"

A moment passed. "Just enough to know you were in a room with him. That is all."

Rosie sucked in a sharp breath as the hand in her lap curled into a tight fist. Had he overheard them? Revulsion churned in her stomach. She wasn't sure she could trust that he was being honest about not hanging around and listening, because truth was, she didn't know the man sitting before her. She'd thought she did at one time, but not anymore. "Did you . . . did you hear us?"

He hesitated, and Rosie knew. She freaking knew that he'd heard something, and that was enough, but before he could continue or she could respond, a waiter in a white button-down appeared.

"Would you like to order something?" the waiter asked, his gaze moving back and forth between them.

As Ross shook his head, she forced her hand to unclench. Her nails had dug into her palm, leaving little indents behind. "We're not ordering anything," she said.

The waiter raised a brow but wisely backed off, moving to check on other tables while Rosie focused on taking a deep, slow breath.

Ross briefly closed his eyes. "Rosie—"

"Shut up," she hissed. "I'm not here to hear about your perverted, creepy stalker tendencies. Why was this picture—"

"The de Vincents killed my girlfriend."

Every muscle in her body locked up as she stared at Ross, her body reacting to what he said before her brain caught up.

Ross leaned forward, holding her wide gaze. "You want to know about this picture?" He slapped his palm down on the photo, rattling the glasses and silverware. "They killed my girlfriend and covered it up. I know they did. I just can't prove it. Not yet."

She still clutched the strap of her bag. "What are you talking about?"

The lines of his face were tense. "Do you remember a woman named Andrea Joan?"

She gave a little shake of her head as she searched for the name. "It's familiar."

"She was an intern for Stefan de Vincent," he replied, his voice hushed.

The intern—the *missing* intern. Holy crap balls. Rosie's eyes widened even further. Now she remembered the name. It had dominated the news for months before everyone just . . . stopped talking about her, stopped discussing what could've happened to her and if she was alive or dead.

"I see you remember now," Ross said with a dry, broken-sounding laugh. "That woman in the picture with me? That's Andrea."

"Holy shit," she whispered, her mind going in a thousand different directions as she drew in a shallow breath. "I thought she was missing—"

"Missing?" His lip curled as he coughed out another dry, broken laugh. "That's what *they* want everyone to believe. After all, they made it look like that. To the world it looks like she just up and left, leaving everything behind, but I don't think that's what happened to her."

She felt cold as she stared across the table. "I don't know what to say, but that doesn't answer how a photo of you two is hidden in my closet."

Ross took a drink of water and cleared his throat. "We met at Tulane. Never believed in love at first sight. Thought it was a crock of shit until I saw her sitting in my comm class freshman year. Thought she was the most beautiful woman I had ever seen and the first time she argued with me—told me that three elven rings were not forged by Sauron—I fell in love with her."

Her brows lifted. "*Lord of the Rings?*"

"Huge fans." A quick smile appeared and then faded. "When she was offered the internship with the senator, a paid internship, she thought this was her foot in the door. It was a big deal. Andrea had been so excited, and before she . . . she disappeared, I . . ." He halted and then took another drink of his water. "I was going to propose. She . . . vanished a little over two years ago and people have already forgotten she even existed."

Sadness seeped into her as she watched him curl his fingers over the photo. She was still angry with him, but this . . . God, this was sad.

"Before she disappeared, she started acting strange." He slid his hand off the table and left the photo there. "Working odd, late hours and she became detached and distant. She was—I don't know how else to describe it other than she became paranoid. Convinced that someone was following her. I couldn't get her to open up to me, to tell me what was going on. She would always tell me she didn't want me to get involved, because she knew me—knew everything about me, and knew that I would, most definitely, get involved."

He paused, glancing around the mostly empty restaurant. "Something was going on with the senator—with the de Vincents. That much I knew, because I . . . I started to follow her. A week before she went missing, she met with Lawrence de Vincent at the Ritz."

Keeping her expression blank, she couldn't help where her mind went with this information. To her, it sounded like Andrea might've been having an affair. "How do you know it was Lawrence and not Stefan? They were identical twins, right?"

"Right. But I got close enough to him to tell the difference. I did my homework, Rosie. Stefan always wore a gold Rolex on his right wrist. Lawrence wore his on his left," he explained. "Besides, Stefan was at some event in Baton Rouge that night. She met with Lawrence."

As much as she probably shouldn't continue this conversation, she couldn't stop the curiosity from growing. "But what does that mean? Why would she go to Lawrence?"

"I think that she went to Lawrence over whatever she knew Stefan was involved in. I don't know why she would've trusted him, but I guess that doesn't matter now." His jaw flexed. "Because Lawrence is dead."

"Lawrence committed—"

"No. No, he did not, Rosie." Ross flattened his hands on the table again. "That's utter bullshit. The police knew it. That chief? The one who died?"

"The one who had a heart attack while driving?"

"The man was in his forties with no known preexisting heart problems, but he had a massive heart attack that caused him to lose control of his vehicle and crash?" He snorted. "Come on."

Many people didn't know they had heart conditions until they woke up dead from a heart attack. "Ross—"

"I know it sounds weird, but hear me out. The de Vincents are involved in some bad shit and they have unlimited money and resources behind them to cover up said bad shit," he said, keeping his voice low. "Look at what happened with the Harringtons. Parker's dead. Sabrina's missing?"

Rosie stilled. The reporter had no idea that Nikki was involved in Parker's death, and she sure as hell wasn't going to tell him. "Okay. What if the senator was doing something shady that your girlfriend got mixed up in? What does that have to do with Devlin and what does that have to do with your picture being in my closet?"

Dipping his chin, he lifted his gaze to hers. "I think Devlin killed his father."

Her mouth dropped open, and for a long moment she couldn't think of anything, but then the night with Sarah came rushing back to her.

Murdered.

That was what Sarah believed the spirit had said, and if they'd been correct in assuming that the spirit was Lawrence?

But to suggest that Devlin was a murderer? Rosie shook her head. "Why do you think that?" she asked.

"Besides the fact that man has the cold, dead stare of a sociopath?" he asked.

Rosie flinched. "He does not."

"Really?" Ross leaned in. "You're involved with him, aren't you? Rosie, God, you need—"

"What I am or am not with Devlin is none of your business," she said, cutting him off. "But what is my business is why that was in my apartment."

Ross fell back, lips pursed. Several moments passed. "Your place used to be Andrea's."

Her stomach pitched. Words completely left her. Holy . . . A tremor coursed through her. She'd moved into her apartment two years ago. Andrea had gone missing a little over two years ago, and there'd been a delay in moving in, because the previous tenant had left . . . their belongings behind.

"Oh God," she whispered. She was living in the same apartment as the missing intern? The apartment owned by the de Vincents? Did Ross know that? Did he . . . ? "Wait." Her gaze centered on Ross. "Wait a second."

"What?"

"You . . . you came to me to do that piece on ghost tours in the Quarter. It was, like, a month after I moved into the apartment. I never saw you before then."

Ross tipped forward again, clutching the side of the table. "Rosie—"

"Did you know that I moved into her place when you sought me out?" she demanded, eyes widening. "Is that why you sought me out?"

"You don't understand," he said. "I started investigating the de Vincents and their staff. You came onto my radar when I saw that you were back from Alabama and were friends with Nikki, the daughter of their main house staff."

Stunned, she sat back. "Holy God, Ross, you sought me out because I was friends with Nikki and living in your girlfriend's old apartment?"

"Listen, you still don't understand. You were connected to the de Vincents in a way and you moved into my missing girlfriend's place," he explained. "That's suspicious as fuck."

Everything . . . everything was suspicious as fuck at this point.

"I didn't know about the hidden thing in the closet," Ross said. "That's really strange she'd hide a photo album in there. Are you sure that's the only thing that was in there, Rosie? It's really important. If there was anything else, it could be really important. Are you sure?"

"Yes." Rosie lifted her gaze to his. "I'm sure."

Chapter 28

For the second time in one day, Rosie was about to do something that sort of made her want to punch herself.

And it wasn't even noon yet.

Fingers tightening around the strap of her heavy bag, she lifted her other hand to knock, but before she could make contact, the door swung open.

Richard Besson stood in front of her, the lines in his forehead increasing as his brows lifted. "Rosie! What a surprise."

"Hi." She smiled as the man stepped forward, giving her a quick, warm hug.

"Are you here to see Nikki?" he asked, clasping her shoulders. "She's in Gabe's quarters. I can take you there—"

"I'm not here to see Nikki. I'm here to see Devlin."

The surprise that filled the man's face was tangible. "You're here to see Devlin?"

"Yes." She fixed what she hoped wasn't a creepy smile on her face. "I know that sounds weird, but I really do need to see him. Is he here?"

Nikki's father's expression smoothed out and for a moment she feared that he was going to tell her no and shoo her away. "He is here, actually. He hasn't left for his office yet." Richard stepped back, holding the door for her. "I can see if he's available."

"That would be awesome. Thank you." She followed him inside, stopping in a massive, grand foyer that she was positive was the size of her entire apartment.

Richard closed the door behind them. "Come. I'll have you wait for him in the sitting room."

Her wide eyes swung from the sparkling chandelier to the grand staircase to, finally, Richard's back. He was leading her to the right, through an archway that connected to a long hallway. Everywhere she looked, there was something to gawk at. "The woodwork is amazing. My word," she said, staring at the trim that had what appeared to be vines engraved into it.

"Yes. Isn't it?" Richard walked them past several closed doors before stopping in front of one that looked like others they'd passed. "Gabriel did all the woodwork you see in here and most of the furniture."

"Wow." Nikki had mentioned Gabe's side business, but Rosie really hadn't realized how talented he was until that moment.

"Why don't you have a seat in here, and I'll go see if Devlin is available. Okay?" When Rosie nodded, Richard smiled at her. "Would you like anything? A drink?"

Rosie shook her head as she glanced around the sitting room—a room that had the kind of fancy chairs and sofas that looked like people didn't sit in them. "I'm fine."

Richard nodded and then started for the door. He stopped and turned back to her. "I didn't get a chance to thank you for being there for my daughter."

"Oh." She felt her face warm. "It's no big deal. That's what friends do."

"That's what real friends do, Rosie. There is a difference."

Richard left before she had a chance to respond. Watching him shut the door, she closed her eyes and let her head fall back.

She'd left Ross sitting in the café and gone straight to her apartment and grabbed the rest of . . . Andrea's belongings. Devlin's paranoia must be catching, because she waited to make sure Ross hadn't followed her before she got in her car and drove out to the de Vincent manor.

Part of her hadn't been thinking, because she could've called Devlin, but this was something he needed to see and not hear over the phone. Rosie exhaled loudly as she neared the velvet-cushioned sofa. Coming here could be a mistake, but for some reason, and maybe it was instinct, she didn't believe what Ross had told her. That Dev had killed his father. But that didn't mean the family—possibly the senator—didn't have something to do with that poor woman's disappearance or Lawrence's death.

Rosie honest to God had no idea what the hell was going on, but she didn't trust Ross. Not after what she'd learned, and she did know that Devlin had no idea that her apartment was owned by his father until this weekend. He sure as hell hadn't known what was hidden in that closet.

Whatever was going on, he needed to know about this.

Biting down on her lip, she turned in a slow circle and checked out the room. It was beautiful. Stunning furniture set around a large fireplace. Interesting artwork adorned the walls. Placing her bag on the Victorian-style sofa, she walked over to one of the paintings. It appeared to be of a cemetery—tombs shaded in grays. Goodness. The artwork was so well-done that it nearly looked like a photograph. Only upon close inspection could you see the brush strokes. Her gaze fell to the right corner, to the initials LDV.

Rosie's head cocked to the side. "LDV . . . ?"

"Stands for Lucian de Vincent."

Letting out a little shriek, Rosie spun around and found that she wasn't alone. "Oh my gosh." She pressed her palm into her chest. "I didn't even hear you come in."

The blond de Vincent smiled. "I can be very quiet when I want to, which isn't very often." He grinned as he leaned against the fireplace mantel. "We haven't had the chance to meet . . . officially, have we?"

"No." She stepped away from the painting. "I'm—"

"Rosie," he answered for her as his grin turned into the kind of smile she hadn't yet seen on his brother's face. "I know who you are and I have so many questions for you."

DEV WAS FEELING the effects of too much bourbon and too little sleep as he stepped off the treadmill and grabbed a fresh towel.

He was sweating liquor, Jesus.

Probably would've been wise of him to take the day off, but running shut his head down. Always had. The moment his sneakers hit the belt or the pavement, he thought of nothing. His head was quiet, and he realized this afternoon that the quiet he experienced when he was running was different from the quiet he felt around Rosie. He'd mistaken that time for the same kind of quiet, but it wasn't. When he was with her, he didn't think about Lawrence or his brothers, Sabrina, or what was in Nebraska and now in his condo. But he was still thinking. Not like when he was running, but his mind was solely focused on her when he was with her, and damn, if that was just about as good as the silence he got when he was running.

"You can trust me."

Fuck.

Those words were going to haunt him.

Wiping his face, he tugged the earbuds free as he walked toward the laundry hamper. He tossed the towel in and then opened the door. He made it about three feet when Besson rounded the corner.

"I've been looking for you." Besson's long strides were that of a much younger man. "You have a visitor."

"Please tell me it's not Stefan," he remarked, stopping.

The man was too professional to show a response. "No. It is Rosie Herpin."

Dev blinked. "Excuse me?"

"It's Rosie Herpin," Besson repeated, clasping his hands behind his back. "She's a friend of—"

"I know who she is." He couldn't believe that she'd come here. "Where is she?"

"In the formal sitting room."

Pivoting around, he started down the hall, his heart thumping heavier than it did when he was running.

"Devlin," called Besson. "A moment please?"

He stopped and looked over his shoulder, impatient. "Yes?"

A look of confusion settled into Besson's expression. "Would you like to take a moment to . . . get ready?"

For a second, Dev wasn't sure what Besson was referring to and then the man looked pointedly at Dev's bare chest.

"I can have Nikki keep her company while she waits," Besson offered.

That would be the appropriate thing to do. His shirt and body were soaked in sweat. "That won't be necessary."

There was a flash of surprise that replaced the confusion on his face, and he couldn't blame the old man for that look, but he wasn't going to waste time on showering and changing. He prowled to the end of the hall and hung a right. Within moments he was nearing the sitting room, and his steps slowed as he heard laughter coming from the room.

What the hell?

His steps picked up and he cursed under his breath as he reached for the handle. He heard Lucian's laugh joining Rosie's. Shit. Rosie alone with Lucian was not going to end well for him. Yanking open the door, his gaze immediately found Rosie. Weird as hell, but the first place he looked was where she was, sitting on the sofa. In that moment, he completely forgot that she wasn't alone. There was only her.

Her gaze flew to him and those hazel eyes widened. Those wild, thick curls were loose, falling over her shoulders and framing her heart-shaped face. She was dressed casually, wearing a long-sleeve shirt that slipped, exposing the tantalizing skin of one shoulder. Who knew a shoulder could be so . . . enticing?

Dev had seen Rosie less than twenty-four hours ago and he was still rattled by the sight of her, still caught off guard by . . . by everything about her. He was held immobile by it, absolutely enthralled. There was something wrong with that, he was sure.

A throat cleared, and with great effort, he pulled his gaze from her to where Lucian was sprawled in a chair. "What are you doing in here?" he asked.

Lucian's smile was a warning of mischief. "I was keeping Rosie company while she waited for you. I told her it might take some time since you were working out, but obviously I underestimated how eager you'd be to join her." His gaze drifted over Dev. "I was just telling her about the time you were suspended from boarding school for breaking curfew."

Dev's brows shot together. "What are you talking about?"

"He's playing coy. Don't let him fool you," Lucian said, winking at Rosie. "Dev is a lot wilder than he lets on. He's such a rebel."

"Is he?" Rosie murmured, lips twitching like she was struggling not to laugh.

"I know what you're talking about. However, I believe you're not telling the whole story," he remarked dryly. "I was caught breaking curfew because Gabe and Lucian decided they were going to sneak out by tying bedsheets together to climb out the window. I was there to stop the two from breaking their necks."

"You're always there to stop us from doing something foolish," Lucian replied with sarcasm.

"Mostly and definitely not always." Dev's gaze shifted back to Rosie. "If you'd excuse us, Lucian?"

"Of course." Lucian rose, turning to Rosie. "Have your team members contact me directly about the house."

Rosie nodded. "Will do."

Dev opened his mouth.

"Perfect. I will handle it from here," Lucian continued smoothly. "Don't forget my offer. I hope you will join us, Rosie."

"Join you for what?" Dev demanded, his gaze swinging back to his brother.

Lucian just smiled at him and then brushed past him as he walked out of the sitting room, closing the door behind him. Turning back to Rosie, he asked, "Join him for what?"

"Wow," she said, staring at him. "You do own something other than trousers. I'm shocked."

He tilted his head to the side.

"Lucian invited me to dinner with him and his girlfriend at the end of the month," she answered. "And with Gabe and Nikki. There's some kind of party they are having."

"He did?" The party that she spoke of was where Lucian planned to propose to Julia. Why he'd invite Rosie, a woman neither of them knew, meant he was surely up to something. "So, you would be the third wheel?"

Her lips curved up on one side. "Actually, I would be the fifth wheel if I'm the only other person attending, but I'm under the impression that it's a *party* and not a dinner date, and I also assume that you would be there also."

Dev would be. "Is that why you would go? Because you assume I would be at this party?"

A long moment passed and then she exhaled heavily as she pressed her hands to her knees. "I'm not planning on joining them. So, you don't have to worry about me being there."

Disappointment flickered through him, but he ignored it. "Why are you here, Rosie?"

She looked away from him, to the purse sitting next to her. "I found something I thought you should see. Actually, I've learned something, too, I thought you should know." She glanced back at him and frowned. "Do you think you could find a shirt that's not glued to your skin?"

He lifted a brow. "Why? Does it make you uncomfortable?"

"Yes."

Dev stepped toward her. "You've seen . . . and felt far more than my chest."

"I know." She shifted on the couch and she stared at him in such a manner that made him wonder if she wished to touch him. His cock liked the idea of that. "You must . . . work out a lot."

"I run daily. So, it's not that it makes you uncomfortable," he clarified. "It distracts you."

Slowly, her gaze lifted to his. "If I said yes, would you find a different shirt?"

"No."

A quick grin appeared and then disappeared as she shook her head. "Then I'll have to make do."

"Yes. You will."

Rosie reached for her bag. "Whatever. I've seen enough nice bods in my life. Yours is nice, but not special."

His brows flew up, but before he could get her to elaborate on that statement, she went on, "After you left last night, I remembered something. The other day when I was rage cleaning my closet—"

"That thing apparently only people with human emotions do that I'm unfamiliar with?"

"Yes. That thing. Anyway, when I was organizing my closet, I saw that there was something jacked up about the back wall, but I forgot about it until after you left."

His curiosity was officially piqued. "What do you mean by 'jacked'?"

"It was like the wall had come apart, but it hadn't come apart. It must've been a hidden door or something," she said. "I pulled it apart and there was something back there. Actually, there were three things back there."

The sweat cooled on his skin. "What did you find, Rosie?"

She wet her lower lip and then picked up her purse. "I'm really hoping I'm making the right call by bringing this to you and I don't end up like the last tenant of my apartment."

"What do you mean about the last tenant?"

"You don't know? I moved into my place about two years ago and you know who went missing around that time?" She clutched the top of her bag. "Andrea Joan. Your uncle's intern."

It felt like the floor moved under his feet. "Andrea Joan lived in your apartment?"

"Apparently. Not only that, she was Ross Haid's girlfriend." She let out a nervous laugh. "Something I just learned this morning." Reaching inside the bag, she pulled out a maroon photo album and laid it on the coffee table. "This was back there. It's just a bunch of pictures of a vacation. Ross is in them. Did you know that was his girlfriend?"

Dev picked up the album and opened it. "I knew."

"Of course," Rosie murmured. "Did you know the only reason he searched me out in the first place was because I moved into that apartment and he knew I was friends with Nikki?"

His gaze flew to hers as his back tightened. "I suspected he befriended you because of your relationship with Nikki, but I didn't know she'd lived there. That wasn't the address that was on file for her."

"Ross confirmed it was her place," she said. "I met with him this morning, because I saw the photo album and I didn't know who she was at first."

Dev tensed as he closed the photo album. "Is that so?"

"Yeah. He asked if that album was the only thing I found and I told him yes, but that's not the truth. I did find two other things." She reached into the bag and pulled out a slender jewelry box. "It's a diamond bracelet. Kind of weird someone would hide that with a photo album, right?"

"Right." He took the box and opened it. His jaw clenched as he stared at the bracelet.

"But that's not the strangest thing. There was also an iPad in there." She pulled it out, and Dev damn near fell over. "It's dead, but I figure it just needs charging and . . . a man with your talents and money can probably find someone to unlock it." Leaning over, she placed it on the coffee table. "I have no idea she lived there or that any of this stuff was there. And I have no idea what is on that iPad, because there has to be something, right? Because why would you hide that?"

Hell.

Dev placed the box on the table as he stared at the iPad. God only knew what was on that device, but Rosie was right. He had the means to find out. Part of him could already hazard a guess. Whatever was on that tablet was probably why Andrea disappeared.

"That's not all," Rosie said, glancing at the closed door. "It's what Ross also said, and maybe you already know this—"

"He thinks we have something to do with Andrea's disappearance? He's made that abundantly clear in the past."

Rosie placed her bag back on the couch. "That's not all he thinks."

"I can only imagine," he replied dryly.

"He told me that . . . that he thinks you murdered your father."

A muscle thrummed along his jaw as he thought back to the photograph he'd received at the Red Stallion. "Did he say why he believed this?"

"Not really."

"And what do you think, Rosie?"

"Honestly? I don't know what I think. I mean, I think Andrea might've been having an affair with your uncle. Why else would she hide a bracelet? And the way Ross talked, it sounded like she was having an affair, but maybe . . . maybe whatever was going on with Andrea has to do with your father," she said. "Ross said that Andrea was acting paranoid and she also met with Lawrence a week before she disappeared. Maybe she did know something and she told him— told him what she knew and . . ."

"He was murdered for it?" he supplied.

She dragged her hands over her thighs and then rose. "Maybe? Look, I have no idea what is going on here, but you came to my apartment because you found out that your father owned it. And then I find out the place was rented by this woman who was tied to your uncle and then went missing. Something is going on here. I don't know what, but it's freaky." She started to pace in front of the couch. "I just thought you needed to know."

Dev wasn't sure how to process this—that she'd brought these items to him. "And you didn't think Ross needed to know?"

"Ross is a liar," Rosie shot back. "Not that I don't get his need to find out what happened to his girlfriend, but he's never been honest with me. He's a liar."

Moving without thought, Dev stepped in front of Rosie. She drew up short and tipped her head back. As close as they were, he could see the flecks of green in her eyes. Her lashes lowered and he knew she was staring at his sweat-defined chest. She stepped back, and it took everything in him to resist the urge to follow her.

Rosie drew in a visibly deep breath. "Have you gotten in contact with the property manager?"

"Left a message first thing this morning."

"Good. Can you let me know . . . ?" Her nose scrunched in a rather adorable way. "Wait. I don't think I want to know if you find out anything."

A twisting motion swept from his stomach to his chest. If this was some elaborate plan put in place by Ross, then wouldn't she want to know?

Holy shit.

Dev felt close to faint as he stood there. Could it be possible that she hadn't been lying this entire time? That the little voice that whispered that over and over could be telling the truth?

"Anyway, that's why I came here and I hope . . . I hope I made the right choice." She turned from him and picked up her purse, sliding the strap up her arm. "I don't know what is going on with your family. Seems like a lot of . . . just a lot, and I pray that it doesn't end up affecting Nikki any more than it has—"

"It won't." His gaze dipped to that one bare shoulder. "That I can promise you."

She stilled as those eyes latched on to his again. "I . . . I believe you."

It felt like his entire body jerked, but it was just his heart. Shock rippled through him. "Why would you trust me?" he asked, genuinely confounded. "If what Ross suspects is true and Andrea went missing because she found something implicating Stefan, then why would you come to me? The same thing could happen to you."

"That's a good question, especially considering how much you don't trust me, but what I do know is that Ross has lied to me since the beginning," she said, holding his gaze. "And as far as I know, you haven't lied to me. That's why."

Dev looked away, and then for the first time in a very, very long time, he wanted to tell the truth. That he was nothing more than a liar, worse than what she could ever think Ross had lied about.

Chapter 29

*D*ev didn't make it far before he ran into Lucian. His brother took one look at what Dev held in his hands and frowned.

"Do I even want to know why you're carrying a photo album, a bracelet, and an iPad?" he asked.

"No. You don't."

"Kind of looks like you're up to some MacGyver shit right there." Lucian fell into step beside him. Several moments of surprising silence passed. "I like her."

Dev stopped and looked at Lucian.

"I'm talking about Rosie, just in case you're wondering."

"You spoke to her for how long and you know you like her?"

"I spoke to her long enough to know she's nothing like Sabrina."

"That doesn't say much, you know that, right?"

Lucian laughed. "It doesn't and does."

He eyed his brother and then asked, "What do you think of her?"

"Are you asking me that as a serious question?"

"Yes."

Lucian blinked once and then twice. "You never ask for my opinion nor do you ever care what I think—"

"I care about what you think," Dev interrupted, and waited until his brother looked up at him. He hated the look of surprise he saw in his brother's eyes. "I do."

"That's not . . . what you usually say to me."

That was the truth and Dev wasn't sure how to respond to that. "I mean what I just said."

"And I . . . I believe you." Lucian looked like a feather could knock him on his ass. "Nikki has nothing but good things to say about her. She's quick-witted and funny as hell. Beautiful, too."

Dev took a breath, but it didn't go very far. "She is . . . very beautiful, but she—"

"She introduced Nikki to Ross. So what? What else has she done?"

He couldn't really answer that. God, he couldn't. Everything else was suspicious, but these weren't things she had done.

"You can trust me."

He hadn't trusted her, but she had trusted him—trusted him enough to bring him the evidence that in Ross's hands could bring the entire family down, even though his brothers didn't know what had been happening.

"I've done crazier and less trustworthy things in my life, as you know."

The corner of Dev's lips twitched. "God, don't I ever."

"I like her," he repeated. "Most of all, I like the way you are with her."

"What?" Dev frowned. "You haven't—"

"You forget that I did see you with her at the Masquerade. I saw you step in front of her to block her from me. I saw you goad me away from the door so she could come out," Lucian said, grinning when Dev's eyes narrowed. "And I just saw you walk into a room that she was in without stopping to shower and put *appropriate* clothes on. You, Devlin de Vincent, who is always the definition of put together, was decidedly . . . unkempt."

"Unkempt?"

"Sweaty. Half-naked. That's unkempt. I've never seen you like that. Not even when we were boys," Lucian pointed out. "And I've never seen you like that with a woman. Ever. So yes, I like her and I like how you are with her."

And with that, Lucian clapped him on the shoulder and said, "Don't let what Sabrina did or what Lawrence did screw up any more than they already have. Now, I have a woman to go annoy the ever-loving crap out of. She likes it when I do that, though."

Dev watched Lucian go, once again reminded that his youngest brother was far more observant than anyone, including he himself, gave him credit for.

ROSIE WAS IN the kitchen of the bakery the next morning, placing the sheets of pralines on the counters to cool, currently doing everything in her ability to not think about what she'd found in her closet, what Ross had said, or how Devlin had responded to it.

She wasn't thinking about any of that.

Instead, she was focused on what she was going to do from here. Restlessness had invaded her senses again, and that usually ended with her enrolling in college yet again, but seriously, she already owed enough in financial aid that she'd be paying for that crap well into retirement.

So no more college for her. Duh.

Which meant she either needed to put one of those degrees to use in some way or . . . or maybe it was time to move. Tossing the oven mitts aside, she glanced up toward the front of the bakery. She hated the idea of leaving her family, but Bella was going to inherit this bakery, as it should be. She'd put the time and effort into it, and besides, Rosie wouldn't go far. Maybe—

Her entire body locked up.

Who was she kidding? She didn't want to leave New Orleans. This bizarre, crazy, cultured city was her home—her only home. But this restlessness? It was an itch that came every so many years. She hadn't felt this way before Ian, but she'd been young then and—

Her sister appeared in the doorway, and her black Pradine's shirt didn't have a single fleck of flour on it. Whatever magical ability her mother had that made her resistant to flour had passed on to Bella.

Rosie was covered in it.

She probably even accidentally snorted some of it.

"Hey," she said.

"You busy?" Bella asked.

"Nope. They just need to cool." Rosie stepped back from the counter. "You need help up front?"

"Not exactly." A smile appeared. "You have a visitor. Perfect timing, too, since Mom and Dad are coming in later today and aren't here right now."

She lifted her brows. "Why would . . . ?" She trailed off as someone joined Bella in the doorway of the kitchen. Her breath caught as she watched Devlin step around her sister. "All righty. I understand why you would say that."

Bella smirked and then pinned a look on her that said, yet again, that Rosie had a lot of explaining to do.

At that moment, Rosie felt like God had a lot of explaining to do.

Devlin nodded at Bella as she left the kitchen and then that intense gaze landed on her. He was dressed like she normally saw him, like he was leaving an important business meeting, but all she saw was the white shirt that had clung to his muscles, leaving little to the imagination.

She would never be able to forget that. Nope. Not as long as she lived.

"Making pralines?" Devlin asked, looking down at the counter. His presence was so odd in the kitchen and it seemed like he took up the entire space.

"Yep." Picking up a damp towel, she wiped her hands off and then tossed the towel onto the counter. She figured he was here over what she'd brought to him yesterday. "Do you want to step out back? It's more private."

He looked at her strangely and then nodded once more.

Wondering why her heart was racing, she turned to lead him out the narrow back door and into a small courtyard her parents had placed plastic table and chairs in for the workers during breaks. The tall, ivy-covered brick walls afforded a level of privacy from the alley in the back and when the rosebushes were in bloom, it was quite beautiful back here.

Sitting down in one of the old chairs, she clasped her hands together. "What can I do for you?" she asked.

Devlin didn't sit, but stood in front of her, and when she asked that question, he cocked his head. "That's a loaded question, Rosie."

A lick of heat curled low in her stomach. "Not really."

"Hmm," he murmured, turning from her.

She drew in a shallow breath. "Why are you here? I'm assuming it has something to do with what I brought you yesterday."

"It doesn't." Devlin picked up the white plastic chair with one hand. "Not really."

"Okay," she drew the word out as she watched him carry it to where she was sitting.

He placed the chair in front of her and sat down. "We need to talk."

She thought he looked rather strange sitting in the old plastic chair, dressed like he was. Her gaze lifted to his face. "About what, Devlin?"

"About a lot of things." He leaned toward her, resting his arms on his knees. "I've been thinking."

"Congratulations."

One side of his lips kicked up. "I've been thinking about *us*."

"Us?" Rosie squeaked. "There isn't an us."

"There is most definitely an us."

Dumbfounded, all she could do was stare for several moments. "What is there to talk about when it comes to us?"

"A lot."

Her expression was pinched as she stared at him. "Okay. You're going to have to be way more detailed than that, because I tried talking to you, Devlin. Did you not get that? When you came over to my apartment and after what we did, I tried talking to you. Do you realize that?"

Thick lashes lowered, shielding his eyes. "Yes. I do."

"I don't think you do." She tipped forward, keeping her voice low. "And there really isn't anything to talk about. You don't trust me. You don't trust anyone, and I don't even know how someone can build a friendship out of that."

"What do you think we're building here, Rosie?" His voice was now just as low as hers.

She sucked in a sharp breath. "Nothing—we are building nothing."

"That's not true. We've been building toward something since you brought me peonies in the cemetery." He moved slightly, pushing one leg out so his knee pressed against hers. "We're not working on a friendship."

Her eyes widened. "Wow, Devlin. You could've just texted that to me or kept that to yourself."

"You're not getting what I'm saying." A small grin appeared. Not a big one. Just a tiny hint of emotion. "Look, I'm not good at this, at . . ."

"Talking?" she suggested. "Acting like a human?"

His lips thinned. "I guess both."

"Glad we're on the same page." Placing her hands on the arms of the chair, she started to rise. "I need to get back to work."

"I was wrong about you."

Rosie halted.

Eyes the color of the sea in winter focused on hers. "And I judged you unfairly. I thought the worst about you, because I . . ." He sat straight and looked away. "I've seen the worst in people. That's not an excuse. Not at all. But I know that I misjudged you and I . . . I want to make that up to you."

"Make it up to me?" she repeated dumbly. "What? Do you want to buy me a new car? Fix my closet for me? Because I really do need to fix that."

That small, lopsided grin appeared again. "I meant something more along the lines of dinner at Firestones."

"Firestones," she whispered. "*The* Firestones?"

"There is only one of them."

"But . . ." Rosie trailed off. She'd never eaten at Firestones, because it was so expensive you felt like you had to give them money when you passed the restaurant. Everyone in the city knew of their food. They were legendary, with melt-in-your-mouth steak and fresh, tasty seafood you never had to worry about getting a flesh-eating bacteria from. Normally, she'd give her left arm for a chance to go to Firestones, but she couldn't fathom eating dinner with Devlin anywhere. "You're asking me to go to dinner with you? At Firestones?"

He reached between them and caught the curl that had fallen against her cheek. "I am."

"We don't even like each other."

"I don't think that is necessarily true. I've given you plenty of reasons not to want to like me, but I can change that," he said, tucking the curl behind her ear, causing her arm to jerk. "I like you, Rosie."

"You have a really terrible way of showing someone you like them."

"I'm trying to fix that," he replied with an arch of his brow. A moment passed. "I want to fix that."

She laughed, but the sound died among the dead rosebushes as her gaze searched his face. "You're being serious, aren't you?"

"I am."

All she could do was stare at Devlin. She was not expecting this. Not after he'd walked out on her when she told him he could trust her, when she tried to start things over between them. Hit rewind. Devlin had made it abundantly clear, but here he was, sitting in front of her, asking her on . . .

"Is this a date?" she asked, and her heart did a silly little jump. "Like a *date* date?"

"I am under the impression there is only one kind of date."

"No. Not true. There are all kinds of dates. There are friend dates. Getting-to-know-you dates. Dates where you take someone out only because you want to hook up. There are dates—"

"It's a *date*, Rosie. Between two people who are undeniably interested in being more than just friends," he cut in. "That's the kind of date I'm talking about."

She opened her mouth, closed it, and then tried again with no success. No words. She had absolutely no words. She'd be less shocked if a full-bodied apparition appeared directly in front of her.

"I know I've been . . . difficult—"

Rosie laughed. She couldn't hold it back. "I'm sorry? You've been 'difficult'? That is not the word I'd use."

"You probably have a lot of words you'd use and I'd deserve every one of them, but . . ." He drew in a deep breath. "But I shouldn't even be entertaining the idea of us. If you had any idea of what was going in my life, you'd understand why I'd be hesitant to start anything."

"I think I know some of it, obviously, but you haven't told me anything about your life, Devlin. Nothing."

"That's not exactly true. I've told you stuff I haven't shared with anyone."

"You've given me the CliffsNotes version, Devlin. Telling me that you believe your house is haunted isn't exactly sharing your life with me. You told me you had a near-death experience, but you gave me no details about how that happened. You've told me your father was a horrible man, but it wasn't something that apparently other people didn't know. You've shared with me, but you've held back on everything you've shared."

"And I want to change that. For the first time in my life, I want to change that, because I . . . I can't stop thinking about you." Pink flushed his cheekbones, but he didn't look away. "I've tried. God, I've tried, but I can't, and I've never experienced that. Not like this."

Rosie sucked in a sharp breath. Was he being for real? Everything about him screamed that he was, but Devlin . . . He was gorgeous and he was complicated and he was . . . a little broken. She'd already realized all of that about him, and that was a lot. *He* was a lot.

A riot of emotions roared through her. There was sweet anticipation mixing with hesitation. Anger swirling itself around confusion. Hope tinged with doubt. Rosie wanted Devlin. Obviously. And that went beyond the physical. Obviously. She wanted to like him, and a huge part of her did, but Rosie couldn't help but hold back.

"Devlin, I want to say yes, but . . ."

"But that's not a yes."

"No," she whispered, feeling a burn crawl up her throat. "You don't trust me."

"I was wrong about that. I should've trusted you from the beginning. I know better now."

A sad smile tugged at her lips as she shook her head, looking away. "But I don't trust you, Devlin."

"You brought that stuff to me yesterday. You have to trust me."

"With that stuff? Sure. But not with what's really important," she admitted. Pushing the curl that had fallen free once more out of her face, she sighed as she looked around the courtyard. "You asked me the night of the Masquerade how my husband died and I didn't answer. I don't even know why. I guess it was something I just didn't want to talk about then."

He leaned toward her again. "And it's something you can talk about now?"

Rosie drew in a deep breath as she reached for the necklace and pulled it out from underneath her shirt. Her fingers closed around the ring. "Ian and I were high school sweethearts. Married as soon as we graduated. Cliché, right? But it was real. We loved each other. He worked long, hard-as-hell days while I went to college. He supported me and I wanted nothing more than to be the best freaking wife ever. He liked my weirdness and I liked his . . . quiet. It wasn't perfect. We argued and fought over stupid shit, but we never went to bed angry at one another. I thought we'd be together forever." She laughed softly at that as she dragged her finger around the ring. "And I thought I knew everything there was about him. I was wrong."

"How were you wrong?"

Her finger stilled, but she didn't look away from the ring. "My husband, who was my best friend, used a gun I didn't even know he owned and shot himself in the bathroom."

Devlin swore softly under his breath and when he spoke, his voice was soft. "Rosie . . ."

She didn't look at him. She couldn't. "He called the police before he did it, so I wouldn't come home from class to find him like that. He also did it in the bathroom so it . . . it would be easier to clean up. You know, we had just begun looking for our first home, and I had no idea that he was suffering like that. Looking back, were there signs? Yes. But he hid it well. And I think he hid it because he didn't want me to be upset." She lifted a shoulder as she dragged her teeth over her lower lip. "It's been ten years and as long as I live, I'll never really understand what led him to that point and I'll never stop feeling a little guilty, like there could've been something I should've done or seen. Even knowing that what he did wasn't my fault doesn't change how the human mind works. So, I know what it's like to live with someone I thought I knew. I know what it's like to lose someone that was your entire world. And I know what it's like to be so damn mad at someone while still missing and loving them. I can't even tell you how many times I wished he'd shared what he was going through with me, but all that wishing isn't ever going to change the past."

Letting go of the ring, she took another deep breath. "I'm telling you this because you don't know me, Devlin. You don't know what I've lived. Just like I don't know what you've lived and are living and you've used your past to judge everyone you've come into contact with. If I did that, I'd never open myself up to anyone again. I wouldn't even want friends after going through losing someone the way I did. But that's not me. That hasn't been my choice. That's your choice.

"And I guess I'm telling you this because I . . . I want to like you." Rosie looked at him then, and she found that he was watching her. "I think that underneath it all, there's something really good here, but I thought I knew my husband and I didn't. And I don't even know what to think or feel when I think about you. One minute you're making me laugh, even if you're not trying to, and the next you make me want to ninja kick you in your face. If someone had said you'd come here today wanting to take me out on a date and prove that there is an us, I would've laughed in their face. Hell, I did laugh in your face. I've never in my life met someone so infuriating and confusing as you, and I . . . I just don't know, Devlin. You want to trust someone and you're saying that you want to try that with me, but are you really willing to do that? Really?"

Devlin looked away and a muscle thrummed in his jaw. "Damn, you really did get a bachelor's degree in psychology, didn't you?"

She grinned at that. "I did." Her grin faded. "And I have to be willing to take that risk with you. Because it would be a huge risk."

His gaze came back to hers.

"I could *really* like you, Devlin. And I know nothing in life is guaranteed, but I thought I knew my husband and I didn't. With you? I already know I don't know the real you. I don't know what makes you tick. What secrets you haven't shared yet or why you're the way you are."

He was quiet for a moment. "I don't know what to say other than

I'm so sorry. No one should have to experience that. I cannot even imagine what you went through."

"But you have," she whispered.

"None of us believe Lawrence killed himself," he admitted quietly, and saying those words out loud seemed to have some kind of effect on him. His shoulders appeared to loosen. "Not Gabe. Definitely not Lucian."

She was thrown by the statement. "So, you do think he was murdered?"

"All I know is that whatever happened to him, he brought it on himself."

Rosie didn't know what to think of that. What he'd said about his father was enough for her to know that he wasn't a good man, but as his son, wouldn't he care to seek justice? Wouldn't the brothers? Or was Lawrence that bad? "But your mother?"

"She didn't kill herself, Rosie."

At first, she didn't think she heard him right. "What?"

He didn't look away. "My brothers and I believed that she'd killed herself. So, I do understand in a little way what you went through, but it's not the same. I don't think any two losses are the same, but what we always believed about our mother's death wasn't true."

Rosie's thoughts raced as she stared back at him. "What do you mean?"

"Do you remember my sister? Madeline?" When she nodded, he drew in a deep breath that lifted his shoulders. "This is something that only my brothers, Julia, and Nikki's parents know. Nikki may know if Gabe shared it with her, but very few people know the truth. If it ever got out, it would be a media circus." He wasn't speaking loud enough to be overheard by a cricket as he said, "Our sister went missing the same night as our mother died. Lucian always thought that Madeline found Mom and had flipped out. Gabe and I . . . well, we weren't as close with Madeline as Lucian was. We had no idea why she disappeared that night. Not at first. So, we always believed that she saw our mother and maybe she couldn't handle it. Madeline was always . . . a little unstable. She was proof that the de Vincent curse could very well be accurate."

"The whole thing about de Vincent women either dying mysteriously or not being exactly the sanest people in the room?"

"Exactly." He dipped his chin, staring at his hands. "Anyway, come to find out our sister had run off and hooked up with our cousin Daniel. Lived with him this entire time. He kept her hidden."

"Holy moly," Rosie whispered. "For real?"

"For real. Nice, right? Cousins. She reappeared this spring. We found her in the pool, facedown and unresponsive. Lucian thought that she'd been held by someone against her will and she'd escaped. Truth was, she and Daniel ran out of money and they plotted to kill Lawrence. It was a terrible plot."

"Wait." Rosie rocked backward. "Did she . . . ?"

"She did a lot of things, Rosie. A lot. Daniel, who was never the sharpest tool in the shed, blew his cover and endangered Julia, who'd been hired to take care of Madeline. There was a horrible fight that night. Daniel tried to shoot me, and he died in the process, and Madeline slipped from the roof. Died this time, for sure." He swallowed, and Rosie was absolutely thunderstruck. "Come to find out our mother caught her with Daniel. They'd gotten into a fight over him and Madeline . . . she pushed our mother, causing her to fall. That's why she ran away that night."

"Oh my God . . ." Rosie placed her hands on his forearms. If his sister had killed their mother, then it was quite possible she'd killed Lawrence, with the help of the cousin, and Devlin just didn't want to say it. "Good God, Devlin . . ."

"We kept it quiet. There's no reason for anyone to know what really happened. What justice would come from all of it? Madeline had been missing for a decade as it was, and she was definitely gone now. We buried her in a private ceremony in our tomb and . . . and those skeletons returned to the closets." A wry grin appeared. "And to never be spoken about again."

She was shocked that he was telling her this. My God, she could make a fortune if she sold this story to the tabloids since it was more dramalicious than a soap opera. Not that she'd ever do that, but she was surprised that Devlin would share this with her without forcing her to sign a non-disclosure in blood.

"Sometimes we've got to wonder if that curse is true. I mean, you know the stories about the accidental deaths and crazy ways people have died on our property. But there's another part of the curse. It's not a bad part, but people only ever focus on the bad."

"I know everything there is about that curse. I've never heard there was another part."

His gaze lifted to hers. "I'll make you a deal. I'll tell you what the other part is if you go to dinner with me."

Her stupid heart did another happy jump. It felt a little less stupid now but still. Even as big as what he'd just shared was, it didn't mean he was going to do a one-eighty. "Devlin . . ."

"Give me a chance, Rosie. Just one chance."

"I don't know. You've just shared something pretty major and completely scandalous." She laughed dryly, still processing what he'd shared. "So, yeah, you're trying, but—"

"A chance, Rosie," he repeated. "One night. Dinner. Tonight."

Her stomach dipped like she was on a roller coaster. "I can't tonight."

"Then tomorrow night."

She opened her mouth, but Devlin leaned forward suddenly, curling his fingers around her chin. The contact was like touching a live wire. "Just dinner, Rosie. Please." *Please.*

Rosie had the distinct feeling he didn't say please a lot, if ever, and that one word, so softly spoken, punched a truck-sized hole through the wall she was desperately trying to build up between them. "Okay."

"Okay?" His eyes widened.

"Okay."

"I was prepared to get on my knees and beg."

She grinned. "You can still do that if you want."

He let out a low chuckle. "I would, but I have a feeling if I got on my knees, I'd end up doing something your sister would not want to walk in on."

Oh dear.

Her entire body flushed hotly. "You're probably going to regret this dinner."

"There are few things I regret. This would definitely not be one of them."

"We'll see," she murmured.

"You're right. We will. I'll pick you up at seven tomorrow night. Wear something formal." He touched the tip of his thumb to her bottom lip, startling her. She sucked in a sharp breath. The touch was as soft as velvet and light as air, barely there, but her entire body felt it. A frisson curled low in her stomach as her heart lodged itself somewhere in her throat.

"You have beautiful eyes, Rosie." His thumb smoothed along her lower lip and then his hand was gone. "Tomorrow night."

"Tomorrow night," she repeated, and she had the distinct feeling she had just made a deal with the Devil.

Chapter 30

*S*abrina is dead." Archie's gruff voice was lanced with frustration as Dev stared down at the iPad.

"What?" Dev was unsure if he'd heard him correctly.

"The Mercedes was found abandoned in a small town near the border and she was in it. I'm thinking she was going to make a run for Mexico."

"What happened?"

"Shot in the back of the head, execution-style."

"Jesus." Dev sat back in his chair.

"I'm not a magic crystal ball, but if she was involved in what Lawrence was doing, she could've reached out to the wrong person and they deemed her a risk," Archie responded. "That means you need to be careful."

A muscle flexed along Dev's jaw as he picked up the iPad. "I'm always careful."

"You need to be more careful. You don't know if she talked before they took her out," he pointed out. "There's nothing more for me to do at this time. I'm heading back."

"Understood."

"I'm also emailing off some info I've ferreted out that has to do with Stefan and Lawrence. Various contacts within and outside the States." Archie paused. "What are you going to do with this information?"

Dev smirked. "Burn their entire worlds down."

"Good. Call if you need me." Archie disconnected the call.

Dev was hoping he wouldn't need Archie again, but he had a distinct feeling that he would.

"Fuck," he said, closing his eyes. Sabrina was dead, and he wasn't sure how he should feel about that. He hadn't wanted her dead. At least not until she answered some questions for him, and he knew that sounded cold as hell, but the woman was a wretched human being. He opened his eyes, unsure of how to process the news of her murder. The whole thing left a bad taste in his mouth, but as terrible as this sounded, it was good news—great news for Gabe and the family he was trying to build, because as long as Sabrina was out there, they wouldn't be safe.

What Archie suspected was probably true. Sabrina had reached out to the wrong person for help and in the process, they deemed her too much of a risk.

His gaze returned to the iPad. Once it had been charged, it had been shockingly easy for it to be hacked and unlocked. After only a few moments of having access, Dev knew why Andrea had hidden the iPad.

Andrea had screenshots of files of suspicious campaign donations and activity. The same kind of deposits that Dev had discovered himself, and now Dev's suspicion of Stefan's involvement, however limited in comparison to Lawrence, was confirmed.

What was also on the iPad proved Rosie's suspicions correct. Andrea had been having an affair with Stefan. There were copies of hotel receipts, detailed notes on the time spent with Stefan, some fairly graphic.

There were . . . intimate pictures of Stefan.

Ones that Dev could've gone his entire life without ever seeing. Either Andrea was planning on exposing Stefan or blackmailing him, and by some horrible twist of fate and misguided trust, she'd gone to Lawrence. Andrea had learned a de Vincent couldn't be blackmailed.

Or trusted.

The truth was, if she had gone to her boyfriend, what had most likely happened to her would've also happened to Ross.

Lawrence and Stefan would do anything and everything to get away with their crimes.

Sickened, he placed the iPad in the bottom drawer of his desk and locked it. Something had to be done about Stefan, but like with Lawrence, Dev knew the man had just as many connections. It would be hard to make any charges stick let alone come to light for public scrutiny.

The general public had truly no idea of how much money could really buy.

All the information he was collecting would be turned over. Most if not all of the de Vincent involvement would be scrubbed, but even if it got out or if the others Archie had emailed him about implicated Stefan or Lawrence, it was a risk Dev was willing to take if it meant shutting down at least one bracket of an international issue.

Rising from behind his desk, he shelved the Stefan issue for later. There was something else he must do. Leaving the office, he went in search of Gabe and found him in the kitchen, thankfully alone.

Gabe was at the island, watching . . . water boil. He looked up as Dev walked into the kitchen. "Yo."

Stopping at the island, he frowned. "What are you doing?"

"Gonna make some hard-boiled eggs." He gestured at a small bowl, and Dev saw a half dozen eggs stacked in it. "Just waiting for the stupid water to boil." He straightened. "Anyway, learned something interesting."

"From boiling water?"

Gabe snorted. "I'm not supposed to say anything, but I have to. I'm proud of you. Well, I hope I'm right for being proud of you."

His brows lifted. "For what?"

A small grin appeared on his brother's face as Dev picked up a chocolate bar that was on the island. "Do you know where Nic is currently?"

"I assume she is upstairs or at her own place?" He peeled back the wrapper.

"You'd assume wrong." Gabe grinned. "Nic is over at Rosie's, because Rosie is getting ready for a date—a date with you."

Dev tensed. He was doing everything he could not to think about Rosie at the moment. Not because he didn't want to, but after dealing with what he had been looking at this morning, he wanted all thoughts of her nowhere near that shit.

When he didn't respond, Gabe's eyes narrowed. "You do have a date with Rosie tonight, right?"

Breaking off a piece of chocolate, he popped it into his mouth. "I do."

The water was starting to bubble. "And why are you going out on the date?"

He chewed thoughtfully. "Why do most people go out on dates, Gabe?"

"There's lots of reasons, but you're not most people." Using tongs, he picked up the eggs and began to place them in the water. "So, when I heard you asked Rosie out, I was surprised, but then I remembered Lucian saying he saw you with her the night of the Masquerade."

He broke off another piece of chocolate. "He did."

Gabe stared at him. "And that's all you have to say."

"Pretty much." He ate the other piece of chocolate.

His brother sighed. "Are you into Rosie, Dev? Or is this some kind of weird thing that's going to end up pissing off Nic, which is then going to piss me off?"

Tossing the chocolate bar back onto the island, he went over to the fridge and grabbed a bottle of water. "This isn't something weird. I'm . . . I'm into Rosie. I like her. A lot."

When Dev turned around, Gabe was just standing there, staring at him with an egg gripped between the tongs. "What?"

"I . . . I think that's the first time in I don't even know how long you've answered a question directly," Gabe replied. "I'm shocked. I think I'm about to have a heart attack. Or maybe hell just froze over. Or—"

"It's not that shocking." Dev came back to the island. "Rosie is . . ." He trailed off, unsure of how to describe her. "There's something about her that I like and that's all I have to say about that."

Gabe was still staring at him. "You're . . . you're smiling."

Was he? It took him a moment to realize that he was smiling.

"You're not anymore," Gabe added dryly.

Dev blinked and shook his head. "I was actually looking for you and not to discuss Rosie or my facial expressions."

Gabe laughed as the eggs knocked around inside the pan. "I'm all ears."

Dev knew he wouldn't be laughing for very long. "As you know, I've had someone looking for Sabrina."

Everything about Gabe changed in an instant. His jaw hardened. "Any updates?"

"Yes. She was found near the border," Dev told him. "She's dead."

"What?" Gabe planted his hands on the island as his chest rose with a deep breath. "You for real?"

"Yes. It appears she was murdered," he said. "That's all I know. I'm sure it will hit the news soon enough." He took a deep breath. "The only good news is that you don't have to worry about her anymore. Not with Nikki or your son."

Gabe stared at him and several moments passed. "You're right. I'm . . . I'm relieved, and I . . . That's a shitty thing to be relieved about, isn't it?"

"No." Dev was quick to correct him. "That woman was dangerous, Gabe, and maybe we would've gotten lucky and she would've left the county or maybe she would've come back. We don't know, but at least with her, it's over."

"It is." Gabe kept staring at him. "Did you do it?"

"What?" Dev pulled back.

"Did you have her killed?" he asked point-blank.

"No." Dev held his gaze, not even surprised that his brother would've thought that about him. Which was, notably, messed up. "I sure as hell did not. That is not a lie, Gabe. I swear to you."

"Okay. . . ." Gabe turned off the burner. Several moments passed. "I've got to ask, Dev. I've got to ask this again. Why were you with that woman?"

Dev lifted his gaze to his brother's, and for the first time, he wanted to tell his brother why, but he couldn't, because Gabe was the reason why, and he didn't want to put that on his brother.

So, all he said was "It's complicated."

"I AM STILL in a state of shock," Nikki said from where she was perched on Rosie's bed. Nikki finally looked like the woman Rosie knew, bruises gone and face bright. "I mean, I think this is a dream."

Rosie turned from her closet, a dress in each hand. "Yeah, well, you're not as shocked as I am that Devlin wants to go out on a date."

"At Firestones, no less." Sarah wandered into the bedroom, a bottle of wine in one hand and a glass in another. Bree was behind her, towing a garment bag.

Since Rosie had never been to Firestones or been on a date with Devlin de Vincent, this was a five-alarm, code-red situation.

She'd already showered, shaved nearly *everything*, lotioned herself up, picked out the sexiest matching bra and panties she had just in case the date went very, very well, and had done most of her makeup. Problem was now she didn't have a dress. Correction. She had lots of dresses, but none that she wanted to wear.

"No, you guys don't understand." Bree laid the garment bag on the bed. "Nikki and I know the de Vincents."

"And we know Devlin, so him wanting to go on a date is breaking news," Nikki chimed in as Bree sat beside her.

"The man was engaged," Sarah said, pouring a glass of wine. "I'm sure he's been on plenty of dates."

Rosie exchanged a look with Nikki, thinking she probably knew that the relationship between Sabrina and Devlin wasn't filled with dates, flowers, and happy kisses.

"What do you think of this dress?" Rosie held up the one on the left.

Bree lifted a dark eyebrow. "If you were reading tarot cards on Jackson Square, then sure."

"Hey, what's wrong with that?" Sarah set the wineglass on the nightstand.

"Nothing." Bree held up her hands. "But Rosie is going to Firestones not Woodstock."

Nikki laughed. "Yeah, not that dress."

Sighing, she hung that one back up. "And this one?"

"Are you going clubbing?" Sarah asked, sitting down in the chair in the corner *with* the wine bottle. "Because that little black dress is going to have your ass and your breasts out."

Rosie looked at the dress. "Nuh-uh."

"Actually, you wore that to a club in Alabama and you had to keep pulling it down," Nikki pointed out.

"Oh yeah. . . ." Turning around, she hung that back up and then went to her wineglass. Her stomach fluttered in a way it hadn't in many years when she thought about her upcoming date. She didn't think she was making a mistake by accepting his offer. If she had, she wouldn't have said yes, but she was nervous, because . . . because she liked him and she, well, she wanted this to be the start of *something*.

"Drink," Sarah ordered from the corner. "You look like you need a drink."

That she did.

Picking up her glass, she took a sip as she eyed the black garment bag behind Bree. "I'm hoping there's a magic dress in there that won't look like I'm attending a club or Woodstock."

"There is." Bree smiled brightly and then reached behind her, picking up the bag. Hooking it on the closet door, she unzipped it. "I knew you weren't going to be able to pick out a dress, so I brought this one over. I only wore it once since I haven't had a good reason to wear it twice, but since we're the same size, I think you can work this."

Sarah lowered the wine bottle. "Oh wow."

Deep hunter green material peeked out between the folds of the garment bag, and when Bree tugged the bag off completely, Rosie really thought her heart had stopped.

"Now, that is a beautiful dress," Nikki announced, eyes wide.

Rosie clasped her hands together as she stared at the stunning dress. Beautiful, flattering color. Point one. It had quarter-length sleeves that were off the shoulder, but it looked like she could still wear a bra and not a strapless one. Point two. The neckline was low cut, but it didn't look like she would fall out of it. Point three. The waist was gathered high and the dress was fitted over the hips and thighs. Point four. It didn't appear to be too short or too long, and that was point five. If it fit, that would be a point explosion.

"Try it on," Nikki ordered. "I've got to see this on you."

Grinning, Rosie pulled it off the hanger and quickly slipped it open. The dress fit perfectly.

"I want to borrow that dress," Nikki said.

Bree grinned. "You can borrow it next."

"And me?" Sarah asked.

"You, too."

Turning in front of the mirror, the fluttering in her stomach increased. The color brought out the green in her eyes and it really did work with her complexion.

"That is beautiful," Nikki said.

"And your ass looks amazing," Sarah added.

She twisted sideways, checking out the back. It was cut low, and her ass did look pretty nice.

This . . . this was definitely the dress.

"You have those black stiletto booties still?" Bree asked, starting around her. "They would look perfect with that dress. Whoa." Bree drew up short. "What in the hell happened to your closet?"

Oh crap, she'd forgotten that the mess was visible. "Oh. Um, yeah, there was an issue with the drywall. It's being fixed." Slipping past Bree, she found the shoes in question. "Are these the ones you were talking about?"

"Yep." Bree turned from the closet. "Ah, look at the time. He's going to be here soon, and we should probably go—Sarah, did you drink all that wine?"

Sarah lifted the bottle. "Uh, no. There's at least two glasses left."

"Really?" Bree sighed. "You owe me drinks tonight."

"You guys going out?" Rosie planted her hand on the wall as she slipped her foot into the shoe.

"Yep. She's my date." Sarah grinned. "I hope she's not expensive."

"Girl, I'm always expensive."

After promising to provide them with an update about the date as soon as she could, she said goodbye and tried to ignore the way the butterflies in her stomach and chest had turned into flesh-eating carnivores hell-bent on chewing their way out of her.

Why in the world was she this nervous?

Everyone had left except Nikki. She hung back as Rosie did the final makeup touches. In other words, she was one more coat away from making her eyelashes look like spider legs.

Nikki leaned against the doorframe, arms crossed loosely over her chest. "What are you thinking, Rosie?"

"Honestly? I don't know." She glanced down at the tube of mascara. "Can I ask you a question? Do you think this whole thing is absurd? Me going out with Devlin? *Me?*"

"I think it's pretty far up there on the list of things I never expected to happen. That has nothing to do with you, but mostly Devlin. I have a hard time picturing him going out on a date with a cardboard cutout of someone."

She shot Nikki a look. "You know, he's not that bad."

Nikki raised her brows.

"Okay." Rosie grinned a little as she returned to her reflection. "He can be difficult, but he's far from boring and he's . . . well, he's just different."

"Indeed," Nikki replied dryly.

Rosie laughed as she lifted the wand. "It's weird, Nikki. I mean, we did not get along, but there's something there between us. Anyway, any advice?"

"It's you usually giving me advice," she stated as Rosie swiped the mascara over her lashes. "How the times are changing."

Rosie snorted. "I know."

"The only advice I can give you is that these brothers, these men, haven't exactly had the easiest of lives even with all the wealth and power," she said. "They all are complicated, and I have a feeling that Devlin is the most complicated of them all."

Rosie lowered the wand and shoved it back into the tube, thinking that even Nikki, who grew up in the shadows of the de Vincent brothers, didn't know exactly how complicated Devlin was.

Chapter 31

From the moment Dev saw Rosie in that stunning dress that picked up those flecks of green in her eyes to this very second while she was scouring the dessert menu, he was absolutely and irrevocably *entranced*.

And he'd never felt that way about anyone or anything. Unlike his brothers and even his sister, he didn't have any special hidden talents. He wasn't good at painting or working with wood, and even though Gabe claimed Dev could sing, it wasn't something he did often and couldn't even recall the last time he had. But in this moment, he found himself wishing he had Lucian's talent. His fingers itched to capture the striking lines of her face and the fullness of her mouth. He wondered what colors he'd have to mix to replicate the shade of her eyes and her skin.

Dev was beguiled by the way the candlelight flickered over the curve of her cheek and how she dragged her teeth along her lower lip when she was thinking hard about something. She toyed with her hair a lot, brushing this rebellious little curl that kept ending up in her face no matter what she did. He sensed a nervousness about her that he found . . . adorable, which was a word he didn't use in his normal vocabulary, but he'd never seen Rosie nervous before. He'd seen her irritated and angry. He'd seen teasing and relaxed. He'd seen her aroused and satisfied, but never nervous.

Rosie was this beautiful, confident, and strong woman he'd believed was incapable of nervousness. But she was, and that didn't make her seem weak or delicate. It made her . . . adorable.

He couldn't remember ever being so engrossed in someone before and actually enjoying sitting back and listening to them talk. During the course of the dinner of crab cakes and pan-fried Cajun shrimp, he learned a lot about her.

How she'd met Nikki. Why she'd decided to go to the University of Alabama, which turned out to be a side effect of wanderlust, and he found her ability to make a decision like that and leave inspiring, especially when he often felt . . . trapped here, with his name and his legacy. He'd learned about the first time she saw a full-bodied apparition, and he was fascinated by the way she leaned forward when she spoke about it and the way her eyes lit with interest and eagerness. The excitement in her gaze and tone did the most inappropriate things to him.

Sitting in Firestones, he became hard—so hard he'd spread his legs as far as he could. That physical reaction made dinner fairly uncomfortable, but he wouldn't have changed a damn thing.

And never once during this was he bored or distracted by anything going on in his life or with his family. That part of him that had to . . . do things to ensure the safety of his family didn't exist when he was with her, but strangely, he wanted her to see that part of him, too.

Placing the dessert menu on the table, she glanced up and her gaze flickered away from him for a half second and then returned. "People are staring again."

He picked up his glass of water as he glanced around the restaurant. There were a few stares, mainly from those who were familiar with him. "I think they're just curious."

"Because you coming here and eating food is something to be curious about?" she asked.

Dev grinned. "Because me coming here with someone as beautiful as you is something to be curious about."

"Oh that was smooth." Rosie laughed softly as she reached for her wineglass.

He lifted a brow. "It was, wasn't it?"

"Yes, but I know what Sabrina looks like. She's beautiful."

"I guess you could say that." He lifted a shoulder. "But whatever beauty that woman possesses is only skin-deep. She's . . ."

"What?" Rosie asked.

Dev drew in a shallow breath as he placed his water back down. They were in one of the more private booths, where their conversation wouldn't be overheard.

Her teeth moved on her lower lip again. "You don't have to answer that. I'm sorry—"

"She was in love with Gabe," he answered. "Well, obsessed with him. Ever since college."

Rosie's eyes widened. "Seriously?"

"You didn't know that?" he asked, curious. "I'm surprised Nikki hadn't told you."

"Nikki doesn't talk about that kind of stuff." Rosie knocked the curl back out of her face. "I have to ask. If you knew she was into Gabe, then why in the hell did you stay with her?"

And there was the million-dollar question. His gaze dropped to the tea light candle. "It's a long story."

"We have time, right?"

A faint smile curved his lips. "We do." There was a quick pause. "How much did Nikki tell you about Gabe's past?"

"You're talking about his son and the mother of his child? I think she died in a car accident a few months ago? I can't remember her name, but yeah, I know about that."

"Her name was Emma. They had this on-again, off-again relationship that was pretty intense. Something happened to her in college. She was assaulted."

"No," she whispered, placing her hands in her lap.

Dev nodded. "Gabe had a pretty strong reaction to it—to the guy who hurt Emma. It did not end well." He paused, lifting his gaze to Rosie's. He waited to see if she had a response to that. Rosie was a smart woman. She knew what Dev was alluding to, and other than the initial reaction to the news, she wasn't throwing her napkin down and rushing out of the restaurant. "Emma must've shared that with Sabrina."

"Why would she do that? Didn't she know how Sabrina felt about Gabe?"

"Emma was a very kind soul, the sort of person who never met a stranger," Dev replied, thinking of the woman. "She believed the best in people, and unfortunately that didn't always work out for her. Her trusting Sabrina gave Sabrina the upper hand. She knew things about Gabe that could be a problem, and Lawrence was pushing for a Harrington to marry a de Vincent, even back then. Sabrina wanted Gabe and would've used what she knew to force him. He would've been stuck with her, and that was . . . unacceptable to me."

Her brows snapped together. "Wait a second. Did you . . . ?" She placed her hands on the table. "Did you agree to be with her so she'd stop going after Gabe?"

Uncomfortable, he shifted in his seat. "I was with her because I believed that the merger of our business with her family's would be a smart endeavor."

"And because it got her attentions off of Gabe?" she insisted.

"Well, I thought it did, but it really didn't in the end. Sabrina was still obsessed with Gabe. You know what happened between Nikki and Parker." He picked up his water. "And it's worse than that."

"How can anything be worse than Parker attacking Nikki?" she whispered.

"Parker said something to Nikki during that attack that leaves us with the impression they had something to do with Emma's accident."

She folded her hand over her mouth. "Dear God . . ."

"Luckily, Parker is no more and I . . . I don't think Sabrina is going to be a problem any longer."

"Did you all go to the police with that information?" she asked and then immediately rolled her eyes. "That's right. The de Vincents don't go to the police."

"Not usually. Besides, none of us wanted Nikki involved any more than necessary and Parker is dead and Sabrina—"

"Is somewhere out there?" She picked up her wineglass. "She shouldn't be out there, waiting to become someone else's nightmare."

"I agree, but I just learned that Sabrina is dead. The news hasn't broken yet, but I'm sure it will shortly."

"What?" Her eyes widened.

Dev told her a somewhat edited version of what had been told to him. "I don't know what happened to her," he said, and even though that was partly the truth, there was a festering of guilt. Something he'd never quite felt before.

"I don't know what to say. I feel for her and Parker's family, but I can't . . . I can't find any sympathy in me for her or her brother. Both sounded like terrible human beings." She took a sip. "Does Gabe know this? Why you really were with her?"

"Like I said, I was—"

"What you said is bullshit, Devlin. Maybe a part of the reason was because of her family's companies, but you were trying to save your brother from a terrible future . . . by sacrificing your own. That's pretty . . . amazing."

Feeling his face heat, he looked away. "I'm not a white knight, Rosie. Or some kind of selfless human being."

"I know." She studied him for a moment. "There's still something I don't understand. If Sabrina was obsessed with Gabe, why would she be with you? I mean no offense, but—"

"No offense taken." Dev had to really think about how to answer a question he wasn't quite sure about himself. "I think . . . I think Sabrina thought by marrying me she'd be close to Gabe. That the proximity would eventually work in her favor. Sounds utterly ridiculous."

"It does." Rosie nodded.

"But she obviously didn't see things the way they truly were. Sabrina was spoiled by her parents. So was Parker. I guess she thought she'd eventually get her way." He lifted a shoulder. "Other than that? I honestly don't know."

Rosie stared at him for a long moment and then whispered, "All you . . . all you rich people are just weird. Legit weird."

It happened.

Just a small curve of his lips, but it quickly turned into a grin that became a smile. Dev laughed. Tipped his head back and laughed loudly and he didn't care who saw him or heard him.

She was grinning at him when he looked back at her. "You have a nice laugh," she said. "You should do it more often."

"Yeah, I should," he said, aware of eyes on them again. "So, what I told you doesn't bother you?"

Rosie didn't answer immediately. "I feel like that's a loaded question."

"It is."

The curl fell back across her cheek. "I try not to judge people, especially when it involves bad things happening to bad people. Maybe that makes me a bad person, but I can't get too torn up over a rapist meeting an unsavory end."

Surprise flickered through him. "Really?"

She lifted a shoulder. "I have this weird opinion on that kind of thing that a lot of people don't agree with. I mean, I think there are some people who've forfeited their rights to live once they've taken another life or have done something heinous that goes beyond human decency, but at the same time, I wonder if any human has the right to decide to take another life. I go back and forth on this. I think . . . I think sometimes it's understandable that when someone they care about is hurt horribly that a person has a break—they snap. Psychosis is a real thing and good people experience it under extreme distress. And people are weird."

That appeared to be an understatement.

"Some of the most popular books and movies and television shows feature vigilante justice, whether it's the ordinary everyday person next door or a superhero. People love that stuff, where the bad guys get taken down through violence or the legal system. And yeah, it's fiction or made up, but what people enjoy speaks to their basic desires and fantasies. When you have a parent that goes after a molester, that parent is cheered. I mean, look at the Old Testament. An eye for an eye and all that jazz. That doesn't mean going out there and killing people is okay, but I don't know . . . like I said, sometimes you can understand why someone has done that. People are weird and they are complicated." Rosie glanced at him. "A lot of things exist within a gray area. Some people just don't want to acknowledge that."

Dev wasn't sure what to say.

"Anyway, the dessert here looks amazing, but I am stuffed." Her lips twitched as she grinned. "That was a bizarre change of subject, right?"

He barked out a short laugh. "It worked, though. By the way, chocolate is my weakness."

She lifted a brow. "Really?"

His lips twitched. "Yes. I try to eat healthy, but you put a chocolate bar in front of me, I'll eat all of it."

Rosie grinned. "I still can't picture you eating pralines or having a hidden stash of chocolate in your drawer."

"You'd be surprised."

Her gaze met his again and held. "So, dessert?"

Dev knew what kind of dessert he wanted and it was nothing that was offered on the menu.

"I don't want dessert," he said.

Rosie didn't look away. "What do you want?"

"I want you to come home with me."

There wasn't a moment of hesitation. "Yes."

ROSIE HAD NEVER seen the de Vincent mansion at night. Granted, she'd only ever seen the section Gabe lived in and the part Richard had led her to when she'd brought the items she'd found in the closet to Devlin.

She'd asked about those things on the drive to his home, if he'd found out anything about them. He'd told her that he'd been able to get the iPad charged and unlocked, but he didn't elaborate beyond that. Rosie didn't sense that he was holding back because of distrust, but more like it wasn't something he wanted to talk about right then, and for that, she couldn't blame him. Their conversation had already gotten pretty dark during dinner, and now she didn't want any more darkness to seep into their night.

And while there was definitely no love lost between Devlin and Sabrina, she suspected he was still processing news of her death.

When she walked out of the garage and waited for Devlin to join her, she couldn't get over how quiet it was here. "This is kind of crazy."

"What is?" Devlin joined her.

She scanned the lit grounds. A floodlight had kicked on when they neared the garage and there was landscaping lighting dotting the property. There were outdoor lights placed between the windows of all the floors, casting a soft, muted glow that gave just enough light for you to find your way. Even now, she could see all the ivy climbing the home. "It's just so quiet."

"A circus would be quiet compared to what you must hear every night where you live."

Rosie laughed as she glanced at him. He stood with his back to the shadows and it was almost like he could seep right into them, vanishing. "True, but listen. I don't even hear insects or animals."

Devlin was quiet for a moment. "Huh. You're right. I've never noticed that before."

"Really?" Rosie figured that was something you'd notice right away. "How can you not notice that?"

"I grew up here," he reminded her. "This is normal to me."

That was a good point, but Rosie still couldn't suppress the shiver that danced over her skin. It was common for animals and insects to avoid places with a lot of spirit activity.

Without saying a word, Devlin took her hand and led her to the back outdoor staircase. His hand was cool against hers, the grip firm, and for some reason, she found herself grinning like she was sixteen again just because he was holding her hand.

"Dinner was nice," she said as they climbed the wide steps.

"Just nice?"

"Okay. It was more than just nice."

He squeezed her hand and she felt that in her chest. "I'm waiting."

She looked over at him as they reached the third flight of stairs. "For what?"

"For you to admit that you were wrong."

"What exactly was I wrong about?"

There was almost a teasing tone to his voice as he said, "You thought I was going to regret the dinner and it was going to be an absolute failure."

She dipped her chin, grinning. "I didn't think it would be an absolute failure."

Reaching the third level, he let go of her hand as he pressed his finger to some kind of contraption above the lock. There was a click-ing motion and the door unlocked. Super high-tech, right there. "Still waiting," he said as he opened the door and stepped inside, flipping on the light.

"Okay. You're right." Rosie laughed as she followed him in. "Happy now?"

"Yes." He tossed his car keys on a narrow, dark wood entry table. "Do you want anything to drink?"

"I'm fine," she said, looking around as she placed her beaded clutch on the table beside his keys. His living area was the same size as Gabe's and followed the same minimalistic design. There was a couch and a large TV mounted to the wall. With the exception of the entry-way table and the end table, there was nothing else. No paintings. No additional seats. "You don't have a lot of guests, do you?"

"No." A small smile appeared as he made his way to a kitchen area outfitted with all the typical kitchen stuff. There was a fully stocked bar, and he picked up a bottle of what appeared to be bourbon. "Do you mind if I pour myself a drink?"

"Of course not."

He turned back to the bar. "Is it obvious that I don't have a lot of guests?"

"Well, you only have a couch and one barstool at the bar, so . . . yeah, it's obvious." She laughed.

"There's not many people I want in my personal space." He poured himself a drink and then placed the bottle back. "I want you here, though."

Her breath caught as he turned to face her. "Why?"

"I like you, Rosie." He came around the bar. "And I don't like a lot of people."

She snorted as she tucked a curl back behind her ear. "Never would've guessed that."

He chuckled. "Do you want to see the rest?"

Rosie nodded.

Sipping from his glass, he turned to his left and started down a narrow hall. The walls there were also bare. "You know what the first thing I liked about you was?"

"My shining personality?"

"Shockingly no," he replied, and she grinned at his back. "It was the peonies."

"Ah."

He opened the door at the end of the hall. "It was kind of you to do that. You were kind."

"So, you now believe that I didn't know who you were?"

"I should've believed you then," he said, stepping aside. "This is, obviously, a bedroom."

That it was, and she knew that only because of the large king-size bed in the middle of the room. But like with the living area, there was nothing personal about the nightstands or the long, narrow bureau. No photos or paintings. There wasn't even a book on the nightstand or a piece of clothing lying on the bed.

"Do you actually live here?" she asked, turning to him.

"What?"

"Do you live here?" she repeated, gesturing to the room with a wide sweep of her arm. "I mean, it's a beautiful room, but it's empty. There's nothing . . . intimate about it."

Devlin stared at her for a moment and then said, "That's the second thing I like about you."

Her brows lifted.

"You speak your mind." He walked over to the bed and sat down. "You're not afraid to say anything to me. Even if you know I won't like it or if it's uncomfortable to hear, you speak your mind."

"Most people don't like that."

"Most people are idiots."

A laugh burst from her. "Wow."

"It's the truth." He lifted a shoulder and took a drink. "You stand up to me. You get in my face. You tell me what I don't want to hear but maybe need to. That is . . . unique in my experience."

She glanced to the curtained French doors that led out onto the balcony and then her gaze fell back to him. "You're starting to make me feel special."

His gaze lifted to hers. "You are special."

Feeling her cheeks warm, she inched closer to him. "Thank you."

Devlin didn't look away as he took another drink. "Probably the most special thing about you is even after how I behaved toward you, you're still standing here. I've given you very little reason to be here, right now, with me."

"That's not true." Drawing in a shallow breath, she walked over to him and stopped in front of him. "Yeah, there were a lot of times that I didn't like you. At all."

He was silent as he stared up at her.

"But I . . . I always felt like there was more to you than just being an arrogant asshole."

A grin tugged at his lips.

"There. That small smile." She plucked his glass out of his hand and placed it on the nightstand. "The first time you smiled in front of me, the first time you laughed, I could tell it wasn't something you did often."

"You're very observant."

"I am." She placed her hands on his shoulders and then sat in his lap, straddling him. He made this low growl as his hands came to her hips. "We didn't get along, but there were moments when we did, and during those moments, I . . . I liked you. A lot."

"Is that so?"

"Yeah." She lifted her hands to his face and dragged her fingertips along his jaw. "I still like you a lot and I know . . . I know that liking you isn't always going to be easy, but I want . . ."

His hands tightened on her hips. "You want what?"

"You're a lot of things." She cupped the back of his head. "And I want you. All of you."

"You have me." He ran his thumb over her smooth cheek, tracing the bone. His touch was featherlight, but she stirred restlessly in his lap. Lust pricked her skin. He moved his fingertips down her throat, over her shoulder. A small sigh escaped her.

Slowly, he moved his hand to the neckline of her gown, his palm pressing against the swell of her breast. "You have all of me," he said.

Rosie placed her hand on his side, moving it toward his back, kneading the cords of bunched muscles. He caught her wrists and re-placed them on his chest. Before that could fully register, he dropped his hand to her hip and tugged her down and against him. All soft curves pressed against hard lines. His erection, straining against his trousers, pressed against her core, and when he moved her against him in a slow, undulating grind, she gasped and stiffened.

"I want you." He rocked his hips again. His next words came out as a low, harsh growl. "I want all of *you* tonight."

Her hips rolled down, and he lowered his head, moving his lips across the cheek he'd caressed moments before. "Then take me."

His remaining hand slid up the flare of her hip, up her stomach. He stopped just below her breasts, his thumb brushing over the swell. Her breath caught as his kisses reached the corner of her mouth. She turned her head slightly. Their lips brushed.

"And if I want to keep you?"

Her fingers curled into his shirt as she rocked against him. "I will have to take that under consideration."

"Or I just need to work harder at convincing you?" He dipped his head to the space between her neck and shoulder. Lowering his hands to her hips, he nuzzled her neck. He let his hand stray higher, nearly reaching the peak of her breast, and then his hand closed over her breast, the heat of his skin searing her through the thin material of her dress and bra.

Her back arched, pressing her breast into his grasp. He answered, pushing the material aside, exposing her bra. He smoothed his thumb over the taut pebble.

His eyes remained latched on to hers as he teased her nipple through the cloth. She moved her other hand down his chest, and her stomach muscles tightened. "I need to see you, touch you . . . taste you."

His words sent a dark shudder through her. *"Yes."*

Moving his hand down, he slipped it under her dress and then lifted the material up. She lifted her arms, and within seconds, the dress was lying on the floor. His sharp intake of breath was lost when he found the clasp on the back of her bra and unhooked it. That, too, joined the dress on the floor.

"You are so beautiful." He lowered his head, flicking his tongue over one pert nipple.

She moaned as both of her hands now clutched his sides. And then she was tugging his shirt up. He chuckled as he pulled away from her aching breast and helped her get the shirt off. Her eyes devoured every inch of his exposed skin. He was ripped, satin stretched over rock-hard muscles. Her hands flattened against his lower stomach, and his muscles bunched.

Rosie lifted her gaze as her fingers trailed over each hard ripple. "You're perfect."

"I am far from perfect." He moved his hand to her other breast. His tongue swirled over the nipple. "That's something you need to know."

Her head went back as her breath came out in short gasps. "Perfection isn't a constant state."

He drew the rosy peak into his mouth as he caught her other nipple between his thumb and forefinger.

"God," she moaned, rolling her hips against him. "See, *this* is perfect."

Desire swirled inside her, leaving her feeling out of control and dazed. Why did she feel this way? Was it more than lust? But then his mouth tugged on her breast and his tongue rasped over her nipple, and she stopped thinking. It was all about feeling and the raw, exquisite sensations shooting down to her core, warming and dampening her. All she knew was that she wanted every part of him, the smooth, chiseled edges along with all the rough, frayed ends.

Her hands slipped over rock-hard abs that dipped and rippled. Masculine perfection. Her hips rocked against the thick length pressed against her core. God, he was *huge*.

He lifted her suddenly and turned, placing her in the center of the bed. Her heart raced as she rose onto her elbows and watched him shuck off his pants and tight boxer briefs. Within moments, he was naked and she . . . she was still wearing her heels. She started to sit up, but he caught her ankle.

"Keep them on," he ordered in a smoky, thick voice.

Her stomach twisted.

Devlin reached for the nightstand. A drawer opened and a condom landed on the bed beside her. He climbed over her and then lowered himself onto his side beside her.

Reaching for him, she gasped when he caught her hands and pinned them to the bed. He shifted over her and then he let go of her wrists, letting his hands trail down her arms and over her breasts as he worked his way down. When he caught her nipple between his teeth, she cried out again, wantonly rolling her hips against his hardness. Tension between her legs built quickly, stealing her breath, shocking her. She'd never come this way before, but oh—*oh sweet Jesus*—the coil tightened deep inside her womb. Her movements became almost frantic. His growl of approval burned her skin, igniting the fire as he lifted his head to stare down at her.

She reached for him again, but this time she ran her fingers along his smooth jawline. Their eyes met, and her throat tightened with unexpected emotion.

He dipped his head as his hand slipped down her stomach, resting just below her navel. "You make me want . . . so much, Rosie. You have no idea."

She lifted her head, brushing her lips against his. "Show me."

His large, powerful body shuddered beside her, and hot, sweet darts of fire sped through her blood. Her lashes lowered and her breath caught in her throat as his hand slipped farther down, gently palming her.

"There's just one problem." He kissed her and then pulled back. His tongue slid over her lips, then inside, matching the slow, languid thrust with his fingers. Tremors started in her stomach. Muscles quivered.

"What problem?" she gasped.

"When I want something, I don't let it go." He tormented her until she moved her hips against his hand, but anytime she tried to get more, to take control, he nipped her lip, her throat. "Ever."

That one word stirred so many raw emotions in her that for a moment she was lost. A small, keening whimper escaped her as her release came out of nowhere. Devlin pulled her to him, holding her close as her body shuddered. Sweat coated his skin, muscles taut and rigid from holding back. And then he turned her around, easing her onto her side. He used his thigh to separate hers. She arched her back, grinding her rear against the length of his erection. "What if I don't have an issue with your problem?"

"Don't make a promise you won't keep." His warm breath danced over her cheek. He cupped her breast, running his thumb over the hard nipple.

Her breath was quickening. "I don't make promises I don't plan on keeping."

Devlin slowly slid into her, inch by inch. It had been a while, so it took a few moments for him to stretch her, but when he did, she felt so unbelievably full. He was moving so deep that she felt like she'd come apart in a shower of sparks. The steady friction sent her body blazing. Slow and steady strokes soon became not enough. More—she wanted more. She moved her hips, and his low growl had her blood pressure skyrocketing.

"Harder," she whispered. "Please."

The things he whispered in her ear as he shifted her onto her knees and thrust into her from behind, each stroke harder and faster than the one before, could probably be classified as depraved, but they excited her. Every thrust mounted her pleasure and deepened her cries. And when she started to spasm around his cock, he caught her chin and forced her head back and to the side, claiming her mouth with his as he spent himself.

"God, that was . . ." He dropped his forehead against her shoulder and shuddered again. "That was fucking amazing."

"Hey," she murmured as she wrapped her arm through his. "We agree on something again."

Devlin laughed quietly against her shoulder and then he lifted his head, kissing her cheek. "I'll be right back."

She pouted as he pulled away from her and rose from the bed. Not one to miss a prime opportunity of seeing him in all his glorious nakedness, she rolled onto her back. The first thing she saw was that unbelievably firm ass that just begged her to take a bite out of it, but then she lifted her gaze.

"My God," she gasped, jerking upright.

Devlin halted, looking over his shoulder at her. Realization dawned in his shadowy expression. He whipped around, but it was too late. She'd already seen.

"Your back," she said, scooting to the edge of the bed. His back was a mess of scars, old faded scars that crisscrossed over one another, forming a disturbing map of what could only be one thing. "Dear God, Devlin, what happened to you?"

Chapter 32

*D*evlin couldn't move. Couldn't breathe as he stared at Rosie. He'd forgotten. Holy shit, he'd been so lost in Rosie that he'd remembered to not let her touch his back but he'd forgotten when he walked away.

He immediately turned, walking toward the door. Where he was going buck-ass naked, he had no idea, but he had to get out of here. Had to get away from the horror building in her eyes.

"No. No." She sprang from the bed, completely nude, and darted in front of him. Surprised, he didn't know what to do when she planted her hands on his chest. "I just told you that I wanted all of you and whatever that is, it's a part of you. You don't get to run from me now."

Another ripple of shock made its way through him. He opened his mouth, but he didn't know what to say. This was something no one saw. This was something he didn't talk about.

Her gaze searched his as she pressed lightly on his chest. "What happened to you?"

Dev couldn't find the words as his brain raced through the years. He stepped back from Rosie and kept retreating as if he were in a daze. He sat on the bed, his gaze following to the dress lying on the hardwood floors. He was so fucking stupid. How did he forget about his back? No one saw it. No one touched it. *No one.* And now this beautiful, strong, confident woman had seen just how weak he'd once been.

"Please," Rosie said as she bent down and picked up his discarded dress shirt. Slipping it on, she tugged it closed. "Please talk to me."

Maybe it was the way she asked him or maybe it was just because it was her asking. Either way, he found a voice—his voice—and he gave sound to something that never had words before.

"Lawrence," he muttered out in a coarse voice.

"Your father?" She sat beside him. "Your *father* did this to you?"

He kept staring at the dress on the floor, but he really didn't see it. He saw the first time Lawrence had hit him. That may not have been the first time. It was just the first memory. It was before the *incident*. Dev had been running outside. Lawrence had grown annoyed and had backhanded him. "He's not . . . Lawrence is not my father, Rosie."

"What?" she whispered.

It was like some kind of seal deep inside him had been snapped in two and everything—*everything*—he'd been holding back flowed to the surface. "He was the biological father of Lucian and Madeline, but not Gabe and me. Obviously that isn't something widely known. Hell, we didn't even know that until this past year, but that man . . . was not my father."

"Do you know who your father was?" she asked after a terse heartbeat.

Dev finally lifted his gaze and glanced at Rosie. Another truth he hadn't spoken rose to the tip of his tongue. "I think I know who it is and I don't even know if Gabe thinks this or not. It's not something we talk about, but I think . . . I think our father is Stefan."

Rosie's eyes widened.

"Twisted, isn't it?" He barked out a short, humorless laugh. "It's the only thing that makes sense to me. Both Gabe and I look too much like Lawrence and Stefan. Hell, I'm practically a spitting image of them when they were younger. Lucian and Madeline obviously took after our mother and I know my theory isn't exactly scientific, but if I'm right, it's Stefan."

She slowly shook her head. "Is there any hard-core proof other than that?"

"No. We could find out, but . . . if there was a record of whose child was whose, that could affect a lot of things. Lucian could end up with the company, and he doesn't want that. I offered it to him, but he doesn't want that kind of life."

"That was . . . that's huge of you to offer it, though."

Dev pressed his lips together. Was it really huge of him? He didn't think so, not when there were days when he'd love nothing more than to leave all of this shit behind.

"Now it makes sense. Why I've never heard you call him Father or Dad," she said and then, "What did Lawrence do to you?"

"What did he not do?" Another short, harsh laugh. "He always knew we weren't his kids and I think he hated us for it, and for some reason, he hated Lucian and Madeline even more for being his kids. The man was a sociopath." Tipping his head back, he closed his eyes. "He'd lose his temper quite easily and if I was nearby, it didn't end well. The day I almost died or did die? He hit me and I lost my balance, cracking my head on the corner of his desk. Besson—Nikki's father—had found me and provided CPR."

"Wait. Are you saying Lawrence caused that and didn't even call for help? Didn't try to help you?"

"Nope. He apparently walked out of the office and Besson just happened to be walking past it when he saw me." Dev dragged a hand through his hair. "He didn't know exactly what happened and I didn't say anything when he took me to the hospital. Everyone just assumed that I'd fallen like kids often do and hit my head."

"But . . . but it didn't stop there, did it? It couldn't have."

"You know, the odd thing was that it did stop . . . until Lucian and Madeline were born, and then it . . . yeah." He lowered his hand. "As I grew older, I knew how he was, so I stuck close to him, because I was . . . I was the oldest. The scars are from the night I got in trouble at school, when Gabe and Lucian were trying to sneak out. Lawrence was furious. I was the oldest, the one to set an example, and whatever bullshit he spewed when he found out. Who knew a belt could leave that many scars?"

"God, Devlin, I'm so sorry—"

"Don't. I don't want your sympathy or pity."

"You have my sympathy."

"It was my job to protect them—"

"It was *not* your job, Devlin. That is no child's job."

His gaze shot to her. It wasn't like he didn't realize that now, but it was still hard to shake that role. "If I hadn't been the one to take the brunt of it, he would've done worse to them. I know it."

Her gaze flickered over his face. "How in the world did Nikki's parents not see this? Not know it was happening?"

"Lawrence was very good at hiding what he did, Rosie. They are not at fault. I never spoke up. I was too weak and too scared to say a damn thing. I could've stopped it. I could've—"

"Dear God, Devlin, you weren't weak. You were a child." She cupped his jaw, forcing him to look at her when he started to pull away. "Don't put that on yourself. That is all on the fucking monster who I am *glad* is dead."

His lips twitched. "You're a little bloodthirsty."

"You have no idea." She smoothed her thumb over his jaw. "There are few things in life that enrage me. Abusers. Molesters. Those who take advantage of others." She paused, wrinkling her nose. "And irresponsible pet owners. Pretty much in that order of the rage-out scale."

Dev folded his hand around her wrist. "No one has seen those scars."

"Not even your brothers?"

He shook his head. "Never been shirtless around them." He brought her hand to his mouth. He kissed her palm. "The times I was with Sabrina or anyone else, I never got completely undressed. I was always careful."

"I'm glad you weren't this time," she whispered. "You can't hide them away forever, Devlin. It would eat away at you."

Hadn't it already eaten away at him?

Closing his eyes, he kissed the tips of her fingers. "What Lawrence did to me wasn't even the worst thing, Rosie. He was involved in some horrific things. I've said that to you before, but you have no idea."

She swallowed as she leaned into him. "Then tell me."

Dev opened his eyes as he lowered her hand to his thigh. "My brothers know nothing about this and I want it to stay that way. I don't want them to know what he was involved in, because it's being handled. I've ensured it."

"I wouldn't say anything and betray your trust like that."

He believed her. For the first time, he believed her without hesitation. "Lawrence, one of the wealthiest men in the world, was involved in human trafficking."

"God." Rosie lifted her other hand to her mouth as her eyes filled with horror. "Oh God."

"Before he died, I started to suspect he was involved in something. There were strange trips he took and deposits that looked odd to me. It took months for a forensic accountant to sift through the bullshit. I think that is what Andrea Joan had discovered."

"So, Stefan is involved, too?"

"Either he is or he was aware, and Andrea trusted the wrong person. That was what was on her iPad. Evidence," he said. "She went to Lawrence, right? That's what Ross claims. If so, she walked right up to the viper."

"That's terrible." Her eyes glimmered. "Dear God, I don't even know what to say. I . . ."

"What can you say? It's . . . it's fucked-up. Worst part is that so many people are involved, either actively or covering it up." Dev thought of the old police chief who'd met an . . . untimely fate. "The evidence that Andrea had gathered implicated a lot of people and that evidence is being handed over to the appropriate people. It's not going to stop it, but . . ."

"But it's going to take a lot of bad people down and that's important," she insisted. "That's huge, Devlin, and you're going to be the reason. You and Andrea and anyone else who is trying to do the right thing."

But Dev hadn't always done the right thing. Maybe he did what he deemed necessary, but the right thing? That was debatable. "You don't know everything, Rosie."

"Then tell me everything. Look, if we can talk about this while you're completely naked and I'm wearing your shirt, we can pretty much talk about anything."

That brought a smile to his face. "Good point."

"I always have good points." Leaning in, she kissed him and it was too quick. "Devlin, I can handle whatever you've got to say."

Could she? He wasn't sure. "I don't deserve you."

"What?" She tried to pull her hand away but he held on. "Don't say that."

Dev was done with the lies—all of them—and he knew if he shared this, there was a good chance this truth could cause him to lose Rosie before he ever really had her. He drew in a deep breath, knowing that he had to tell her if there was any hope of a future.

He lifted his gaze to hers. "That wasn't me in the cemetery that day."

Confusion clouded Rosie's face as she stared back at him. "What?"

"That wasn't me. That was my twin."

Chapter 33

Rosie's brain sort of shut down for several moments. That was how it felt as she looked at him.

He said her name and when she didn't answer, concern spread into his face. "Say something. You're starting to worry me."

She blinked. "You have a twin?"

He nodded. "Yes."

Rosie opened her mouth and then closed it. Several more moments passed. "I don't understand."

This didn't make sense to her. Out of everything he'd just shared with her, this was the one thing that she couldn't wrap her brain around. What she'd just learned about his father was shocking. What she thought as Devlin told her was even more unsettling, because as Devlin spoke, she thought . . . God, she thought it really might have been him.

That Devlin had killed Lawrence.

And she'd still sat there, not horrified by her suspicions but by how that *hadn't* disturbed her. How she didn't look at someone who might've killed another person and feel anything but horror. How she felt sympathy for everything Devlin had lived through and had dealt with to protect his brothers. As he told her about what Lawrence had been involved in, there was a huge part of her that had understood why he did what he'd done.

What did that say about her?

Her training and education suggested that she might have issues, but how could she loathe or fear a man who had stopped someone so inexplicably evil? How could she be okay with it? Two wrongs didn't make a right, but sometimes . . . sometimes they did.

Like she'd said during their dinner conversation, life often existed in the gray area and for people like the de Vincents, even more so.

But it was *this* that had thrown her completely for a loop. He had a twin? And it hadn't been him in the cemetery? Feeling numb, she pulled away and this time, Devlin let her. Needing space to think, she rose from the bed, clasping the edges of the shirt.

"I'm going to need a thoroughly detailed explanation of this," she said, pacing as she held the shirt closed. "Because I'm confused. You just said that the peonies were one of your favorite things—"

"They are." He rose and picked up his pants, pulling them up, leaving them zipped but unbuttoned. "You just didn't give them to me. I wasn't even in town yet. Didn't get back until that afternoon. I didn't even know he was here, but he went to the cemetery to see our mother's grave. He told me that he ran into someone. I figured it out when I saw you the next day."

She stopped as realization dawned. "That's why you didn't recognize me at first."

"The morning in your apartment was the first time I saw you, Rosie."

A horrible thought occurred and her stomach churned. "Are there any other times where I thought I was dealing with you and I wasn't?"

"No. Absolutely not. Every other time was me. A hundred percent."

She wanted to believe that. "And how do I even know if that is the truth?"

"I have no reason to lie about it now," he said, sitting back down. "I told you because I want . . . I want a future with you, Rosie, and to have that, I need to tell you everything."

God, she wanted that, too. She really did, but she needed more information on this. She needed to understand how Devlin could've hidden something like this. "Your brothers don't know?"

"No. I only found out myself back in the spring. My brother— his name is Payton. The man who adopted him told him the truth. Come to find out, the woman who raised him passed away a few years back and then his father got sick. Told him before he died that he'd been adopted and that he had brothers. Payton reached out to me, and at first, I didn't believe him, but he sent me a picture. We're nearly identical, Rosie. I think if we were side by side, you could tell the difference, but . . ."

Her heart was pounding in her chest. "How did he end up being adopted?"

"I didn't even know I had a twin. None of us did. My mother never mentioned it. Lawrence sure as hell never did, and the Bessons—Nikki's parents—only started working for our family shortly after I was born. I have no idea how Payton ended up being adopted, but I know without a doubt that it was Lawrence who did it. Maybe it was because he knew we weren't his kids. Maybe he was just a psychotic fucker who did it just because he could. I don't know and will never know. Neither will Payton." Anger sharpened his tone. "But Lawrence took that from both of us. We are twins, Rosie, and I always felt . . . I always felt like I was missing something. You know? Like I grew up thinking it was because I almost died. That maybe I came back wrong or something, but I think . . . I think it's because I had this person out there who was a part of me, in a way."

Dear God.

Rosie turned away, swallowing hard. She obviously didn't know what it was like to have a twin, but she had a sister and if she'd just found out about Bella after all these years, she would've been heart-broken, especially if there was no good reason for the separation. But to be separated from a twin? She knew that was an intense bond forged in the womb and she'd seen many studies on twins separated. Many had gone their entire lives feeling like they were missing a part of them.

"Payton explained that when his father died, he was told about us. There was some kind of relationship between Lawrence and the family that adopted Payton. What, we don't know, but he lived in this small town in Nebraska. Grew up there. Hadn't even heard of us until his father told him." Devlin drew in a ragged breath. "I didn't tell my brothers because Payton asked me not to—not until he was ready. I had to . . . I had to honor that."

Rosie faced him as pressure clamped on her chest and twisted her insides. This family was . . . was a disaster. No, she corrected herself. One man was a disaster and he nearly ruined an entire family, and that man wasn't Devlin.

He drew in a deep breath. "He's actually been in town, staying at my place at the Port. My brothers don't even know I have a place there. It's just somewhere I go to get away. I didn't know Payton was coming in again. He'd left after you saw him at the cemetery, but he said . . ." He trailed off, shaking his head.

"What?" she asked. "What did he say?"

"He said he had a weird feeling. That he needed to be here."

She considered that. "There's a lot of research that says twins share this bond that helps them know when the other is going through something. Maybe it's that."

"Maybe," he murmured.

Rosie was quiet as she tried to process everything he'd told her. "I don't know what to say or what to think. But your brothers are going to be upset, Devlin."

"I know." He smoothed his hands over his knees. "And I'll have to deal with that."

Staring at him a moment longer, she looked away. "The first time I met you it wasn't even you. It was a lie."

"Everything after that wasn't. You saw the worst of me. You saw the best of me, and you've seen parts of me that no one else has." He rose, letting his arms fall to his sides. "And I know this is going to sound out there and this isn't the right time, but I think—no, I know that what I feel—"

"Dev? You in there?" Fists pounded off a door somewhere nearby, causing Rosie to jump and turn. "You need to get out here. Now."

Devlin cursed as his gaze swung from Rosie to the living area. "I'm sorry. It—"

"It's okay." Rosie stepped back.

He hesitated for a moment and then prowled out of the room like a caged lion. She turned to watch him. Her eyes widened. "Wait."

Stopping, he turned around.

"Your back. You're shirtless." Hurrying over to him, she shrugged off the shirt and handed it to him. "Here."

His face had paled, but then his gaze dipped and everything about him heated. "God," he growled, snapping forward. Wrapping a hand around the back of her neck, he kissed her deeply, fiercely. "I'm sorry."

She was a little dazed when he let go and stepped back, shoving his arms into his shirt.

"Thank you," he said, and then he turned, making his way down the hall.

Rosie watched him for a few seconds and then she spun around. Quickly finding her bra and panties, she pulled them on and then slipped the dress back on. Luckily, it wasn't too wrinkled. Picking up her shoes, she started out of the room, really having no idea what she was going to do. Call an Uber? Stay and wait? She needed time to really process everything she'd just learned, but—

"What do you mean Stefan is here?" Devlin sounded furious. "How in the hell did he get into the house?"

"I have no idea." That was Lucian. "But he was in your office. Gabe was just leaving to go to Nikki's when he saw him."

"What the fuck?" Devlin exploded as Rosie entered the living area.

Lucian was standing in the doorway and he couldn't look any more surprised if a ghost had strolled out behind Devlin. Magically, he managed to not comment on her rumpled appearance.

Not that he got a chance.

Devlin was out the door and Lucian was right behind him. Rosie stood there for a moment, not quite sure what to do, but instinct took over. Something she couldn't quite explain. She dropped her shoes on the floor and followed, catching up with them in the long hall.

Neither of them said anything, but Lucian glanced back at her. She figured if they didn't want her to follow, they would say something.

The upper hallway was just a blur of closed doors and the second floor was the same way, just less of them. Up ahead, she saw double doors open and heard voices coming from inside the room.

"You need to get out of here," Gabe was saying. "This is unacceptable."

"I'm family. Am I not allowed to be here?"

"At night, when you're not invited?" Gabe shot back. "Hell no."

Rosie's stomach pitched as Devlin burst into the office.

"How did you get in here?" Devlin demanded, stalking into his office. "You do not have keys to this house, let alone my office."

"Of course I have keys," Stefan replied, and when she neared the open door, she saw the tall man walk over to a small sofa. On the table in front of the sofa was a bottle of bourbon and two glasses.

Any other time she would've been checking out Devlin's office, but she was riveted by what was going down.

"How did you get keys, Stefan?" Devlin asked again.

The senator poured himself a glass as Lucian walked over to Devlin's desk and sat down, propping his legs up on the desk like this was a normal Tuesday night.

Stefan arched a brow as his glance slid past Devlin to where Rosie stood. "I figured you'd be busy longer, Devlin. Sort of disappointed in you."

She sucked in a gasp as Devlin stepped toward Stefan. "Don't speak to her or look at her. You need to tell me—why the hell were you in my office?"

"I wanted to spend time with you." He reached for the glass he poured. "You were busy. Understandably so. I heard both of you went to Firestones tonight. How surprising, considering you never took—"

"Answer my damn question," Devlin cut in.

Rosie stood there while Gabe walked past her, shaking his head. He said something to her about stepping out, but she was stuck. Something nagged at her as she watched Stefan sit back and lift the glass of bourbon with his left hand. The light glimmered off the gold watch, catching her eye.

She suddenly thought about her reading with Sarah. What had that spirit said?

"He shouldn't be dead."

Her gaze latched on to Stefan's hand as the brothers and he went back and forth. Realization dawned, rocking her to the very core of her being.

It hadn't been Lawrence's spirit trying to come through Sarah that night.

"Oh my God," Rosie whispered, lifting her gaze to the man's face. Identical twins. Just like Devlin and his brother. "That's not Stefan."

Devlin whirled toward her. "What?"

"That's Lawrence. Look at his watch." Horror threatened to choke her. "Stefan wore his watch on the other wrist. That's what Ross told me. That's how he was able to tell them apart. That's *Lawrence*."

Chapter 34

Dev turned to Stefan, his gaze dropping to his wrist. Rosie was right. The watch was on the wrong wrist, but that alone couldn't mean . . .

Dev lifted his gaze to Stefan's face. Everything in him rebelled at the idea that this man in front of him was Lawrence.

He arched a brow at Devlin from his lazy, arrogant sprawl on the sofa.

"What?" Lucian laughed. "This is most definitely Stefan, the bumbling senator."

Gabe smirked as he leaned back in his chair, crossing his arms.

"Devlin," Rosie whispered, rooted to where she stood by the window.

There was no way. His heart lurched in his chest as he stared at the man. This couldn't be Lawrence, because if this was, then that meant . . .

He suddenly thought about what Rosie had said to him about the spirit that supposedly came through to her. That it had claimed to have been murdered, but not only that, she'd said the spirit had said it wasn't supposed to be him.

Holy shit, was it possible Stefan's spirit had come through? And was he really starting to believe a psychic medium?

"You look like a ghost walked over your grave," Stefan noted, tilting his head. "Do you need to sit down, Devlin?"

His heart rate kicked up as a sense of dread filled him. His thoughts raced, and they ended up on the day Nikki brought them tea. What had Stefan said to her?

"I see some things never change." Stefan had said that and more. *"You're still incapable of not making noise."*

Sharp tingles danced along the nape of his neck. Stefan had never paid attention to Nikki when she was a child. Lawrence, on the other hand, couldn't stand how much noise she made even when the girl was barely making a sound. And Lawrence . . . he'd always been watching Nikki, paying too much attention to the young girl.

"I want to see your watch," Dev demanded. "Now."

Stefan laughed as he leaned forward, placing his bourbon on the table. "Why would you want to see that?"

Gabe twisted in his seat toward Dev. "You're not . . . ?"

"Let me see your watch," Dev repeated. "Now."

The laugh and smile faded from his face as he leaned back. "You already know what you're going to find."

Shock splashed through Dev, freezing him for a moment.

"What are you going to find?" Gabe demanded, turning toward the couch. He started to rise.

"The initials." Stefan unhooked the clasps on his watch, catching it as it slid off. He tossed the watch to Lucian, who caught it with ease. "He wants to know what the initials are."

Brows snapping together, Lucian turned the Rolex over in his hand. The smirk faded from his face.

"Rosie," Dev said softly. "You need to leave."

"No, I think she needs to stay." The bastard on the couch lifted his brows.

"Lucian?" Gabe had turned to his brother. "What do the initials say?"

Lucian slowly pulled his legs off the desk and dropped his feet to the floor. "LDV. . . ."

A chill coursed down Dev's spine as he turned back to Rosie. "Please. You need—"

"She's going nowhere."

Rosie's voice came out as a whisper. "Devlin. . . ."

"What the fuck?" Gabe exploded, and Dev whirled.

Fury poured into him as he saw that the man they thought was Stefan held a gun.

"Lawrence de Vincent." Lucian dropped the watch like it scalded his skin and looked up. Horror filled his expression.

"Silly of me, right? But it was a custom-made Rolex. I just couldn't part with it." The slow smile that spread over his face was a hundred percent Lawrence.

Dear God, how did this happen? How did none of them see this? How had he not noticed the watch when Ross had?

Gabe stumbled back a step, bumping into the table. He paled. "Jesus. . . ."

"Yeah, I don't think he's going to help you now." Lawrence smirked. "I raised all of you. Whether you like it or not, the three of you are my sons, and you had no idea that it was me this entire time? I don't know if I should be impressed by my ability to assume Stefan's place or by the stupidity of you three. Then again, this isn't the first time Stefan and I switched places. That was a favorite pastime of ours, after all."

Dev got tunnel vision, not taking his eyes off Lawrence. He hoped that Lucian remembered the gun he kept in his desk. If he could just keep Lawrence's attention on him, Lucian could get it.

"But none of you knew it was me this whole time? Really? *She* figures it out?" Lawrence laughed out loud. "A fucking Creole girl with a sweet ass and what, a few hundred bucks to her name?"

Rosie jerked her head back. "Fuck you."

Lawrence smirked. "I would be down for that, but I don't think we're going to have the time."

Fury exploded into rage as Dev's hands curled into fists. "I'm going to kill you."

"But didn't you already try that?" Lawrence replied smoothly. "In the very room underneath this one? One late spring night?"

Dev's jaw locked down as he could feel his brothers' and Rosie's eyes land on him.

"Didn't you already do that, Devlin?" Lawrence insisted as he rose, still holding the gun. "Oh that's right. You murdered Stefan, instead."

"God," whispered Gabe.

"Oh yes." Lawrence chuckled. "He killed Stefan, because he thought he was killing me."

"Is it true?" Gabe demanded.

"Oh yes, it is true." Lawrence laughed once more. "He killed Stefan thinking it was me and staged it as a suicide."

Devlin could feel Rosie staring at him, but he couldn't bear to see the condemnation he knew had to be in her gaze.

"I didn't ask you," Gabe snapped back at the man who'd raised them. "Dev, did you do it?"

"He doesn't want to say it, but I'll tell you. Devlin thought he had it all figured out. And I'll give you credit." Lawrence winked at Dev. "You discovered what I was doing, but did that matter in the end?"

"How?" Dev demanded, voice hoarse. "How did it end up being Stefan? He was wearing your suit. He was—"

"When you confronted me about my . . . business entanglements—"

"Business entanglements," gasped Rosie, drawing Lawrence's attention. "You were trafficking human beings. That's not a business, you sick creep!"

Lawrence tsked. "Honey, that's the oldest business in the world, and the most profitable."

"Why?" Rosie demanded, surprising Dev and his brothers. She showed no fear as she glared at Lawrence. "Why would you do that? You have all the money in the world."

"It was never about the money. It was about the power," he said, tone condescending, as if he couldn't believe he had to explain this. "When you hold someone's life in your hands, you are their god."

"That's repulsive," she replied, shaking.

Lawrence lifted a shoulder in a half-hearted shrug. "Don't you think murder is repulsive?" he asked.

Rosie didn't respond, but Dev thought he already knew the answer to that.

"But back to the biggest plot point of them all. Devlin confronted me, and from that moment on, I knew." Lawrence stepped around the table, gun in hand. "I saw it in your eyes, boy. Just as I saw it in your eyes the day you came back. You were only five then, but yeah, I saw it. I saw your hatred. You wanted me dead then and you wanted me dead the night you confronted me."

"Came back from what?" Gabe demanded.

Lawrence smirked. "Punishment got a little rough when Devlin was younger. The boy needed a firm hand."

"Hitting me so I fell and cracked my head open is a firm hand?" Dev spat back. He heard his brothers curse. "If Besson hadn't found me, I would've died."

"No, Devlin, you would've *stayed* dead."

"How did we not know about that?" Gabe demanded. "How in the hell did we—"

"Because Devlin is a liar, too. Why don't you tell the truth now?" prompted Lawrence. "Tell them what *you* did."

Dev lifted his chin. "I did what was necessary. What you were doing had to be stopped, and I knew the police weren't going to be able to do it. You'd get away with it, like you've gotten away with everything else."

"I wouldn't have stopped unless you killed me? You're right. I wouldn't have. But you didn't kill me. I switched places with Stefan. He owed me. Told him I had a meeting that night. We did that often, by the way, so often. And you didn't succeed in killing me, but you did succeed in killing your real father."

Rosie's gasp was lost in the explosion of Gabe, but it was like Dev lost his hearing for several minutes, and when it came back up, Lawrence was talking. His lips were moving and Dev was hearing him, but the world was tilting all around him.

"Your mother didn't know. Not until Lucian and Madeline were born." Lawrence smiled in Lucian's direction. "I told her then—that you and your sister were my actual kids. The look on her face . . ." One side of his lips kicked up. "Just between us, I think she always knew."

"God," Dev murmured.

"Oh don't let it tear you up too much," Lawrence said. "Stefan was an utter fool."

"Why did you come here tonight?" Gabe asked.

"Why? Heard through the grapevine that someone had been snooping around," Lawrence said, and Dev immediately thought of Archie.

"I knew that meant Devlin got his hands on something. I came here to find it. Figured it had to do with Stefan. He was in on everything. You know that fucking reporter? Ross? If Stefan had kept his dick in his pants and his mouth shut, we'd never have to worry about him. But no. The dumb son of a bitch fell in love with the intern, fucking spilled his damn guts in regret or something."

"Andrea," whispered Rosie.

"She came to me, thinking I'd help her expose him. And wasn't that awkward?" The evil fuck chuckled. "Because he started feeling bad, he brought it all down. Now he's dead—by your hands—and that poor little intern is . . . well, she's at the bottom of the ocean floor."

Rosie covered her mouth.

"And let me guess, you had Sabrina killed, didn't you? She was a risk, because she knew. She knew it was you all along, didn't she?" Dev demanded.

"Sabrina was a lovely woman who should've married one of you, but she . . . well, we know she had issues and she could no longer be trusted. Both Stefan and Sabrina did this."

"It wasn't Stefan or Sabrina, you dumb fuck." Dev stepped toward Lawrence. "Your greed gave you away. It was all on you. You brought this down on yourself."

"Was it just my greed? Tell me one thing, Devlin. Nebraska? You weren't looking for property there, were you?"

His spine stiffened. "No."

"How long did you know about it?" Lawrence asked.

"Long enough," Dev replied.

"Hmm." Lawrence glanced at the brothers. "So, the past came a-knocking and the pieces all started to fall into place for you?"

Dev smirked. "Like I said, you're a dumb fucker."

The man sneered. "Do they know? I'm guessing not."

"I want to know what in the hell you two are talking about." Gabe looked close to losing it.

"It was bad enough having to deal with one of Stefan's bastards but two of them? You'd be amazed by what people will do for money. Paid off the hospital staff. Told that bitch one of them died. Fucking pointless, wasn't it? This other one came along." He gestured at Gabe with his hand. "I did it because I wanted to know what it was like to sell a child."

"Jesus," gasped Gabe.

"He wasn't my kid." Lawrence shrugged.

"You're a sick fuck," Dev said, shaking his head.

"Wait a minute. We have . . . we have another brother?" Lucian's tone echoed the riot of emotions swirling through the room. "You knew we had another brother?

"What in the hell?" Lucian gasped, and out of the corners of Dev's eyes, he saw Lucian had the top drawer open.

"Dev had a twin," Lawrence explained. "Well, apparently he still does."

"Is that . . . dear God, is that true?" Gabe questioned, his face pale.

Dev nodded. "I didn't know until—"

"He knew long enough," Lawrence cut in. "Just like he knew that Sabrina had something to do with the death of the mother of your child."

"I did not know that for sure," Dev argued, taking his gaze off Lawrence. "I had my suspicions, but I did not know that for sure."

Gabe gaped at him.

Refocusing on Lawrence, he could taste the rage building inside him. "What do you think is going to happen now? Did you plan on masquerading as Stefan for the rest of your life?"

"Why not? It was working out quite well and it's going to continue to," Lawrence said. "You see, you're going to let me walk out of here. And I'll go away. I have the money and the means, and none of you will have to worry about seeing my face again."

"That's not going to happen," Lucian said, and Dev's gaze shot to him. He held the gun as he stepped out from behind the desk.

"You're not leaving," Dev agreed.

Lawrence's laugh was devoid of humor. "How are you going to do it, Devlin? You going to strangle me like you did your father?"

Dev flinched.

"Shut up," growled Lucian. "Shut the fuck up."

"What? You going to do it? Shoot me? Your father?"

"Don't tempt me."

Lawrence smirked as he carelessly flicked the wrist of the hand holding the gun. "Like you've ever followed through on anything in your life, Lucian. I'm not worried."

That insult struck home and Lucian's arm trembled. Gabe, ever the mediator, stepped forward, lifting his hands. "This doesn't have to go down this way."

"Yes, it does," Dev cut in. "He knows that, because the only other option is prison time for him."

"And for you," Lawrence shot back. "You think if I go down, I won't bring you down with me? You killed Stefan. You think I won't throw you under the bus and drive right over you? You're out of your mind if you think that."

Dev's shoulders tensed as he glanced briefly at Rosie. God, he'd give up everything for her to not be here for this. His reputation. His money. His life. Everything for her to not witness what was about to go down.

"No," Gabe said. "No one is going to believe you, Lawrence. Not with everything you've done. You're going to prison, you sick fuck."

"People will believe me. Especially when they dig up Stefan's body and have another coroner, one not paid off, examine the body." Lawrence's cold gaze shifted to Rosie. "How does it feel to fuck a murderer?"

Rosie jolted.

"Don't look at her," Dev warned, stepping toward Lawrence. "I swear to God, if you even look in her direction one more time."

"Or what?" Lawrence laughed once more. "You're going to kill me?"

"That's what he wants," Gabe reasoned. "We're not going to give that to him."

"How does it feel?" Lawrence asked again. "To know you've been fucking a man who killed his father in cold blood?"

Dev charged, but Gabe threw his arm out, stopping him. "Don't," his brother ordered in a low voice. "Don't give him what he wants."

"You set him up," Rosie cried out, and Dev's head swung in her direction. She was . . . she was defending him? "You knew he was going to come after you and you set up your own brother. How does it feel to be a sociopath?"

"Feels amazing, actually. You should try it." Lawrence winked. "I may not have been his biological father, but I raised him. I made him who he is today and I can assure you that the apple doesn't fall far from the tree."

Rosie's hands clenched. "He is nothing like you."

"Is that so?" Lawrence's wide eyes came back to Devlin. "Did you fuck brain cells out of her?"

"Shut the fuck up," Dev growled, pushing at Gabe. He made it another foot. "You son—"

"You are a sick, twisted excuse for a human being," Rosie gritted out. "For what you've done—for what you've been a part of—you deserve being cut up in tiny pieces and fed to hogs."

Lawrence's gaze sharpened. "And did the police chief—"

"He was covering up for you!" Dev shouted. "He was covering up for you and you were providing him with *girls*. Little girls, you sick son of a bitch. He was just as sick and depraved as you."

The man ignored him. "Tell me, Rosie, do you think two wrongs make a right?"

"I swear to fucking God, if you speak to her one more time, I will kill you where you stand!" Dev exploded, straining against his brother.

Lawrence stared back at him, his head cocking slightly to the side. "Goddamn, you're . . . you're in love with her."

Dev's heart stopped in his chest.

"You don't even have to say it. I see it." A look of wonder crossed Lawrence's face. "You love her and you're going to . . . you're going to throw it all away for her."

Slowly, Dev's focus shifted to Rosie. She wasn't staring at Lawrence. No. She was staring at Dev, her chest rising and falling heavily.

"Yeah," he whispered, and it was like an earthquake. He did love her. He didn't know when it happened. If it was when he first saw those god-awful beaded curtains as bizarre as that sounded or the first time she called him a dickhead. It could've been the first kiss or the first time she put him in his place. It could've been the first time she sat there and listened to him. It could've been right then, when she defended him even knowing the truth. Devlin was in love with Rosie.

Their gazes connected and held and then he said louder, "Yes."

Tears filled her eyes, and that was all that he allowed himself to see. He refocused on Lawrence and he knew what he had to do.

This was it, Dev realized.

Everything was over.

Gabe was right. Even though he wanted to take Lawrence down and watch the life seep out of the bastard's eyes, he wasn't going to do that. Not in front of his brothers. Not in front of Rosie. She'd already been pulled into this too far.

Of all people, she didn't deserve this.

"Call Troy," Dev said.

"What?" Lucian demanded, still pointing the gun at Lawrence. "Are you for real?"

"Devlin," Rosie whispered, stepping toward him, surprising him yet again, like she always did. "Think about this. . . ."

"I have." He focused on her. "It's going to be okay."

"You're going to go to prison right along with me," Lawrence said.

"No, he won't," Gabe growled out.

Lawrence chuckled darkly. "Oh I'll make damn sure of it."

"Shut up," Devlin yelled. "Just shut the hell up." Turning to Lucian, he said, "Call Troy. Get him here."

"You really want to do this, Devlin?" Lawrence asked, lifting his brows.

Dev drew in a deep breath. "It is what it is."

A broken sound came from Rosie, a gasp that ended in a sob. He couldn't look at her now as he stared back at the man who'd raised him.

Who'd made him who he was today.

"No," he said out loud, stepping back from Gabe's grasp.

Lawrence frowned as Gabe looked back at him.

No, it wasn't true, Dev realized, and hell if that wasn't another earthquake. If he was the man Lawrence raised, he would've killed the bastard the moment he learned it was him and not Stefan. He wouldn't be giving it up.

He wouldn't be in love.

Devlin smiled as the muscles in his back and neck loosened. And that smile *felt* real and right, and dear God, it was freeing. It spread across his face as he met Lawrence's stare. "I'm nothing like you."

His words slammed into Lawrence like a well-placed punch. Blood drained from his face as he held Dev's gaze. The grandfather clock ticked away.

"You're right." Lawrence's voice was hoarse. "You're not."

Lawrence lifted the gun, and it was like the entire world slowed down to an infinite crawl. Gabe cursed, and Dev knew what he was going to do. Lawrence was going to end it—end it right in front of them—and all Dev could think of was Rosie. She didn't need to see this of all things. He turned to her, her name on his tongue as he heard Gabe shout out a warning.

Dev whipped back around, and saw with rising terror he was wrong, so damn wrong.

Lawrence wasn't going to kill himself.

He was pointing the gun. Not at them. Dear God, not at them. Lawrence was aiming the gun at Rosie.

Lawrence smiled. "And you're going to have to live with that."

There were screams. Rosie's. His brothers'. His. And the crack of gunshot was like thunder.

Chapter 35

Lucian's face paled as he gasped, "Holy shit."

Stumbling back a step and against an empty chair, Rosie tried to draw in air, but it went nowhere as she stared at Lawrence. Her heart raced so fast she thought she might actually be sick.

Lawrence was going to shoot her. He'd aimed the gun at her and was going to shoot her.

But not anymore.

The utterly evil man was lying in front of the sofa, a bullet to the center of his chest and a pool of ruby-red liquid spreading across the hardwood floor. His eyes were open, fixed on the ceiling.

The man . . . the man was dead.

"Lucian," Gabe started and then stopped.

"It wasn't me." Lucian was staring past Devlin and Gabe. "I was going to do it. I was going to shoot that bastard, but it wasn't me. It was *him*."

Rosie turned as if she were stuck in a dream. A man stood in the doorway, a man who looked so much like Devlin that she jolted, thinking at first that it was Devlin standing there, holding a gun, but it wasn't, because Devlin was beside her, wrapping an arm around her. Devlin was touching her, skimming his hands over her body as if he were searching for a wound. The man who was utterly identical to Devlin was his twin.

"I was following him. Took me a while to get in here, though." Payton lowered the gun. "He was going to shoot her. I had . . . I had to do something."

Gabe was saying something else, but there was a buzzing in Rosie's head that was drowning out what he was saying, drowning out everything around her.

There was a dead man right there.

She thought after everything she'd learned and what she'd experienced in her life, this wouldn't be so shocking, but it was. Her entire being was rattled and there was a humming in her ears, in her veins.

Hands suddenly landed on her, gripping her arms and startling her. Devlin's face was in hers. "Are you okay? Rosie, talk to me? Are you okay?"

She strained to see around his shoulder. She wasn't even sure why. It was like she had to keep looking so she could keep telling herself that he was dead.

"Don't. Come on, don't look at him." Dev lifted his hands, cupping her cheeks. He tilted her head back. "Look at me."

Her gaze latched on to his and the next breath she took finally felt like it went somewhere. The room came back into focus as the buzzing in her ears receded.

"You know," she said, her voice sounding hoarse and unused. "You could've picked a better time to say you loved me."

Devlin let out a rough laugh. "Yeah, I probably could've picked a better time." Dipping his chin, he kissed her forehead and then pulled back, scanning her entire body. "You sure you're okay? You're not hurt?"

She swallowed hard as she kept her gaze trained on his. "I don't think he fired."

A sound of relief poured out of him as he pulled her against him, folding his arms around her. "I'm so sorry," he said, a tremble rolling through his body. "I'm so fucking sorry you had to see this. You had to hear this."

"It's okay." Rosie dropped her head to his shoulder as she wrapped her arms around him, holding him as tightly as he held her. "It's okay."

He curled his hand around the back of her head, fisting her hair. "It's not okay, Rosie. None of this is okay."

Her heart squeezed painfully. "I know," she whispered. "But it's going to be. It has to be now."

Another shudder rocked him, and then all hell seemed to break loose.

A scream pierced through the room. Devlin pulled back, twisting his body so he kept Rosie behind him. Over his shoulder, she saw Julia in the doorway, behind Payton.

"Oh my God." Julia had her hands up in front of her, as if she was warding off what she was seeing.

Rosie saw Julia race toward Lucian. He was no longer holding the gun he didn't even fire. That was in Gabe's hands as Julia clasped Lucian's pale face. "Babe, what happened?" Panic clogged her voice. "What's going on? Lucian, babe—"

Her cries were lost when Lucian pulled her to him, folding his body around her. He held Julia like . . . like Devlin had just held her, like he would sink if it weren't for her.

All she could think was thank God Nikki was back at her place now and wasn't here to witness this.

Everything happened in a blur at this point. Gabe put the gun down on the desk and he was on the phone, talking to someone. Rosie was ushered out of the room, along with Lucian and Julia, who was staring at Payton and Devlin like something was wrong with her eyes, and somehow the three of them ended up downstairs, in a cozy, comfortable living room that actually looked like a real one.

Lucian sat on the couch, his head in his hands while Julia rubbed his back. She'd been filled in, and her concern for Lucian was evident in every pained look she sent Rosie. Lucian hadn't pulled the trigger, but he had been ready to, and that had gotten to him. That much was evident.

Rosie . . . she couldn't sit still as Devlin and Gabe were doing God knew what upstairs. She paced the length of the living room a hundred times over. At some point she thought she heard voices—voices that weren't Gabe's or Devlin's.

Who did they call?

Someone who was going to take care of it all, remove the body and scrub the evidence away until it was like this person never existed?

God, a part of her couldn't believe she was even thinking that, but this . . . this had become her life, because not once since the gun was fired and Lawrence went down did she even consider calling the police.

And when Devlin had decided to call the police, she had panicked. That wasn't . . . that wasn't like her. Or maybe it was and she was now just discovering that? She couldn't find it in herself to judge Devlin.

She may have nightmares and she might need many, many years to deal with that, but she knew she wasn't going to regret not calling the police. What she did regret was being put in that situation by an evil, out-of-control person.

Just like Devlin and his family had been put in that position all these years.

Rosie shuddered as she wrapped her arms around herself. Glancing over at Lucian and Julia, she bit down on her lip. She was worried about him. Julia drew him in toward her. Their heads bowed together, and Rosie turned away to give them some level of privacy.

She had no idea how much time had passed, but it was still dark outside when Devlin and Gabe appeared in the doorway. Payton wasn't with them, and for a moment, she wondered if he'd even been there.

Before she had a chance to move, Lucian spoke for the first time since he came down to this room. "Where is *our* brother?"

"He left," Devlin answered. "He thought it would be wise to come back at a . . . better time."

"Better time?" Lucian coughed out a dry laugh.

Unfolding her arms, Rosie rushed over to Dev as Gabe dropped into the recliner. She gripped his arms, her gaze searching his. "Is everything . . . everything okay?"

Devlin didn't respond as he pulled her to his chest and dropped his forehead to hers. Her hands went to his chest and she could feel his heart pounding under her palm.

"Everything has been taken care of." Gabe sounded tired. "It's over."

Rosie pulled back, lifting her gaze to Devlin's.

"Don't ask," he said, cupping her cheek. "You don't want to know."

Part of her did want to know and maybe that was the part of her that existed in a pool of morbid curiosity, but she could tell from Devlin's shattered face, he didn't want her to know the grittier details. At least not right now. So she asked, "What's going to happen now?"

"We're going on like we always do." It was Lucian who answered, causing Rosie to twist around. He was leaning back against the couch now. "Stefan will be reported missing since Lawrence was already presumed dead. Another strange de Vincent disappearance to be whispered and gossiped about."

Rosie winced.

"And we will go on like nothing happened, won't we?" Lucian's laugh lacked humor once again. "I mean, we should. That bastard . . . he didn't deserve to live, but how are we . . . how are we any different?"

"Oh babe." Julia cupped his cheek. "You are nothing like that man. Nothing like either of them."

"We're not like him. We've never been like him," Gabe stated. "But you?"

Rosie sucked in a sharp breath when she realized Gabe was staring directly at Devlin.

"What the hell, Dev?" Gabe continued. "You did do it."

"Come on," Lucian said, shaking his head. "That's not exactly surprising."

"Maybe not to you," Gabe shot back.

Devlin didn't jump in. The whole time he stood there, taking it. Taking it all like he always had.

"Like you didn't have your suspicions," Lucian countered.

"I did, but I at least had hope that I was wrong." Gabe's jaw hardened. "Call me an optimistic fool for wanting to believe he wasn't capable of that."

"Believe he wasn't capable of what?" Lucian inched forward on the couch. "You know damn well we are not any better when it comes to that."

Julia opened her mouth.

"Emma," Lucian said, and Gabe drew back at the mention of the mother of his child. "Can you really say what we did was any different than what Dev did?"

"I had to do something," Dev finally said. "You know going to the police wouldn't have stopped Lawrence. Half of them were involved and he would've paid off the rest or they would've ended up dead. You don't understand—"

"No, you're right. We don't understand." Gabe rose. "You never told us any of this. Not once did you tell us what they were involved in. What they were doing."

"I didn't want you to know!" A crack showed in Devlin's composure, surprising both brothers and Julia. But not Rosie. This—all of this—was a long time brewing. Devlin stepped around Rosie. "Would it have made your life better or easier knowing that the man who raised you and his brother were selling humans? Trafficking women and children? Little girls?"

Julia covered her mouth with her hand.

"Would it have helped you sleep better at night knowing that half of those people were sold against their will or were tricked into believing they were leaving their families for a better life? Or that the other half were murdered? Did you want to know that?" Devlin demanded.

Neither brother answered.

"I didn't think so. Because I know what happens once you learn about that. You start doing research. You start learning what they do to people, how they drug them and threaten them to get them to do what they want." Devlin's shoulders stiffened. "You won't sleep very much once you know. So, excuse the fuck out of me for trying to save both of you from that."

Gabe thrust his hand through his hair. "But we're family. You shouldn't have had to do this by yourself—know this by yourself. How could you not know that as much as it would've fucked us up, we would've been there to shoulder that with you?"

"We didn't even know that he almost killed you," Lucian said, drawing Devlin's attention. "Shit. Richard had to know about that. Livie, too?"

"They knew I was hurt," Devlin said after a moment. "It was Besson who found me unconscious. He gave me CPR, but neither he nor his wife knew how it happened."

"And you never said anything?" Gabe lifted his hands. "And what you knew about Sabrina? You knew—"

"I was trying to protect you," Devlin cut in, and Rosie's breath caught. Was he going to tell him about Sabrina? "I was trying to protect both of you."

It took great effort for Rosie to not speak up at that point, because this was something Devlin needed to say, needed to get off his chest.

"Just like you were trying to protect us from knowing we had another brother?" Lucian demanded, and Julia slowly lowered her hand to her knee. "Is that why you never told us?"

A muscle flexed along Devlin's jaw. "I didn't know until the past spring that he even existed."

"That was nearly six months ago!" Gabe exploded.

"I didn't know how to tell you," Devlin returned. "And he didn't want it known. Jesus. He'd just found out that he'd been adopted and that he was related to us. I didn't plan—"

"On ever telling us?" Lucian asked.

"No," snapped Devlin. "We both planned on telling you when he was ready."

Gabe shook his head as he started to turn away and then he spun back to Devlin. "His name is Payton. I just learned that tonight. You had months knowing that Lawrence . . . that he sent him away out of spite. Lied to our mother, because he . . . he could."

"He was a monster," Julia whispered, placing her hand on Lucian's thigh. "And I am glad he is dead for real now."

Rosie had to agree with her. Might make her a terrible person, but that man and his brother were pure evil with a human face.

"You should've told us," Gabe said, turning and walking toward the fireplace. He placed his hand on the mantel. His head bowed. "I don't even . . . Jesus, Dev. I don't even know who you are."

Pressure clamped down on Rosie's chest as Devlin stepped back.

She twisted toward him, but he was already walking out of the room and he was gone before she could say a word.

Unbelievable.

That was all Rosie could think as she slowly turned back to the brothers. She'd just learned some crazy stuff herself and before what had happened . . . just happened, she wasn't sure where she stood with Devlin.

Now she knew.

She didn't look at Julia when she spoke. She looked straight at them. "You guys are clueless. Seriously. Fucking clueless."

Lucian's gaze snapped to her. "Rosie—"

"No. Everything he's *ever* done has been because of you all. What he's *become* has been because of both of you. You have no idea."

"We wanted to know." Gabe pushed away from the fireplace. "He kept us in the dark."

"No. Absolutely not." Rosie's voice shook with anger. "He didn't keep you in the dark. He kept both of you in the light."

Lucian's entire body seemed to jerk in response to that.

"He put up with a psychotic woman who was obsessed with you to protect you. She knew everything and if it weren't for Devlin, she would've held that over your head. If it weren't for him, you wouldn't be with Nikki right now. You'd be saddled with *that* woman," she said to Gabe before swinging toward Lucian. Anger pumped through her veins. "And you remember that funny story you told me about the three of you at school? How Devlin got busted for you all breaking curfew? What is really funny about all of that is Lawrence beat him so badly after that, his body still bares the proof. You didn't know that, did you? Have either of you seen his back?"

Both brothers had gone silent as tears crowded her throat. "Have either of you ever seen the scars? All over his back? I'm guessing you haven't. And I'm guessing neither of you pulled your heads out of your asses long enough to even wonder why Devlin is the way he is or to realize that while both of you were out there living your lives and doing whatever the fuck you all wanted to do, he was trapped with those monsters. So, no. He didn't keep you in the dark. He kept you all in the light. Think about that while you're dragging him through the mud he's been living in for years."

Rosie didn't wait for them to respond, she left the room and started looking for Devlin. She found him standing in the foyer, under the gold chandelier. He was staring up the grand staircase.

"This . . . this fucking house," he said as she walked up to him. Her gaze followed his, but she didn't see anything. That didn't stop the goose bumps from spreading across her skin when he said, "This house is haunted by the dead and the living. I wish I never brought you here."

"Devlin. . . ." She touched his arm, but he didn't look down at her. "Are you okay?"

He laughed.

"I know that's a dumb question."

"It's not, but you shouldn't be asking me that."

"Your brothers—"

"They have every right to be mad. I did lie to them."

"No." Her grip on his arm tightened. "You protected them. You gave them their lives while sacrificing your own. Yeah, they get to be mad, but they also need to get the fuck over it. Which I pretty much just told them. So, hopefully you don't get too mad at me over that."

Devlin turned to her then, his eyes wide with surprise. "You did . . . what?"

"Um, well, I did basically tell them to pull their heads out of their asses. I said other things, but um, yeah, that's the gist of it."

He stared down at her.

She started to get a little worried. "They needed to know what you've done for them. They—"

"Thank you." Devlin's head swept down and he kissed her. "No one . . . has done that. Stood up for me. Thank you."

"You don't need to thank me. I did it because I—"

"Don't," he said quietly, as if he sensed what she was going to say. He kissed her again, softly at first, but the touch of his mouth quickly deepened. The kiss turned fierce, desperate even, and when he finally lifted his mouth from hers, she was shaken and felt . . . felt a little like the end. "What I need from you is to just go home. Okay? You were never here."

"What? I thought everything was taken care of?"

"It is, but just in case. There's something I need to do."

He held on to her cheeks, his gaze pleading. "All right? I just need you to leave. I'll be in touch. I promise."

"I don't want to leave."

"But I need to do this alone and I need you to leave."

"Do what?" she asked.

He turned from her and stared up at the staircase. "I think it's time to rid this land of those ghosts."

"Then I'm your girl. I'm—"

"Not those kinds of ghosts, Rosie." He made his way to the stairs. "Please go. This is something I need to do myself."

A different kind of anxiety blossomed to life.

Blinking back tears, she felt herself nod and she heard herself say yes, but she reached for him, coming up with nothing but air.

"What I said was true." Devlin's gaze met hers. "I love you, Rosie. I know it seems impossible, but it's real."

"Devlin—"

He'd already started up the stairs, and Rosie heard the door swing open behind her. She spun, expecting to see someone, but no one was there. Just her and the wind, stirring the ivy.

DEV WAS A MURDERER.

He'd long since accepted that.

He'd killed Stefan thinking it was Lawrence. He'd ordered the death of the police chief who covered up Lawrence's crimes.

Dev had killed.

He didn't and wouldn't regret what he'd done, and maybe that spoke of the darkness in his soul—he didn't know and he didn't care.

Earlier that night, he'd been ready to turn himself in. Now he was ready to do what should've been done decades ago.

His brothers were gone when he returned downstairs, bag in hand.

He placed the black duffel bag by the front door and then he picked up the can he'd retrieved from the garage. He wasn't all that surprised. Instinct told him that Gabe had gone to Nikki, and Lucian and Julia were together, safe and far from here.

Would they forgive him? Understand?

He took in the intricate woodwork Gabe had crafted with his own hands and the arched doorways as he moved through the house. There were no photos, just the morbid yet beautiful paintings rendered by his brother's and sister's fingers. He stopped at his office and thought about the irony of paying off the medical examiner. If he hadn't, the coroner would've surely discovered that it wasn't Lawrence's body wheeled into the morgue, but Stefan's.

Both men had been complicit in some of the most atrocious crimes out there. Both men had been not only a curse upon this land and home but also everyone they came into contact with.

His steps echoed through the silent, dark third-floor hallway as he passed the bedroom of his mother, who had been just as trapped as he'd been. He walked past Lawrence's private quarters and tasted the bitter fear that always consumed him as a child and the red-hot hatred that had festered from that. He made his way through the second floor, throwing open all the doors as he went, remembering Nikki as a child, running through the halls, and then he stopped, and he could recall him and Pearl doing the same.

A tickle danced across the back of his neck, and he swore he heard the faint sound of a man laughing.

Dev started walking, slowly, meticulously making his way downstairs. He stopped at the back window, the one that overlooked the rose garden and the pool.

And he saw his sister, not facedown in the pool but standing by it staring up at the window, her pale blond hair blowing in the wind. Maybe it was just a memory. Or it was a ghost. Maybe he'd lost his fucking mind, but he saw her, and in those quiet moments, he heard his mother whisper thank you.

Maybe they'd all be freed now.

Dev returned to the foyer and breathed in the pungent scent of gasoline as he picked up his duffel bag. Reaching into his pocket, he pulled out a lighter he'd found in the pantry. His thumb rolled over it. It clicked and a flame sparked to life.

The walls of the house were like the scars on his back, the floors like the bones Lawrence had tried to break over and over, and everything inside of the house was nothing but tainted meat and torn muscle, stretched too far.

And it was all going to burn.

Chapter 36

*S*candal after scandal consumed the local news and newspapers, and then, like a wildfire, it spread nationally.

First it was the report of Sabrina's death, and somehow, and Rosie was guessing the de Vincents had had a hand in this, what was fed to the public was a tragic robbery gone wrong. Nothing of what Sabrina was involved in was revealed.

Then the . . . Senator Stefan de Vincent was reported missing by Gabe. That news replaced the talk of Sabrina. Rosie had no idea what truly happened to Lawrence's body and she didn't want to know, and as sick as it was, the only thing she cared about was the fact that two very evil men, Stefan and Lawrence, were no longer walking this earth.

The news of fake Stefan's disappearance had overshadowed something else, something that Rosie understood but had not expected. Something that was so heartbreakingly powerful.

Devlin had burned down the de Vincent mansion.

The whole thing was gone. The fire was ruled an accident—the home was razed to the ground and, according to what Nikki told her, no one could understand how the whole place had gone up, leaving absolutely nothing but charred wood and ashes.

There'd been something unnatural about the fire, and that had been Gabe's wording.

The brothers and Julia and Nikki knew that Devlin had started the fire, and Rosie had thought they'd be angry, but all of them had seemed oddly . . . relieved that the place was gone.

And at first, Rosie had experienced mind-numbing panic. Devlin was . . . he was gone, and she'd feared that he'd burned down with the house, but then she'd learned that he'd been seen after the fire.

He'd been to Nikki's parents' house, to Richard and Livie, and apparently given them a duffel bag full of money, shocking the Bessons, Nikki, and his brothers.

But it didn't come as a shock to Rosie.

There was an innate goodness inside of Devlin. It was just buried under a lot . . . a lot of darkness.

Two weeks had passed since that night—a night that had started so beautifully and ended so darkly.

She had not heard from Devlin. Neither had Gabe or Lucian. He, too, seemed to have disappeared after going to Nikki's parents' house, and Rosie . . . God, she was heartsick with worry and then furious that he'd left her.

"You okay?"

Jarred from her thoughts, she blinked and focused on Jilly. She was at Jilly and Liz's place and she was supposed to be paying attention, but obviously wasn't.

"I'm sorry." Rosie forced a smile.

"It's okay." Concern filled Liz's gaze. "We can talk about this later."

"Totally," chimed in Sarah. "We don't have to talk about this right now."

"It's fine," she insisted.

The three women stared back at her and their looks said they knew it wasn't fine. She'd told them what she could, which wasn't a whole hell of a lot, but they knew Devlin had left and they knew . . .

They knew that Rosie had fallen in love with him.

When that had happened, she had no idea, but she knew it was either the first time she'd seen a hint of a smile from him or when she first heard him laugh. How corny was that? Totally. But it was true. She just didn't realize it until after he was gone, and how . . . how ironic was that?

But she realized it when she'd heard that Devlin had given Nikki's parents more money than they'd ever need and it was confirmed when she heard from Ross and he'd told her that the photo album had been anonymously delivered to him. He'd believed it had been her, but Rosie knew it had been Devlin.

Ross was having a field day with all the recent developments, and Rosie knew it would be a long time before he let his quest go, but she also knew he was never going to find out the truth. It was hard not confirming his suspicions about Andrea being dead, but she feared if he did discover that, then he'd learn that the woman he'd loved and lost had been having an affair with Stefan.

Sometimes secrets were better left buried.

"Okay." Sarah nodded. "So, I've done a walk-through of the Mendez house, and I can tell you there are no spirits there now. I've saged the hell out of it and put up a barrier just in case any spirit tries to worm its way back in."

"You mean when the ghosts decide to leave Lucian's place again?" Jilly supplied.

After her walk-through, Sarah believed that the ghost pestering the Mendez family had originated from Lucian's house, which was not exactly something Julia had been happy to hear.

"Like I told Lucian, when the remodeling is done, I will do the same to their home, but I don't think they're going to have a problem anymore." Sarah's gaze met Rosie's. "I think someone else got rid of those ghosts."

Rosie's breath caught. She hadn't told Sarah about what Devlin had said to her before the fire.

Sarah smiled, and yeah, that kind of creeped out even Rosie.

The discussion ended there and Sarah followed her out onto the porch. "Man, it's gotten really cold," Rosie said, tugging the thick cardigan close. "I can't remember—"

"I know," Sarah cut in.

Rosie turned to her. "Know what?"

"He just needs some time to get his head in the right place." She winked. "To get that . . . light back in him."

"Okay." Rosie glanced around, unable to suppress a shiver. "Is there a spirit whispering this in your ear or something?"

Moving down one step, she grinned up at Rosie. "He'll come back,"

Sarah said, and she said this in a way that made Rosie wonder if she really did *know*. "And when he does, try not to yell at him too much."

A weak smile tugged at her lips as a bubble of hope swelled in her chest. "Can't make any promises with that."

HE WAS SITTING on a bench in the middle of a meadow full of peonies and even with his back to her, Rosie knew who it was and she couldn't believe it as she walked up to him.

Tears filled her eyes, threatening to choke her as she walked around the bench. Her heart didn't stop in her chest, but it felt like it was being squeezed in a juice grinder.

It was *him*.

And that was how she knew she was dreaming.

"Ian," she whispered as she sat down on the bench beside him.

He didn't look at her, but stared out over the bright meadow. "Rosalynn."

Her breath caught on a knot of raw emotion. His voice. Oh my God, that was *his* voice. "This . . . this is a dream."

Ian smiled as a warm breeze rolled through the meadow, stirring the crisp white peonies. "Is it?"

She drew in another breath but it ended in a soft sob. "I don't know. I don't want it to be."

"Does it matter?" he asked, and then he lifted his hand, opening it. Resting in the center of his palm was her gold wedding band. "It's time."

"I don't understand." There was a chirping in the distance, growing louder and louder.

The wedding band vanished. "It's time to let go."

Rosie woke, gasping for air as she jerked upright. The chirping was the alarm on her cell phone. She reached for it, turning it off as she tried to slow her breathing. In the darkness of her bedroom, she reached for the chain around her neck and pulled the ring out from underneath her shirt. She folded her fingers around the warm metal.

It's time.

The knot in her throat expanded and she closed her eyes tight against the sting. In the ten years since he'd been gone, she'd never dreamt of him. Ever. Not even once, and this dream, God, it felt so real. She could still hear his voice, see that smile, and feel the warm breeze on her skin.

It's time to let go.

Her shoulders shook as the tears snuck through, coursing down her cheeks. The dream could've been some kind of subconscious message or maybe . . . just maybe Ian was finally reaching out to her from the beyond.

She didn't know what to think.

Falling backward, she shifted onto her side and pulled her legs up to her chest as she held on to the ring. The tears . . . they came, quiet at first, and then they shook her entire body. She had no idea if she was crying because of the dream or because it really was time to let go or because of everything she'd learned about Devlin and what she'd seen or because she hadn't heard from him.

And maybe it was because there was this fear that she'd never get the chance to tell him that she loved him.

It was as if a seal had cracked inside her, letting the raw emotions slide through, but they'd gathered behind that crack, pushing and piling on until the fissure gave way and the seal exploded.

She didn't know how long she cried for. It felt like hours, but finally, she got it all out of her.

Eyes blurry and achy, she sat up and folded her legs under the blanket.

It was time.

Lifting the ring, she pressed a kiss to it and then she lifted the chain, removing the necklace. She rose from the bed and walked over to her dresser, picking up a small wooden cigar box that had belonged to Ian. He hadn't smoked cigars, but he liked to collect the boxes. After his death, she'd given the boxes to his family, all except this one. Opening it, she placed the ring, along with the chain, inside the box and closed the lid.

It *was* time.

A STRANGE BOX showed up on her doorstep the next afternoon, after she returned from a shift at Pradine's.

"What the . . . ?"

Rosie picked up the medium-sized box. It wasn't all that heavy. Her name was written in a rather elegant scrawl on a white shipping label. There was no address on it—not hers or a return one. This package was definitely dropped off here.

Frowning, she quickly unlocked the door and stepped into her apartment. She nudged the door shut and then carried the box over to the table.

She dropped her bag on the couch and then walked over to the kitchen area, flipping on lights. A buttery soft glow filled the large room as she grabbed an old steak knife out of the drawer. A box cutter would work better, but box cutters kind of creeped her out. It was the whole blade breaking off in whatever it was cutting into thing.

Rosie shuddered.

She stabbed the steak knife into the packing tape on the box, slicing it open. A woody, almost sweet smell greeted her. She recognized the scent immediately. Sandalwood. Yum. Brown paper hid whatever rested beneath it. She wanted to rip the paper apart, but there was a small white card folded in the center.

Knocking a curl out of her face, she reached into the box and plucked it out, placing it aside. She reached for the brown paper and pulled it apart.

"Holy moly," she gasped.

The brown paper slipped from her fingers and floated to the worn, hardwood floor, landing with a dry whisper.

Inside the box was the most stunning display of carved wood she'd ever seen, but it wasn't just a plank of wood. It was sandalwood, which she knew was absurdly expensive. The pieces were round and cylinder-shaped beads separated by shorter, oval-shaped pieces.

Stunned, she reached in and picked up the beautiful, tan-colored pieces, eyes going wide as the strings of wood delicately knocked off one another.

It was a beaded curtain.

A beaded curtain that probably, no joke, cost more than her Toyota Corolla. A tremor coursed through her arms as she stared at the beaded curtain, openmouthed since it felt like her jaw had come unhinged.

Her gaze fell to the card on the table.

With her heart now somewhere in her throat, she snatched up the card and all but tore it open. There was just one sentence. No name.

Thought these would be an improvement.

Slowly, she turned to her old Walmart beaded curtains that hung between the bedroom and the living room/kitchen area.

Her fingers curled around the smooth beads as she whispered, "Devlin."

A knock sounded from her front door.

Clutching the card in her hand, she didn't let herself feel too much hope as she raced over to the door and threw it open.

Her heart did stop then.

Devlin de Vincent stood before her, his hair not as styled as normal and a few days' worth of growth along his jaw. He made that look good, real good.

But there was something utterly shocking about him as he stood in her doorway, those sea-green eyes fixed on her with hope, hunger, and something far more powerful.

"You're wearing jeans," she blurted out.

"What?"

The card dug into her palm. "You're wearing denim jeans."

"Yeah," he said, confusion seeping into his gaze. "They're jeans."

"Wow," she murmured. "I didn't think you owned jeans. Seriously."

One side of his lips twitched. "Is that all you have to say to me?"

"No." Snapping forward, she hit him on the chest. Not hard. It was more of a gentle love tap. "Where have you been? I was so afraid you weren't going to come back. And everyone—"

Devlin stepped into her apartment, and before she could say another word, his mouth was on hers and he was kissing her and she was kissing him back. His lips moved over hers, kissing away anything she was about to yell at him. Devlin kissed like a man staking a claim, like someone who'd never had the luxury of doing so before.

When he lifted his mouth from hers, somehow he had the door closed behind them. "Did you like the beaded curtains?"

She still held the card in her hand as she clutched his shirt with her other hand. Resting her head against his chest, she swallowed back tears. "Yes. They are an improvement."

"Perfect."

Drawing in a shaking breath, she pulled back and didn't get very far, because the hand that was around the back of her head slipped to her neck.

"Where is it?" His gaze searched her face. "The necklace? The ring?"

"Oh. It was time."

His brows lifted.

She fisted his shirt. "I thought . . . I was worried you weren't going to come back."

"I told you I was." He cupped her cheek. "Besides, I had to. I never did get to tell you the other part of the de Vincent curse."

She laughed as his face blurred. "No, no, you didn't."

He smoothed his thumb over her jaw. "Our great-great-grandmother claimed that when de Vincent men fell in love, they did so fast and hard, without reason or hesitation."

"Really?" she whispered.

"Really." He dropped his forehead to hers. "I didn't believe it."

"Obviously."

"But that changed. I met you," Devlin said. "And now I do believe it."

Rosie smiled. "I guess that's a good thing, then."

"Why?"

"Because I love you." She slid her hand to his cheek as he drew in an audible breath. "I'm in love with you, Devlin de Vincent, so it's a good thing you're cursed, isn't it?"

"Yeah." His arms swept around her. "For once, it is."

Epilogue

*D*ev lost himself.

He lost himself every time he was with Rosie, and each time, he found a piece of himself that had been hidden away. This time was no different, even though her father had plied them both with enough liquor and pralines the night before that both him and Rosie were made of nothing but sugar and alcohol, so much so that any physical activity seemed unreasonable when they both collapsed into her bed, him grumbling about the damn glow-in-the-dark stars and her giggling like his drunken curses were the funniest thing ever. They'd passed out together in a tangle of arms and legs, arguing over whether or not the stars would adorn the ceiling of the bedroom in the house they were building together. There may have been a discussion about particleboard, and Dev had already accepted that there'd be beaded curtains in his home.

Now their arms and bodies were tangled in a much different way.

Dev moved above her and in her, one arm curled under her head, the other lower, his hand gripping her hip as he thrust between her thighs. Her legs were wrapped so deliciously around his waist, dragging him in as she lifted up, meeting every plunge. Passion soaked their skin, drenched their muscles and bones, and he wanted more.

He always wanted more of her and he was never not ready for her—never not seconds away from tearing off his clothes and baring his body and his soul to her warm, welcoming arms. He could never get enough of the taste of her mouth or the salty musk of her skin. He could just never get enough of Rosie and her glow-in-the-dark stars, her ghost investigations that he now knew way too much about, and her damn beaded curtains.

Being with Rosie was a revolution of the soul, and who in the hell would've thought he'd be so damn poetic now?

He chuckled as he dragged the bridge of his nose down the elegant slope of her neck.

"What are you laughing about?" she asked, her hands skating over his back, tracing the ropy lines of the scars with a care that nearly broke him each time.

"Just . . ." He lifted his head and stared down at her, his thrusts slowing as he went deep enough to cause her to gasp. "Just thinking we're probably sweating sugar and liquor."

"True." She giggled.

"And I was also thinking that you're . . . you're a revolution of my soul," he admitted, pressing his hips flush to hers and feeling a little silly for speaking it out loud, but there were no secrets between them now. None at all.

A wide, beautiful smile tugged at the corners of her lips as a sort of wonder filled her gaze. "You . . . you really think that?"

"I know that."

Lifting her head, she curled her arm around his neck and kissed him—kissed him in a way that almost caused him to come right then. "I love you, Devlin."

He groaned as the words skated down his spine and he lost all semblance of control, just like Rosie knew he would, just like he did every time she said those words. He lifted her to him as he thrust in her, over and over, his mouth finding and claiming hers, and when she tightened and spasmed around him, there was no holding back. He lost himself in those moments of bliss, and as his heart slowed and their bodies stilled except for the heavy, sated pants of breath, he discovered that he had no problem with the power her love had over him.

No problem at all.

Who knew how much time had passed before he rolled off her. He didn't go very far, snagging an arm around her waist and pulling her along with him so that her cheek rested on his chest.

Staring down at the mess of curls, he idly dragged his fingers up and down her back as he thought about who he was and who he was now becoming. It had been a year since the night he'd started to lay his demons to rest and everything had changed. Not just for him.

Julia and Lucian had married—eloped, actually—and were planning to welcome their first child in the summer in a ghost-free home. Gabe and Nikki had also married, but in a ceremony that had dominated the local news for weeks. They'd moved to Baton Rouge, to be closer to his son, William. After all, Nikki wanted William to spend as much time as possible with his younger half sister. Livie, who had been named after Nikki's mother, was only three months old.

Even Payton, his twin, was starting to come around. He was in town, staying at Dev's place at the Port, and tonight they were all going to have their first family dinner. It was a beginning.

And Dev . . . well, he was a different person . . . mostly.

He felt no remorse nor shame for what he'd done to stop Lawrence and his father. Maybe that made him a bad person, but he didn't care and he knew Rosie didn't, either. He wasn't haunted by his actions even if his past still followed him into his sleep, but Rosie had always been there for those nights. With her kisses and her touches, her sighs and her very breath, she chased away those ghosts.

Dev had to say he was a better man because of Rosie, but he would utterly destroy without a second thought anyone who harmed one strand of hair on Rosie's head. That brutal part of him still existed. Always would for those he loved and cherished, and there was no one he was more in love with than Rosie.

And it was time he proved it.

"Hey." He scooped a few of the curls from her face. "Could you do something for me?"

"Depends." She shifted so that her breasts pressed against his side in the most distracting way possible. Resting her chin on his chest, she grinned. "If you're going to ask me to cancel the ghost investigation of Waverly Hills—"

"I would never dream of doing that." He laughed as he crooked his arm behind his head. "Can you lift your pillow up for me?"

The corners of her lips turned down. "Um, what for?"

"You'll see."

She stared at him for a few moments and then she raised up onto an elbow as she reached over and lifted the pillow, revealing what he knew was under there, and he knew the exact moment she saw the small black box. She became so still, he wondered if she breathed. "Devlin . . ."

He bit down on his lower lip. "Open it."

Her gaze swung back to him and then she sprang onto her knees, snatching up the box as she rested back on her haunches, completely comfortable in the nude. Slowly, she opened the box and gasped. *"Devlin,"* she repeated.

Sitting up, he, too, rose to his knees as he took the box from her trembling fingers and plucked the ring from the velvet interior. His heart started pounding as he met her gaze and saw that her beautiful eyes were gleaming.

"How long was that under there?" she asked, voice hoarse with emotion.

The corners of his lips curled. "Just two days."

"Two days!" She clasped her hands together. "You had that under my pillow for two days and didn't say anything?"

"I was waiting for the perfect moment."

"Every moment is the perfect moment!"

His grin spread. "I'm making this the perfect moment right now if you let me speak."

"Go ahead. Speak. I'm waiting."

He chuckled as he cupped her cheek with his other hand. "I never believed in love until I met you, Rosie. At least not for me, but you proved me wrong. I wasn't lying when I said you're a revolution for the soul, but what you don't know is you're so much more than that. You're a balm to my soul, and while I know I don't deserve you, I will spend every damn day of my life becoming worthy of you. Will you marry me, Rosie?"

"No," she whispered.

"No?" He blinked.

"You already *are* worthy of me," she insisted, and the tightness in his chest loosened. "You already deserved me and that is why I will marry you."

"Thank God," he growled.

Devlin de Vincent wasn't sure who moved first or how the ring got on her finger, but he was kissing her and guiding her back to the bed, sinking into her, the woman who was to become his wife—the woman who stood up to the Devil and proved that even he could love.

Acknowledgments

None of this would've been possible without the TV show *The Dead Files*. I know. That sounds weird, but an episode about cursed land is what gave me the idea to write the first de Vincent book.

I want to thank Tessa Woodward and the amazing editing, marketing, and publicity team, along with Kristin Dwyer; Jenn Watson; Social Media Butterfly; my agent, Kevan Lyon; my sub-rights agent, Taryn Fagerness; and my assistant and friend, Stephanie Brown. It really does take a team of people to publish a book.

Special thank you to my friends, family, and fellow authors who help support me. You know who you are.

And last but not least, thank you to YOU. Without you, there would be no stories.

Have you met all the de Vincents? Make sure to check out the first two books in the spellbinding series.

MOONLIGHT SINS

Julia Hughes has always played it safe until she learned a very painful lesson. Now Julia's starting over with a job in the Louisiana bayou, working for the infamous de Vincent family, the massively wealthy brothers who are haunted by a dark reputation and whispers of misdeeds. Hired to care for their troubled sister, Julia can't afford any distractions, but the menacing presence in the mansion and the ever-present temptation of the handsome Lucian de Vincent isn't something anyone can ignore.

Julia knows better than to get wrapped up in Lucian. He's from a world she can't relate to. Plus, he's her employer. But his wicked touch and sensual promises are too much to deny. What starts with a kiss ends with so much more.

Lucian is the youngest brother—the wildest, most unpredictable one. He's the unrepentant bachelor of the family, known for his escapades in and out of the bedroom, and he *wants* Julia. There's something about her that makes Lucian want to lay himself bare, but some secrets are better left buried, right along with a past that could not only bring down a dynasty but also destroy Julia in the process.

MOONLIGHT SEDUCTION

Nicolette Bresson never thought she'd return to the de Vincents' bayou compound. It's where her parents work, where Nikki grew up . . . and where she got her heart broken by Gabriel de Vincent himself. Yet here she is, filling in for her sick mother. Avoiding Gabe should be easy, especially when so much of Nikki's time is spent trying not to be stabbed in the back by the malicious hangers-on who frequent the mansion. But escaping memories of Gabe, much less his smoking-hot presence, is harder than expected—especially since he seems determined to be in Nikki's space as much as possible.

Gabriel spent years beating himself up over his last encounter with Nikki. He'd wanted her then, but for reasons that were bad for both of them. Things have now changed. Gabe sees more than a girl he's known forever; he sees a smart, talented, and heartbreakingly beautiful woman . . . one who's being stalked from the shadows. Now, Gabe will do anything to keep Nikki safe—and to stop the de Vincent curse from striking again.